PanEuro

Stick and Lipstick

Thomas Brant

CHAPTER 1 – Disappointment in Lockdown

Wednesday 17th March 2021

London Manston Airport, Hayley Northcott decided, was not like the airport she had grown up with as a child, having lived in the Isle of Thanet all her 21 years of life. The irony that the formerly defunct airport, now the new hub of PanEuro, an airline which had gone back to the 'Golden Era of Flying', where men were pilots and women wore gloves and matching lipstick, was not lost on her.

PanEuro Airways, a brand-new airline launched mere months ago with brand new Airbus A320neo and Airbus A321neo aircraft, mainly from cancelled and deferred orders that had Airbus had scooped up on the cheap during the pandemic downturn, had positioned itself as a no-expense-spared antidote to soulless low-cost travel. The concept, a British Overseas Airways Corporation-style resurrection for the twenty-first century, had caught the public imagination in a way no one expected. White-gloved stewardesses—never flight attendants—distributed menus rather than QR codes, and gin and tonic was poured from glass bottles into real tumblers rather than thimble-sized plastic cups. Flying PanEuro, according to its flamboyant press launch, was to be "a restoration of civility in the skies."

The daughter of a British Airways Captain, sister of a Virgin Atlantic First Officer and granddaughter of a British Midlands Captain, Hayley knew from a young age that she wanted to be a pilot. She had trained hard, and at 16, had started her training in smaller, lightweight, planes that would lead, at 18, to being accepted at Cranfield Flight Training Centre, the L3Harris Airline Academy, as part of a cadet programme designed to fast-track the most promising young aviators. She had been taken on by Easyjet a few months prior to the Coronavirus pandemic, but when COVID-19 hit and the world locked down, her dreams were mothballed like so many grounded planes. EasyJet had withdrawn its cadet intake indefinitely. Her final flight, flight EZY8682 from Naples to Gatwick, one of 6 actual in-flight deck First Officer line training flights she had been assigned to, had ended in the eerie calm of March 2020, with the airport silent and the terminal dark, its occupants—staff and passengers alike—anxious and uncertain.

Now, one year later, Hayley Northcott was back at an airport, but not as a pilot. Not even as cabin crew, which she might have reluctantly accepted if it got her back in the air. She was here as she had just had an interview to be a pilot, one which, the interviewer had said, that if she had been born with XY chromosomes and a square jaw, she would have walked into.

The interviewer, a former British Airways Captain who she knew was a former colleague of her fathers, before the flag carrier had 'adjusted staffing levels in accordance with unprecedented global demand reductions,' had said, off the record, that had it been up to him, with her spotless record from Easyjet and that she had trained on the A320 family, he'd have hired her without a second thought. But PanEuro, despite all its press about reviving the "glamour and glory of aviation," had an image to maintain—one that didn't allow for short haircuts, slightly scuffed shoes, or ambition worn too boldly by someone in a skirt.

And then he had said something that had made her stop.

"You know, the Head Purser reports to the Head of Flying, the latter of who is an ex Flybe guy who's not as strict on the criteria for pilots as the brass wants."

Hayley looked at the man, Captain Richard Parker, who had said those words with a kind of hushed guilt, as if saying them aloud was an act of sabotage rather than solidarity. He hadn't met her gaze when he said it.

"Do you know Toby Radcliffe?" he then asked, and Hayley looked up at Captain Parker, the sterile filtered air of the Manston departure lounge suddenly thick with implication. Of course she knew him, as they were in the same cohort at L3Harris and had both applied to Easyjet as cadets. Toby Radcliffe, shy, good looking in a geekish sort of way, had once offered to swap study notes with her on final approach calculations and fuel vectoring. The two had been thick as thieves, as they had both struggled to be accepted, Hayley as she was female and Toby as he was gay, meaning that they had been whispered about by some of the older instructors as "the ones with an agenda."

"Yes, he and I were in the same cohort," she replied cautiously, watching Parker's expression for signs of where this conversation was really going.

"He's on the 1505 to Berlin, as he's one of the First Officer cohorts in the Manston pool. If you just happened to be on that flight as a passenger, maybe..."

Hayley looked at the man with a grin, and knew what he was hinting at, that he was suggesting that if she happened to get on that flight as a passenger, and that as she was carrying her pilots licence, passport, medical certificates and other documentation, then just maybe, if something were to happen to one of the scheduled flight crew—or if someone needed a jump seat observation—then she might find herself logging hours not as a paying customer but as an unexpected professional presence. It wasn't unheard of. In fact, it had happened before, especially in the early days of post-lockdown operational chaos.

Hayley's grin faded slightly. She knew what Parker meant. He was offering her a gamble: not a guarantee, not even a proper backdoor, but an opportunity built on thin air and the hope that she might just be in the right place at the right time, with the right paperwork, and the right person noticing.

She thanked him, left the interview room, and crossed the newly refurbished Manston terminal, her shoes clicking with more determination than certainty.

*_*_*_*

Walking through the terminal, Hayley had to admit, the refurbishment from its 2000s EUJet era beige generic chic to a 1960s inspired retro-futurist glamour was oddly convincing. The floors had been laid in a mosaic of polished tile and jet-age grey-blue linoleum, and the walls were decked out in walnut panels that shimmered under conical pendant lamps. Above her, digital flight information screens sat inside rounded chrome frames, built to look like CRTs even as they showed 1080p clarity. The PanEuro logo—a stylised globe with silver wings— was everywhere. It was theatrical. It was nostalgic. And to Hayley, it was infuriatingly seductive.

Pulling her iPhone from her pocket, she loaded up FlightRadar, to see what the historical schedule for the plane she was going to get to Berlin Tegel, the only airline serving the former West Berlin airport, showed. It was PanEuro Flight PE107, operated by an A320neo registered G-POEL. Looking at the previous day's schedule for the 1505 flight, she noticed that the plane, G-POEK, had done in one day Belfast - Manston, Manston - Berlin, Berlin - Birmingham, and then a ferry flight from Birmingham back to Manston without passengers. Curious. That suggested a potential for crewing shortages or inefficiencies in roster planning. That, or the crew for the Manston to Berlin sector were Manston based crew, which meant that those crews did a triangle style triangle-style routing: out to Berlin, then on to Birmingham, before deadheading back home. Looking at previous days, she noticed the same pattern, that the Manston - Berlin flight was always followed by a Berlin–Birmingham leg and then the empty hop back to Manston. A fixed pattern. A routine in a world of disruption.

Looking at the departures board in the concourse prior to the check in and sales area, she noticed that other flights, from Kiev, Paris Charles de Gaulle and even a flight to Moscow Sheremetyevo, along with one, single, flight to New York JFK, an obvious Airbus A321LR ran service due to the fuel limits of the A320.

The irony, she noticed, of PanEuro starting a brand new airline from Manston, mirroring the same destinations as the likes of British Airways, Virgin or even BOAC in its heyday, albeit from Manston and not Heathrow, was not lost on Hayley either. The move had been marketed as 'giving jobs to the people of East Kent' for the Manston base, as 'improving Birmingham's standing' for the West Midlands base and 'improving Scotland's West Coast' for their Prestwick Airport operations.

Looking on the map that was on the wall of the terminal, Hayley noticed that the thin golden arcs emanating from Manston gave the appearance of a resurgent empire: lines to the heart of Europe, sweeping curls reaching across the Atlantic, and narrow threads probing eastward into territories that once felt impossibly distant. The branding read "PanEuro: Connecting the Continent Again", with retro serif typography that tried to straddle prestige and adventure.

She lingered there for a moment, absorbing it all. It was a map that offered possibilities, and as someone whose wings had been clipped, it pressed on her heart like a promise she wasn't sure she was allowed to accept.

Hayley smoothed her blazer once more and approached the faux-wood counter of the PanEuro "Ticket & Guest Relations Desk," as the glinting brass plate proclaimed. A woman stood behind the counter, mid-thirties perhaps, with perfect hair and lipstick to match—just like the posters. Her uniform, with its gold pinstripes and crisply tailored cut, was clearly a throwback to the BOAC aesthetic, though the headset perched incongruously at her ear betrayed the twenty-first century.

"Good morning," Hayley said, summoning the voice she'd used in simulator briefings and interviews—the one that said confident, professional, not to be underestimated.

"Welcome to PanEuro, madam," the woman returned, her smile wide and brittle as cellophane. "How may I assist?"

Hayley leaned in slightly. "I'm hoping to purchase a same-day to Berlin Tegel please," she said. She knew she could buy her ticket on her phone, as, like most of the airlines in the world, PanEuro had a website with a fully functioning booking engine, but she also knew that face-to-face interaction might just be the better route in this theatre of appearances. If she wanted to get noticed, to catch the eye of a crew manager or duty pilot, it was better to be seen and to be remembered.

The woman at the desk nodded primly. "One way or return, madam?"

Haylcy glanced at the departures board again, as if contemplating some grand tour of the continent, before settling back on the woman with a composed smile. "One way. I'd also like to book the 2031 Berlin Tegel to Birmingham, if possible, please?"

The woman's fingers danced across the keyboard with balletic precision, her manicured nails clacking softly as she navigated through the booking system. Hayley watched with a measured gaze, heart pacing not with nervousness but with anticipation, a pilot's calm before take-off. She was calculated, poised. This wasn't a whim. It was a strategy.

"Of course, madam," the woman responded after a beat, her smile never faltering. "Would you like Classic or Executive class?"

Hayley hesitated for the briefest moment, weighing the cost of visibility against the reality of her bank account. Executive class would place her squarely in the line of sight of the cabin crew—and possibly the cockpit—but it came with a price tag she wasn't exactly prepared to swallow casually. Then again, opportunity rarely arrived gift-wrapped.

She knew that travelling in First, or Executive as PanEuro called it, was the norm for her when she was with her father or sister on BA or Virgin as they had staff benefits, or when her EasyJet cadet pass still meant something. Now, she was very much on her own—no staff standby fares, no jump seat privileges, no special favours. Just her, her ambition, and the dwindling digits in her current account.

"Executive," she said, committing to the gamble. "Window seat, if available."

The agent gave a soft, approving nod, as though pleased to be serving someone who understood the experience PanEuro was trying to sell. "Seat 2A is available. You'll be served a choice of salmon terrine or roast guinea fowl for luncheon. If you would like to visit the Executive Lounge prior to departure, you may enjoy a glass of Laurent-Perrier before boarding. The total cost will be £581, and that is the total for both flights. Will you be paying by card, mobile wallet or cash?"

Hayley knew that she had her Starling card on her Apple Wallet, though she wasn't sure if the balance would clear the full amount. Swiping the screen open with a practised flick, she double-checked the available funds. Just over

£720. It would hurt—there was no doubt about that—but not as much as staying grounded would. Not as much as watching another opportunity drift by while she played it safe.

"Apple Wallet," she said, tapping her phone against the terminal.

The reader beeped softly. The agent smiled again, this time with something a little more genuine—almost approving.

"Thank you, Miss Northcott," she said after confirming the payment. "Your tickets, boarding pass and lounge invitation are here." She slid across a pale blue envelope, discreetly embossed with the PanEuro crest. "Boarding begins at 1425. Gate 3."

Hayley accepted it with a nod, feeling the weight of her decision settle in the pit of her stomach. This wasn't just a boarding pass—it was a statement. It was a message to the universe, to PanEuro, to the ghosts of flight plans past: *I am not done.*

* _ * _ * _ *

The PanEuro Executive Lounge at Manston was a strange echo chamber of a past no one there had lived through. Hayley had stepped through the polished chrome doors expecting something slightly above your average airport business class area—a few comfy chairs, some token snacks and a barista machine. Instead, she'd found herself in a world that smelled faintly of sandalwood, aviation fuel, and old money. Brass fixtures gleamed under warm recessed lighting, and thick carpets muffled every footstep. There were no phone-charging kiosks or digital vending fridges. Instead, a white-gloved attendant in a fitted navy uniform approached with a silver tray.

"May I offer you a glass of Laurent-Perrier, madam?"

Hayley smiled faintly and nodded. She accepted the flute and made her way to the far end of the lounge, where wide windows overlooked the freshly tarmacked runway. Her A320neo, G-PANL, stood proud against the backdrop of a watery spring sky, its livery an elegant white trimmed with navy and gold. A staircase vehicle lingered near the forward door. Fuel trucks hissed in the distance.

She sipped slowly, letting the bubbles settle both her nerves and her thoughts. She wasn't just waiting for a flight. She was waiting for fate to blink, especially as, legally, she was on a sticky wicket as the UK was on the 'path to returning from Covid', and that as the third lockdown of the United Kingdom had not yet officially ended. Hayley knew that travel was still largely restricted, even if the messaging from Downing Street had grown more ambiguous by the day. But business travel— particularly under the guise of essential logistics, repositioning or professional obligations—was a murky enough category to let things slide. Technically, she knew that, upon arrival in Berlin, she should also present her Covid vaccination certificate, which she had on her NHS app, and a negative PCR test, which she'd arranged through a private clinic in Ramsgate the day before, as her interview had required one.

Loading up the website for the German digital entry registration, she continued filling out the details with the precision of a seasoned pilot filing a flight plan. She selected the reason for entry—"professional meeting and assessment"—which wasn't a lie, not really, if she considered the unspoken potential of the day. Every field she ticked, every form she uploaded, was a reinforcement of her intention: that she was serious, that she belonged in the cockpit, not the cabin.

When the confirmation screen flashed green, she took a screenshot for good measure and allowed herself a brief glance back towards the tarmac. G-POEL shimmered slightly in the midday light, having arrived moments ago from Belfast. Looking on the FlightRadar app, she noticed that its earlier move to Berlin had been from Moscow, and so it had obviously been rostered into a new triangle, one that spanned further east than before—another sign of PanEuro's aggressive expansion and a tantalising clue that crewing needs might be changing faster than public statements implied.

She watched as a ground crew member extended the forward air-stairs and a catering truck reversed into position at the rear service door. Two pilots disembarked: both male, both in their early forties if she had to guess, one clutching a leather flight bag while the other rubbed his temples as if warding off a headache. They both wore navy epaulettes trimmed in gold thread—PanEuro didn't skimp on the embroidery, it seemed.

Hayley Northcott: *Hey, Toby. Which base does the flight deck crew for the Belfast - Manston and the Manston - Berlin come from?*

She knew that her friend was the same age as her, as they both graduated L3Harris in the same month, and though they'd never been especially close outside of simulator rooms and debriefs, they had a sort of battle-born camaraderie that had endured. She wasn't sure he'd reply immediately—flight crew were hard to reach in the air—but if he was on the ground and in uniform, there was always a chance he'd be checking WhatsApp between duties.

Toby Radcliffe: *Belfast does the leg into Manston, then its Manston pilots, Birmingham cabin crew for the Berlin. Why?*

Hayley's thumbs hovered over the screen for a moment, debating just how much she should say.

Hayley Northcott: *Got an appointment in Berlin, so I'm flying on PE107.*

She knew she was lying about an appointment, but the truth would have been far too complicated to type out. It wasn't strictly a lie either, she rationalised—after all, her "appointment" was simply unconfirmed, contingent on fate. Hayley closed WhatsApp and took a final sip of champagne, letting the delicate fizz tingle down her throat as she watched the cockpit crew from Belfast stride across the tarmac towards the terminal, probably to grab lunch and rest before their next rotation.

Toby Radcliffe: *Wait... you're on my flight to Berlin?*

The WhatsApp message from Toby appeared on Hayley's screen almost instantly, interrupting her contemplation.

Her pulse quickened, and she tapped out a rapid reply, fingers fluttering over the screen.

Hayley Northcott: *Yep, seat 2A. I'm on the 2031 Berlin Tegel to Birmingham as well. Is that one of your flights too?*

There was a pause.

Toby Radcliffe: *Bloody hell. Yes, I'm flying both sectors. What the hell are you up to?*

Hayley let out a small breath of air that might've been a laugh, though it didn't quite make it to her lips. She tapped her reply slowly, deliberately.

Hayley Northcott: *Just... sightseeing. And maybe reminding someone that I've still got wings.*

Toby Radcliffe: *I'll speak to the Captain, as I might have a surprise for you.*

Hayley looked at the WhatsApp message and Hayley looked at the text message and allowed herself a smile— not smug, not hopeful, just something caught in the static between fear and possibility. It was the kind of smile a person wore when they were balancing at the edge of the diving board, feet curled just over the drop, heart full of questions but ready to fall forward anyway.

She didn't respond straight away. She didn't want to seem overeager. Not that Toby would misread her—he wasn't like that—but still, she had to walk the line carefully. There was dignity in the pose she'd assumed, in the performance of professionalism. Even when her stomach was tying itself into knots at the thought of being so close—again—to the sky.

She stared out of the panoramic lounge window once more, her gaze locking with the aircraft's nose, as if willing the A320 to blink first.

****

CHAPTER 2 – Back on Board
Wednesday 17th January 2024

"This is a call for all PanEuro passengers travelling on Flight PE107 to Berlin," came the crisp, clipped tones of a voice that seemed piped in directly from a 1950s BBC newsreel, full of poise and precise pronunciation. "Executive Class passengers, PanEuro Platinum card holders and those requiring assistance are invited to approach Gate 4, where your boarding process will now begin."

Hayley felt her stomach jolt. She stood, gathering her pale blue envelope, smoothing down her blazer once more as if it were armour, and slinging her handbag over one shoulder. The lounge attendant—who looked like she'd been cast by a particularly exacting director of The Crown—inclined her head gracefully as Hayley walked past.

"Have a pleasant flight, madam," she said, with the kind of trained warmth that suggested her ancestors might have offered the same to first-class passengers aboard the Queen Mary.

Hayley offered a quick smile, the kind that didn't quite reach her eyes. Outside the lounge, the world felt sharper, cooler. The departure concourse at Manston wasn't busy—still throttled by international restrictions and the hangover of lockdown uncertainty—but the few passengers present had already gathered by the gate in a neat, orderly line. Some wore masks, some didn't. The rules were still in flux, guidance reshaping itself daily, but all wore that same tentative look of people unused to airports, still reacclimatising to the rhythms of travel.

The PanEuro ground agent—tall, in a vintage-inspired navy skirt suit with white piping and a navy pillbox hat perched immaculately on a slick chignon—scanned Hayley's boarding pass with a little nod of approval.

Hearing the chime which meant that her pass had been approved, she noticed that the ground agent looked at her.

"Miss Northcott, you've been upgraded to the jump seat," she said, a look of confusion upon her face, as if she hadn't expected such a change herself. "You're to report to the flight deck prior to boarding."

Hayley blinked. Her lips parted, but the words didn't come. For a half second, her brain refused to process what she'd just heard.

"The… jump seat?" she managed finally, careful to keep her voice even, her pulse not.

"Yes, ma'am." The agent smiled again, this time with a flicker of genuine curiosity. "Captain Livingstone has personally placed your name there. You are to board via the front doors and then pass the Purser this."

The agent gave Hayley a laminated card with the symbol of a golden wing and the word "Observer" embossed beneath it in italic serif. Hayley knew that it was very rare a gate agent would be giving a member of the public such an Observer pass, as they were usually held by the flight crew, or by the flight operations supervisor back-of-house. For it to be handed over at the gate, printed and laminated, meant it had been arranged with urgency—and a touch of theatre.

Hayley nodded, her grip tightening slightly on the plastic card. She forced her steps to remain measured as she stepped down the airbridge, its chrome and Perspex styling a continuation of the 1960s aviation cosplay that PanEuro had made its brand. With every stride, her mind replayed Toby's message: *"I'll speak to the Captain. I might have a surprise for you."*

This was no mere surprise. It was a chance—a sliver of sky carved open just wide enough for her to step through.

* _ * _ * _ *

Looking at the Executive Class cabin of the A320neo, Hayley had to admit that if she had travelled in it, it would have been like a trip to a bygone era, the 2+1 seating, leather armchair style seats with polished wood-effect tray tables and brass reading lamps giving the distinct impression that the aircraft had stolen its fittings from a retired Pullman train. Each seat had its own curtained pod, a feature that harked back to first-class rail travel more than any modern flight. Even the cabin lighting was deliberately warm, set to a golden hue that mimicked mid-century incandescent bulbs rather than the sterile LEDs of modern fleets.

Hayley took it all in with a glance and a breath before turning left, not right, at the bulkhead—towards the cockpit, not the cabin. As she stepped past the Purser's galley, a woman with a platinum chignon and sharp eyeliner intercepted her, her smile frozen but her eyes alert.

"Miss Northcott?" she asked.

Hayley nodded and presented the Observer pass.

"Right this way, dear," the Purser replied, gesturing towards the flight deck door. She tapped a code into the keypad beside it, then added, with a tone that was too composed to be surprised but too curious to hide it completely: "Captain Livingstone is expecting you."

The door slid open.

The first thing Hayley recognised as she looked at the flight deck was the standard layout of the A320neo, the dials, screens and switches the same as the configuration that Easyjet used. Despite PanEuro's obsession with retro aesthetics in the passenger cabin, the flight deck was modern to the bone: all clean lines, glass displays, sidesticks instead of yokes, and the familiar scent of aviation sealant, plastic, and recirculated air. Comforting, almost. Familiar. Like home.

"Miss Northcott," came a voice from the left seat.

Hayley looked up and met the eyes of a man in his late forties, salt-and-pepper hair beneath his captain's hat, and a square, sun-lined face that spoke of long-haul experience and long hours above cloud level. His epaulettes gleamed with four thick gold stripes, his shirt crisp. This, she presumed, was Captain Livingstone.

"Yes, sir," Hayley replied, slipping into the tone she'd used a hundred times in the simulator briefings at L3Harris.

"Welcome aboard," the Captain said, his voice even but with a flicker of warmth. He extended a hand, which she shook firmly. "Captain Max Livingstone, ex-Flybe Exeter, pleased to meet you."

"Likewise, sir," Hayley replied, voice steady though her heart was knocking against her ribs.

Max gestured to the jump seat behind the centre console. "Stow your bag wherever you like. My First Officer mentioned you're a classmate of his from L3 and Easyjet. Got any time on A319 or A320s?"

Hayley nodded, sliding into the jump seat and securing her handbag beneath it with a hook of her foot.

"Yes, sir. Logged just over seventy-six hours of in-flight time on A319s and A320s with EasyJet. Six line flights before the programme was paused. Most of the rest was sim time—LOFT scenarios, base checks, and a few emergencies."

Livingstone glanced back at her, then at a slim tablet mounted to his side. He tapped a few things in. "Good. I see you're on the Berlin to Birmingham leg too. Stopping over in Birmingham or getting a train back to London?"

Hayley facepalmed, as she had forgot that she had to find a way back to Thanet from Birmingham as it had been a last-minute decision to book both legs of the journey without considering the return from the Midlands.

"Hadn't got that far, sir," she said with a wry smile. "Probably a train, unless I can get a Premier Inn—"

"Nah, I wouldn't suggest that. Look, do you have your certs and licence with you?"

Hayley blinked in momentary confusion at the question—one that was simultaneously casual and heavy with implication. Then she nodded, unzipping the outer pocket of her handbag and drawing out the soft leather wallet that held her EASA licence, her Class 1 medical, and her L3Harris training documents. She handed it over without a word.

Captain Livingstone took it with the casual professionalism of someone who had done this many times before, flicking through it quickly, pausing only to confirm her name and licence number.

"Right, I'm going to let you into a little secret. The cabin crew for this flight and the one from Berlin are Birmingham based, so they'll be getting off in Brum, but Toby and I have to fly a ferry flight back to Manston after the Berlin to Birmingham leg. It's just us and the aircraft on that hop. You interested in sitting in on the return as well?"

Hayley blinked. Her fingers curled tighter on her lap belt. "You mean—another jump seat?"

Livingstone chuckled, still looking at her paperwork. "Not exactly. Toby's got to do some Pilot in Command hours, so even though he's right seating, he's got the logbook priority. But I can see you're rated on A319s, A320s and the neo variants, so if we've got operational clearance—and I don't see why we wouldn't—you can take the left seat for the ferry leg. It won't be logged as PIC time for you, but its SIC time, and I'll log it as H Northcott in the official aircraft movement log. You'll like the flight plan, as I'm an ex-Exeter guy, I don't like approaching here on a landside approach. We'll be taking the departure and approach over Ramsgate... brings back old memories of Exeter and leaving over the Channel. Let's just say... I know who you met earlier."

Hayley chuckled, as she remembered her interview with Captain Richard Parker, the man who'd once flown with her father, and who had suggested taking this specific flight. That quiet nod of solidarity now unfurled into something more tangible—a series of steps, of chances, which had not just fallen her way but had been nudged by hands that remembered.

"I'd be honoured," she said, and her voice came out softer than she intended, almost reverent. She cleared her throat and added more firmly, "Absolutely, sir. I'd love to take the opportunity."

Livingstone gave a single, satisfied nod, then returned the paperwork to her, placing it delicately on the fold-out tray behind him. "You'll brief with us for both legs, then. Nothing ceremonial—we'll go over the same ops bulletin we'd use with any other crew member. Make sure your seat harness is locked, and if you're uncomfortable during any stage, say so."

Toby walked in, and Hayley noticed that he was wearing an engagement ring. She knew that he and his (then at L3) boyfriend, Owen Heart, were both part of the cadet intake, and she smiled instinctively, as she knew that the duo had been inseparable back then—even when instructors had smirked or given 'old school' nods about "recruiting couples." Hayley made a mental note to ask him about Owen later.

"Look at you," Toby grinned as he settled into the right seat, flicking the arm of his headset forward as he ran through his pre-flight checks. "Been months since we were at Luton—and now here you are, about to fly into Berlin like it's just another sim session. Todays a special flight anyway. It's our last day at Berlin Tegel."

Hayley knew that Brandenburg, the new Berlin airport, had opened nearly opened nearly six months ago, but PanEuro had applied to use it for their first 3 months while the Germans transitioned from Tegel and Schönefeld, something about allowing an efficient handover of long-haul and mid-haul routes before consolidating at BER permanently. It made sense in the chaos of post-lockdown Europe—PanEuro was one of the few new airlines to negotiate temporary retro-access to Tegel on a full-service basis, a move which played perfectly into their retro branding.

"Last day?" Hayley echoed, watching as Toby flicked through his checklist with an easy, practised rhythm.

"Yeah," he said, voice tinged with something just shy of melancholy. "Final PanEuro arrival into TXL. From tomorrow, it's all Brandenburg. Bit of a shame, really—Tegel has charm. It's like Heathrow's weird German cousin who never renovated."

Captain Livingstone snorted. "Never did like Brandenburg's design. All glass and no soul. Tegel's got character. Besides, you can walk from gate to curb side in under five minutes. Try doing that at BER."

The overhead panel came alive as systems whirred and clicked into readiness. Hayley stayed quiet, absorbing it all. Watching. Learning. She felt herself settle into a calm that only ever arrived in a cockpit—something bone-deep and peaceful, a steadiness that anchored her even as turbines spun up outside the fuselage.

"ATIS reports slight crosswind, nothing dramatic," Livingstone remarked, adjusting a frequency with fluid fingers. "Toby, your leg to Berlin. Miss Northcott, you'll monitor. I'll handle radio. We're not doing the planned Westbound departure, Toby, as I've told the Tower that we need an Eastbound departure for procedural training purposes, told them that I'd heard that the RAF were planning on doing some training over the West Kent patch around departure time—complete fabrication, but they bought it. Better visuals over Thanet anyway, and it'll give Hayley a nicer send-off."

Toby smirked, making a note on the flight log. "Appreciate the detour, Captain. I'll make sure she gets a full tour of the clouds."

Hayley smiled back, but said nothing. The truth was, she could hardly speak. It was happening—really happening. She wasn't just watching from the ground anymore. She was back in the seat that felt like home, where decisions had consequences and purpose hummed through your fingertips.

They taxied without delay, the ground team at Manston clearly efficient—likely due to the light schedule still imposed by Covid. As the aircraft eased into position at the end of the runway, Hayley could feel the engines spool up, the familiar pitch of the Leap-1A engines on the A320neo a comforting hum in her bones. She kept her eyes forward, scanning instruments even though it wasn't her leg, mirroring Toby's calls, letting her muscle memory revive itself.

And then they were off, wheels screaming against tarmac, nose lifting, and with a kick to her spine, Hayley felt it: lift. The glorious, sacred moment when ground became a memory and sky became the new certainty.

* _ * _ * _ *

"You know, Hales," Toby said as they were midway over Dortmund, the flight having overpassed Bruges, Antwerp and Eindhoven on its way to Berlin, "I think Owen's going to be thrilled when he hears about this."

Hayley turned her head slightly, the static hum of the cockpit filtering around her like a second skin. "What's he up to nowadays?"

"He's applied to Southeastern as a Trainee Train Driver, as he's been unable to find a flying role yet," Toby replied, adjusting the throttle ever so slightly as the A320 cruised smoothly at FL360. "Says he still wants to stay in transport—still wants control, responsibility. But the job market's a mess, and he got tired of waiting for something that might never reopen."

Hayley nodded slowly, the comment striking closer to home than she'd expected. "Yeah. I get that. I almost applied to become a paramedic at one point," she admitted, surprising even herself with the confession. "Thought about doing an Open Uni course too, retrain in IT or something else stable. But every time I opened the application page, I'd find myself on FlightRadar instead, tracking aircraft, checking registration histories, imagining myself in the left seat again. It's like gravity— no matter how far you drift, it pulls you back."

Toby gave her a glance, his expression softening. "That's because this was never just a job for you. It was never just a dream either. It's who you are. Remember when you used to show us Insta photos of your sister on her Virgin Atlantic flights, back when we were midway through L3 and she was finishing her training at Virgin for her First Officer upgrade? You used to talk about how she was hopping the Atlantic near enough daily and was living the life you'd been aiming for since you were a kid."

Hayley noticed that her hand was simulating Toby's movements on the side stick, as he was, unlike most of their generation, not using the auto throttle for this part of the cruise. The two of them, when they had done simulator exams, had, instead of relying on the autopilot too early, insisted on hand-flying up to FL180 at least once every session. Once, the examiner had asked her why she did it, and her response was simple.

"Sometimes it's useful to be able to control it manually, so if the tech failed, then you're not just a passenger with a licence. Instead, you're able to fly the aircraft no matter what." That answer had earned her a rare nod of approval from an old-school instructor who rarely looked impressed. That mindset had stuck. It wasn't just about being in the air—it was about command.

"You know, there's some captains here who don't agree with the whole 'women should be in the galley, men in the flight deck'," Livingstone said, his voice cutting across the soft symphony of cockpit hums and airband chatter, "and I'm one of them. PanEuro talks about bringing back the glamour, the golden age of aviation. But I think what they forget is that the only thing golden about those days was the illusion. There's actually some cabin crew... yes, I prefer that to the term 'stewardess'… who have licences and only do the job because... well, it keeps them in the air instead of instead of on the dole," he continued, adjusting a dial with deliberate calm. "Captain Powers allows us to invite them, if they're current and type rated, to either do a bit of right seating or jump seating, as the Head Purser reports to him, so he makes sure those who can fly, fly—no matter what uniform they're wearing. As long as they've got a pair of flats and their docs handy, I just tell them to leave the lipstick and silver tray behind and get their hands on the sidestick. Simple reason—if they took the time to get the certs and licences, and they've took the time to keep the sim and medicals up to date, then they're good enough to fly. Good enough for me, anyway."

Hayley noticed the underlying hint, the suggestion, that if she applied for a stewardess position just to get into the system—just to get on the books—it might not be the end of her ambitions after all. Not if the likes of Captain Livingstone and Captain Powers were quietly subverting the more archaic parts of PanEuro's branding from within.

She turned that thought over as the landscape drifted by beneath them. Fields, towns, rivers, all rendered hazy by altitude and distance, but somehow sharper in her mind than ever.

"You really believe that?" she asked quietly, though not with doubt—more as if she were asking permission to hope.

Livingstone looked over, not unkindly. "Look, I've seen pilots be unable to get jobs for years because of redundancies, cuts, airlines going under and even age discrimination. You've got a licence, the hours, and the grit. So yes, I believe it. And more to the point—I believe you've earned it."

There was a beat of silence. Not uncomfortable, but potent. Hayley sat back in the jump seat and let herself exhale. Not with resignation, but with release.

The A320 continued its cruise over the hazy lowlands of central Germany. Their descent would begin soon. Berlin Tegel was less than half an hour away. She could already feel the slight shifts in the pressure and tone of the aircraft's structure—the subtle tremors that came before a new phase of flight.

"Right, pop quiz, Toby, Miss Northcott," Livingstone said as they approached the point of descent. "You've got a pounding noise, accompanied by severe vibrations, and the cabin crew are reporting smoke in the cabin. What don't you do?"

Hayley had a feeling that Livingstone was hinting to British Midlands Flight 92, a simulation she'd seen time and again during CRM training—the 1989 Kegworth air disaster. She and Toby responded nearly in unison.

"Don't shut down the wrong engine," Toby said dryly.

"Or you'll end up in the M1 central reservation with a salvage team picking through luggage," Hayley finished, the corner of her mouth quirking in a grim echo of a smile. "Instead, you check your readouts, do a visual inspection if possible, and follow QRH before making assumptions."

Livingstone chuckled, a low, approving sound that settled into the background like the idle rumble of engines at cruise. "Good. Both of you. Thought I'd check. Why did Captain Hunt close down the wrong engine?"

Hayley didn't miss a beat. "Auditory misperception and confirmation bias. He assumed the loud bang and vibration was from the left engine, because it was closest to his seat. That, combined with no visual confirmation and a lack of clear diagnostic data in the cockpit, led to a fatal assumption."

Toby nodded. "Back then, instrumentation wasn't as advanced, and CRM wasn't enforced the way it is now. The flight engineer didn't push back hard enough, and co-pilot procedures weren't robust enough to challenge the decision. It was a textbook case in why we train for multi-layered redundancy now."

Captain Livingstone gave a curt nod, visibly satisfied. "Good. You've both done your homework. I bring it up every now and then with crew who are less than 2 years in the seat or back from extended leave. It's a reminder.

Doesn't matter if you're wearing four stripes or none at all—aviation doesn't forgive arrogance, or assumptions."

He let the words hang in the air for a moment, like contrails across a morning sky. Then, as if flicking a switch, he returned to business.

"Alright, Toby, you've got control, as you know, so you're responsible for getting this down on the ILS 26L approach. Hayley, I want you on radio monitoring, but shadow the decision process. If ATC throws a curveball, I want to see how quick your planning mind still is."

"Aye, Captain," Toby replied with a touch of humour as he adjusted the MCP for descent. "Let's bring her home."

Hayley leaned forward in her seat, locking her harness tight and watching as Toby began configuring for descent. The cockpit became a hive of precise, mechanical coordination. Frequencies were changed. Descent was initiated. The aircraft began to tilt nose-down ever so slightly, its pace steady and deliberate.

"Berlin Radar, PanEuro 107 descending FL360 to FL240, direct HAVEL."

"PanEuro 107, roger. Descend FL240, expect ILS 26L, maintain present heading."

Livingstone acknowledged the call, his tone clipped and professional. "FL240, ILS 26L, PanEuro 107."

Hayley reached for the approach plate clipped onto a spare kneeboard she always travelled with—it had become habit, even when she was just a passenger. Within seconds, she had the procedure memorised again: altitudes, fixes, glideslope intercept, go-around protocols. Tegel's setup was still fresh to her, owing to simulator runs during cadet training. The only thing different now was that it was real.

The descent passed smoothly through FL240, and then FL180. The city began to take form far below, fractured into blocks by canals and tree-lined boulevards. A grey March mist hung over the rooftops, half-shrouding Berlin in mystery as it prepared to receive what could be its final PanEuro arrival.

"Gear down," Toby called, voice steady.

"Three greens," Hayley confirmed, glancing at the gear indicator lights with trained eyes.

Livingstone nodded from the left seat, his eyes scanning his side of the panel while his hand hovered near the thrust levers.

"Flaps full."

Hayley noted the configuration silently, instinctively checking the slats on the wing through the side window.

"Speed... Vapp 137," Toby read off.

"Check," Hayley and Livingstone said in near unison.

Hayley watched the glideslope come alive on the PFD, the purple diamond sliding towards centre. She could feel the aircraft almost shift into focus—a thoroughbred eyeing the finish line.

"Localiser alive."

"Glideslope alive."

"Final approach."

The callouts passed between them like poetry—carefully rehearsed, deeply ingrained. For Hayley, each one was like oxygen to a drowning woman. Every checklist ticked, every switch flicked, every call was a reminder: this is what I trained for.

"Landing checklist complete," Toby said softly, and there was something reverent in his tone, too.

Outside, Berlin shimmered into clearer view. The Tower came alive.

"PanEuro 107, wind 280 degrees at 11 knots, cleared to land Runway 26L."

"Cleared to land 26L, PanEuro 107," Livingstone replied.

As the runway stretched ahead of them, flickering into view beneath the cloud base, Hayley felt her breath catch in her chest—not from nerves, but from awe. The lights on the tarmac danced like stars in alignment, guiding them in. Her hands itched to feel the sidestick again, but she restrained herself.

"Minimums."

"Landing."

The main gear kissed the runway with surgical precision. A moment later, the nose wheel touched down. Spoilers deployed. Reverse thrust roared. The aircraft slowed with a confident grace.

"Seventy knots."

"Manual braking."

Hayley released a breath she hadn't realised she was holding.

"Ladies and gentlemen," came the voice of the purser over the cabin PA, as the aircraft slowed on the taxiway, "we are pleased to announce the safe arrival of PanEuro Flight 107 into Berlin Tegel. Local time is 17:16. The temperature is a mild nine degrees. We bid you farewell on what is likely to be PanEuro's final scheduled passenger arrival at Tegel Airport. Thank you for flying with us."

There was a brief, stunned pause in the cockpit before Toby broke the silence.

"Well… that's going in the logbook," he said, almost under his breath.

Hayley turned her head and caught the glance between him and Livingstone. Both men wore that odd half-smile pilots sometimes wore after a particularly meaningful flight—part professionalism, part pride, part silent communion with the skies.

****

CHAPTER 3 – Birmingham - Manston

Wednesday 17th March 2021

The flight from Berlin to Birmingham was smooth, Hayley would later note in her diary, apart from a small spot of turbulence as they crossed the North Sea and approached the East Anglian coast. It hadn't been the sort that prompted concern, but rather that momentary rush of adrenaline—the soft, rolling tremor that reminded every soul on board, from Executive Class to the flight deck, that they were indeed airborne, and not merely gliding on rails.

The descent into Birmingham had been routine: vectored over Lincolnshire, a brief handover between Maastricht and London Control, and a calculated drop into the Midlands' grey dusk. The runways at Birmingham were still damp from earlier drizzle, and their touchdown on 33 had been smooth enough to earn a discreet nod from Captain Livingstone as Toby brought the aircraft down with measured finesse. The reverse thrust, although louder than necessary for the lightly loaded aircraft, gave the A320neo a sort of theatrical flair, as if it, too, knew it was participating in something just a little outside of the ordinary.

They pulled onto a remote stand near the old cargo apron, away from the passenger terminal. PanEuro, still lacking full integration into the main pier allocations at BHX, was temporarily operating from the stand-off bays once used by Flybe and the occasional charter. There was no jet bridge here—just a ground stair vehicle and a skeletal crew of ramp agents, who looked mildly bemused at the sight of a white-and-gold trimmed jet pulling in from Tegel in the middle of the Covid-quieted night.

Hayley waited in the flight deck as the few passengers disembarked. She listened to the low murmur of the APU kicking in, the hiss of air-conditioning lines, and the clipped exchanges between the Birmingham-based cabin crew gathering their bags. Their shift was done. The aircraft would soon be handed over to its ferry crew— which, tonight, included her.

Livingstone removed his headset and turned slightly in his seat, addressing her with a relaxed ease now that the formal flight was complete.

"Alright, Hayley, I've filed a revised flight plan for this leg, as sometimes I like to do something different. We've got a touch and go at Bristol, one at Lille, and then a westbound approach to Manston. Officially it's to give Toby knowledge of alternates for here and Manston, as officially, Lille and Heathrow is the Manston diversionary airports we have in the SOP, and Manchester and Bristol is Birmingham's diversion pair, and while we don't normally serve them, it's best to have the knowledge and the practical experience in case there's an incident and we're required to divert at short notice."

Hayley knew it was common to have knowledge of diversionary and alternate airfields—pilots were often required to demonstrate familiarity not only in theory but in practice, particularly at airlines that liked to pride themselves on procedural robustness. But she also knew this wasn't just about procedural robustness.

It was about time in the seat. It was about creating opportunities in a world where they were few and far between. It was about captains like Livingstone bending the rules, just enough to let someone fly through them.

"Does anyone want a brew while we've got an hour here on the tarmac?" Toby asked, undoing his belts so he could stand up. "I can nip into the Birmingham crew room and grab a few cuppas and that, as, Hales, there's a base for pilots and cabin crew here, as we have flights to most of Europe and JFK, as it's a base for PanEuro like Manston. Even though the canteen part will be shuttered, the coffee machine is proper coffee, not that Costa or Starbucks swill you get from the landside terminal. Real espresso beans, real milk froth if you're brave enough to try the cappuccino option."

Captain Livingstone waved a hand without looking up from the EFB tablet mounted beside him. "Latte for me if the machine's working. No sugar. I've had enough sugar today watching PR videos of PanEuro's new Berlin service—makes Ryanair's safety card seem humble."

Hayley chuckled lightly, unfastening her shoulder straps. "Flat white, if it does one. Otherwise, I'll take a tea— milk, no sugar."

Toby chuckled. "Yeah, you like it lots of milk, no sugar, and the teabag still in the mug like some kind of monster," he teased, nudging her lightly on the arm as he stood. "I'll grab a few sarnies from the vending machine too, chicken and stuffing do?"

"Perfect," Hayley replied with a grin. "As long as it's not curling at the edges. If it's doing an impression of a Ryvita, leave it for the pigeons."

Toby made his exit down the forward airstairs, zipping up his jacket as the spring chill nipped through the open doors. The sound of the Birmingham night—distant engine hum, flashing beacons, a squawk of ground radio—drifted into the cockpit. Inside, the A320neo's flight deck remained a warm, glowing cocoon of glass panels and soft backlit controls. Hayley sat in silence for a moment, simply letting the hum settle over her.

"So, what was your first flight as pax?" Livingstone said after a few minutes, to which Hayley grinned, as she remembered it faintly, being 3 at the time, and it being a famous flight, as it was the last flight of the British Airways operation of the Concorde from New York to Heathrow.

"BA002," she said softly, her voice tinged with a mix of pride and nostalgia. "October 2003. Well, that's what I remember. Dad was a First Officer, close to promotion to Captain, and my sister, mother and me had gone to JFK as he'd been slated to be on a regular transatlantic rotation, but we ended up flying back on the Concorde because Dad had managed to pull a few strings, and was Concorde trained, and as the FO had gone of ill, he'd been bumped to that. He finished conversion from DC10 to Concorde in '00, days before Air France Flight 4590 was lost. He still says how airports should do checks between departures just to ensure that there's no foreign objects on the runway, but they don't do it because time is money, and the owners would rather sacrifice a bit of safety than delay a departure slot," she said, shaking her head slightly. "He always prays every time he does a departure from CDG, something about once a Concorde pilot, always a Concorde pilot. He still keeps a tiny model of her in his flight bag. Calls it his lucky charm."

Captain Livingstone looked at her, a flicker of something between admiration and wistfulness in his expression. "Concorde… now that was a machine," he murmured. "Flown her in the sim once, years back when BA let a few of us at Flybe have a go for charity. Different world. You didn't just fly it—you tamed it."

Hayley nodded slowly, her mind wandering momentarily to the stories her father used to tell. "He said the cockpit was hotter than most ovens during cruise, and the switches were from the Ark. But once she passed Mach 2, it all just... stabilised. He used to say it was like flying a missile on autopilot—but in high heels and a dinner jacket."

They shared a quiet laugh, the kind that only aviators could fully appreciate. Outside the cockpit window, the ramp lights flickered faintly on the tarmac, casting long shadows across the fuselage of a parked DHL freighter a few stands away. The airport was beginning to settle into that uniquely eerie calm that descended after the last commercial banks had landed but before the red-eye cargo haulers fully took over.

Hayley tapped gently on the glareshield, idly tracing the etched panel lines. "It's funny… how things change. A year ago, I was grounded, wondering if I'd ever get back up. Now here I am, logging hours again—even if unofficially."

Livingstone turned to look at her properly, his tone measured. "Don't discount this, Hayley. Just because it's not on a rostered duty sheet doesn't mean it doesn't matter. You've sat in for two sectors today. You've briefed, observed, assisted. And you'll fly next. That's not nothing. And you'll remember this more than you will any textbook route check."

She smiled gratefully, glancing down at her Observer pass. "It's strange. This little bit of laminated plastic feels like a golden ticket."

"It is," he said. "But not because it was given to you. Because you're making it count."

Just then, a rap on the airstair door echoed faintly through the aircraft. Toby returned, cheeks slightly pink from the cold and hands full with cardboard coffee trays and a tote bag full of premium sandwiches that, if they were in Waitrose in Ramsgate, would be part of the premium meal deal and accompanied by a complimentary quinoa salad and a smug sense of superiority.

"Fresh delivery," he said. "The tech was filling the vending machine up and had no space for half a dozen of these beauties, as well as some other bits and bobs, so he let me grab the lot for nowt. I've got pasta, chocolate, and a peanut and raisin flapjack that was made, looking at the label, by a Coventry bakery. One thing I will say about PanEuro, they may be sexist, misogynistic pigs in the brass, but they don't skimp on using local suppliers."

Hayley accepted the flapjack with a thankful grin, turning the cellophane-wrapped bar over in her hand. "Local flavour," she murmured, before adding dryly, "Probably the only thing that is local about this airline—other than the press releases claiming to be 'revitalising British regional aviation.'"

Toby chuckled as he passed the drinks around, carefully balancing the cardboard tray on the centre console. "Flat white, Captain. Latte for you. And yes, Hayley, yours still has the teabag in like the absolute wrong 'un you are."

"Much appreciated," Hayley said, taking the mug and inhaling the familiar scent of over-brewed tea. "At least it's not from the machine at L3. That one brewed everything with the flavour of despair and floor cleaner."

"Oi," Toby protested, settling into his seat again. "That machine got me through three back-to-back CRM assessments and a sim check where the rudder pedals jammed."

Captain Livingstone arched an eyebrow. "And you passed?"

"Miraculously," Toby replied with a smirk. "Mainly because Hayley spotted the error in the FMS before the instructor did. He looked very unimpressed, which is always the sure sign you've done something right."

Hayley sipped her tea and allowed herself a soft laugh. The memory of those sim sessions, the grey-and-blue instructor booths, and the almost absurd pressure of cadet assessments came back like phantom turbulence. There had been little room for mistakes then, even less for camaraderie. And yet somehow, she and Toby had managed to keep each other sane through it all.

"Alright," Livingstone said, brushing crumbs off his lap and reaching for the aircraft's documents folder. "We've got a scheduled slot at Bristol in forty minutes for the touch-and-go. Lille is slot-less but we've filed. Manston has cleared the visual approach request—local tower want us in before 2300 so we're not clashing with their overnight repaving works. I'm going to quickly use the loo, so get comfortable in the left seat, Hayley, and I'll sit in the jump seat behind you two."

Hayley froze for a moment at the instruction, not out of fear, but reverence. The left seat. Captain's seat. Even unofficially, even unlogged, it was a place she hadn't occupied since before the pandemic. Since before everything changed. She slipped into the seat quietly, reverently almost, adjusting the rudder pedals and seat height by muscle memory alone. Her fingers hovered briefly above the sidestick before she pulled them away, resting them instead on her thighs. No need to seem overeager.

Toby threw her a knowing look from the right-hand seat as he reattached his headset. "Look at you. Queen of the skies again."

"You'll have to settle for Duchess," she said, sliding her own headset over her ears and pulling the mic into place. "Captain Livingstone still holds the crown."

A flush of the forward lavatory followed by the opening of the cockpit door signalled Livingstone's return. He climbed in and settled into the jump seat behind them with the relaxed confidence of someone who had once flown in full fog into Belfast with a failed ILS and a crosswind gusting 40 knots—and had still made it to the crew room in time for breakfast.

"Right," he said, fastening his seatbelt. "Hayley, you've read the routing. You know what to expect. Bristol's standard left-hand pattern, runway 27. Touch and go only—don't flare too early, it's a short hop and we want clean contact, not a ballet recital."

"Copy that," Hayley replied, setting the trim and checking her initial inputs. "Shall I call for clearance?"

Toby gave her a nod. "You've got the radios, Captain."

She couldn't help the twitch of a smile that rose at that, before keying the mic. "Birmingham Ground, PanEuro 738F, requesting startup and pushback, stand Echo Four."

"PanEuro 738F, startup and pushback approved, facing west. Expect taxi to Alpha Five for Runway Three-Three. QNH 1007."

"Startup and push approved, Alpha Five for Three-Three, QNH 1007, PanEuro 738F."

With the clearance in place, she began the flow checks, reading through the laminated card. The comforting choreography of aviation returned like an old friend. With every switch, every system check, she felt the scaffolding of her confidence tighten, lifting her higher.

Toby ran through the engine start sequence as Hayley called for pushback. The nose gently eased away from the stand as the tug whined beneath them, and the twin Leap-1A engines spooled up in sequence, their start-up chime rising through the flight deck.

Livingstone leaned forward slightly. "And just like that, you're a flight crew again."

"Feels like coming home," Hayley murmured.

* _ * _ * _ *

"Bonjour, Lille Control, this is PanEuro Flight Seven Three Eight Foxtrot, 10 miles out, descending Flight Level Zero Niner Zero, Runway Two-Six, over," Hayley called out on the radio, knowing that although some pilots would group the numbers, she preferred to keep to the formal ICAO phrasing—clear, measured, and textbook-perfect. The French ATC replied with professional calm, thick-accented but intelligible.

"PanEuro Seven Three Eight Foxtrot, cleared for approach Runway Two-Six, surface wind two seven zero degrees at six knots, report established."

Hayley acknowledged smoothly, her voice low and crisp. "Cleared for approach Two-Six, will report established, PanEuro Seven Three Eight Foxtrot."

The approach into Lille was calm, uneventful—by the book. But to Hayley, seated in the captain's position, every second was electric. Her grip on the sidestick was light but firm. She followed the glidepath markers like a seasoned professional, mind parsing the raw data on the

PFD instinctively, like music read by a pianist. She felt the aircraft in her bones—its weight, its attitude, its tiny corrections in the crosswind.

As they intercepted the localiser, Toby began a running commentary—part mentoring, part banter.

"Right, you're a smidge high but trending back nicely. Watch that sink rate on short final. Winds are steady. You've got the flare point marked?"

"Got it," Hayley replied, flicking her eyes down to the radar altimeter, then back up again.

Livingstone's voice crackled in her headset. "Take her in, Hayley. But remember—touch and go. Don't love the runway too much. She's only yours for a second."

The wheels kissed down with just the right firmness to register—a crisp, professional contact. Not showy, but sound. In a flash, she advanced the thrust levers. The aircraft surged forward again, lifting its nose with eagerness, obedient to her every instruction.

"Positive rate."

"Gear up."

"Climb power set."

She exhaled with a grin forming, her eyes flicking to Toby's approving nod. It was no longer a dream. This was flying.

* - * - * - *

Back in the cruise towards the English Channel, the chatter on the radio thinned. French airspace drifted behind them. Hayley relaxed in her harness, fingers running lightly across the throttle levers like a pianist testing ivory.

Toby passed her another flapjack and twisted to glance back at Livingstone. "Not bad, eh?"

The captain's reply was characteristically understated. "I've flown with worse. Ones with lanyards and job titles."

Hayley laughed softly, a flush of pride colouring her cheeks.

As they reached the FIR boundary approaching Kent, London Control handed them back to Southend Radar, then Manston Tower. It felt almost poetic.

"PanEuro 738F, good evening. Cleared for visual approach, Runway One Zero. Winds light and variable. Report established final."

Hayley replied smartly, adjusting their heading. "Visual One Zero, Wilco, PanEuro 738F."

Outside the cockpit windows, East Kent unfurled below like a patchwork quilt in twilight. Ramsgate's harbour lights twinkled near the coastline, and the dark mass of Pegwell Bay stretched to the south.

"You know," she murmured, "Living in between Ramsgate and Broadstairs, I remember when EUJet used to fly into Manston, faintly but I remember once going to the beach at Ramsgate, and a Fokker went lower than they normally go—made the seagulls scatter like they'd been slapped by thunder."

Toby chuckled, eyeing the altimeter. "Well, don't go showing off just to relive the glory days. This isn't a flypast for the Turner Contemporary."

Hayley smirked. "Spoilsport."

Captain Livingstone leaned forward, his voice calm but precise. "Right, let's see how much muscle memory you've got left. Winds are calm, no traffic, and the tower's practically falling over themselves to welcome us back. Treat it like a short field—Runway 10's not Heathrow."

Hayley's hand hovered over the sidestick, the calm confidence radiating from her fingers even as her eyes danced across the Primary Flight Display and Navigation Display. The A320neo was now descending smoothly through 3,000 feet, just east of Sandwich, Kent, with a clean vector in towards the final approach fix. The Channel was a silver sheen to the south, and Manston's solitary runway was now clearly visible—Runway 10, gleaming under its simple but reassuring PAPI lights.

"Manston Tower, PanEuro Seven Three Eight Foxtrot, visual Runway One Zero, three miles final."

The tower came back almost immediately. "PanEuro Seven Three Eight Foxtrot, runway 10, cleared to land, surface wind calm. Welcome back."

"Cleared to land, PanEuro Seven Three Eight Foxtrot."

There was something about that call—'Welcome back'—that made Hayley's chest tighten. Not in fear, but in awe. This was her home airfield, in a way. The one closest to where she'd grown up, trained in simulators just a few miles west. The one her dad had flown over hundreds of times. The one that never really saw much commercial use… until now.

She shifted her focus. This was a short runway, and while there was no performance penalty on an empty ferry flight, precision was still everything. The last thing she wanted to do was float the landing and have to go around on a perfectly clear evening. That wouldn't do—not here. Not tonight.

"Gear down."

Toby read back, "Three greens."

"Flaps full."

"Vapp 132 knots set."

"Confirmed."

The aircraft slowed obediently, slats and flaps fully deployed now, the sound of wind whistling just slightly higher-pitched around the fuselage.

Livingstone leaned forward behind them. "Watch your flare height. Manston's runway sits on a slight plateau—don't let the illusion mess with your depth perception. No heroics. Just plant it on and keep it straight."

Hayley nodded, eyes focused. The PAPIs were perfectly on slope. The localiser was nailed. She centred the sidestick with an almost imperceptible pressure.

"Hundred above," Toby called.

"Minimums."

"Landing," she replied.

She gently flared at thirty feet, pulling the nose up just enough, throttles to idle, rudder trim neutral. The main gear touched down with a firm but elegant thud, followed by a slight squeak from the nose wheel.

"Speed brakes up."

"Reverse green."

"Seventy knots."

She applied manual braking. The aircraft decelerated quickly, the runway centreline lights slipping past the cockpit in a rapid, evenly spaced rhythm until they turned off at the mid-runway exit.

"Nicely done," Livingstone said, his voice entirely devoid of sarcasm. "That was sharp. Controlled. You'd have passed your line check with that one."

Hayley grinned, wiping a small bead of sweat from her brow. "I had a good FO," she said lightly, glancing sideways at Toby.

"Don't think flattery gets you out of post-flight checks," he said with a mock frown.

After taxiing onto the remote stand beside Hangar 2, they ran through the full shutdown sequence. The auxiliary power unit kicked in with a low hum, keeping the cockpit warm while the electrical systems powered down methodically.

"Right," Livingstone said, unfastening his harness, "let's sign the airframe log and get her locked up. Engineering will pick it up in the morning. This one's staying parked here overnight."

Hayley chucked as she and Toby simultaneously reached for the tech log binder stowed in the side compartment. She flicked through to the current page as Toby unclipped a pen from his flight bag and handed it over.

"I'll log her as H. Northcott in the SIC column, just as agreed," Livingstone said, peering over her shoulder. "Callsign, routing, weather conditions, remarks—you can jot down the touch-and-go entries for Bristol and Lille, too. Operational training. Completely legitimate."

Hayley did so with care, her handwriting neat and precise, as if the significance of this moment would be carried forever in the ink. Under "Remarks," she added simply:

Dual-sector observational and SIC flight. Satisfactory handling.

She signed beneath it, alongside Livingstone's bold scrawl. The weight of those signatures felt more meaningful than any exam certificate she'd ever earned.

Stepping outside, the tarmac was lit in that half-washed hue of sodium lamps and cold halogen floods. Hayley noticed Livingstone looking at her personal flight log, a pen in his hand, writing something down in a quick, looping script. He handed the small black book back to her with a quiet nod.

"Just endorsing your log with the ferry flight and a few extra notes, so if you do apply for a stewardess role, and another friendly Captain, or Powers, is piloting, they'll know I've seen you in action. There's a couple, mind you, who think the gimmick of male flight decks and female cabin crew is a good thing, mostly a few who are bloody arses who think groping a lady is acceptable and don't realise half the women they're mocking could probably hand-fly an ILS to minima better than they could with all the autopilots in the world. So, I've left it clear—you're not cabin crew with a hobby. Just promise me one thing. If you do apply for a cabin crew position, apply for Manston, and as soon as BA or another airline start wanting FOs again, get back on the proper track. Take that rating, use it, and get yourself a cockpit door that closes behind you because it's yours, not borrowed. This seat's too rare to waste."

****

CHAPTER 4 – Sisters
Thursday 18th March 2021

Hayley was sat cross-legged on the sofa, FlightRadar24 on her laptop, the virtual replay of the ferry flight tracing a ghostly arc from Birmingham to Manston via Bristol and Lille. The magenta line—a silent echo of a mere few hours ago playing out with the elegance of a flight which, looking on the list of 'trending' flights, with forum users confused why the route was via Bristol and Lille.

She knew that, even though it was tempting, if she responded to the speculation threads on PPRuNe or Reddit, she'd be breaching every unspoken code of aviation humility she held dear. Still, there was a pull—something deeply satisfying about knowing that the obscure routing was now part of someone else's aviation trivia. A line of magenta and mystery. And she had flown it.

Her hands hovered over the keyboard for a moment, the cursor blinking in the "comment" box under a thread titled "What the hell is PanEuro doing with BHX–MSE via BRS + LIL?" Someone had replied, half-joking, "Scenic route? Or someone's hour-building on the sly?" Another user had already tried to track down the tail number and confirmed it had no scheduled passengers onboard between BHX and MSE.

Hayley smiled to herself and shut the lid of the laptop gently. Let them guess. Let the enthusiasts chase the truth through speculation and ICAO routing codes. The truth was far more nuanced, and far more personal, than any of them could guess.

She leaned back into the throw cushions of the Northcott family home in Broadstairs, coincidentally only a few doors down from the famous Bleak House, knowing that Dani, her sister, was due to be up in a few hours to make her way to Heathrow for flight VS505, a short hop at 0715 to Brussels on a Airbus A330, before returning to Heathrow on flight VS506, the same aircraft, within four hours—a perfectly timed daylight rotation for a widebody check-ride assessment.

Her dad, Alan, on the other hand, was slated for a later wakeup, as he was on a 1530 Heathrow to Chicago British Airways flight. As he was one of the senior Captains at BA, he often took the more choice long-haul assignments, such as JFK, Chicago, Johannesburg, Cape Town, Doha and Tokyo, flights that, prior to the pandemic, had been run-of-the-mill staples of a long-haul pilot's schedule, but in the Covid era were now carefully selected slots, weighed down by logistics, layover restrictions, and crew bubbles. He'd spent the evening before triple-checking his documents, because while seniority had its perks, it didn't stop the layers of bureaucracy airlines now wrapped around every international movement like bubble wrap around crystal.

"You know the AvGeeks on Discord think that the FO on that flight was full of new blood?" A voice behind Hayley said, and she knew instantly that her 27-year-old sister was on the stairway. Looking at the time, Hayley realised it was 0342, and that Dani had woken up because of the drive to Heathrow looming on the horizon. Hayley didn't even have to turn her head—she knew that voice, knew the way Dani's soft South London-tinged vowels always seemed to carry a mix of irony and affection.

"Yeah?" Hayley replied, keeping her voice low so as not to wake their mum. "I know who the PIC and SIC was. Pair of FOs... well, one FO and a trainee FO with a dodgy teabag habit and a penchant for flapjacks," she added, letting the smirk reach her voice. "You need driving to Heathrow?"

Hayley knew her sister's car, a BYD Seal, electric, with a range that could allegedly get her to Heathrow and back on a single charge, had been in and out of the charger socket since 10pm. But she also knew Dani didn't trust the infrastructure yet—not when the alternative was a lift from her sister with aviation-level punctuality and a shared history of laughing at M25 diversions.

Hayley's car, however, a Ford Focus with a petrol engine and a reassuringly analogue dashboard, was Dani's preferred option for airport runs—reliable, predictable, and free from any anxiety-inducing battery range indicators. Hayley had a habit of always keeping the tank full, an ingrained aviation mindset of ensuring adequate fuel reserves. Dani appreciated that kind of preparedness. After all, pilots, whether airborne or grounded, lived by the principle that planning eliminated panic.

"Not yet, they've just messaged me. My flight's been cancelled. I'm on a 2005 Heathrow to JFK now, as the FO has got Covid and the Captain planned for it has tested negative but is quarantining. A350, so, like Dad, I'll be crossing the Atlantic. Except I don't get his comfy layover—mine's out tonight, back tomorrow. Pity it's not a 787 I've got as I need to get more hours on that side of things."

Hayley twisted around on the sofa, drawing her knees to her chest as Dani padded softly into the room, pulling an oversized Virgin Atlantic crew hoodie tighter around her slender frame. Despite the change of flight, Dani seemed remarkably calm—years of scheduling chaos, crew shuffles, and disrupted patterns had clearly hardened her against any unexpected disruption. Her long, dark hair, normally meticulously tied into a sleek chignon under her captain's hat, hung loosely now around her shoulders, giving her a relaxed, almost carefree appearance that was rarely visible when she was fully in uniform.

"You look remarkably chill about being booted off a nice, easy Brussels hop onto a redeye to JFK," Hayley observed quietly. "Last-minute long-haul out of nowhere? I thought you'd be fuming."

Dani shrugged, leaning against the kitchen counter opposite. "To be honest, Hales, at this point I'm just glad I'm still flying. Brussels would have been easy—just long enough to tick the boxes without needing a nap, back home for dinner—but I'd rather cross the pond at night than have another cancellation. My roster looks like a Christmas tree, all reds and greens, with cancellations, standby, and simulator checks every other day. I've got a nice one coming up for the 10th of April, A330 to Barbados, but who knows if it'll even happen. I just hope the Government keep that 12th April date of the easing of restrictions, because if it does, we'll be back to a full schedule in no time." Dani's eyes drifted for a moment, her thoughts fleeting as she absentmindedly traced the rim of her coffee cup with a fingertip. "I can get you, Mum and Dad a cheap flight out if the restrictions ease up. It's a standby ticket, but if you want to come out to the

Caribbean, just say the word." Dani's smile was playful, but there was an edge of longing in her eyes. It was the kind of smile that said 'I'm tired of all this uncertainty, but I'll make the best of it'.

Hayley chuckled softly, knowing that her sister had longed for the days when full flight rosters were the norm. A short hop to Brussels was a chance for an easy day, and a long-haul flight to JFK was an opportunity to cross the Atlantic with purpose. But she also understood the deep fatigue that Dani felt, buried beneath layers of aviation bureaucracy and the sense that everything was subject to change with little notice.

"Barbados, huh? Maybe I'll take you up on that," Hayley said, rubbing her face with a sigh. "If I get back in the air, that is." Her fingers brushed against the laminated Observer pass she had left on the table, the one Livingstone had handed her after the ferry flight.

"You're serious about this, aren't you?" Dani asked, her voice low but full of curiosity.

Hayley took a deep breath and shifted her legs, sitting up straighter. "I don't know, Dani. I don't know what's next. I've flown more in the past 48 hours than I have in the last year. A year ago, I was grounded, uncertain, wondering if I'd ever get back in the cockpit again."

She paused for a moment, the reality of her situation weighing on her chest. There was something about being in the air again that felt like coming home, even if it was unofficial and unlogged. Her heart longed for it, but her mind was more cautious, reminding her of the risks and the hard road ahead.

"I might apply for a cabin crew... sorry, Stewardess... post at PanEuro," Hayley suddenly said, sighing. "If it's the only way to stay in the air, then so be it. I'm not proud of it, but it might be the only option left. At least it's a wage and when Easyjet, Wizz or TUI at Gatwick have job openings, I could slip back into a flight deck sooner rather than later. But if not, it might be a way to get in, even if the brass doesn't want to see women in the cockpit unless they're in the galley, stirring up the tea." She sighed, staring at the Observer pass again, fingers absent-mindedly tracing its edge. "I don't know what to do next. What I want, what I'm capable of, or even how long I can keep waiting for an opportunity that might never come. And hey, at least Manston's only a 15 minute drive and not god knows how long to get to Heathrow, right?" she added, with a slight chuckle to herself, trying to lighten the weight that had settled around her words.

"Wizz or Easyjet? Really? Why not go for something more stable like British Airways or Virgin?" Dani's voice was tinged with disbelief, her eyes narrowing as she watched her sister's conflicted expression.

"Because the business market is dying, Dani, but the leisure market will be alive soon enough," Hayley replied, running her fingers through her hair, still tangled from a restless night. "There's always a demand for people to fly on holiday, and those low-cost carriers are going to be first off the ground once everything starts to pick up again. They'll want pilots, trained or half trained, quickly, as you know what people are like when a £9.99 fare pops up.

They'll be scrambling for crews. If I can get into PanEuro as part of cabin crew, it means I'll have access to the grapevine, know when sudden opportunities might come up. And when the market recovers, I might just find myself on the flight deck sooner rather than later. It's not glamorous, but it's a foot in the door." Hayley paused, looking at her sister. "It's not the ideal situation, but it might be the only option left."

Hayley glanced up at Dani, who was silent for a moment, processing her words. The room was quiet, save for the soft hum of the radiator and the distant sound of the sea, which had been a constant companion throughout Hayley's childhood. A sense of calmness washed over her as she sat back and let the soft waves of nostalgia help ease the heaviness in her chest.

"I get it," Dani finally said, her voice softer now. "You just want to be in the air again. And I'm not going to pretend like I don't get that either. We've both grown up surrounded by it—Dad, always flying somewhere, and us glued to the airport windows watching planes take off. But Hayley, if you're doing this just for the 'foot in the door'... it's not worth it. You deserve more than just a door with a crack. You deserve a cockpit."

Hayley smiled faintly at her sister's words. Dani had a way of putting things into perspective, but it didn't change the facts. The pandemic had forced the aviation world into hibernation, and even as flights slowly resumed, the road back to a cockpit felt more like a winding trail than a straight path. She had no illusions—her training, her hours, her ambitions—all of it seemed like distant dreams some days. But here she was, perched on the edge of hope and reality, unsure of where the next step would lead.

"I know, I know," Hayley replied, tapping the side of her mug absently. "But you know what they say... You take what you can get. And if this is what it takes, then it's better than just waiting. I'd rather have my foot in the door than just sit here hoping for a miracle."

Dani shook her head, walking over to the sofa and sitting down beside her sister. "Don't make excuses. You don't need to settle. Maybe I don't have the right to say this, but I know how it feels to push for something you really want. I didn't get where I am by accepting second best. Yeah, things got disrupted, but you're still here, and you're capable of so much more. Don't let this moment—however frustrating it feels—become the point where you stop fighting for what you really deserve."

Hayley looked at her sister, her eyes searching for the confidence Dani always seemed to exude, even when things were uncertain. Dani had always known what she wanted, even when the world around them seemed uncertain. Hayley, on the other hand, often found herself floating between decisions, unsure of which path to take.

"I don't know, Dani," Hayley said, her voice tinged with doubt. "I've been on the ground for so long. The dream feels so far away. I keep thinking that if I just take a step back, maybe something will fall into place... but it doesn't. And I'm not sure how much longer I can wait around like this."

Dani leaned back into the cushions, her arms crossing as she studied her sister thoughtfully. "Look, Hales, I know it's not easy. And I get that you're frustrated. But I've seen you in action—you're not a 'maybe' kind of person. You don't wait for things to fall into place. You go out and make it happen. You've got a strong head on your shoulders, and you're damn good at what you do. Maybe the flight deck isn't open right now, but that doesn't mean it won't be again."

Hayley sighed deeply. Her fingers traced the edge of her Observer pass again, the same laminated card that had felt so much like an invitation to something greater just hours before. But now it felt like a piece of paper—something symbolic, but not quite tangible.

"I wish I had your certainty," Hayley muttered, feeling the weight of her uncertainty press against her chest. "I really do. You've always known what you wanted, and you're out there, living it."

"Maybe I look certain," Dani said softly, "but I'm just as lost as you are sometimes. This job, this lifestyle, it's all changing. And just like you, I've had days where I felt like I wasn't going to make it. That maybe I was going to be stuck in limbo forever. But I got through it. I kept pushing, even when I didn't feel like it. That's how it works."

Hayley raised an eyebrow, intrigued. "How do you keep going, then? When the uncertainty gets overwhelming?"

Dani smiled, her lips curling into a soft, knowing grin. "I remind myself why I'm here. Why I started. And when I forget, I think about what I'm fighting for. You're fighting for the same thing, Hales. To be in the air again, to take control, to live your dream. Don't let the setbacks change that. They're just part of the journey."

"I don't know," Hayley murmured, glancing down at the pass again. "Everything feels so much harder now. The world is so different, and I just... I don't want to be stuck."

Dani's expression softened, and she placed a hand gently on Hayley's shoulder. "I get it. But that's why you don't stop. You're not stuck, Hales. You're just waiting for the right time. And when it comes, you'll be ready. We both will."

Hayley looked at her sister, a sense of comfort settling in her chest. Dani had always had that way of making things seem simpler. And maybe it was. Maybe she had been complicating her own journey by overthinking every step.

For the first time in a long while, Hayley felt a glimmer of hope. It wasn't a grand, sweeping wave of certainty, but a small, steady pulse of belief that perhaps she wasn't as far from her dream as she thought. Maybe it wasn't about waiting for an ideal moment. Maybe it was about finding a way to make that moment happen.

"I've got time," Hayley finally said, her voice soft but firm. "I'm not giving up. I'll figure this out."

Dani's smile widened, and she leaned back against the couch, looking satisfied. "That's my sister."

The sound of the clock ticking steadily in the background filled the silence between them, but for once, it didn't feel oppressive. It felt like time, rather than something to be feared. Time was on Hayley's side—just like it had been for Dani, just like it had been for her dad all those years in the cockpit.

****

CHAPTER 5 – First Day at Stewardess School
Monday 29th March 2021

Hayley had to admit, apart from the girdle, heels, lipstick and the need to have her bust professionally measured by a woman named Marlene in a lab coat, it wasn't the worst first day she'd ever had.

PanEuro's "Stewardess Academy"—yes, that was the official title, emblazoned on a faux-marble plaque next to the entrance to the basement classroom—was less a training centre and more a fashion shoot on a loop. The place smelled of furniture polish, Elnett hairspray and filtered coffee. Everything was gold trim, pastel-blue walls and pretend sophistication; the kind of set you'd find in a 1970s sitcom, if that sitcom involved a lot of thinly veiled sexual politics and a manual titled Smiling Through Insubordination.

The irony that the school, as it was, was at Birmingham, not Manston, as they had appropriated funds from the West Midlands Combined Authority to "provide City and Guild Qualifications in Air Cabin Crew", the words that the website had specifically promised in large, swirly font beside a photo of a smiling girl in a pillbox hat offering a tray of Buck's Fizz to an elderly man in a flat cap. Hayley had looked at it, once, late at night, after too much wine and too little hope, and thought, Well, if I can't fly the bloody thing, I might as well get on board somehow.

Technically, she muttered to herself, it is another qualification, and that means one more bullet point on her

CV, one more notch in the belt of survival, one more way to stay near the aircraft rather than locked out of it. The girdle pinched, the shoes bit into her heels, and she hadn't worn this much eyeliner since sixth form prom. Still, she was in.

The classroom—if it could be called that—had wall-to-wall carpeting in pale peach, six mock airline seats bolted to the floor, and a podium that looked like it had once been used for a beauty pageant in Rhyl. Everything was framed in gold-effect plastic, the sort of aesthetic one might find in the lobby of a mid-tier wedding venue near the M6

Joining her to form the class of 6 was a former RAF Typhoon Flight Lieutenant named Sarah Marsh, a college dropout named Tannie Keyworth, a former Easyjet cabin crew member named Agatha Dean, a former Manic Radio Manchester, Bee Manic, host named Emma Lang and a barely 18 year old girl named Poppy Knight.

Their Poise and Profile tutor, a former Deportment teacher named Mrs Rosemary Havers, who insisted on being addressed as Mrs Havers, not Miss or Ma'am, stood at the front of the classroom like a porcelain relic of finishing schools past. She wore pearls the size of gobstoppers, a stiff navy skirt suit and an expression that conveyed equal parts disdain and distant fondness for her charges. Her hands were perpetually clasped at her waist, and her perfume—Chanel No. 5, so strong it clung to the walls—seemed to precede her like an aura.

Of all the students present, Hayley knew that she and Sarah were the most experienced in terms of being at the controls of a plane, Sarah in military Quick Reaction Alert jets at RAF Lossiemouth and her in the Airbus family of civilian airliners. It had been a fact they had bonded over prior to Mrs Havers entering the room.

"You know," Sarah said, eating a peanut from a bowl that had been left out on the fake walnut side table next to a pile of PanEuro Stewardess Standards handbooks, "I've done g-force turns in a Typhoon over the North Sea and been on QRA calls that meant going full throttle with less than five minutes' notice, but nothing—and I mean nothing—prepared me for Marlene and her steel measuring tape. I'm only doing this so I can get contacts to get me into civil flying. I miss being at the controls and feel like I'm drying out just standing here, all hairspray and pantyhose."

Hayley gave a sideways glance, amused. "Same. Though I suspect you've got better stories than me. I don't have any Russian intercepts, or afterburner climbs on my CV."

Sarah chuckled, running a hand through her sculpted blonde bob. "I've got a couple of good ones, yeah. But you probably didn't get booted from the flightline for refusing to do a photo shoot in heels next to a Tornado."

"No," Hayley said, smirking. "But I did once get told I'd be 'less intimidating' to passengers if I smiled more during boarding. By a man who smelt of egg mayo and wore his tie like a noose."

Sarah snorted. "Christ."

Behind them, Poppy Knight tried to discreetly lower her tray-table, only to realise that the fake seats were screwed shut. "Why is this like a theme park but sadder?" she asked no one in particular, her Essex accent bright and unfiltered. "I thought this'd be, like, I dunno... posher."

Emma Lang, leaning against the wall with the natural ease of someone who'd spent years in front of a microphone, raised one eyebrow. "Darling, it's PanEuro. They market themselves as posh, but it's all brass spray paint and budget eggshell carpet. I've seen better sets on 'Homes Under the Hammer.'"

"You were on the radio, right?" asked Agatha, the former EasyJet crew member, whose perfectly smooth bun and default resting-smile hadn't yet slipped. "You were that drivetime girl from Manchester. I used to listen on my breaks."

"Guilty," Emma replied, flicking a fake eyelash back into place. "Bee Manic. Until I got made redundant. Covid. Miss the place to be fair, lots of orgies, coke and booze. My old co-host at one stage, Kyler Thompson, a walking red flag, but he was a good shag. Would fuck me however I wanted with no questions asked. He's shacked up with some whore named Cassie from Altrincham now, got a sprog on the way. Shagged her rotten once, I did. Got her off her tits with cocaine and had her eating my pussy like it was her last meal. She didn't even know I'd slipped something into her WKD. Classic Bee Manic days."

There was a pause.

Mrs Havers, who had just stepped back into the room with a clipboard and a scent trail of Chanel so potent it could've grounded a drone, narrowed her eyes. "Miss Lang," she said, her tone glacial. "This is not Bee Manic.

This is PanEuro. I will remind you—again—that poise begins in thought and ends in expression. Kindly rein in the anecdotes."

Emma raised her hands, palms open. "Yes, Mrs Havers."

"You are not here to indulge in the language of locker rooms or Lime Street," the older woman went on, her pearls catching the overhead fluorescent lighting. "You are here to represent British excellence. To be ambassadors of sky and service. You may think this is just theatre. You are wrong. It is performance—and performance is everything."

Hayley fought not to roll her eyes. Sarah, beside her, gave a subtle military-style smirk.

"Now," continued Mrs Havers, stepping daintily toward the front of the room, "today we begin Module One: The Embodied Stewardess. This is not simply about serving tea or opening the emergency slide. This is about presence. Posture. Profile. The way you walk, the way you sit, the way you pour a glass of orange juice in turbulence and still look dignified. You are to be both hostess and heroine. If you are squeamish about lipstick, deportment, or dealing with a drunken stag party while maintaining a facial expression best described as benevolent neutrality, then you are not cut out for PanEuro."

Poppy's hand shot up. "What's 'deportment' again?"

"Have you ever heard of Ladette to Lady?" Sarah smirked. "It's like that. But with less booze, more lip gloss, and a fire extinguisher if someone sets the galley bin alight."

Poppy blinked. "So… posh manners?"

"Yes, dear," Mrs Havers said, tight-lipped. "But with consequence."

Hayley looked down at her training folder—three rings, plastic cover, pale pink paper. "PanEuro Training Manual: Module One – Embodied Stewardess." The subtitle beneath it made her mouth twitch.

"A Stewardess is Grace in Altitude."

She turned the page. There were diagrams of walking posture, an actual list of approved lipstick shades (Coral Command, Mauve Majesty, Crimson Class), and an entire section on 'Teacup Temperament'—how to serve hot beverages without 'jostling' or 'excess facial engagement.'

This wasn't training. It was choreography. And the deeper Hayley got into the pages, the more she felt like she was studying for a West End audition rather than preparing to handle turbulence and medical emergencies.

"Now, later in the course, we have an original Pan American Purser, who our service and style is modelled upon, who will demonstrate how to serve an in-flight dinner tray without breaking eye contact, disturbing your coiffure, or—God forbid—allowing your stocking seam to twist."

Mrs Havers swept across the classroom like a duchess arriving at a budget tea party. "But before that, we begin with your walk. Line up, please, all six of you. Against the back wall. Posture is the foundation of poise.

Shoulders back, chest proud, chin parallel to the floor. Think Princess Diana on a windy balcony, not Cheryl Cole in a Wetherspoons."

The six women shuffled into position with varying degrees of enthusiasm. Hayley found herself beside Sarah, both standing marginally straighter than they had a moment earlier. Poppy bounced in place like a toddler at ballet class, while Emma blew a stray eyelash off her cheek and muttered something about being "too old for this bollocks."

Mrs Havers took a small wooden baton—God only knew from where—and pointed at Agatha.

"Miss Dean. Please walk to the front, turn, and return. Elegantly. Without clatter."

Agatha stepped forward with a grace clearly honed over years of trolley service. Her steps were measured, her head high, her arms swinging just enough. Hayley couldn't help but admire her fluidity. She'd seen captains do worse taxiing into position.

"Acceptable," Mrs Havers said, making a small mark on her clipboard. "Miss Marsh?"

Sarah stepped forward and began to walk—not stiff, not swaggering, but with the practiced neutrality of someone who had marched in formation with actual purpose.

"Too military," Mrs Havers sniffed. "You're not guarding the Queen, dear, you're presenting a breakfast roll at 37,000 feet. Try again, with softness in the knees."

Sarah tried again, this time with an exaggerated hip sway that made Hayley snort quietly behind her hand. It drew a nod from Poppy and a suppressed giggle from Emma.

Hayley's turn came next.

She moved forward, every inch of her screaming with the quiet dignity of someone who would rather be conducting a before-start checklist in the flight deck, but was now instead being assessed for "flirtatious balance."

"Mm," Mrs Havers murmured. "Decent effort. But I'd suggest a little more confidence in the hips. You walk like you've got purpose. Admirable in a doctor. Less so in a stewardess. You're here to serve, not save."

Hayley didn't reply. She didn't trust herself to.

Poppy's walk was something between a Love Island entrance and a drunken Bambi attempt. Mrs Havers physically winced. "Your arms," she said. "Are not paddles. Keep them close. You are not flagging down a minicab."

"Sorry, miss," Poppy muttered. "I just get excited when I've got heels on."

"Then bottle it," Mrs Havers said.

Emma sauntered next, chewing invisible gum, her hips moving like she was still on a club night promotion run in Deansgate.

"That," Mrs Havers said, once she'd finished, "was a lap dance with a lanyard."

Emma grinned. "So I pass?"

"You pass a nightclub audition," Mrs Havers replied, ticking something anyway. "PanEuro, we shall see."

By the time the sixth attempt was over, everyone's cheeks were either flushed or contorted in barely concealed fury. Mrs Havers stood, clipboard clutched, and announced, "You may take ten minutes. When we resume, we shall begin the seating routine: a perfect perch, knees together, ankles tucked, back straight. No slouching. No spread. Legs are for elegance, not expression."

The group dispersed like misbehaving schoolgirls released from detention.

Hayley drifted to the coffee corner where the "PanEuro Blend" was a tepid, watery brew that tasted like something squeezed through the seatbelt fabric of a Vauxhall Corsa. Sarah joined her, chucking two sugar packets into her paper cup with the resignation of a woman who had eaten ration packs in Arctic drills and still found this worse.

"I had an instructor at Lossiemouth who once screamed at me for breathing too loudly on approach," she said, sipping. "But even he never made me sashay like I'm auditioning for Eurovision."

Hayley nodded grimly. "And we're paying for this."

"Technically," Sarah said, "the City and Guilds are. Or the Combined Authority. Or some panicked MP who thinks 'aviation heritage' means women in gloves handing out peanuts."

Poppy wandered over, highlighter in hand. "So is this… like, really how it was back then?"

"Yep. Remember when we got weighed before coming into see the seamstress?" Hayley said, pouring some milk into her coffee with the same precision she would've used to measure fuel flow. "Apparently, it's for 'uniform consistency'. Can't have the hem rising awkwardly if your BMI creeps past a 22. The Yanks did a drama with Margot Robbie a few years ago, called Pan Am. They've even took the age and marital rule Pan Am had here, according to a friend who's a First Officer, for stewardesses. Can't be older than 32 when hired. Retire at 34 or go to selling tickets. Can't be married. Can't have children. And if you fall pregnant during your contract? Termination. Not metaphorically. Actually, fired."

"Technically I've only got 2 years as a stewardess," Sarah said, sipping her coffee with a look of gallows humour. "31, 32 in October. Served 10 years as a RAF officer, so this is what you'd call my encore."

Emma drifted by, having lit a cigarette that she clearly had no intention of smoking indoors but wanted everyone to know she could if she fancied it. "God, remember when I was twenty-two and I thought a bad day was a producer telling me I couldn't use the phrase 'cock-socking knobhead' before the 5pm travel bulletin. Now I'm being told my knees aren't demure enough for 'teacup posture.'"

Hayley sighed into her cup. "I logged four sectors on an A320 and got complimented by a Captain who's flown more hours than most MPs have told lies. And now I'm being told my walk has too much intent."

"You're not wrong," Sarah muttered. "Apparently 'intent' isn't ladylike. We're air geishas now. Trim the aircraft, trim the waist."

Agatha, the ex-EasyJet pro, had pulled her hair down from its regulation bun and was gently massaging her temples. "Y'know what gets me? I used to do Palma rotations on two hours' sleep, with a toddler at home and a nosebleed from a pressurisation fault, and nobody ever once asked if my lipstick was 'Crimson Class.' They just wanted the chicken or the pasta without a fight."

Emma smirked. "Yeah, but at EasyJet you're allowed personalities. PanEuro wants Stepford Slags."

"Stepford Slags," Sarah repeated, with a sudden laugh. "Put that on the lanyard."

Poppy had perched herself on the edge of a seat, legs swinging beneath her like a schoolkid. "I only applied 'cause the dole told me I needed to apply or get sanctioned."

Hayley stared at Poppy, her paper cup halfway to her lips. "Wait—seriously?"

Poppy shrugged, swinging her legs a little higher. "Yeah. Was doing hairdressing at college but got bored. Got sanctioned for skipping too many job centre appointments, so they said I had to do 'aviation entry' or lose Universal Credit. This came up. They said it sounded glamorous. Mum said it'd stop me getting pregnant."

Emma barked out a laugh. "Oh love, if anything, this course's more likely to get you pregnant. Have you seen the uniform? It's like asking for turbulence in the back row."

Agatha made a noise that was somewhere between agreement and despair.

The overhead Tannoy crackled—not a real one, just a speaker mounted above the training classroom's fake bulkhead—and Mrs Havers' voice, clipped and contemptuous, came through.

"Ladies, your ten-minute respite has concluded. Kindly reassemble with your folders, your lipstick reapplied, and your minds focused. It is time for seating posture and tray etiquette."

"Tray etiquette," Sarah muttered as she pushed herself off the wall. "Sounds like something you'd get points for on Bake Off."

"More like Downton Abbey meets Ryanair," Hayley said, draining her coffee and binning the cup.

Back in formation, they were instructed to sit in the mock airline seats with the grace of coronation guests. Back straight, knees pressed together, feet angled at a demure tilt—as if the act of merely existing in a chair was a ballet of deliberate submission.

"This is the 'elegant recline,'" Mrs Havers intoned. "You may not be reclining in reality, but your body language must never suggest stiffness or strain. You are the vessel through which calm is transmitted. You are a stewardess. You are serenity, with a smile."

Emma raised her hand. "What if I've got a bladder infection?"

"Then you excuse yourself with discretion and return with composure," Mrs Havers said, not missing a beat. "We do not announce medical concerns to passengers, nor do we squirm. We glide. Always."

Hayley felt the muscles in her lower back begin to ache from the pose. It was less 'glide' and more 'vertebrae protest,' but she kept her expression fixed. It wasn't unlike holding a level-off after a bad vector. Endure, trim, adjust.

After thirty minutes of simulated smiling and non-verbal grace, they were handed plastic trays and instructed to balance them with one hand, elbow tucked in, while opening a faux bottle of Prosecco and pouring it at a precise 30-degree tilt.

"You are not dinner ladies," Mrs Havers snapped as Sarah over-poured her glass and Hayley accidentally nudged the fake cutlery askew. "You are choreographers of comfort. Conductors of class."

Agatha's tray clattered as it was placed too firmly on the folding table.

"You are not fencing a microwave meal, Miss Dean. You are presenting an experience."

"An experience of what?" Emma muttered under her breath. "A last supper before Ryanair steals your landing slot?"

There was a dull thud as Poppy dropped her bottle entirely, the fake fizz rolling along the floor. She tried to chase it but got her heel stuck in the carpet.

"Miss Knight," Mrs Havers said, her expression fixed somewhere between scandal and disappointment. "We serve beverages. We do not chase them like cats after gobstoppers."

By lunch, everyone's patience was thinner than the sandwiches. They were given half an hour to themselves in a nearby staffroom, a space that doubled as an overflow area for security interviews and smelled like bleach, burnt toast and trauma.

The sandwiches were triangle-cut and wrapped in clingfilm, the type that sweated under fluorescent lighting and always tasted faintly of office sadness. Hayley found a seat beside Sarah and unwrapped hers with surgical precision.

"Egg mayo," she said, grimacing.

"At least it's not coronation chicken," Sarah replied, peeling back her own. "I had a trauma over that after a week in Belize. Something about lukewarm mayonnaise in 40-degree heat haunts a person."

Poppy, sitting cross-legged on a counter, had managed to coax the vending machine into releasing a Penguin bar by sheer persistence. "So, like… do we get wings at the end?"

"Wings?" Agatha blinked.

"Yeah, like… proper little wings. Like pilots get," Poppy said, holding her Penguin bar like it was a sceptre of ambition. "My cousin got some on a Ryanair kids' flight when he was four. Wore them for weeks."

"You get a badge," Sarah said. "Well… a pin. And a certificate, I imagine. I doubt it'll be a framed calligraphy scroll. You only get wings if you're a pilot, love."

Poppy pouted, unwrapping the foil with exaggerated delicacy. "Well, that's a bit stingy, innit? We should get wings. Or tiaras. We've got to wear tights in July and serve fizz to creeps who don't know the difference between 'stewardess' and 'stripper.' Might as well get a badge for it."

Emma cackled around a mouthful of turkey and something-supposedly-cranberry. "Tiaras. Now that's a vibe. Give me a bloody coronation and call me Queen of the Cattle Class."

Agatha stirred her tea, lifting her gaze with the gentle weariness of someone who'd endured too many sunrise turns from Luton. "You'll get a brooch with the PanEuro logo, gold plated if you're lucky. Just don't lose it. You're charged a fiver if it goes missing."

"Five quid?" Poppy squeaked. "What is it made of? Unicorn hair?"

Hayley leaned back in her chair and folded her arms. "I reckon it's made of broken dreams and varnished regret."

The whole table dissolved into exhausted laughter, the kind that came not from joy but survival—worn-out women bound together by lipstick regulations, posture drills and a mutual loathing of plastic Prosecco bottles.

Sarah tapped the lid of her yoghurt pot like it had personally offended her. "Honestly, I can't work out if this is a joke, a satire or a highly elaborate piece of performance art."

"It's definitely performance," Hayley said, sipping her own tepid tea. "Just not the kind that deserves a standing ovation."

Their conversation lulled, not quite comfortably but with the resignation of those who'd reached the halfway mark of a long-haul flight with two hours of turbulence behind and three more ahead. The staffroom buzzed with the low hum of vending machines and muffled footsteps in the hallway.

Emma, always the first to break silence, reached into her handbag and pulled out a battered paperback—Confessions of an Air Hostess, its cover art all golden lighting and gravity-defying hairdos. She dropped it onto the table like a holy text. "This is what I thought I was signing up for. Love triangles, dashing pilots, a suspicious number of sequins."

"Trust me, shagging is normal in the airline industry," Hayley said with a cheeky grin. "My sister, Dani, is a First Officer at Virgin at Heathrow, and she's shagged half the flight deck at Terminal 3. It's mainly the long haul lot who get up to it, though. Jetlag, layovers and hotel minibars are a dangerous combination."

Hayley then laughed as she saw Emma and Poppy were believing what she was saying as if it were true. "Nah, seriously," she then continued. "Most pilots are in long term relationships, married to someone or to the job. Yes, there's casual hook-ups, yes, there's scandal now and again, but mostly it's trying to grab a Pret sandwich before your slot time and hoping the weather holds over wherever you're heading. One of my close friends is a PanEuro First Officer, and he's engaged to someone, he's as strait-laced as they come. Dani, my sister, she's married to the job, and my Dad? He's been happily married 30 years, never cheated on my mum once, and that's saying something considering he's been flying international for most of that time. There's temptation, sure, but most of us just want eight hours' sleep and a decent coffee before pushing back."

Emma leaned in, mock whispering, "Still sounds like a better deal than the bloody WKD-swigging antics of Bee Manic. I once got propositioned live on air by a bloke who thought cunnilingus was a pasta dish."

Poppy snorted, mid-Penguin. "What even is cunnil—?"

"Don't," Agatha said sharply, holding up a hand. "Don't finish that sentence."

****

CHAPTER 6 – Turbulence in Training

Wednesday 7th April 2021

Hayley arrived at the Stewardess Academy that morning fifteen minutes early, her navy PanEuro-issued heels clicking across the tiled hallway that led to the changing room. She'd learned by now not to be surprised when the room still smelled like a blend of Chanel No. 5, stale clingfilm and the aggressive artificial lemon of industrial surface spray. The fluorescent lights buzzed faintly, as though fatigued by the sheer force of Mrs Havers' expectations.

The previous night, she had not been at the hotel that she and her fellow trainees were officially meant to use, but instead at the home of a PanEuro First Officer who she had, admittedly, slept with as the two were former school friends in Kent, with him having moved to Birmingham at 16 when his family had got a mortgage on a new-build in Solihull. His name was Theo Sullivan, and he'd ended up at L3Harris two intakes ahead of her, had flown for Wizz for a year pre-COVID, and now wore the crisp navy stripes of PanEuro's mid-seniority FO roster. It hadn't been planned, not really; she'd bumped into him by chance outside the staff canteen when she'd gone to fetch a half-dead cup of tea and a KitKat to cope with another afternoon of 'Elevated Teacup Poise'.

What had followed was a blur of nostalgia, too much supermarket rosé, a shared Uber, and a night spent tangled in each other's bodies, their lust spilling over into passion. The two had been sexual partners before, so she knew that the familiarity between them had made the line between comfort and complicity blurrier than it should have been.

Theo's flat was a modest two-bedroom off the Stratford Road, nestled between a halal butcher and a chain gym that never seemed to have more than three people inside. It had the smell of engineered air and fabric softener—impersonal but oddly clean, the sort of place a man lived in when his job was both his lifestyle and his escape. The bedroom, dimly lit with one of those faux-hipster filament bulbs that gave everything a tawny, sepia hue, still bore the marks of their night together: a rumpled duvet, a half-empty wine bottle on the windowsill, and her bra looped, almost shyly, around the arm of a bedside lamp.

They hadn't talked much. There had been laughter, a brief, fumbling catch-up that skipped over emotional details in favour of easy laughter about old instructors and worse simulators. When she woke at 06:15, Theo was already in the kitchen, shirtless, cooking eggs and humming to himself.

"Scrambled or fried?" he'd asked over his shoulder, his voice too casual, too breezy, for the knot that had already started forming in her stomach.

"Fried," Hayley had replied, buttoning up her blouse without meeting his eye. "And strong coffee. Very strong."

Now, as she adjusted her uniform in the mirror of the changing room, dabbing at a faint smudge of mascara that had survived her morning shower, she tried to silence the small voice in her head that whispered mistake over and over. It wasn't that she regretted the night. Not entirely. But she knew, deep down, what it had been—a moment of weakness masquerading as warmth.

"You look like you've had a good fuck," Hayley heard from behind her, and she turned to see Emma Lang had walked in, a smile on her face that danced the line between amused and approving. The ex-radio host dropped her handbag on the bench with an exaggerated sigh and began undoing her coat, flicking her long, manicured nails in the air as though to dissipate invisible drama.

"Or," Emma continued, "a terrible night's sleep, which is basically the same thing but with less dopamine and more regret. But let's not split hairs."

Hayley gave a weary smile. "Bit of both, maybe."

"So come on, girl, how was he in bed?"

Hayley glared at her in the mirror, but the humour behind it softened her response. "Not that it's any of your business, but… better than the coffee machine in the staffroom and worse than a Boeing 737 sim session at 3am."

Emma barked a laugh and began pulling her long red hair into a regulation bun. "Sounds about right for a man with pressed uniform trousers and three different varieties of hot sauce in his cupboard."

Hayley didn't reply. She was too busy smoothing her skirt, checking for any signs that she hadn't slept on a proper mattress. The heels still pinched. The bra still cut into her ribs. She felt like a costume version of herself—

something airbrushed and polished, a performance stitched into seams and stitched smiles.

The rest of the group began to trickle in shortly after. Sarah, ever the stoic, nodded curtly at both Hayley and Emma before heading straight to the lockers. Agatha arrived looking like she'd spent the night meditating and drinking hot lemon water—immaculately fresh and as well-put-together as ever. Poppy, on the other hand, had half an eyelash dangling off her cheek and was muttering something about buses and men who couldn't read Google Maps.

"Today's the slide drill, yeah?" Tannie asked, her voice still scratchy from sleep and several late-night fags. She was rubbing at a spot of foundation that had smudged onto her blazer sleeve and looked like she'd wrestled with her pillow rather than slept on it.

"Slide and ditching," Agatha confirmed. "With 'life jacket presence and poise' review by Mrs Havers herself." She sighed like someone who had faced down a firing squad and survived, but not without trauma.

"Bloody hell," Emma groaned, slipping into her heels and wincing. "There goes my pelvic floor. I haven't jumped out of anything since the time I got kicked out of a moving Ford Mondeo in Sheffield."

Poppy blinked. "Wait, what?"

"Long story. Terrible breakup. Great playlist."

They filed out into the corridor together, a mismatched parade of posturing, perfume and varying degrees of poise, just in time to be intercepted by Mrs Havers herself. She stood at the junction like a particularly stern headmistress, clipboard in hand, lips pursed like she was assessing the curvature of their souls.

"Ladies," she said with clipped precision, "today we begin the Emergency Response component of your Stewardess Formation. This module is both physical and psychological. You will demonstrate courage without crassness, urgency without panic, and assertiveness without vulgarity. You are not to scream, unless on fire. Even then, you must do so with dignity."

Emma muttered something about making sure her screams were pitched in B minor.

Mrs Havers, either ignoring her or refusing to acknowledge the comment, turned on her sensible heel and led them through a set of double doors into the mock training bay. The room was colder than the rest of the facility, dominated by a full-sized cabin mock-up built onto a hydraulic platform. The slide, covered with a protective tarp for now, loomed at the end like an inflatable promise of embarrassment.

There were also life vests lined along a table, plastic emergency doors, and a mock galley complete with extinguishers, trolleys and tray carts bolted to the floor.

"This," Mrs Havers said with theatrical gravity, "is where image meets impact. Your role in an emergency is not to be ornamental, but operational. However—" her eyes swept over them like a radar locking onto the weakest target, "—PanEuro demands that even crisis should be met with composure. A stewardess does not simply survive. She leads."

Hayley felt a pang of resentment twitch under her ribs. It was the same old story dressed in a new uniform—be excellent, but don't overshadow the men. Be capable, but never authoritative. Be prepared, but not… ambitious.

Still, she nodded along like the rest. Survival, after all, sometimes meant saying nothing.

"Miss Marsh," Mrs Havers snapped, drawing Sarah forward with a single, imperious wag of a finger, "demonstrate the vest procedure."

Sarah stepped forward, face expressionless. She lifted one of the standard yellow life jackets from the table, unfolded it smoothly and slipped it over her head. Her movements were military-efficient—too efficient, as far as Havers was concerned.

"You're deploying, not donning tactical gear," Havers said, with a withering look. "Smile. You are the harbinger of hope in the event of water impact, not a parachute instructor on day release."

Sarah didn't smile, but she tightened the straps and mimed inflating the vest with such mechanical precision that Hayley almost applauded.

"Next," Havers called.

They rotated through the drill, each of them demonstrating how to secure the vest, instruct passengers, inflate only outside the aircraft, and respond to cabin smoke with calm authority.

Hayley's turn came. She executed the sequence perfectly, her hands steady, voice clear.

"Better," Havers said. "Though you could look less like you're preparing for an execution."

Hayley bit back the retort that almost reached her lips.

They moved on to the slide. The hydraulic platform groaned into life, elevating the mock door until it was level with a designated jump height. The slide, once deployed, coiled down like a fat, expectant tongue.

Emma raised an eyebrow. "I've had worse landings on Tinder dates."

"Miss Lang, you will go first," Havers said icily.

Emma gave a mock salute and stepped up to the door. "Brace, brace," she muttered under her breath, then launched herself forward. The slide caught her awkwardly and she bumped halfway down on her side, coming to rest in an undignified pile of limbs.

Poppy cheered.

Agatha was next. She landed with elegant precision, knees together, arms crossed, looking like someone emerging from a royal engagement rather than an emergency landing.

Hayley followed, her leap precise, posture tight. She hit the slide and rode it down with controlled grace, hitting the mat at the bottom with a roll that surprised even herself.

As she stood up, brushing imaginary dust off her skirt, she noticed Mrs Havers glaring at her with an expression that hovered somewhere between grudging approval and deep internal disappointment. As if Hayley had executed the move too well, too confidently—like she'd robbed the drama of the moment by actually being competent. Again.

"Miss Northcott," Mrs Havers said, marking something down on her clipboard with a dramatic flick of her biro. "Adequate. Although do remember, it is not a gymnastic dismount. Maintain restraint. Control is commendable, but a stewardess must never appear like she is enjoying the emergency."

Hayley blinked, unsure whether to laugh or weep.

"Understood," she replied flatly, joining the others who had congregated near the life raft demo area, where Sarah was already half-through inflating the bright orange monstrosity with a look of quiet disdain.

They were split into pairs for the next drill. Hayley was paired with Agatha, while Sarah ended up with Emma—something that made Hayley briefly wonder if the world was attempting to trigger another Cold War. Poppy and Tannie, meanwhile, formed the kind of duo that would either get themselves knighted for heroism or reported to Ofcom for excessive profanity.

"Right," Mrs Havers barked, her voice cutting across the echoey chamber, "water ditching drill. Your objective: evacuate passengers via the over-wing exit, direct them to the slide-raft, assist with boarding, deploy the survival canopy, and maintain passenger morale while not appearing hysterical, flustered, or above your station."

"What about snacks?" Emma deadpanned. "Do we get to hand out a KitKat and a quick cry before we open the exit?"

"No," Havers snapped. "Though I suggest you consume less sugar. Sarcasm is not a vitamin."

Emma turned to Sarah. "She wishes sarcasm was a vitamin. I'd be indestructible."

Sarah didn't respond, instead focusing on buckling the raft's support ropes with the meticulousness of a woman used to securing ejection seat harnesses.

As Hayley and Agatha took their positions, they were handed emergency scripts laminated in thick plastic. It included lines like "Sir, please remain calm while I assist you into the life raft" and "Madam, this is an emergency, not a negotiation about your handbag." Hayley resisted the urge to ask what to do if Madam in question had just decked a pensioner over the last seat in Row 26.

They ran the drill.

Hayley moved quickly, calling instructions with a clarity that echoed across the mock-up bay. Agatha followed, smooth and poised, ushering phantom passengers with the grace of a West End understudy. When it came to boarding the raft, they executed the hoist manoeuvre with precision—Hayley on the 'injured dummy', Agatha guiding from the rear. It worked flawlessly.

"You're a solid team," Agatha noted quietly as they climbed into the raft together, pretending to shield against imaginary wind.

"You've done this before?" Hayley asked, still panting slightly.

"Only for real," Agatha replied. "Palma. 2018. Fire in the galley. We didn't evacuate, but we were seconds from it. Two passengers fainted. Captain made the right call, but the smell of burnt plastic and fear still lives somewhere in my sinuses."

Hayley nodded slowly. "Still here though."

Agatha offered a small smile. "Always. It's the lipstick that keeps us going."

They crawled out of the raft as the others completed their drills. Sarah and Emma had managed to perform the evacuation while bickering about fuselage integrity, while Poppy had accidentally slapped Tannie in the face with the inflation cord and was now laughing so hard, she couldn't speak.

"Ladies," Mrs Havers said crisply, clearly deciding to pretend the slap hadn't happened. "Now that you have completed your initial exposure to slide deployment and raft boarding, we move on to the psychological component."

Hayley felt her stomach drop. She had no idea what that meant, but from the glint in Havers' eye, it involved at least one deeply patronising roleplay exercise and possibly a monologue about the 'strength in submission.'

They returned to the classroom, still slightly damp from the raft's synthetic material, to find the lights dimmed and a projection screen lit up with the PanEuro logo and the words:

Module 4B: Composure Under Crisis – Passenger Management and Emotional Scripting

"This," Mrs Havers intoned, "is where we discover who among you will truly earn your wings."

Emma leaned across to Sarah and whispered, "I'd settle for not earning a criminal record."

They were each handed a script packet.

Hayley flipped through hers. Each page was a scenario: *"Engine Failure Mid-Flight (Secondary Cabin Role)"*, *"Aggressive Passenger in 21D (Redirect to Duty-Free Distraction)"*, and *"Medical Emergency – Unresponsive Child (Calm Demeanour Vital)"*. The instructions included prescribed facial expressions, acceptable language choices, and 'suitable tonal approaches for reassurance.'

"It's like a GCSE drama class written by an airline HR department," Hayley muttered.

Each trainee was called to the front, one by one, to perform a randomly assigned crisis script. Emma got "Misbehaving Hen Party, Row 15" and absolutely nailed the 'authoritative but ladylike tone,' despite finishing the scene with a wink and the line, "Please fasten your seatbelt, madam, and kindly remove the inflatable penis from the aisle."

Somehow, Havers still gave her a pass.

Sarah's performance of "Sudden Turbulence and Cabin Disruption" was executed with the precision of a woman who once flew a jet at Mach 1, and although Havers sniffed that she was "too brusque," she also added "decisive under pressure" to her clipboard.

Hayley's script was one she hadn't seen yet: *"Dead Passenger, Rear Galley"*.

For a moment, she froze.

Not because the situation was unfamiliar—she had read countless case studies, attended medical response lectures, even done CPR drills—but because the idea of standing in front of her peers pretending to react to a death in a space designed to serve stale lasagne made her stomach twist.

She took a breath and stepped forward.

"Begin," Havers said.

Hayley adopted the posture she'd been taught—upright, open, reassuring but authoritative.

"Captain," she said to the imaginary interphone, "we have a Code Red. Passenger unresponsive in the rear galley. Pulse absent. I am commencing CPR. Request medical diversion priority."

Her voice didn't waver.

She mimed the compressions, counted aloud, described the AED use and the moment she realised it was too late.

Then she stood upright and faced the room, lifting her chin.

"I've covered the passenger respectfully. The area is cordoned. I've asked Emma to move the trolley and assist with nearby passengers. Sarah is calming the immediate cabin."

It was clinical. It was detailed. It was textbook.

It was everything she knew a real moment like that demanded.

"Miss Northcott," Havers said after a pause, her voice devoid of sarcasm for the first time that day, "that was... acceptable."

Hayley nodded, relief flooding through her bones.

The rest of the afternoon was a blur of evaluations, clipboard ticks, minor humiliation and grim sandwiches with egg or prawn, no other option. By the time the day ended, most of the group were flagging—heels in hand, hair pulled loose, lipstick long since faded.

In the locker room, Emma dropped her bag onto the bench with a groan. "I swear to God, if tomorrow's module includes *emotional labour under hydraulic stress*, I'm going to throw myself out the emergency exit headfirst."

"Tomorrow's grooming inspection," Agatha said, slumping onto the bench. "Full uniform, full makeup, no exceptions."

Hayley muttered something unprintable.

Tannie produced a small hip flask and passed it to Poppy.

"Is that...?" Poppy asked, blinking.

"Rum," Tannie confirmed. "And trauma support."

They passed it round like survivors of a minor war, each sip a reminder that they were still standing, still in this game, no matter how absurd it was.

As Hayley laced up her trainers for the walk back to her digs, she looked down at the Observer pass that still lived in the inside pocket of her uniform blazer. A talisman. A reminder. A future, however faint.

Because amid the poise drills and posture lectures, amid the sexist pageantry disguised as procedure, she hadn't forgotten.

She wasn't here for the tray service.

She was here for the flight deck.

And one day, they'd have no choice but to see her for what she truly was: a pilot, not a passenger in a pencil skirt.

* _ * _ * _ *

Hayley was sat in the terminal at Birmingham International, as she had had a WhatsApp message from a friend that a British Airways flight from Washington had been diverted from Heathrow due to being held in an holding pattern, and, instead of waiting as it was getting low on fuel, it was diverting to Birmingham as there was ATC issues at Heathrow.

Looking at her watch, Hayley noticed it was half past 6, and that it had been scheduled to arrive at Heathrow nearly an hour earlier. Curious, she pulled out her phone and tapped open the FlightRadar24 app again, fingers navigating with ease to the inbound BA216 from Dulles. Sure enough, it was on final approach to Runway 15, squiggling in from the northeast after a brief orbit around Warwick. The aircraft, a Boeing 777-300ER, G-STBB, was painted in British Airways' signature Chatham Dockyard livery and had been airborne for over seven hours.

She watched as it touched down—smoothly, professionally—and felt a familiar pang, that silent twist in the chest that ached whenever she watched an aircraft arrive and knew she wasn't the one bringing it home.

The terminal was quiet, save for a few bored travellers and a smattering of airline staff sipping from take-away Costa cups. It was one of those post-peak hours when airports seemed suspended in a kind of artificial dusk, the lighting never quite matching the mood.

A few minutes later, she spotted the crew descending the airstairs on a remote stand, led by none other than her own father, Captain Alan Northcott.

Even from a distance, Hayley recognised his stride—measured, confident, the sort of presence that only came with years in the left seat. He wore his navy BA overcoat against the chill, epaulettes gleaming under the sodium glow of the floodlights. His hat was tucked beneath one arm, his other hand gesturing politely to the co-pilot beside him, a younger man who looked to be about her age. They paused for a moment by the waiting shuttle bus, the two conversing briefly before boarding.

Hayley hesitated. She hadn't seen her father in person in weeks. He had been flying mostly long-haul, with quarantine rules and roster pressures keeping him away from home more often than not. They kept in touch, of course—video calls, text messages, the odd voice note sent from a hotel room in Boston or Doha—but it wasn't the same. Seeing him now, in full uniform, the hero of her childhood, made something stir uncomfortably in her chest.

Her phone buzzed. It was a message from Dani.

Dani Northcott: *Saw on the system that Dad's flight got diverted to BHX. I've just got off a JFK that diverted to MAN.*

Hayley knew that Virgin served Manchester as well as Heathrow, and it didn't surprise her that Dani had ended up at the other end of the M6 while their father was parked just a few hundred metres away. Still, the coincidence of all three Northcotts being in the UK on the same evening—and diverted from their usual airports, no less—felt surreal. A family of aviators, scattered like contrails in a shifting wind.

Hayley Northcott: *You're kidding. What are the odds?*

Dani Northcott: *Might be time to start blaming Mum. She did always say we were drama magnets.*

Hayley Northcott: *Or maybe just victims of Heathrow's ATC being held together by duct tape and passive-aggressive tea rounds.*

Dani Northcott: *Are you going to speak to him?*

Hayley stared at the message. Her eyes flicked toward the airside windows, where the shuttle bus carrying the BA crew was just pulling away from the remote stand.

Hayley Northcott: *Don't know. He looked tired.*

Dani Northcott: *He always looks tired. You should still say hi. It's been weeks.*

Hayley Northcott: *I will. Maybe. I just... don't want to tell him I'm in girdle school.*

Dani Northcott: *Tell him you're undercover. Deep ops. Subverting the patriarchy in heels.*

Hayley Northcott: 😄 *Noted.*

The bus disappeared from view. Hayley stood up slowly, her back still aching slightly from the ridiculous posture drills, and made her way out of the terminal into the cool evening. The car park lights buzzed overhead. Her breath hung briefly in the air.

It had been a long day. A long month. A long bloody year.

And yet, despite everything, she didn't feel broken. Bent, maybe. Twisted into a shape she didn't quite recognise, wrapped in PanEuro pastel and trussed up in lipstick codes and shoe-shine lectures. But not broken.

And she knew that things could happen in the future beyond her control.

****

CHAPTER 7 – The Mistake
Friday 25th June 2021

Hayley knew she had just made the biggest mistake of her life with Theo that the passion the two had just let themselves sink into, again, had been a comfort, not a connection. As she sat on the edge of his bed, blouse re-buttoned and tights rolled up halfway, her stomach twisted in quiet regret.

The reason for the regret?

They had just had 3 rounds of sex, drunken sex, and neither she nor Theo had used protection.

At her most fertile time.

The worst possible time for her to be careless.

Her eyes wandered to the wine bottle on the windowsill, then the empty condom box on the floor. Empty. She didn't even remember seeing it before—probably from before lockdown, judging by the dust. Theo was now in the en suite bathroom, brushing his teeth to the rhythm of a soft hum. Blissfully unaware. Or maybe just pretending. He was always good at avoiding reality, especially when it was tangled in bedsheets.

Looking at the clock on the bedside table, she noticed that it was barely past midnight, and that it had been 7 hours since she had finished the days training, 6 hours since she had had a takeaway with her father before he got a taxi, at the expense of British Airways, back to his plane where the crew would do a ferry flight, as the later traffic around Heathrow would be impossible to slot into with any guarantee of punctuality. BA had decided to take the unusual step of moving the aircraft overnight to Cardiff Maintenance for an upcoming C-check, leaving Alan Northcott and his crew responsible for a quiet hop westwards.

Hayley hadn't expected to see her father, let alone share a rushed meal of overpriced carbonara and lukewarm white wine at an Italian chain restaurant inside Birmingham's Grand Central complex. He had looked tired—more so than she remembered. Their conversation had been functional, distracted. She'd made small talk about PanEuro training, avoiding the more surreal aspects like Mrs Havers' obsession with 'emergency grace' and the silent war between Emma and Sarah. Alan had asked about Dani too, naturally. Hayley had lied and said she'd spoken to her just the other night.

And then she'd bumped into Theo, when she had arrived at Birmingham Airport, as he had finished a Moscow in-and-out, the flight back barely loaded with passengers, mostly Russian business types and a handful of returning Brits. She hadn't been expecting it—one minute she was heading towards the station platform, scrolling through the evening's rail delays with a growing sense of irritation, and the next, a familiar voice called her name. Not the name shouted across a playground or yelled during a sim crash in training, but that tone. Warm. Familiar. Dangerously so.

Now, hours later, sat on his bed with her tights bunched at the knees, Hayley's chest tightened with a swirl of guilt and fear. It wasn't just the sex—it was the recklessness of it. The collapse of her usually methodical brain into something soft and stupid, like overcooked pasta.

Especially as it had been 3 rounds of virginal sex and 2 of anal sex, as she had always wanted to experiment with that.

But now she was regretting it.

Not the fact that she had pleasure from it all, but the fact that the lack of protection now hovered over her like an emergency oxygen mask—dangling, ominous, and completely outside her control.

Hayley pulled her tights the rest of the way up, the nylon catching slightly against her dry skin. Her knickers—still damp—had been discarded somewhere under the bed, but she didn't want to crawl around looking for them. Not now. Not with the gravity of what she'd done beginning to settle like turbulence at cruising altitude.

She stood up, steadying herself on the corner of the IKEA dresser. Her reflection in the mirror caught her off guard: makeup half-removed, hair slightly mussed, blouse wrinkled where Theo's hands had been. She didn't look ruined, exactly. But she didn't look right either.

The door opened.

Theo emerged, a towel draped loosely around his waist, his dark hair wet from the steam, a toothbrush still in his mouth.

"Didn't realise you were up," he mumbled through the foam.

"I didn't sleep," Hayley said. Her voice came out flatter than intended.

He raised an eyebrow, spat into the sink, and rinsed. "Too warm? Or was it the radiator? It rattles like mad—been meaning to bleed it."

Hayley shook her head. "No, Theo. It wasn't the radiator."

Theo paused in the doorway, finally sensing the shift in her tone. He leaned one shoulder against the frame, mouth twitching.

"I know what you're thinking," he said, sighing. "I remembered after I woke up myself about 20 minutes ago that we'd forgot to use... well, that, as... well, I'd ran out. My cousin's on her way round... she's been to a 24 hour pharmacy, as she's a GP and knew the name of the pharmacist on shift. It's sorted, alright? She's picking up the morning after pill for you. She also called me a pillock and that if I loved you like I used to and still cared about you enough that I should... shit... did I just say that?"

Hayley watched as Theo started to clam up after he realised what had just slipped from his mouth. His face reddened, the cocky confidence of the past few hours melting into awkward tension. He scratched behind his neck and looked down at the floor, towel slipping a little too low on his hips before he tugged it back up.

Hayley blinked.

"You're a bloody idiot," she said at last, voice tight. "And you really should've led with the part about your cousin. Instead of talking about bleeding radiators."

Theo winced. "Yeah. That was… not my finest moment."

"No," she agreed. "It wasn't."

She crossed her arms, fingers brushing the creased seam of her blouse. Her skin still felt flushed, not from warmth or shame, but from the sudden shift—lust to logic, the crash that always came after a high. The morning after hadn't even arrived yet, and already the guilt was setting in like condensation on cabin windows.

"Why didn't you say anything earlier?" she asked, not unkindly.

"I didn't want to make a big deal out of it," Theo replied. "You seemed… I don't know. Like you needed something tonight. Something easy. Familiar. So did I."

Hayley closed her eyes for a second. He wasn't wrong. That was what made it worse.

"I did," she admitted quietly. "But I didn't need a pregnancy scare."

There it was. Spoken. Out loud.

Theo's face crumpled slightly. "I know. Look, I know it doesn't change what happened, but I'm taking responsibility. The second I realised—well, I called Sophie. She was out on a call anyway. She'll be here in ten, tops. Anyway... erm... if you do... well, y'know... then I'll do the right thing by you... I mean if you'll let me."

Hayley's breath caught in her throat.

There was something both noble and naïve about the way he said it—as though 'doing the right thing' was as simple as announcing it. As if it solved anything. She didn't want nobility. She didn't want a crisis to draw them together. And she definitely didn't want to be someone's "reason to settle down" just because they'd fumbled their way into a shared consequence.

She exhaled sharply, her voice lower now, and oddly calmer. "Theo… don't say things like that unless you mean them."

"I do mean it," he insisted, stepping into the room now, more clothed in guilt than cotton. "I'm not that kid from school anymore, Hales. I know I mess about, but when it counts—"

"This shouldn't have been the thing that made it count," she interrupted.

There was a silence.

The kind of silence that hangs over a cabin during final descent—everyone strapped in, no further announcements, just the long wait for the landing.

Hayley finally stooped to pick up her knickers from beneath the chair, when she noticed Theo get down in front of her, down on both knees, and kiss her stomach, not once but twice—soft, reverent, as if he were apologising to something not yet real, something that existed only in the cruel imaginations of "what ifs."

She froze.

"Theo…" she purred as he then started getting up, pecks of kisses on her …stomach, then lower ribs, then up to her collarbone. It wasn't lust. Not this time. It was something desperate and muddled, a clumsy attempt at reassurance. Hayley didn't stop him at first, too caught in the confusion, the sobering weight of consequence and history and muscle memory.

She knew that, if she was honest with herself, she had feelings for Theo, feelings that had never really gone away, even after all the time and distance.

She knew that, unlike the other men she had slept with, Theo never played mind games, never said one thing and then disappeared behind a wall of silence and unread messages.

The next thing she knew, she was undoing her shirt again, and that she felt herself losing herself in the moment. This time, however, she heard, while Theo was kissing her, the sound of a bedside cabinet drawer opening, the sound of rummaging around it for something, and then the sound of a box being lifted out.

Theo paused his kisses as he brought it into view: a crumpled, half-forgotten pack of condoms—new, unopened. Not from the dusty empty box on the floor.

"Turns out," he said, breathless but genuine, "I'm more of a muppet than a monster. Thought I'd ran out, but it seems I'd still had one last bit of sense left in me. These were in the drawer with my passport and a half-eaten pack of Strepsils. Romance, eh?"

Hayley laughed. Not a full, free laugh, but one of those reluctant ones that escape when tension finally tips into absurdity. She sank back down onto the bed, the crumpled duvet beneath her knees, blouse half-undone again.

"The passport drawer," she said. "Of course. Every man's chaos corner."

Theo grinned, flashing her a boyish look that had once been charming in sixth form, and somehow still carried weight now. He sat beside her, quiet for a moment, the box of condoms resting between them like a ceasefire treaty.

"I didn't expect any of this," he said softly. "Seeing you. Tonight. Us."

"Neither did I."

"And I know it was reckless. But I don't regret seeing you again. Even if you do."

Hayley pulled the collar of her blouse tighter around her. She didn't want this to be a scene from a bad soap, where one night led to declarations of love and a morning filled with saccharine promises.

"I don't regret seeing you," she said. "I just regret letting myself get swept up without thinking. That's not who I am anymore."

Theo looked down at the crumpled sheets. "Maybe not. But it was who we were, once. And for a few hours… maybe we needed to be that again."

She didn't answer.

Instead, she just sighed.

*_*_*_*

By the time Sophie arrived, the flat had quietened. Hayley was fully dressed again, sat in the small kitchen with a mug of water cupped between her hands. She felt no need to make small talk with Theo now. The mood had shifted—less charged, more reflective. Like cabin crew in the galley after a rough patch of turbulence, assessing the damage with bruised professionalism.

Sophie was brisk, efficient, and blessedly devoid of judgement, well, devoid of judgement for Hayley. Theo on the other hand wasn't so lucky. She handed Hayley a pharmacy bag and nodded.

"Take it now," she said. "You've got twelve hours of grace left, but best not leave it. It's levonorgestrel. No prescription required. I've also got you a petrol station sandwich and a bottle of water, it's in the bag. Cheese OK for you?"

Hayley nodded, grateful for Sophie's pragmatism and no-nonsense approach. "Cheese is perfect, thanks."

"Good," Sophie replied briskly, turning sharply to her cousin with a glacial stare. "And you—what exactly were you thinking?"

Theo had the grace to flush deeply. He shifted his weight uncomfortably from foot to foot, as if trying to find solid ground under Sophie's withering glare. "It was a mistake, Soph. I'm handling it."

She raised an eyebrow. "Clearly."

The flat fell into a strained silence, punctuated only by the distant sounds of traffic on the Stratford Road. Sophie, sensing that further interrogation would yield diminishing returns, softened her tone slightly. "Look, mistakes happen. I'm not here to lecture either of you, but for God's sake, Theo, get your act together.

Theo opened his mouth to protest but thought better of it, settling instead on a sheepish nod. Sophie turned back to Hayley, her voice losing its icy edge.

"You okay? Any concerns or questions?"

Hayley managed a weak smile. "I'll be fine. Thanks for sorting this."

Sophie offered a brief nod, eyes sharp but compassionate. "No worries. And don't overthink it. Just take the pill, get some rest, and if anything else comes up medically or otherwise—call me."

Hayley nodded again, feeling absurdly emotional at Sophie's kindness. She watched as Sophie swept out of the room, her departure punctuated by the firm click of the front door, leaving a vacuum of awkward silence behind her.

Theo remained rooted to the spot for a long moment before sinking into the chair opposite Hayley. His gaze fell on the pharmacy bag between them, something unspoken but heavy hanging in the air.

"I'm sorry," he finally said quietly, not meeting her eyes. "I genuinely didn't want to put you through this."

"I know," she sighed, reaching into the bag to retrieve the pill and quickly swallowing it down with a swig of water. The bitter taste lingered at the back of her throat, like a tangible echo of their shared recklessness.

The sandwich sat untouched on the counter, suddenly unappealing despite her hunger. She felt emotionally drained, the adrenaline of panic and anxiety now ebbing into weariness. Theo watched her silently, clearly wanting to speak but unsure what words could possibly make things better.

Eventually, Hayley broke the silence. "It was my mistake too. We both should've known better."

He gave a small, rueful smile. "I think we've always known better; we just ignored it. Anyway, I meant what I said, that I still have feelings for you."

Hayley's hands tightened slightly around the mug. Her heart didn't jump. It didn't flutter. It just… stilled. As though someone had opened a pressure valve in her chest and let out the last of the hot, tangled emotion. Maybe a few years ago, those words would have undone her completely. Now, they just settled somewhere between melancholy and fatigue.

She didn't reply immediately. Instead, she stared out of the kitchen window, where the sodium-orange glow of the streetlamps cast long, broken shadows across the pavement. Somewhere outside, a fox yelped in the distance—sharp, eerie. The city didn't sleep. Not really. It just shifted gear.

"I know you mean it," she said eventually. "But it's been a long time since meaning something was enough."

Theo didn't argue. He just nodded, the smile slipping from his lips like condensation down a galley door. He understood. Or at least, he understood enough not to push her when she was already doing the emotional labour for both of them.

The silence that followed wasn't heavy now. It was gentle. Worn out. Like two people sitting at the end of a long-haul flight, knowing the journey's over but neither quite ready to stand up and reach for the overhead locker.

"I need to get some sleep," Hayley said, rising slowly from the chair.

"You can stay here, you know," Theo offered. "I'll take the sofa. Promise."

She paused, considering. Part of her wanted the comfort—the proximity to someone familiar, the safety of knowing she wouldn't have to face the night alone.

But she knew that if she was stopping here, that she'd rather Theo be laying next to her, not banished to the lumpy IKEA sofa with the squeaky springs and the smell of someone else's laundry detergent. She didn't want more sex. She didn't even want a cuddle. What she wanted—needed—was the warmth of someone who'd known her since before the uniform, before the lipstick drills, before the endless posture lectures and life raft roleplays.

So, she made a decision.

"You can sleep in the bed," she said quietly. "But no funny business. And if... that's if... we do this again tomorrow night, I'm bringing a spare set of uniform and a toothbrush. I am not showing up to Mrs Havers with mascara flake on my eyelids and a bra strap burn like I've been rolling in a thistle bush."

Theo raised both eyebrows, arms lifted in mock surrender. "Understood, ma'am. No funny business. Strictly side-by-side, PG-rated proximity. You have my word."

She gave him a look—somewhere between withering and weary—then padded back towards the bedroom. She'd left her shoes by the dresser and found her overnight bag slumped by the wall where it had half-fallen during their earlier escapades. A pack of face wipes lay half-pulled from its sleeve beside it.

As she wiped her face clean in the mirror, she studied the eyes that stared back. Still her, just softer at the edges, like a photograph left too long in sunlight. Her expression was unreadable, even to herself. She wasn't angry. Not really. She wasn't even sad anymore. Just... sobered.

Theo appeared behind her in the reflection, now in trackie bottoms and a plain T-shirt, barefoot. He stood silently for a moment before quietly reaching past her to tidy the loose pillow from the floor and shake out the duvet. Hayley watched the gesture. It was small, almost absurdly domestic. But there was something disarming about it too.

When she climbed into the bed, she made sure to face the wall. Not as a rejection, but as a boundary. Theo followed, wordless, slipping in on the other side and lying still. The gap between them wasn't large, but it was definitive. They didn't speak again that night.

* _ * _ * _ *

It was half past 7, and Hayley woke up to find that Theo was spooning her, his hand on her breasts, his involuntary erection against her. She knew that it wasn't his fault, that in the night couples sometimes do that sort of thing, and that she was, surprisingly after the scare the previous night, comfortable with his position.

And then the alarm clock sounded, the JD and Roisin breakfast show on Free Radio mid-laugh about "workplace disasters that involve superglue, a managerial arse, and one very unlucky intern." The usual chirpy, chaotic energy of local FM filled the dim bedroom, the alarm too loud for the early hour. Hayley groaned softly, one arm flopping over her face as Theo mumbled something unintelligible into the back of her neck.

She could feel the length of him pressed against her, his morning arousal evident. But she wasn't alarmed. They weren't mid-fling anymore, not after last night. It wasn't about lust now. It was about consequence, about reckoning, about navigating the minefield of intimacy without making another mess of things.

And then he shifted.

Not because he was asleep, but as the alarm was on her side, and his mobile, that was on charge on a wireless

112

charge while hers was plugged on, was ringing, a phone call.

She saw his hand grab the phone and she could see that it was the Dispatch Office of PanEuro—displayed in bold on the screen, the company number unmistakable even in its early morning blur—sent an immediate jolt through Hayley's still-sleepy brain. She twisted around in Theo's arms, her voice dry and still thick from sleep.

"Isn't that your ops line?"

Theo groaned and rolled onto his back, squinting at the glowing screen. "Yeah," he muttered, then cleared his throat. "Shit. That's not good."

He tapped the green circle to answer, the volume still audible enough that Hayley could hear the muffled voice on the other end, even through the distorted speaker.

"First Officer Sullivan? Morning. Sorry for the early call—standby allocation just changed. We've had a crew out sick on the 10:04 sector from Birmingham to Tallinn. Report time 09:03. Are you available?"

Hayley knew that he was slated for a Belfast, but that was in the evening, and he was only on short call today— meant to have a few more hours before he could be legally roped in.

The irony that she also had to be at the airport, albeit for another day in Stewardesses Academy, at the same time, meant that they were now on the same countdown clock. Different destinations, different uniforms, but both racing toward the same chaos of a shift that neither had emotionally prepared for.

Theo cleared his throat again, voice thick with sleep but soft with professionalism. "Yeah, I'm available. I'll be there. Thanks."

The dispatcher confirmed the report time again before hanging up, and Theo let the phone fall to his chest with a soft exhale. He stared at the ceiling, the silence between them stretched thin with reluctant anticipation.

Hayley sat up slowly, brushing her hair back from her face. "You're flying today."

He nodded without looking at her. "Tallinn. Short turnaround. Back tonight, if all goes to plan."

She stretched, her muscles protesting after a night of poor sleep and emotional weight. "I've got life-raft theory and lipstick inspection. If I don't contour my cheekbones to the acceptable PanEuro radius, I may be publicly executed in front of the galley trolley."

Theo chuckled hoarsely. "Ah, the aviation glamour dream. Bet Amelia Earhart never had to master waterproof mascara under duress."

"Or deploy a smile while disembarking pensioners who've spent two hours complaining about the chicken wrap," Hayley added.

They shared a look—a strange, fleeting moment of genuine connection amidst the bleary-eyed fog. No romance, no seduction. Just two professionals, broken in different ways, finding temporary solace in their mutual fatigue.

She swung her legs out of bed and stood, adjusting her bra strap beneath her blouse. "I'll shower first. I need to look less like I've been hit by a catering truck."

"Unless you don't mind us showering together, saves time and water. Don't worry, I'll wear a condom this time. I'm not a complete moron to have forgotten again."

Hayley knew that it would save time, as they both had less than an hour and half to shower, dress, put makeup on and get from Shirley to Birmingham Airport during the rush hour, but she also knew that they couldn't risk getting swept up in the wrong kind of urgency again—not now. Not after everything.

She paused in the doorway of the bedroom, towel in one hand, toothbrush in the other. Her expression was somewhere between amused and exhausted. "Tempting," she said dryly. "But let's not push our luck, shall we? We've already played Russian roulette once this week."

Theo grinned, but didn't argue. "Fair. Solo shower it is. You know we've broke the law, in a way."

Hayley raised an eyebrow as she closed the bathroom door behind her. "Broke the law? Bit dramatic, don't you think?"

"The lockdown laws," Theo's muffled voice said, and Hayley chuckled, as she knew that he was technically right. Mixing households overnight, even in April 2021, while under semi-loosened lockdown rules, still counted as a breach—especially when it involved wine, sex, and zero distancing.

"Don't worry," she called through the door, toothbrush clamped between her teeth as she unrolled her towel onto the heated rail, "I'll write a very sincere apology to Boris on scented PanEuro stationery."

"Toast or grab a Greggs on the way in?" Theo's voice from the other side of the door continued, softer now, like the weight of the morning was finally beginning to settle into something more mundane.

Hayley spat toothpaste into the sink, rinsed her mouth and replied through the sound of running water. "Greggs. Always Greggs. If I have to face Mrs Havers in a pencil skirt with a freshly powdered trauma from last night, I'm at least doing it with a sausage and bean melt in hand."

There was a pause. "Classy," Theo replied.

****

CHAPTER 8 – Gossip
Thursday 8th April 2021

Hayley walked into the training centre for the PanEuro Stewardess Academy clutching the Greggs coffee and Sausage and bean melt that she had and Theo had brought while on their way to Birmingham Airport, the bag of which was now warm and slightly translucent in one corner, when she could feel the chafing in her thighs from the previous night's activities, combined with the corset that she was required by PanEuro to wear beneath her uniform. The garment, stiff with boning and utterly unforgiving, dug into her ribs as she walked with as much grace as one could muster when both arousal and regret still echoed faintly in the body.

The training centre smelled the same as it had all week: lemon surface spray, hot printer toner, and the heavy floral fog of Mrs Havers' Chanel No. 5. As Hayley stepped through the glass doors, she caught sight of her reflection in the panel and quickly adjusted her hat. The angle had shifted slightly since the taxi—thanks to the slightly too enthusiastic kiss Theo had given her cheek as they parted at the curb.

She'd told him "no funny business" this morning. She'd meant it. But his lips had lingered a second too long, and she'd let them. She wasn't sure what that meant, and frankly, she didn't have time to analyse it now.

The reception area was quiet except for the soft hum of the vending machine and the dull whir of the ceiling fan. Hayley made her way toward the changing room, heels clicking against the linoleum, the Greggs bag swinging gently at her side. She'd barely taken two steps past the lockers when a familiar voice rang out.

"Well, if it isn't Lady Morning Glory herself."

Hayley turned to see Emma Lang reclining on the bench like she was holding court in a backstage lounge. She was already in uniform, hair twisted into a sharp, sleek bun that would've survived a category five hurricane, one hand cradling a steaming coffee, the other delicately lifting a blueberry muffin to her glossed lips.

"Greggs?" Emma asked, eyeing the bag like a sniffer dog. "How very… working class of you."

"So says the cow who whored herself out at Manic," Hayley muttered to herself. She knew that Emma had been, like most female Manic hosts, more of a prostitute and cocaine habit, and less of a radio presenter, as, in the locker room two days ago, Emma had revealed all to the group.

*_*_*_*

Tuesday 6th April 2021

Hayley was sat in the locker room, reading the latest Airbus manufacturer briefing, when Emma started talking about her days at Manic. "Honestly, the place was like the set of Geordie Shore meets Narcos. If you didn't leave a trail of white powder wherever you went, they thought you were boring."

Emma had paused dramatically, scanning the circle of women changing around her. Hayley reluctantly lowered her phone, eyebrows slightly raised. Sarah Marsh gave an encouraging nod from behind her locker door, clearly interested in this sordid tale.

"Yeah," Emma continued, clearly relishing the spotlight, "fit blokes, impressionable whores and even bosses who'd have snorted Charlie off their own mother's gravestone if someone told them it would boost the RAJAR figures. Honestly, you think aviation's brutal—radio's like a Game of Thrones episode, except with less integrity and more tequila."

Hayley had glanced around the room, amused by the mixture of curiosity and mild horror on the faces of her fellow trainees. Even Sarah, usually unflappable thanks to her years in the RAF, seemed mildly scandalised. Tannie Keyworth, who'd been quietly trying to wrestle her hair into submission, piped up from behind Emma.

"Hang on—are you saying everyone was at it? Management, presenters, the lot?"

Emma snorted softly, clearly delighted at the captive audience. "Trust me, darling, it was an orgy of excess. And anyone who didn't play along quickly found their contracts mysteriously not renewed."

Poppy Knight had shaken her head, visibly uncomfortable. "And no one spoke up?"

"Spoke up?" Emma laughed dryly, a harsh note creeping into her tone. "This is media we're talking about. You speak up, you vanish faster than last year's Love Island winner. There was this one slut in at the studio, Cassie her name was, Toni Green, she called herself on air. So there

I was, me and Kyler, shagging in the offices, my tits smashed up against the glass, while he was pounding me from behind, when, after he came, Kyler saw that our producer, Cal Ellington, was in the studio, and according to Kyler, the slag had had a baby with Cal when she was 15. Dumped the sprog in care. Anyway, Kyler and I were the mid-morning hosts at Bee Manic at the time, and during the show, she was meant to be shadowing us, learning, and during an advert, I had her on her hands and knees, eating Kyler's cum out of me. Anyway, at Manic, there's a rule that as long as it doesn't interfere with the show, having a shag or doing a line is more than fine. In fact, I've been off my tits so many times that I've lost count. Anyway, Greenie was 19 when she joined Manic, so it's not as it-"

Hayley could see Sarah was getting annoyed with Emma casually all but admitting that she was a sex pest at best and a rapist at worst.

Then the explosion came.

Hayley saw Sarah, the former RAF officer, get right in Emma's face and her expression gradually hardening as Emma rambled on with her usual blend of outrageousness and braggadocio. But the moment Emma crossed the line — that line — Sarah stood.

Not abruptly. Not with theatrics. Just a quiet, deliberate push off the bench, her feet planted shoulder-width apart, and the kind of coiled stillness that only came from military service and knowing exactly when to make your point count.

She stepped toward Emma, slowly, the locker room falling into a hush.

"Lang," Sarah said, voice low but razor-edged. "You might think this is all just a laugh — shock value, bragging rights, another tale to keep you in the centre of attention. But I swear to God, if I hear you talk about another woman like that again — especially one who wasn't in the room to defend herself — I'm going to drag you out of this Academy by your bleached extensions and see how well you handle an emergency slide in freefall."

Emma blinked, taken aback.

"Jesus, calm down, Sarge—"

"No. Firstly its Flight Lieutenant. Even though I'm no longer in the RAF, I earned a commission. I'm not a bloody NCO. Secondly," Sarah snapped. "You don't get to hide behind that smirk and that radio voice. What you just said — that wasn't gossip. That was cruelty, weaponised. And if half of it was true, you should be ashamed. If the other half wasn't, then you've just thrown someone under a bus for your own entertainment."

Emma's mouth opened to respond, but Sarah cut her off again.

"People like you make it harder for every woman who actually wants to be here for the job. Not the drama. Not the clout. The job. You talk about 'shagging in studios' like it's a punchline — but what you described was predatory. And vile."

Hayley could feel the coldness in Sarah's rebuke at the Mancunian, and could see that Emma's mouth opened to respond, but Sarah didn't give her the chance.

"People like you make it harder for every woman who actually wants to be here for the job. Not the drama. Not the clout. The job. You talk about 'shagging in studios' like it's a punchline—but what you described was predatory, vile, and frankly dangerous. And if you ever say something like that again, especially about a woman who couldn't defend herself, you'll be doing it through a disciplinary hearing."

The silence in the locker room was absolute. Even Poppy, who usually had a quip for every situation, had gone still, her eyeliner pencil hovering in the air.

Emma stood rooted to the spot, colour rising in her cheeks—not from shame, Hayley suspected, but from the realisation that the room had turned. That her usual armour of flippancy and shock-value had not just cracked, but failed her.

"I'm just saying it how it is," Emma muttered, brushing a strand of hair behind her ear. "No point pretending the industry's clean."

"No," Sarah said sharply. "There's not. But there's a difference between speaking truth to power and using someone else's trauma as entertainment. What you said about that woman, whether true or embellished, wasn't honesty. It was cruelty. You used her name like a punchline."

Emma looked away.

Sarah took a breath, her voice softening slightly, but still firm. "I've served on Quick Reaction Alert, Lang. I've sat on the edge of a runway at two in the morning waiting to intercept God knows what. I've pulled colleagues out of crash seats and had to tell families their loved ones weren't coming home. I've seen what damage looks like, and I've spent too long in rooms full of men who treated women like jokes. I didn't think I'd have to deal with that here."

* _ * _ * _ *

Thursday 8th April 2021

"You want to watch what you say, Lang, as Sarah won't hesitate to give you another dressing-down if you open your gob like that again," Hayley said, voice low but cool as she passed Emma on her way to the lockers.

Emma flicked a glance at her, lip curling slightly. "Didn't realise we were still doing morning morality plays. What is this, Loose Women at 36,000 feet?"

Hayley ignored her. She wasn't in the mood. Not after last night. Not with her stomach still a knot of caffeine, stress and residual guilt. She popped her locker, retrieved her regulation cabin shoes and makeup pouch, and began the familiar ritual of assembling herself into the corporate fantasy of the PanEuro woman.

By the time Sarah Marsh arrived, the mood in the locker room had settled into a brittle quiet. She exchanged a brief nod with Hayley, who appreciated the wordless camaraderie. Poppy arrived moments later, balancing a giant Costa, a lip-gloss and a copy of Heat magazine under one arm.

"Tannie's not coming," she announced, flopping onto the bench beside her locker. "She rang in this morning, said she had cramps bad enough to fell a horse and couldn't even move. Didn't fancy crawling onto a ditching slide looking like an extra from Holby City."

Sarah snorted. "Hope she phoned Mrs Havers and not just Ops. Otherwise she'll be subject to a cross-examination worthy of a fraud trial."

"Mate, she sounded like she was mid-cramp. I'm pretty sure she just sobbed and hung up," Poppy said. "She told me to tell you lot."

Emma, who had returned to inspecting her manicure, muttered, "Bet she's bunked off to watch Loose Women in a bubble bath with a bottle of Prosecco. I would."

"Not everyone has the stamina to run on cheap fizz and spite, Lang," Sarah said without looking up.

"Some of us have trauma to process through breakfast pastries, actually," Poppy added brightly, unwrapping a cinnamon swirl with one hand and dabbing on lip gloss with the other.

Hayley managed a half-smile. It wasn't that she felt cheerful, but the rhythm of these mornings—the strange alchemy of ritual, banter and bizarre glamour—had its own momentum. Even after a night like hers.

"Morning, girls," came the sharp, gliding voice from the doorway.

Enter: Mrs Havers.

The scent of Chanel No. 5 hit them like a cold compress of rose and powder. Havers floated in like the Queen's less affable second cousin—clipboard tucked beneath her arm, her twinset perfectly pressed, her pearls swinging with every step like they were measuring disapproval.

"Good morning, Mrs Havers," the group said in unison, knowing that any variation in the greeting would be noted, clocked, and potentially deducted as a demerit under 'Conduct – Morning Presence'.

Mrs Havers didn't return the greeting so much as absorb it.

She came to a slow halt just past the lockers, eyes sweeping over the assembled trainees like a General inspecting a firing squad. Her gaze settled on Poppy first.

"Miss Knight," she said crisply, eyeing the half-eaten pastry with distaste. "Is that a cinnamon swirl?"

"Yes, Mrs Havers," Poppy said with cheerful defiance. "Fuel for greatness."

Havers didn't blink. "You'll find greatness more attainable without icing sugar on your lapel. Five minutes to lipstick check. Do see to it."

Poppy blinked slowly. "Yes, Mrs Havers."

"Now, today, Captain Paul Harvester will be taking control of your cohort, as one has an appointment that requires punctuality. Captain Harvester is one of our senior trainers, and... regretfully... more... liberal."

Hayley could hear the venom in the word, as if Havers thought it was a STD and not a legitimate philosophical stance. A ripple of relief — and barely concealed amusement — passed through the group at the mention of a liberal trainer. Anything was better than Havers' emotional Guantanamo Bay.

Sarah leaned slightly toward Hayley, voice pitched low. "Translation: he lets us speak before he sneers."

"I'll take that over being told my eyeliner makes me look disreputable," Hayley muttered back, still massaging her temple where a tension headache had begun to bloom.

Havers's stilettos clicked decisively across the linoleum as she turned to leave, but not before offering a final barb over her shoulder.

"I do hope," she said with syrupy acidity, "that you all conduct yourselves appropriately. PanEuro does not train clowns."

Emma smirked. "Just employs them in upper management."

The door had barely shut before the group burst into muffled laughter. Even Sarah cracked a reluctant grin.

"Clowns," Poppy said through a mouthful of cinnamon. "I can juggle three mini Prosecco bottles and a tray of chicken or pasta, thanks very much."

"Do it on the raft tomorrow and I'll personally start a slow clap," Agatha muttered as she arrived, bun immaculate, heels sensible, eyes sharp.

The door opened again, this time with less perfume and more understatement. Captain Paul Harvester entered with the kind of unbothered authority that only a man used to supervising junior crews and cabin fires could command. His navy uniform was regulation but rumpled, his greying hair a bit wild, and he held a reusable coffee cup with a sticker that read "I Brake for Runway Lights."

He looked around the locker room like a secondary school supply teacher walking into a Year 10 class on a rainy Wednesday.

"Morning," he said simply, and the air in the room shifted.

The trainees stood — not because they were told to, but because there was something about Harvester's presence that made you want to at least pretend you had your act together.

"Ladies," he said. "I'm Captain Harvester. You can call me Paul if that's easier. I was supposed to take you tomorrow, but apparently today's tutor is otherwise engaged in the complex art of judging eyeliner and passive-aggression. So, I'm yours now."

Emma raised a hand. "Just so we know — do you also judge us based on our lipstick shade?"

Harvester sipped his coffee. "No. But if you've got stick time and are only here to stay in the industry because every airline is furloughing and making pilots redundant, then I'm far more interested in your emergency drill response than the Pantone number of your lip gloss. Now, I'm going to say this once, and I don't want it repeated out of this room. I don't care who is up front in the cockpit, if they've got a pair of bollocks or tits, as long as they've got the certs, got the rating, got the hours and can get a plane on a ground. Now, raise your hands if you ever been at the pointy end of an aircraft, hands on a stick, doing flying and not serving drinks or shagging the captain."

There was a moment of hesitation. Then Hayley's hand went up. So did Sarah's, of course—unflinchingly.

Captain Harvester gave a small, approving nod. "Good. You'll find that I don't believe in wasting good pilots in the galley just because some idiot in corporate wants a throwback to Pan Am circa 1965. If you've flown, you've flown. Doesn't matter whether you logged hours in a Typhoon, a Cessna, or a sim that made you puke. Now, if I'm honest, if Ade and I were running this shit show instead of the arseholes that run it from an office that's never smelled Jet-A1, you'd be in the flight deck and not learning how to pour orange juice without disturbing your coiffure. Now, has anyone got cabin crew experience?"

Agatha raised her hand, as Hayley knew that she was, like herself, formerly EasyJet and so was probably the most qualified person in the room when it came to actual airline cabin operations.

"Ten years," Agatha said, her voice calm and composed. "EasyJet. Mostly Europe routes, a few charter specials."

Captain Harvester nodded, his expression unreadable but definitely more respectful than Havers' usual scowl. "Good. Now, that grumpy cow Havers wants us to follow her schedule, but I can't be arsed with that. Instead of being classroom based, who wants to go on an operational A320? There's a lightly loaded Tallinn in and out departing in 45 I'm meant be on. 4 pax, all Classic accommodation. Who fancies a field trip?"

Hayley suddenly felt suspicious, as the flight was in 45 minutes, which, according to her watch, was 1004, and the destination, Tallinn, was where Theo was FO on the morning rotation. Her mind jolted like a thrust reverser mid-brake. Theo. Flight to Tallinn. 10:04. That was his flight.

And Harvester—he was Captain on that flight?

She blinked, the realisation fizzing through her brain like a mis wired warning light.

"Captain Harvester," she said slowly, trying to keep her voice level. "This Tallinn rotation—what's the flight number?"

Harvester shrugged, sipping from his coffee again like it was just another day in aviation purgatory. "PE174. Birmingham–Tallinn. Back same day, unless the Estonians decide to randomly close the airspace again because someone's drone took a wrong turn."

Hayley kept her face composed, but the internal panic began to thrum at the base of her neck.

Theo. She'd said goodbye to him at the curb less than an hour ago, his hair still damp from the shower, his smile doing that crooked thing it did when he was pretending not to worry about being late. He'd kissed her cheek and said, "See you tonight—unless I crash into a Baltic snowbank." Then he'd laughed. She hadn't.

And now Harvester was inviting them on a field trip to that exact flight.

She glanced at Sarah, who caught the micro-expression and raised an eyebrow. Hayley gave her a tiny shake of the head—not now. Not here.

Emma, meanwhile, was practically vibrating with enthusiasm. "An actual plane?" she said, wide-eyed. "With actual passengers?"

Harvester gave her a look. "Don't sound so surprised. We do, in fact, still fly planes. Occasionally. Between the glamour and the pension slashing."

He turned to the group, surveying them with an experienced eye. "You'll be shadowing the actual crew. That means behaving like crew, not tourists. No selfies in the flight deck, no TikTok dances in the aisle, and if anyone drops anything in the galley, you mop it up like a human being and not a drama student at a budget improv night."

Poppy bounced a little on her toes. "Do we get to wear high-vis? I love high-vis."

Harvester rolled his eyes, but not unkindly. "You'll wear what ops says. And if anyone's heels cause damage to the airbridge, I will personally make you swap them for Crocs."

Hayley barely heard the rest of his instructions. Her mind was spinning.

Tallinn. Theo. Shared aircraft. Shared airspace.

There were dozens of reasons she shouldn't go. Professional boundaries. Emotional aftershocks. The sheer risk of being on the same plane as the man you'd had a pregnancy scare with six hours earlier. But somehow, the idea of being on that aircraft—of seeing him in uniform again, in his natural habitat, not tangled in bedsheets and panic—tugged at something inside her that she couldn't quite name.

"Alright," Harvester said, clapping his hands once. "We leave in ten minutes. Meet at the crew security line. If you're not there, I assume you've died of nerves or been eaten by Havers' scent trail."

There was a scramble. Lipsticks reapplied. Buns adjusted. ID passes snatched. Hayley moved on autopilot, clutching her Greggs coffee like a talisman against common sense.

As they headed towards airside, Sarah fell into step beside her.

"You alright?" she murmured, low enough that only Hayley could hear.

"Fine," Hayley lied. "Just… complicated."

"Trust me, Hales, I know that look. Hell, I've been there, got the t-shirt and shagged the pilot."

* _ * _ * _ *

Of all the things Hayley didn't expect, 40 minutes into the flight, being in the toilet, nearly naked, Theo the same state of dress, completely consensual and sweaty, joining the mile high club was not that.

Especially as Sarah was up front, learning in the FO seat, as the former RAF officer was planning to transition into a commercial pilot, meaning that she was getting some actual experience watching a Captain.

She knew that what she was doing was both wrong and irrational, yet as it was a quiet flight, that—

The sound of knocking interrupted her line of thought, as it was 1 of 4 toilets on the A320neo, and as it was the rearmost one, behind all of the passengers, and that as Hayley and Sarah were meant to be covering the rear galley, which was not actually being used, she knew that the only other person could be the purser, a Ukrainian named Dimitri, who was, from what he had told the group of trainees, "gayer than a Pride flag".

The knock was followed by a pause. Then a second, more deliberate one.

Hayley froze, breath caught in her throat. Theo, still half-dressed and blinking like a deer in landing lights, met her gaze. His mouth opened to speak but no words came out.

Then came the unmistakable metallic click of the manual toilet lock being triggered from the outside.

"Oh my God," Hayley whispered. "Someone's opening—"

The door swung inwards a few inches before it caught against the compact shape of Theo's frame. He pressed it shut instinctively with one hand, his face twisted in panic. A voice rang out beyond the panel.

"Sorry to interrupt your little team-building exercise," came a dry male voice, thick with a Slavic accent and steely amusement. "But this aircraft only has four lavatories, and unless we're testing PanEuro's emergency evacuation policy for coitus interruptus, I suggest you tidy yourselves and exit with discretion."

Dimitri. Of course it was Dimitri.

Hayley's face burned. She could barely find the strength to breathe, let alone speak. Theo, to his credit, didn't try to be slick. He just pressed his forehead against the lavatory wall and whispered, "Christ."

From outside the door came a theatrical sigh. "Three minutes. No more. I have seen worse. Trust me."

Hayley chuckled as she knew that there was absolutely no recovering from this.

Three minutes. That was generous, all things considered. They could have been reported. Sanctioned. Ejected via the nearest slide. But Dimitri — fabulous, flawless

Dimitri — had clearly decided that his duty of care extended as far as discretion and no further.

Hayley tugged her tights back up in silence, cheeks still flaming. Theo retrieved his shirt from the tiny sink where it had been hastily discarded, his movements careful, contrite. It wasn't romantic now — not the panting breathlessness of ten minutes ago. It was pure damage control.

As she straightened her skirt, Hayley avoided his gaze. Theo opened his mouth — probably to apologise, or joke, or suggest they "laugh about this one day" — but thought better of it. He buttoned his collar instead.

"Ready?" he murmured.

"No," she muttered. "But let's go anyway."

They slipped out of the lavatory like guilty schoolchildren, trying not to make eye contact with anyone. Dimitri stood just outside the galley with a perfectly folded linen cloth draped over one arm and a smirk that could have registered on seismic equipment.

He gave a pointed glance to Hayley's skewed hat, then to Theo's askew tie. "There is a mirror in the galley," he said simply, "and a God who sees all."

Theo looked sheepish. Hayley gave a nod of respect, too mortified to speak.

"At least you've got good taste, girl. Nice jawline, hot bod, pity he's straight,' the Purser then said with a grin which Hayley knew meant she wasn't being judged for the moment of indiscretion but was in fact being welcomed into the unofficial, unspoken society of crew who had found themselves entangled in emotional turbulence at 38,000 feet.

Hayley tucked her blouse back into her skirt with swift precision, then did a double-check on her hair and uniform in the small galley mirror. Her lipstick had smeared just slightly, but with a deft flick of the wrist and a quick application from the emergency makeup kit she carried in her blazer pocket, she restored her appearance to PanEuro-approved standards.

Dimitri, now brewing a pot of coffee like nothing had happened, glanced sideways. "You know, dear, we all make mistakes. Some of us make them more stylishly than others."

Hayley cracked a smile in spite of herself. "Was it obvious?"

"Oh, darling," Dimitri said, his tone affectionate and laced with mischief, "the entire tail section is aware. But don't worry — the passengers are asleep, the flight deck are men, and I have no interest in complicating your lives further. Just don't make it a habit."

"Wouldn't dream of it," Hayley replied, though her voice lacked conviction.

Theo, now composed, with his hair re-gelled and uniform in proper order, reappeared beside her. "Thanks for not, you know… making a scene."

Dimitri raised one carefully plucked eyebrow. "Sweetheart, I flew for WizzAir. I've seen people do far worse things in the crew rest on a Krakow–Luton. This? This is practically quaint."

And just like that, the moment passed. No scandal. No wrath. Just the quiet understanding that, in aviation, emotional entanglement was as inevitable as turbulence over the Bay of Biscay.

****

CHAPTER 9 – Old Habits Die Hard
Saturday 10th April 2021

It had been two days after that flight from Birmingham to Tallinn, and Hayley was looking forward to a week off.

As promised, Dani had gotten her, her father Alan and her mother a standby deal for Barbados on Virgin, the irony that her father's ID90 pass, a standby pass which pilots and other staff from various airlines used like a magical ticket to the world, was actually slightly less generous than what Dani could wangle as she was a Virgin Atlantic First Officer, and therefore the staff travel perks that Dani could give were unusually excellent, particularly in a pandemic spring. The airline's crew planners, perhaps out of guilt or nostalgia for the days when pilots could hop across the globe without COVID testing or twelve pages of digital paperwork, had managed to find three empty seats on the next VS131 to Bridgetown.

The only catch was the relentless uncertainty of standbys in 2021: the looming possibility of being offloaded at the gate for a last-minute fare-payer, or finding your slot bumped for a "COVID crew" repositioning. But after a year of tarmac dreams and airport commutes that never led further than the security hut, Hayley would have settled for a jump seat, a galley floor, or a night in a deserted outstation.

The irony that they were to be travelling in Upper Class on an Airbus A350-1000, one of the airline's most luxurious machines, was not lost on Hayley. The fact that her sister and father, despite being on rival airlines, were both type rated on the A350 family, while also being

Boeing 787 and Airbus A330 rated due to both airlines having the fleets made Hayley chuckle, especially as she was Airbus A320 rated, due to her start at easyJet before the pandemic caused them to pause all recruitment. Even now, she caught herself automatically running through the flows for the A320's overhead panel whenever she sat in a passenger seat, an old reflex that lingered like a muscle memory. The difference was that this time, instead of straining to see a sidestick from a window seat, she'd have the luxury of a seat that fully reclined and a menu that didn't feature a cheese toastie or a £5 instant coffee.

Hayley had always relished the pre-flight rituals, even when she wasn't technically crew. Her packing routine bordered on ceremonial: a battered Samsonite roller case (scuffed at every corner, with at least three faded "Priority" stickers and a tiny crack by the handle from an ill-fated Malaga trip), a navy blue Roxy backpack, and her trusty logbook tucked inside a zippered side pocket—more out of habit than any real hope of jotting down new sectors. The only additions this time were a linen dress, three swimsuits she hadn't worn since her last holiday in the Algarve, and a multipack of masks ("triple-layered, proper ones, not those limp blue things," as Alan had said).

The kitchen was alive with a nervous energy that morning, the kind that only comes before an airport run. Dani was on WhatsApp with a mate from Virgin crewing, double-checking the loading situation on VS131 and making sure there were enough Upper Class beds for her "VIPs." Alan, meanwhile, was triple-checking his NHS Fit to Fly certificate, flicking through his passport, and grumbling about the online check-in system that "wouldn't recognise a real pilot if they saw the four stripes themselves." Their mother, Karen, seemed to float above it all, serenely buttering toast and humming "Barbados" by Typically Tropical as if it were 1975 and she'd just won the Pools.

Hayley found herself caught between their energies: part aviator, part nervous holidaymaker, but mostly just grateful to be headed for the airport at all. Even the drive up the Thanet Way, traffic surprisingly light for a Saturday, felt like a return to old rhythms. Alan insisted on driving, his "pilot-in-command" attitude manifesting as a rigid 70mph and meticulous lane discipline. Dani, in the back, kept one eye on the VS131 load sheet, refreshing her phone every sixty seconds. Hayley did her best to pretend she wasn't obsessively counting her own lucky stars.

"You're booked in Upper Class, dad," Dani said, as she was cadging a lift, instead of driving her own BYD Seal. "The Clubhouse private security lane is still shut, so you'll have to go through the general Fast Track security at T3. Oh, and the gate is subject to last-minute change, so don't go wandering off to buy any more overpriced sunglasses until you're actually called," she added, nudging Alan with a grin. He rolled his eyes, but Hayley saw a flicker of nerves beneath his bluster. For a man who'd spent most of his adult life in cockpits from the 747 to the Dreamliner, the prospect of flying as a passenger— not a crew member, not in uniform, but as just another "punter"—always left him slightly on edge.

It was the sort of travel day Hayley remembered from her childhood, equal parts anticipation and a relentless checklist of documents, snacks, "just in case" items, and little rituals. Alan insisted on carrying his own battered black flight bag—still sporting the "Concorde 001" pin from a trip decades earlier—while Karen's handbag contained a treasure trove of sanitiser, boiled sweets, and duty-free coupons. Dani travelled light as she was working, and that she'd only be in Bridgetown while the rest of the family were off on their week of sun, sand and, if Alan had his way, at least one trip to the airport perimeter fence to spot anything interesting on the tarmac.

Dani, Hayley knew, was going to be leaving the day after they arrived, as she was booked on the return flight, and then another return, coincidentally timed so she would be the First Officer on their flight back to their eventual return—assuming, as she said, "the border doesn't get shut, someone doesn't test positive, and Virgin doesn't suddenly need all A350 crew to go to Lagos." Such was the ballet of pandemic rosters, where every flight, even to paradise, came with a caveat.

"You know we're breaking the law, Dani," Alan said, and Hayley could see that her father was already warming to one of his favourite soapbox topics—the ever-changing morass of government travel rules. "Only 'essential' travel, they say. Two days away from the restrictions ending."

Karen, as a former operations officer for EUJet when they were based at Manston, looked at Hayley with the kind of quiet smile only a seasoned ops veteran could muster. "Alan, don't start. If anyone asks, we're essential for the morale of the British public. Besides, it's better than hearing the constant repeating headlines of the late Duke of Edinburgh," she finished, a gentle sigh colouring her words, "and if the Daily Mail want to run another headline about 'selfish sunseekers', I'll give them a piece of my mind at baggage reclaim."

Hayley caught her mother's eye and smiled. The week's endless coverage had felt like a national holding pattern, the kind that left you yearning for blue skies and the reliable mundanity of a boarding announcement.

"Even KMFM has gone overboard with the Philip tributes," Hayley said, glancing up from her phone as the A299 changed into the M2. "Dad, you know they're digging up Sevenscore roundabout again when we come back."

Sevenscore roundabout, just outside of Ramsgate, near to the site of Thanet Parkway rail station and where the A256 to Sandwich met the Thanet Way, had been at the start of their journey, and was, Hayley knew, being closed for the one lane to connect the new Airport turn off, with drivers facing the usual, bemused chorus of "temporary" signs, cones, and a random clutch of hi-vis-clad contractors standing around discussing anything but the job in hand. The project, connecting the new tunnel that had been built to access Manston by road, had had a temporary exit on the main Thanet Way, but was now joining the main A256 with a proper roundabout, part of the full, post-COVID, opening of Manston, with PanEuro's full 24 plane a day service, up from the current 8 that had been going on since December when the airline launched.

It was well known in Thanet that the road building, a tunnel under Manna Hutte and the runway, and the temporary exit onto the dual carriageway, was done in record time, nearly 7 months, because the owners of PanEuro, a consortium of Rothschild & Co and several members of the House of Lords, had paid contractors during the initial stages of the pandemic triple the usual rate to finish before the first A321 landed from Berlin on launch day, and that the Development Consent Order, that for years RiverOak Strategic Partners had wanted to build Manston into a full-scale freight hub, had, by a combination of pandemic opportunism, legal threat and sheer brute force of lobbying, finally been flipped into a passenger operation instead. Of course, the only two airlines permitted by RiverOak under an 'exclusivity' clause were PanEuro for passenger services, and for the freight side, a new combined terminal being built at the west end of the runway for DHL, which Alan had spent many an evening moaning about—something to do with "bloody cargo ops and 2am jet noise," though Hayley suspected he secretly liked having the excuse to spout about the old days when Manston had seen 747s and Antonov s dropping in for fuel.

"Stay in the right hand lane," the Waze app, which even though everyone in the car knew the way to Heathrow, as Alan was based there and so was Dani, was a source of travel amusement and mild friction. Alan, naturally, ignored it, muttering about "having a better internal compass than a sat nav, thank you very much." Dani, scrolling through Slack messages from the Virgin crewing desk, barely glanced up.

"We might be quicker just scooting down the A249 past the County Showground, as Waze is suggesting getting off at Blue Bell Hill and taking the 229," Karen muttered, as the they approached the Sittingbourne turn off, where the road to Maidstone and M20, the A249, which was the road that linked the Isle of Sheppey to the Kent's county town.

"All because you want to avoid Waze sending Dad anti clockwise round the M25 and through the Dartford Crossing, and because the M26 goes straight onto the M25 at Sevenoaks instead of doing that awkward turn off to stay on if we went clockwise," Dani smirked, shaking her head. "Honestly, between Dad's navigation and Waze's obsessive need to shave three minutes off every journey, it's a miracle we ever make it further than the Cobham services." She glanced at her phone, checking the live Heathrow arrivals as if confirming that, indeed, aircraft were still landing at Terminal 4, and the world hadn't come to a standstill.

Hayley, curled in the passenger seat, let the patter of road banter wash over her. It was strange, how much comfort she took in this mundane tangle of family logistics and low-key squabbling—how, watching flight deck dreams recede into fog, even motorway stress felt like a luxury.

* _ * _ * _ *

It was on board the A350 when Hayley, sitting in seat 1A on board G-VBOB, Soulful Rebel, the seats nearest the front galley and flight deck, noticed her dad was muttering to himself. The irony that they were being pushed back from the gate, and that Alan was muttering to himself the calls that he'd be making in the flight deck, was not lost on either of his daughters. "Ground to cockpit, brakes released, cleared for push and start, set parking brake," he recited under his breath, his hand unconsciously gripping the armrest as if it were the tiller.

Looking at the closed flight deck door, Hayley knew her elder sister was going to be taking the landing, as CRM, the Crew Resource Management, or as Dani joked, the 'Cockpit Realignment Matrix', dictated that on an eastbound Atlantic crossing the first officer often got the landing, and Dani, as she was only three years as a First Officer, and so being at the 'pointy end' of the Airbus, was still something of a thrill, pandemic or not. Even with a mask on, Dani's eyes had sparkled when she'd messaged Hayley from the crew van, "I'll be up front. Try not to make a scene in Upper."

The aircraft trundled away from the terminal, guided by a marshaller in hi-vis, and Hayley leaned into her cocoon of purple mood-lighting, gazing out at the sloping window as drizzle traced little streams down the plexiglass. The engines purred with that smooth, almost too-quiet A350 growl. The PA chimed: "Cabin crew, please arm doors and cross-check."

Hayley grinned as she turned her head towards her father, his brows slightly furrowed as if resisting the urge to bark a checklist into the void. The sight of Alan Northcott, decorated British Airways Captain with over three decades of long-haul logged in his logbooks, reduced to fidgeting with a complimentary water bottle and adjusting his seatbelt like a nervous passenger, would have been comical had it not also been deeply familiar.

"You've got your licence and certs with you, ain't you, Dad?" she teased, lips curling around the smirk. "Just in case they need someone to cover for a sleepy FO mid-Atlantic."

Alan huffed, his pride caught between a chuckle and a retort. "Of course I do. A pilot never flies without them. Doesn't matter whether I'm flying the thing or not. Old habits die hard, you know."

"Funnily enough, even though I'm only typed on the 320 family," Hayley said, grinning, "I've got my licence and certs. As you said, its force of habit. It'd feel wrong travelling without it. Like turning up to a party without a bottle."

Alan gave a low chuckle, the kind that rumbled in his chest. "Exactly. And besides, who knows when you might get lucky and some poor sod in the flight deck keels over, eh?"

Karen, who was sitting in 1G, next to Alan in 1D, the 1-2-1 configuration and 4 rows of Upper Class, rolled her eyes, though her smile gave her away. "If you two get any more superstitious, you'll be wearing wings on your pyjamas and sleeping with your logbooks under your pillows." She reached across, patting Alan's hand with the kind of easy fondness that can only come from decades of early-morning check-ins, diverted flights, and endless duty-free Toblerone bars. "At least in Ops, we don't have to worry about losing our slot because someone's left their kitbag in the wrong crew room. Or, heaven forbid, Alan, you have to deal with a Spanish handling agent who thinks your last name is 'Northcoat' and not Northcott."

Alan's retort was pre-empted by the whirr of the seat motors as he fiddled with the recline, instinctively checking how far it would go—another pilot's tic, as if he could squeeze another degree out by sheer force of will.

Hayley felt the subtle surge as the Rolls-Royce engines spooled up, the familiar pre-take-off hush broken only by the gentle jangle of seatbelt buckles and the rustle of boarding cards. The crew's announcements had the singsong quality of people who had done this too many times, who had explained mask-wearing and sanitiser stations so often the words had lost meaning. But to Hayley, each line was a comfort, a piece of the choreography she'd missed so desperately.

She sipped her welcome glass of orange juice—no champagne today, not with the pandemic rules and a mother who'd glare at her for "starting early"—and let her mind drift, eyes half-closed as the taxiways slid past. Out the window, an American 777 waited at the next stand, its white livery dull beneath a leaden London sky. On the other side of the aircraft, a Qatar A350 taxied in, and the proximity of familiar types made the world feel briefly smaller and more connected.

There was a different energy in the air: the subdued anticipation of a flight that shouldn't quite be happening, the luxury of travel in a time when most people were still stuck behind closed doors, the sense that the rules— always shifting—might change again at any moment. The weight of that luck pressed in on Hayley, making her both grateful and guilty, elated and restless.

As they lined up on the runway, Alan closed his eyes and breathed in, as if he could feel the aircraft's acceleration through the soles of his shoes. Hayley watched his hand twitch in time with the engine's note, ghosting through the motions of throttling up, holding centreline, waiting for V1, VR, and the gentle pull of rotation.

Dani had promised to flash the landing lights as they rolled past the threshold—an old in-joke from their childhood, when she and Hayley would stand by the fence at Manston and imagine the light was just for them. Hayley watched, heart thudding, as the lights winked once, twice, then the aircraft shuddered into life. G-VBOB surged down the runway, the silence inside shattered by the muted roar outside.

In the stillness that followed, as wheels tucked up into the belly and London fell away beneath broken cloud, Hayley felt her eyes prickle. For a moment, she was a little girl again, perched on her father's shoulders as he pointed out the climb profile of a departing jumbo, or sitting on a picnic rug with Dani by the perimeter fence, counting how many seconds it took for each aircraft to vanish into the haze.

* _ * _ * _ *

By time they had arrived at Bridgetown, Hayley had had 6 hours sleep, allowing herself, even though it was only 8 in the morning that the flight had departed London, and was now quarter past 12 by time the wheels had touched down onto the runway at Grantley Adams International. The tropical light streamed through the A350's oversized windows, bathing the Upper Class cabin in a buttery gold that made the greys and purples of the seats look almost cheerful. Hayley blinked blearily, adjusting to the sensation of warmth—real, honest warmth, not the industrial-grade heating of a crew hotel or the stuffy blast from a cabin air vent. She pressed her forehead to the cool glass for a moment, savouring the sticky-sweet scent of jet fuel, humidity, and sea that seeped through the aircraft's skin.

"This is your First Officer speaking. Unfortunately, we're unable to approach our gate at the present time due to a local equipment reposition, so we'll be holding short for just a few more moments. The weather is a balmy 28 degrees, clear blue skies, and we'd like to thank you for flying with Virgin Atlantic today. We'll have you disembarking as soon as possible. And to the guests in 1A and 1D—Dad, please don't critique my parking when you get off. Thank you."

There was laughter from the cabin crew, as, in the Upper Class cabin, there was only the 3 Northcotts and no other passengers except a solitary American banker in 2A, who had slept through nearly everything but the lunch service and appeared deeply unimpressed by the British brand of familial banter over the PA. The crew, meanwhile, radiated that mixture of quiet amusement and thinly veiled exhaustion that Hayley had come to recognise in anyone still flying in the spring of 2021—a strange breed, at once essential and invisible.

"Y'all family or something," the American said suddenly, and Hayley noticed her dad was smirking, his blue eyes twinkling as he reached up to retrieve his battered flight bag from the overhead. "More or less," Alan replied, his

Kentish accent somehow sharper against the soft vowels of the American. "This one's my eldest, up front, keeping the shiny side up, and this one here"—he jerked his thumb at Hayley—"is my youngest, who can fly an Airbus but is currently on sabbatical, which in our family means 'between adventures'." Karen, unbothered by the mild spectacle, gave the American her most diplomatic ex-ops smile and started methodically distributing masks and anti-bac, as though running an impromptu cabin service.

The air on the apron shimmered in the Caribbean heat, thick with the hum of distant ground power units and the rumble of a 737 taking off for Miami. For a few long minutes, the world held its breath—everyone suspended in that familiar aviation limbo between touchdown and the first hiss of opening doors. Hayley found herself staring at her reflection in the window, sun-bleached and rumpled and just slightly out of time, as if she'd crossed an invisible line and landed somewhere her old self might not recognise.

There was a thump from the hold as baggage carts rattled into place, the gangway finally inching towards 1L. The crew, sensing a moment's respite, gathered their bits and bobs, exchanged a few weary jokes about quarantine hotels, and prepared for the sprint to freedom. In the midst of it all, Dani appeared, her hair tied back and her uniform looking impossibly crisp after eight hours at the controls. She waggled her fingers in greeting before ducking behind the flight deck door, leaving Hayley with a wave of both pride and envy, the old ache of not being at the front—yet—returning with a fresh sting.

When they finally deplaned, the air hit them like a velvet hammer: warm, humid, thick with the promise of lazy days and the faintest undercurrent of jet exhaust. Hayley let her head tip back, eyes closed, just breathing. For a fleeting moment, she felt utterly weightless, as though she'd stepped into one of the postcards Dani used to send from layovers around the world—only now, it was her turn.

The airport was mostly empty; a relic of its usual bustle, the halls echoing with the sounds of a skeleton staff and the low babble of a handful of arrivals. At immigration, the officer barely looked up, flicking through their passports and scanning their QR codes with a practised swipe. "Purpose of visit?" he asked in the flat monotone of someone who'd spent too long behind a Perspex screen.

"Family holiday," Hayley said automatically, earning a raised eyebrow from the officer, who looked from her to Alan, then Karen, then back to Hayley.

"How long will you be here for?" the immigration officer then asked.

"We fly back to Heathrow on VS188 next Saturday," Alan said, pulling out the standby tickets that he'd carefully printed out and annotated with highlighter, as if a yellow stripe of ink could somehow confer official legitimacy. The officer, to his credit, barely glanced at the paperwork before applying a neat, efficient stamp to each passport and waving them through. In a pandemic spring, with tourist arrivals a trickle and airline staff even scarcer, there was a certain deference for anyone who had managed to negotiate the labyrinth of travel regulations and make it as far as the arrivals hall.

Hayley let the cool stamp ink dry as she followed the signs to baggage reclaim, feeling that odd lightness that always came at the end of a long-haul flight: the dull ache in the muscles, the sandpaper eyes, the slightly surreal sense of having skipped several hours of time and weather. She caught a glimpse of herself in a mirror as they passed—a slightly dishevelled blonde in a crumpled linen dress, carrying a battered logbook, looking far more like a runaway than a holidaymaker. She grinned. If only the ground staff knew how much of her life that she'd spent waiting at baggage belts in cities far less glamorous than Bridgetown.

Hayley's gaze lingered on the carousel, watching it shudder into motion as if reluctant to fulfil its only task. The battered Samsonite emerged first, proudly adorned with a new 'Priority' tag, a small miracle, since 'priority' often seemed more like a suggestion than a guarantee on most airlines—unless you had the right uniform or, in Alan's case, a sharp word for the ramp agent.

Alan retrieved his own ancient black flight bag with a veteran's practised ease. Karen's case followed, gliding out as serenely as she always managed to look after ten hours on an aircraft, her composure unruffled by the queue behind her. Only Hayley's little blue Roxy backpack was missing, having vanished somewhere between Heathrow's Upper Class wing and the bowels of Grantley Adams International. For a fleeting moment, she felt the prickle of irritation that always came with lost bags—another airline habit that refused to die, even on holiday.

"First night and already a crisis," Alan quipped, watching Hayley scan the thinning belt. "That's got to be a new record. At least you've got your logbook and your licence, so you'll survive."

Hayley shot him a look that was half exasperation, half affection. "As long as it's not stranded in Miami or Lagos, I'll cope. Besides, I packed spare swimmers in Mum's case." She grinned, grateful for the years of forced redundancy drills and her mother's compulsive habit of triple-packing every essential.

Karen was already speaking to the solitary Virgin agent by the baggage claim, her voice soothing and low, explaining the situation in that "don't panic, but fix this immediately" tone that only former ops staff could truly master. Hayley watched the interaction, reminded of a dozen times her mother had quietly made disasters disappear with a smile and a well-placed phone call.

The American banker drifted by, briefcase in hand, offering a tight nod as he disappeared through customs— another silent footnote in the story of the journey. The family gathered their bags, what they had of them, and stepped out into the arrivals hall, blinking against the brilliant, salt-bright sunlight that poured through the open glass doors.

For a moment, Hayley simply breathed in the warm, thick air, feeling the tension of travel begin to unspool from her shoulders. Outside, the taxi queue was empty save for a pair of minibuses emblazoned with faded hotel logos, and a solitary palm tree bent gracefully over the forecourt, fronds stirring in the slow, syrupy breeze.

Alan led the way, his stride confident, almost swaggering, as if he owned every tarmac from Gatwick to Grantley Adams. Karen followed, unflappable, eyes scanning the horizon as if plotting the most efficient route to the hotel. Hayley fell in step between them, glancing back once at the terminal—half expecting, by old instinct, to be called back to deal with a technical snag or a sudden crew change.

Instead, she was greeted by a wall of heat, the low thrum of cicadas, and the faint sound of reggae wafting from the taxi rank's battered speakers. It was—finally—holiday time.

*_*_*_*

Their hotel, a low-slung sprawl of cream stucco and breezy, salt-blasted terraces, was only a twenty-minute drive from the airport. The taxi, air conditioning valiantly struggling against the afternoon sun, swept them past roadside stalls selling coconut water, a tangle of technicolour buses, and the dazzling arc of Browne's Beach. Dani, who was in a different hotel, the flight time limitations meaning that the 10 hour rest rule for crew put her up at the Crew House in Christ Church parish, would be gone by the next morning, her own layover little more than a blur of sleep, paperwork and a mad dash for a PCR test before the next rostered leg. She waved them off in the hotel lobby with a yawn and a promise to join them by the pool if she got sprung from crew rest, her lanyard already half-tangled with the phone charger, a copy of *Not Without My Daughter* stuffed in her cabin bag.

Hayley, Alan and Karen checked into adjoining rooms on the top floor, the sort of rooms that smelt of coconut soap, sea salt, and just a faint trace of ancient air conditioning. For a family that could probably assemble an Airbus blindfolded, it took them an embarrassingly long time to get the air con working and the balcony doors unlocked, but once the cool air began to circulate and the curtains were thrown wide to reveal an uninterrupted view of blue-on-blue, the trip finally started to feel real.

Alan wasted no time in slipping into a battered pair of BA-branded swimming trunks ("You've had those since Concorde went out of service," Karen reminded him) and was on the balcony with binoculars, scanning the distant approach path to the runway. "Might be a few 737s in before sunset," he muttered, as if the proximity to flight paths was the only acceptable criterion for a good holiday hotel.

Hayley, with the peculiar energy that only comes after a transatlantic flight and three cups of indifferent airplane coffee, found herself standing on her tiptoes, gazing down at the resort pool, where the only sign of life was a pair of American retirees bickering over the last sun lounger. She knew, from experience, that if she let herself sit down for too long, she'd never get up, so instead she unpacked, swapped her jeans for a faded bikini and linen wrap, and announced she was going for a swim.

The pool, shimmering in the late afternoon sun, was warmer than the sea back home even at its chilliest.

Hayley dove beneath the surface, letting the salty water close over her ears, the world narrowing to the slow pulse of her own breath. For a moment, she let herself drift—weightless, silent, free.

When she surfaced, Karen was stretched out on a lounger, sunglasses on, a paperback in one hand and a rum punch in the other. Alan, ever the restless aviator, had migrated to the edge of the pool, feet dangling in the water, phone open to FlightRadar24. "There's a Condor from Frankfurt due in twenty," he informed them, as if the family might want to arrange their afternoon tea accordingly.

Hayley laughed, flopping onto a neighbouring lounger. "We're meant to be on holiday, Dad. No more flight plans, just beach plans."

But Alan just grinned, the lines at the corners of his eyes softening. "Old habits, Hales. Old habits."

They dozed by the pool, the air thick with the scent of frangipani and sun cream, the gentle background hum of resort life—ice clinking, the distant shout of children, the muted whirr of a ceiling fan—lulling Hayley into a contented haze. For the first time in months, maybe years, she felt herself unwind.

****

CHAPTER 10 – Return to Blighty
Saturday 17th April 2021

The holiday, Hayley had to admit, was more than she could have hoped for. Barbados, for all its post-lockdown strangeness—half-empty hotels, the tentative murmur of masked tourists, the odd ritual of "quarantine bubbles" at the beach—had worked its subtle balm on the Northcott family. Hayley had allowed herself to sink into the rhythm of it: lazy breakfasts on the terrace of the Coral Sands, Alan reading the local Nation News aloud with dry captainly wit, while Karen had been busy ushering the duo.

There was one thing Hayley had to admit that she enjoyed doing while she was in Barbados though, and that was thanks to a company that did flight training, even though she and her dad were both still technically on holiday, enabled her to get some time in the air.

The company, Blue Horizon Flight Academy, had managed to reopen—sort of—a couple of months earlier, and their battered Cessna 172s still pottered up and down the south coast, skirting the reef, bobbing over turquoise water in a way that made even Hayley, who was no stranger to hard instrument weather over the Channel, feel like she was flying on the wings of a song.

She'd coaxed her father into hiring one for an hour, just the two of them and the instructor, a smiling, round-shouldered Barbadian named Joseph who, after a quick look at Alan's old ATPL and Hayley's recent logbook scribbles, was more than happy to let them loose after a couple of circuits. Joseph sat back in the rear seat with an air of gentle amusement, while Alan took the left seat for the first half hour, letting the stick-and-rudder memory settle into his bones again.

* _ * _ * _ *

Tuesday 13th April 2021

"Mr Northcott, I believe you booked the Cessna for the day?" Joseph, the instructor, asked as he led them across the cracked apron. The little aircraft—8P-CNA, its tail number covering a patch of sun-faded blue—sat patiently by the low, chain-link fence, its propeller casting a bent shadow across the heat-warped tarmac. The palm fronds at the edge of the aerodrome flickered in a languid breeze, and for a heartbeat, Hayley forgot the world beyond the coral edge of the island—forgot the masked signs, the swabbed noses, the return-flight uncertainty.

Alan Northcott was a different man here, stepping into the role he knew better than almost anything in life. "Just for an hour or two, Joseph—don't worry, we'll bring her back with oil still in the engine and wings attached," he replied, affecting a drawl that Hayley recognised from his old Heathrow days, part RAF, part the gentle banter of British Airways seniority. Karen watched from the shade of a frangipani tree, phone in hand to immortalise the moment, her face soft with nostalgia.

They ran through the pre-flight—Alan slower than Hayley remembered, but meticulous as ever, running a finger along the elevator hinge, rapping his knuckles on the wing-root, checking the fuel sumps for a trace of water. Hayley, meanwhile, let the familiar rhythm steady her.

She'd barely touched an aircraft since PanEuro's hiring freeze and the humiliations of stewardess school. Yet here, under a coconut sky, the controls and checks came back like childhood language: check the pitot, crack open the fuel cap, scan for wasps in the cowling.

Joseph, after a brief check of Hayley's logbook—half a dozen pages of "air experience" flights and simulator time since her last serious line work—smiled, shrugged, and said, "Well, Miss Hayley, you and your dad seem like you have this in your bones. I'm just here in case you decide to try a barrel roll."

Alan cackled, sliding into the left seat. Hayley slid in beside him, headset in place. "Just like the old days," he murmured, and she could hear the smile in his voice, the softening of old scars.

They took off to the west, bumping through the thermals rising off the sugar-cane fields, Alan's hands steady, even if his feet occasionally lagged on the rudder. For half an hour, they turned lazy circuits over the turquoise water, Alan narrating the coast as if he was giving a passenger briefing: "On your left, you'll see the famous Sandy Lane—Sean Connery's favourite haunt. And off the nose, that's the airport, where I first brought a Tristar in on three engines after a bird strike. Don't worry, the passengers barely noticed."

Hayley let him reminisce, watching the shoreline curve away in the morning haze, the island a patchwork of green and gold. Joseph hummed quietly in the back, offering the occasional word but otherwise letting the Northcotts be Northcotts, father and daughter in their airborne element.

When it was Hayley's turn, she slid into the left seat, the old tension dissolving as she nudged the throttle, felt the little Cessna leap ahead, wheels chirping as she lifted into the clean Caribbean air. For the first time since PanEuro had sent that impersonal rejection, she felt the weight shift—she was a pilot, whatever the roster said, whatever the uniform or lipstick.

She turned gentle circles over the surf, dialled in headings, ran through a couple of steep turns and a power-off descent that had Joseph raising his eyebrows in approval. Alan sat beside her, wordless, hands off the yoke, letting her fly. For a moment, it was as if the pandemic, the lost year, and the ache of the denied cockpit were just flecks of cloud in a cobalt sky.

"Mind if I do a bit of island hopping, some touch and just under one. Would be a shame to let all that avgas go to waste."

"Mind if I do a bit of island hopping, some touch and goes?" Hayley asked, her voice crackling slightly over the intercom. She had the Cessna steady, trimmed and level, her fingers loose on the yoke. "After all, we did pay for 5 hours, and we've only used just under one. Would be a shame to let all that avgas go to waste."

Joseph's chuckle came through the headset, a low, easy sound. "You've got the map, you've got the time. Just radio back if anything seems dodgy. Where were you thinking, as the company has got agreements with the FBOs at St Vincent, Grenada, St Lucia, Martinique and Dominica?"

"Let's go for St Lucia first," Hayley said, glancing down at the tablet on the stand beside the throttle quadrant. "Rodney Bay's always been on my list, and Hewanorra will be nice and empty this time of day."

Alan gave a low whistle. "Bit of a stretch for this old kite, isn't it?"

Joseph gave a theatrical scoff in the back. "You'll be cruising over sea and beauty all the way, not dodging icing over Inverness. CNA can manage it in her sleep—as long as you don't push her like a Learjet."

"You know, dad, Dani will be jealous, especially as she's doing a JFK today," Hayley said, pulling up on the iPad that was in the panel's suction mount, one that Joseph had said was part of the companies package deal for visiting pilots. She tapped in a quick route plan—Christ Church to Hewanorra, a pause for tea and a leg-stretch, and maybe even a sunset return via Grenada if fuel and daylight allowed.

Hayley pushed the throttle gently forward and watched as the Cessna's nose lifted over the teal-glimmering sea, the air smooth and obliging. Below them, the rugged coral-fringed south coast of Barbados receded, a postcard of sugar-white sands and gently swaying palms. The afternoon haze gave the horizon a soft blur, as though someone had traced the boundary between sea and sky with a smudge of chalk.

Alan sat back in the right seat now, arms folded loosely, eyes scanning the sky with casual discipline. He might've been off duty, but the habits of a lifetime—of flight plans, checklists, and the subtle vigilance of command—still lived behind his gaze.

"You always wanted to go to St Lucia, didn't you?" Alan asked, as Hayley dialled in their heading and leaned back slightly, relaxed now that they were climbing steadily through two thousand feet.

"Yeah. I had a poster of the Pitons in my bedroom at fifteen," Hayley replied, smiling slightly at the memory. "Mum used to tease me it was more about the airstrip than the view."

"I remember," Alan said. "You'd plot fantasy routes on your wall with bits of string and thumbtacks—like a Cold War general with a Caribbean obsession."

Joseph chuckled from the back, his voice lilting through the headset. "Well, Captain Northcott Junior, shall we see if your fantasy holds up to a real-world approach?"

Hayley laughed, feeling the thrill of challenge twist in her belly like a favourite melody. She trimmed the aircraft, let it settle into cruise, and checked their instruments. "Let's get those Pitons in the logbook then."

The hop to Hewanorra took just under an hour, a ribbon of blue unspooling beneath them. Occasionally, fishing boats left white wakes behind like scratches on sapphire. Over the radio, chatter was minimal—most commercial traffic was still throttled by post-COVID cutbacks—and they were given a straight-in approach with barely a delay.

Hayley flew the descent like she was lining up for an easyJet check ride: gear down, flaps stage by stage, callouts steady and confident. The Cessna kissed the tarmac at Hewanorra's long southern runway with barely a jolt.

"Nice," Alan murmured. "She's still got it."

"You make it sound like I'm an old banger yourself," Hayley replied, rolling her eyes with a smile.

At the far end of the strip, they turned off onto the stubby taxiway and pulled up near the small FBO building. A young ground handler in a mask gave them a thumbs-up and pointed toward the tie-down line. Hayley shut down the engine with a flick of switches, then sat back, letting the silence wash over them.

The heat rushed in when they opened the cabin doors, thick and sweet with frangipani and jet fuel. They clambered out, stretching cramped muscles and drinking in the Caribbean air.

A woman in a bright yellow safety vest walked over, clipboard in hand. "You're the Northcott party from Barbados? Welcome to St Lucia. We've got your fuel arranged and some refreshments in the lounge if you like—tea, juice, snacks."

Alan and Hayley exchanged grins.

* _ * _ * _ *

Hayley descended the metal steps of the Cessna and adjusted her sunglasses, the lenses catching the soft golden flare of early afternoon light. The air at Hewanorra was stickier than Barbados—less of the coral breeze and more of a languid humidity that clung to the skin like syrup. Still, it was wonderful. She didn't feel like a passenger here, or a stewardess playing dress-up. She felt like what she was born to be.

"Tea, juice or rum?" the woman in the yellow vest asked with a knowing smile, glancing between Alan and Hayley as they made their way across the sun-bleached apron to the FBO lounge.

Alan paused, made a show of consulting his watch. "Well, technically it's five o'clock in the UK."

"That's the spirit," Hayley replied, tugging her ponytail tighter under her cap.

Inside, the lounge was modest—white plastic chairs, ceiling fans twirling with the indifference of island pace— but there was a jug of chilled sorrel, a battered kettle for tea, and a tray of coconut drops that Hayley promptly descended on like a schoolgirl at break time. The handler disappeared with a promise that fuel would be sorted within the hour, and for a brief window, the Northcotts simply sat in silence, sipping their drinks and staring out across the shimmering runway.

"Feels strange, doesn't it?" Hayley said after a moment. "To fly again. Not a simulator, not some stewardess demo. Just—fly."

Alan leaned back in his chair, a half-smile teasing the corners of his lips. "Strange, but good. You know, I had half a mind to take early retirement when BA offered the last package. Thought I'd grow tomatoes and play golf."

She gave him a dry look. "You hate golf."

"I do," he admitted. "And the tomatoes never stood a chance against the squirrels. But I still have seniority, so I decided to stay at BA."

Hayley grinned. "So instead, you drag me halfway across the Caribbean in a glorified lawnmower."

"Ah, but a beautiful lawnmower," Alan countered. "And besides, when was the last time you felt this alive, hmm?"

That silenced her. She sipped her tea, staring at the Cessna through the mesh of the window. Joseph had offered to wait until they were ready, but she knew he was enjoying the ride as much as they were. Retired instructors were always the same—itchy feet, always looking for an excuse to climb back into a cockpit, even if it was from the back seat.

"I keep thinking about PanEuro," she said eventually. "How they made it sound like I wasn't good enough. Like I had to put on lipstick and strut down an aisle before I could touch a yoke again."

Alan's eyes softened. "They don't know what they've got. And one day they'll regret it."

She didn't reply immediately. Instead, she pulled her tablet from her bag and started rechecking weather for Grenada. The skies still looked good—calm, clear, the sun angling westward but still hours from setting.

"Think we can do Grenada before sunset?" she asked.

Alan raised a brow. "It's ambitious, but I suppose I didn't pack my sunglasses for nothing."

Back on the apron, they ran through a rapid pre-flight—Hayley doing the walk-around this time while Alan checked oil and fuel. Joseph reappeared from inside the FBO, holding two cold water bottles and a mischievous grin.

"I asked them to skip the full top-off. You'll get better performance with half tanks, and it gives you reason to stop for a refuel in Grenada."

Hayley nodded approvingly. "Smart thinking."

They took off again into the lowering sun, Hayley handling the departure, skimming just above the Pitons before turning west for the diagonal hop to Grenada. This leg was longer, and the skies were beginning to paint themselves in amber and rose. As they passed Saint Vincent, the shadows lengthened over the sea, and the wind began to whisper differently through the cabin vents—cooler, edged with the coming dusk.

The Cessna purred along, steady and responsive, and Hayley let herself imagine a future again: not as a stewardess, not stuck in a legacy airline's pastiche fantasy, but on her own path, whether that meant short hops over island chains or fighting her way back into the right seat of an Airbus.

"You remember flying with Mum to Palma that summer?" Alan asked out of nowhere, interrupting her thoughts.

Hayley blinked, then laughed. "You mean the one where the APU failed and the cabin turned into a sauna?"

"She was not amused," Alan chuckled.

"She nearly threw her G&T at the cabin crew."

"Only because they'd run out of cucumber."

They both laughed, the sound swallowed by the propeller's endless drone and the expansive quiet of sky. The conversation faded again, replaced by the comfortable hush that came from years of shared flight.

They landed at Maurice Bishop International just as the sun kissed the western horizon, bleeding orange fire over the tarmac. A lone tug was moving a JetBlue A320 into position across the field, but otherwise the airport seemed asleep, resting between the chaos of the day and whatever red-eye ghosts passed through after midnight.

They taxied slowly toward a makeshift tie-down near the GA terminal, and Hayley ran through the shutdown checklist like a priest at altar—deliberate, reverent. The propeller stilled. The silence came. And again, the two Northcotts simply sat there, watching the last light fade over the Caribbean.

"Think this'll be our last flight together for a while?" Hayley asked quietly.

Alan didn't answer straight away. Then he said, "Maybe. But not forever."

They didn't go inside the terminal straight away. Instead, they perched on the wing, drinking from their water bottles, watching the stars appear one by one over the darkening bay.

* _ * _ * _ *

Saturday 17th April 2021

"This is a final call for flight VS188 to London Heathrow. All remaining passengers please proceed to Gate 6 for immediate boarding."

The voice on the PA echoed across the high glass dome of Grantley Adams International, a peculiarly British accent superimposed on Bajan rhythms—so familiar and yet, in this place, ever so slightly surreal. Hayley blinked up at the display, half expecting to see a typo, some sign that the return to "Blighty" was a mirage.

The terminal was busier now than when they'd arrived, the air full of quiet tension that belonged as much to the world outside as the echo of wheels on linoleum and the rustle of plastic boarding passes. Masks bobbed everywhere, but so did the scent of sunscreen, perfume, the faintest trace of Jet A-1 wafting from the apron. Hayley stood by the window, watching the pale, heat-hazed form of a Virgin Atlantic A350, G-VLUX, shimmer in the distance as ground crew bustled below.

Like their journey out, they had been on standby tickets thanks to Dani, however, this time, the Virgin Atlantic flight was looking like it may be oversold. Hayley could feel the tension threading through her mother's fingers as Karen compulsively checked her phone, as she had loaded the British Airways staff travel portal, Alan being a Captain and therefore having ID90, the option to try either airline for staff travel, but with pandemic schedules still in flux, nothing was guaranteed. Hayley could sense her father's effort to project calm—the same cool detachment he'd worn during weather diversions or when ATC started playing games over the North Sea—but beneath it, his jaw was tight, hands clasped a little too firmly on his battered leather satchel.

Grantley Adams International was no longer the ghost terminal they'd encountered on arrival. Now, each cluster of seats in the departure lounge was occupied by some motley assortment of families, honeymooners, sunburned soloists, and the perpetual tribe of aircrew zigzagging the globe's barely ticking arteries. The Northcotts—three among many, yet defined by the invisible badge of aviation—blended in as best they could, but Hayley found herself staring at the parade of uniforms and rollaboards, a quiet ache blooming beneath her ribs.

Karen leaned in, lowering her voice, "Theres an AA to JFK, Alan, if we can't get on VS188—at least we'll get partway home, and as you're a Oneworld airline employee, love, you can get your bags checked through. I know Dani said she could call in a favour with someone at crew check-in if we get desperate. But I'd rather not do the JFK dash unless we must. Or there's a BA to Heathrow in the morning, or an Aer Lingus, the first one now the restrictions at home have been lifted, to Manchester. Doesn't BA still do the shuttle from Manchester? We could train it down from there, if it comes to that."

Alan grimaced, half-wry. "It's always a last resort— Manchester after an overnight. Remind me never to let you organise the family holidays again, Karen."

Hayley smirked, rolling her shoulders to chase away the tension that had crept up as departure time approached. "I don't mind the detour, Mum. As long as we're not stranded in JFK—again. I still have nightmares about Terminal 8."

They stood for a moment in companionable silence, staring out through the glass as G-VLUX was loaded, catering trucks and refuelling bowsers crawling like beetles beneath the sweep of the A350's wing. The world was resuming its slow, reluctant churn, but it still felt oddly hollow—every passenger wearing a mask of caution, every crew member moving with the fatigue of months lived on high alert. The Northcotts, at least, had their ritual: flight bags packed to precise dimensions, passports sheathed in battered holders, shoes chosen for speed through security rather than fashion.

Hayley's phone sounded, a text from Dani.

Dani Northcott: *I've checked my end, and there's only one seat available. I know you've got to be back in Birmingham tomorrow, so I'll try to get you the seat, H. Mum and Dad will have to try and get the BA or EI back.*

Hayley let out a small, dry laugh at the message, thumbs flicking a response back before she could quite think through the ache that flared in her chest.

Hayley Northcott: *If it's just me, then I'll take it. Dad has his staff travel as he's a BA pilot, and Mum can always charm her way onto something—she always does. Do you know where I'm sitting?*

Dani Northcott: *As it's a A330, I've got you 4A, if that's all right? Upper Class, window, bulkhead. They might swap you out if a last-minute revenue ticket pops up, but right now, you're golden. Just tell the crew you're my sister, they'll know what to do. And text me when you land. Love you, H.*

A wave of relief—mixed with guilt—washed over Hayley. It wasn't just about flying home; it was the return of agency, the promise of a window seat, the heady, shameful pleasure of being "looked after" by the system she sometimes despised. She caught her mother's eye, reading the answer in her smile before she spoke.

"You got a seat, love?"

Hayley nodded. "Just me, though. Dani pulled a string. She's said that the Aer Lingus will take you and Dad as Dad's got his IAG staff travel card. Manchester, then the shuttle. Or a hire car, worst case. Sorry."

Karen only shrugged, unfazed. "Don't worry about us, sweetheart. We've done enough airport sprints to survive one more. You get yourself home, all right?"

Alan gave her a long look—equal parts pride and melancholy. "Text us the second you're through border control. And for God's sake, don't say anything cheeky to the crew. They'll clock you for one of us in about thirty seconds anyway."

Hayley grinned. "Me? Never."

Their ritual parting was matter-of-fact, the sort of gentle leave-taking that comes from years of departures and arrivals, more "see you soon" than "goodbye." Alan pressed his battered old BA wings pin into her palm—"for luck, if you find you're missing one up front." Karen handed over a Ziplock bag with three ginger biscuits ("so you don't fade away, love"). Then the final embrace: tight, bracing, unspoken.

At the gate, the boarding queue was snaking its way along the windows, a thin line of British holidaymakers, a few islanders clutching branded carry-ons, and a handful of business types nervously clutching phones. Hayley found herself behind a family from Nottingham, the mother humming a football chant under her breath, the little girl—mask askew—pointing at the waiting Airbus, convinced it was going to "fly to the moon."

She watched the weary but professional Virgin crew work the gate: one at the scanner, another fielding anxious questions about connections, a third wielding a tape measure to settle a heated debate over hand-luggage dimensions.

When Hayley's turn came, she offered up her passport and boarding pass with the blandest smile she could muster.

The gate agent, a woman in her late twenties with a familiar tired warmth, barely glanced at the documents before her eyes flicked up to Hayley's.

"Northcott, right? You're Dani's sister?"

"That obvious, is it?"

The agent's eyes twinkled behind her mask. "Dead ringer. Your seat's 4A, Upper Class. Crew's expecting you. If you need anything, just let us know."

Hayley's reply was dry. "Not unless you've got a spare logbook. Or a pilot vacancy."

The agent laughed softly. "Get on board, love. Dream big."

Walking down the jet bridge, Hayley felt the familiar shiver that always came with crossing the liminal space between earth and sky. The gentle thrum of air-conditioning, the faint tang of jet fuel and shampoo, the sense of stepping into an engineered cocoon—all of it pressed nostalgia and hope into the tightness beneath her sternum.

As she stepped into the A350's forward galley, she felt immediately at home in the clinical, companionable bustle. The purser—a trim, grey-haired woman with the unflappable air of a lifelong flyer—smiled broadly at her.

"Miss Northcott? Dani said you'd be joining us. Welcome aboard."

"Thank you," Hayley replied, slipping easily into the banter of her tribe. "She's got all the dirt on me, so I'll behave."

"We'll make sure you're spoiled rotten," the purser winked. "Pop your bag wherever, then I'll bring a drink around before departure."

Her seat—4A—was more cocoon than chair, angled window, a private island of fabric and softly glowing LEDs. Hayley stowed her battered rucksack, ran her hands over the seat's controls, and let herself breathe in the privilege, guilt pricking at the edge of her comfort. For a fleeting moment, she remembered the hours spent wedged into economy, knees knocking tray tables, enduring those rituals that made up the economy-class ballet. And now, here she was—one of the lucky ones, a Northcott, a pilot-in-waiting, a guest in the world her family had built.

The crew moved about the cabin with a quiet precision. Hayley watched as the safety demonstration played, half-listening, half-lost in memory: the careful ballet of demonstration cards, the clipped language of emergency exits and seat belts, the practiced pantomime of calm in the event of a sudden loss of cabin pressure.

Even in this strange twilight of air travel, with the world still unsteady from the pandemic's grip, the rituals held.

She texted Dani a last thank you, a silly emoji, and a request to thank the crew for her. Then, as the doors closed and the engines wound up with that soft, rising whine that vibrated through the fuselage, Hayley settled in for take-off.

Destination?

Home.

****

CHAPTER 11 – Back to Training
Monday 19th April 2021

The air on Monday morning was different—neither the honey-thick humidity of Barbados nor the recycled chill of an aircraft, but the plain, pale damp of a Kentish spring. The tarmac outside the low building was still spattered with overnight rain, glossing the battered kerbs and making the stubby grass beyond gleam. Hayley Northcott stood by the bus stop, her black cabin bag parked at her ankle, and felt a peculiar sense of dislocation. Her skin still carried the faint, clinging warmth of Caribbean sun, and yet here she was, stood in the terminal at Manston, waiting for the PanEuro flight that was one of the few internal Britain flights, where she could get to the Stewardess Academy at Birmingham International.

Straightening her pillbox hat, as, according to the PanEuro Staff Handbook, even when she was off duty and flying with them, she would have to wear full uniform, from the girdle that crushed her waist to the impractically glossy heels. The hat, perched just so, felt alien after days in linen and sandals. She caught her reflection in the shelter's grimy glass, checked her lipstick—'Proper Scarlet', as per Mrs Havers' never-ending memos—and straightened the scarf knotted tightly at her throat.

A bus lumbered past, trailing diesel and puddle-spray. Hayley ignored it. No one else seemed to be waiting for the shuttle to the terminal. The airport was a strange hybrid these days, a holding pen for PanEuro's nostalgia act and a few charters that drifted through like distant relatives. Manston's concrete and fog-bound history pressed in on her. Only three weeks before, she'd stood here trembling with anticipation and indignation, unsure if stewardess training was a step forward or a humiliating detour. Now, after Barbados, after the cockpit of the Cessna with her father, and the odd, healing freedom of those island flights, she felt more certain—though about what, she wasn't sure.

A sudden wind lifted the edges of her skirt, and Hayley clamped it down with a practised hand. She'd mastered the PanEuro walk—small, clipped steps, head high, don't let the elements or the leering van drivers get the better of you. She would not give Mrs Havers, or anyone else, cause to mark her down on "poise under adverse conditions".

Looking at the departure board, Hayley noticed that the next flight, a routine PanEuro trip to Birmingham, was boarding soon. Looking at the queue, there was hardly anyone in the security lane, despite it being a week since the laws had changed to allow airlines to operate full capacity on domestic flights again. Hayley knew the limited passengers for this flight were mostly business people, the kind of regulars that didn't bat an eyelid at a uniformed stewardess nor care for the unnecessary grandeur that PanEuro still insisted upon, despite the rest of the aviation industry trimming the fat.

She adjusted her scarf again, drawing the ends tighter to avoid the chill, and made her way into the terminal. The light inside was artificial, flat and unyielding, the air filled with the faint scent of coffee and polished plastic. The usual bustle was missing, replaced by an eerie calm. No rushing crowds, no hurried ticket counters or grim-faced travellers. Instead, there was just the dull, rhythmic pulse of airport life—a forgotten relic of times when travel had felt glamorous, before the chaos and uncertainty of a pandemic had brought everything to a halt.

She passed through security, where the familiar monotony of the process did little to alleviate the tension in her chest. The guards were either too tired to look her up and down or too distracted by their phones to care much about her uniform. As she walked towards the gate, her mind drifted to the absurdity of it all—how she had come to this point. The flight to Barbados had been a quiet escape from the grind of her existence, a brief respite to reconnect with her roots, but now, as she moved through the terminal, it felt like nothing more than a distant memory, something that belonged to another life altogether.

The gate area for Gate 7 was small, with only a handful of passengers seated. A few of them glanced up as Hayley approached, but their attention quickly returned to their devices or papers. The flight attendants who stood by the desk wore their uniforms like a second skin, their faces painted with forced cheerfulness. Hayley forced herself to smile as she passed, but it was a hollow gesture, the kind that you give when you feel like a cog in a well-oiled machine that's slowly losing its function.

"Are you commuting or leisure?" one of the PanEuro gate agents asked, walking over to her. Unlike the ultra-low cost airlines, who often had gate agents who gave off a sense of hurried indifference, the PanEuro staff were always a bit more involved, even if it was just the aura of propriety they were trying to maintain.

"Commuting," Hayley said, keeping her tone neutral. She didn't have the energy for the usual pleasantries or to explain that her role was far from what it once seemed.

"Ah, of course," the gate agent said, nodding knowingly. She was older than most of the flight crew and had an air about her that seemed to suggest she understood the weight of things beyond just the flight. "The regulars don't get any easier, do they?" she said, referencing the passengers.

Hayley gave a thin smile but didn't respond. The regulars, those frequent flyers who seemed immune to the nostalgia PanEuro so fervently held onto, were a different breed. They expected nothing less than perfection—both from the airline and the staff. Anything less was not tolerated. The idea of being part of an airline that clung so desperately to a past that no longer held any real relevance bothered her more than she cared to admit.

"Seat 1D is available," the gate agent then said, printing out a chit that would allow Hayley to board and settle into a first-class seat, as she was travelling standby as an employee. The irony, Hayley knew, that her own ID90 as a Trainee Stewardess, for leisure, was valid only on the few airlines that PanEuro had interline agreements with, those being Emirates, Qatar, and Etihad Airways, the more 'upper class' style airlines that PanEuro believed aligned with their ethos of not serving the 'plebs' but the more the more cultivated traveller. Hayley had once joked, bitterly, that PanEuro would sooner codeshare with Concorde than let its uniformed trainees fly Ryanair. Not that she'd dare say it aloud in the stewardess lounge; too many of the girls clung to the fantasy that they were queens of the skies, not clowns in couture.

The Airbus A321neo, G-PANT, Hayley saw, chuckling at the unfortunate registration that made it sound like a rejected lingerie brand, gleamed on the wet tarmac. It was one of PanEuro's newer acquisitions, though already retrofitted with faux-vintage interiors that never quite matched the quality of the original aircraft the airline fetishised. Burgundy leather, chrome seatbelt buckles, and floral-patterned curtains—like something from a 1960s Parisian brothel—wrapped the cabin in a skin-deep illusion. It was heritage as performance art.

Hayley boarded without fuss, the crew offering her polite nods but little else—she wasn't on duty, just another commuting minion in their eyes. She settled into seat 1D, placed her handbag on her lap and looked out over the sodden apron. The grey English sky pressed down, low and flat, without promise or movement. Her holiday tan already looked out of place, like a stain on the grey canvas of her return.

"Would you like a complementary pre-departure orange juice?" the stewardess, who Hayley recognised from the training flight to Tallinn, Martha Kempstone, asked, a tray in her hands with 6 glasses, obviously for the 5 passengers in the Executive, or First Class, cabin, the 1-2 seating with the 6 rows of A, C and D seats being the standard layout while the rest was a 2-2 configuration, the usual four-abreast economy, or 'Classic', class.

Hayley offered a polite smile and accepted the orange juice, the crystal-cut glass chilled to the touch. Even that, she thought, had been chosen to evoke a sense of another age—like flying was still something only a few could afford, an event dressed up in gloves and etiquette.

"Thank you," she said softly, balancing the glass on the narrow armrest and letting her fingers rest gently around it.

The stewardess nodded and moved on. Hayley watched her go—her gait smooth, her smile fixed, her hair coiled in a perfect chignon. She could already imagine Mrs Havers' voice praising the symmetry, the poise, the effort. It was all so precise. So manufactured.

The aircraft's engines hummed to life with a subtle throb as the last of the passengers boarded. A pair of suited men took seats a few rows behind her, both already absorbed in their phones, their conversations clipped and dry. A young woman in economy looked nervously around as she struggled to place her bag in the overhead locker, while a crew member gently but firmly stepped in to help.

The aircraft doors closed with a familiar thud. Hayley's ears pricked at the sound—always more reassuring than the mechanical jolt of closing gates or train doors. It was the signal that nothing else could be changed. You were committed. Going forward. The seatbelt signs chimed, and the safety demonstration began, delivered live in the Executive Cabin despite the presence of functioning screens. PanEuro didn't trust automation for appearances. Everything had to be done the old way—manual life jackets, hand gestures, even the forced smiles as the demo played out like a rehearsed dance.

Hayley sipped her orange juice and looked out the window as the aircraft taxied.

Mentally, however, she called out in her head the calls that would be going on in the flight deck, as she knew that she'd wished she was up front.

*_*_*_*

"Hey, Hales," Hayley heard, walking into the locker room of the Stewardess Academy, the cheerful voice of Tannie Keyworth bouncing off the tiled walls like a caffeine shot.

Tannie was already half-changed, adjusting her blouse in the mirror with the same manicured precision she applied to her makeup. Her lipstick—PanEuro's mandated "Proper Scarlet"—was flawlessly reapplied, but her grin was crooked and genuine. The locker room, with its linoleum floor and faint scent of hairspray and industrial soap, was already bustling with the usual morning scramble.

"Back from paradise, are we?" Tannie chirped, turning to give Hayley a quick once-over. "Look at you. Glowing. You must have actually relaxed."

Hayley gave a faint smile, placing her bag down by her assigned locker. "I think I forgot what relaxing felt like. I got sunburnt on day two and wore nothing but cotton for a week."

"That sounds illegal." Tannie laughed. "No girdle rash, no hairspray headaches? You're not allowed to enjoy yourself without at least some minor trauma."

"What did you get up to during 'half term', Tannie" Agatha Dean, the former easyJet cabin crew member, who had just walked in, looking like she had just stepped out of a fashion editorial by way of a Wetherspoons breakfast shift. She was holding a double-shot coffee in one hand and tapping her fingernails against her phone with the other, a look of studied disinterest on her face.

"Didn't go anywhere. Watched Call the Midwife reruns, argued with my neighbour about recycling bins, and nearly punched a bloke at Sainsbury's who tried to tell me masks were 'a hoax invented by Big Soap'," Tannie replied breezily, applying a final spritz of perfume that smelled of something retro and vaguely cloying. "So you know. The usual restorative break."

Agatha smirked. "Sounds about right. I... may... have handed in my notice. Got a new job..."

Hayley blinked. "You what?"

Agatha nodded, taking a long sip of her coffee before continuing. "Yeah. I'm off. Can't be arsed with this retro bollocks, so I may have signed up for training at Lufthansa Aviation Training in Frankfurt. Not as cabin crew, but ground school. Got a cousin who works for Lufthansa, and they're putting me up for the next year or so while I train at Lufthansa."

Hayley stared at Agatha, torn between admiration and a pang of sudden, unbidden jealousy. "Bloody hell," she said finally, her voice caught somewhere between breathless surprise and repressed envy. "That's... that's incredible."

Agatha shrugged, but her eyes gleamed with a hint of pride. "It's sensible, is what it is. This place is a costume drama masquerading as an airline. I didn't sign up to be an extra in a 1960s BA training film, I signed up to fly. If I've got to start from the tarmac to do that, fine. At least the Germans believe in training you for the future, not for the past."

The locker room buzzed with its usual background noise—zippers, perfume spritzes, heels tapping against linoleum—but the announcement landed like a thunderclap. Tannie let out a slow whistle, twisting back toward the mirror with a wink at Hayley.

"She's got a point, you know. If I get one more lecture about the correct angle to serve tomato juice in the 'Classic Cabin', I might flip a drinks cart."

Hayley leaned against the locker, her fingers momentarily clutching the vented slats as if the metal could offer her clarity. She'd only just returned from a rare reminder of what flying could be—real freedom, raw sky—and here she was, back in the imitation. A world of pristine lipstick and polished shoes that pretended it was flying's golden age, while the aircraft themselves taxied through the muck of Brexit logistics and COVID protocols.

"Do they know you've quit?" she asked Agatha, soft-voiced.

"Not officially," Agatha smirked. "But Mrs Havers will have a conniption when she finds out I'm not bothering with her 'Ladies of the Air' graduation ceremony. I'll post her a thank-you card from Frankfurt."

The image of the formidable Mrs Havers, nostrils flared as she opened a pastel envelope with glittery German stamps, nearly made Hayley laugh. Nearly. But instead, she felt the press of something sharper in her chest—doubt, maybe. Or discontent given shape.

"Morning," Sarah said, walking in, and Hayley noticed that her friend had had a haircut, one which was 100% not Havers-approved, but looked almost RAF regulation, as if Sarah had walked into a barber in Brize Norton and asked for the no-nonsense, aerodynamically-efficient special. It was short, sharp, and entirely out of step with PanEuro's 'Bouffants & Beehives' aesthetic. No soft curls, no femininity as per Mrs Havers' cherished handbook. Just clean lines, clipped precision.

"You trying to get court-martialled?" Tannie asked, one brow raised in mock horror as she took in Sarah's new look.

Sarah, shrugging off her navy-blue coat and hanging it in her locker, smirked. "Royal Auxiliary Air Force. Have to do minimum hair standards, don't I? Spent most the weekend in the simulators keeping my QRA skills up to date, as my Squadron is attached to my old RAF squadron. You see, as part of when I was commissioned as a Flight Lieutenant 10 years ago, when I left the RAF, I would have to join the RAuxAF, the reserve component," she continued, matter-of-fact, slipping off her scarf with the ease of someone used to toggling between uniforms and identities. "Turns out I'd rather spend a weekend doing low-level intercepts in a sim than learning the choreography of tea service aboard a narrow-body Airbus."

Tannie whistled again. "God, I feel lazy. I binge-watched Selling Sunset and barely moved."

Hayley couldn't take her eyes off Sarah. That clean new cut—it wasn't just about regulations. It was a statement. Quiet, controlled, a rejection of the elaborate persona demanded by PanEuro's stewardess pantomime. There was a steel to it. A reminder that Sarah had once flown Tornadoes and Typhoons, not just carried tomato juice and smiled through turbulence.

"Do you miss it?" Hayley asked, almost too softly. "The RAF, I mean."

Sarah's reply was immediate. "Yes. Every damn day." She turned to face her properly. "But that's the point, isn't it? We're not here because we forgot how to fly. We're here because someone somewhere decided we had to earn our way back in, via heels and hemlines."

The silence that followed wasn't awkward—it was heavy with recognition. Tannie looked between them both and gave a small shrug, as if to say, Some of us never flew to begin with, but we feel the same. Hayley thought of the Cessna, of her dad glancing over at her in the sunlit cockpit, of the weightless joy she'd felt in those hours. That had been real flying. What she was doing here was a performance.

"Did you get any flying done Hales?" Sarah asked, and Hayley had to admit, the memory of her hands on the yoke, the sun bouncing off the ocean as she banked left toward Grenada, made her heart ache a little.

"I did," she said quietly, a small smile playing on her lips. "Cessna 172. Hopped across the islands with Dad. Grenada, St Lucia… even did some circuits at elsewhere, just for fun. It reminded me why I even put up with this place."

Hayley then noticed Agatha and Tannie look at her quiet, the sound of footsteps behind her softening to nothing as the group turned collectively. Behind her, standing in the open doorway of the locker room with the poise of a drama teacher about to stage a full-cast re-enactment of Brief Encounter, stood Mrs Rosemary Havers.

"Ah. Miss Northcott. I see the tropics have not entirely obliterated your ability to report on time," she said, her voice as clipped as ever, like someone cutting thread with small, angry scissors. Her eyes flicked to Hayley's hatless head, and though she said nothing, the silence spoke volumes.

Hayley, with a smoothness born of many rehearsals, lifted her pillbox hat from her bag and placed it squarely upon her head.

"Of course not, ma'am," she said, her voice butter-smooth. "Uniform regulations remain foremost in my mind."

A faint twitch at the corner of Havers' mouth could have passed for a smirk or a tic. No one dared clarify.

"I expect no less. This academy does not dispense diplomas like pamphlets on the Tube," Havers announced, her gaze sweeping across the room. "We craft ladies of excellence. Ambassadors of civility. Not tanned delinquents or aspiring co-pilots with illusions of grandeur."

The last line was delivered with an almost surgical precision, directed just past Hayley and directly at Sarah Marsh, who met it with the cool, unflinching composure of a woman who'd once landed an aircraft during a hydraulics failure and still made it to her brother's wedding by dinner.

"Understood," Sarah said dryly, buttoning her navy cardigan. "Though I believe we were advised to demonstrate initiative and adaptability. Both of which, I might add, I exercised this weekend."

Mrs Havers stared at her for a long, loaded moment. Then, without breaking eye contact, turned on her heel.

"Briefing Room Three. Ten minutes. Ladies, if you're not early, you're already late."

She swept out as dramatically as she'd entered, her kitten heels clipping down the corridor like disapproval given sound.

* _ * _ * _ *

Briefing Room Three looked much the same as it had three weeks ago: like the waiting room for a Pan Am promotional film, albeit one constructed by someone who'd only ever seen such films from a great distance, possibly on mute. Framed vintage advertisements ("Fly the Friendly Skies—Without the Fat Men") hung alongside yellowing world maps and plastic models of aircraft suspended mid-climb. A kettle hissed on a side table, next to a silver tray of Bourbons and pink wafer biscuits.

The girls filed in quietly, the usual chatter subdued. Something in Havers' tone had pressed a firm hand on their collective mood. Hayley sat between Tannie and Sarah, with Agatha on the far side, checking her phone with one hand and unwrapping a biscuit with the other.

Mrs Havers re-entered, flanked by a man none of them had seen before. He was tall, with a former-military bearing and a distinct lack of facial expression. His suit was grey, his shoes black, and his eyes carried the unfocused glaze of someone who'd once stared too long into a HUD at 30,000 feet.

"This," Havers said, as if introducing a serial killer at a cotillion, "is Mr Douglas Pearce. Mr Pearce is Head of Safety and Security for PanEuro and will be delivering your compulsory Security Procedures Seminar this morning."

Pearce nodded once. "Good morning, ladies," he said, in a tone that suggested the morning was neither good, nor particularly female.

"Security is not about paranoia," Pearce began, his voice gravelly and clipped, like a drill sergeant who'd done time in corporate HR. "It's about expectation management. Yours, and the passengers'. You are, at all times, both the front line and the firewall. Glamour has nothing to do with it."

The slide projector—yes, an actual projector, part of Havers' fondness for tactile learning—clicked into life with a mechanical thunk, casting a yellowish slide onto the wall: Security Threat Profiles: 2021 Onwards. It looked like something a school geography teacher might have thrown together in the 1990s.

"What you see here," Pearce continued, pointing to a chart of threat categories, "is a breakdown of recent incidents affecting civil aviation in Europe. That includes unruly passengers, cyber breaches, contraband smuggling, and, in one case, a service animal trained to detect explosives that instead chewed through the seatbelt of a federal marshal mid-flight."

A few heads turned. Tannie stifled a laugh. Sarah looked impassive. Hayley's attention sharpened. Pearce might be dry as Ryvita, but he spoke the language of the air, not of theatre.

"The important thing to remember," he said, clicking through to a grainy still from a CCTV feed, "is that threats rarely arrive as threats. They arrive as problems. Overheard conversations. Unattended bags. A man with too many questions about door locks. A passenger who suddenly decides to move seats just as you begin taxiing. And sometimes... the threat is wearing a uniform just like yours."

That last line landed with the weight of truth. Pearce paused deliberately, scanning the room. Agatha looked up from her phone. Sarah folded her arms. Even Havers, for once, was silent.

"You're probably wondering what all this has to do with lipstick shades and chicken-or-beef service," he said.

"The answer is: everything. You are, in effect, a security team disguised as hostesses. And if that seems absurd, welcome to the modern world."

He continued, detailing the protocols they'd memorised in handbooks but never truly absorbed. The mechanics of rapid egress in hostile territory. How to identify false credentials. Where to strike if someone attempts to force their way into the cockpit mid-flight. The language was precise. Not gory, but specific. Pearce didn't indulge in theatrics. He simply described what had happened, on real flights, to real people, and what the stewardesses had done to stop it.

Hayley found herself taking notes, real ones, not the pantomime scribbles they all produced for Havers' 'Service with Elegance' workshops. Pearce's words held consequence. Every word implied that the job she'd belittled in her own mind still mattered—just not in the way PanEuro pretended.

After forty minutes, he paused. "We'll take a short break. Ten minutes. Tea's on the trolley. Try not to die of ennui."

Hayley stood, her legs aching slightly from sitting so upright for nearly an hour. The chairs in Briefing Room Three had that rigid, institutional feel—just soft enough to avoid outright complaint, but ergonomically medieval in all the ways that encouraged 'ladylike posture'. Tannie made a noise somewhere between a groan and a sigh as she rose and rolled her shoulders.

"Well," she said, flapping the collar of her blouse like she was trying to air out a corset, "that was cheerful. I was hoping we'd get a seminar on perfume selection or which way to slice lemons for gin and tonics, but no—just casual terrorism and dog-chewed seatbelts."

Agatha stretched luxuriously, looking for all the world like a cat sunning itself in a Berlin window. "I actually didn't hate that. At least it wasn't more of Havers' thoughts on 'grace in the galley'."

Sarah, already pouring herself a cup of builder's tea from the ancient urn, looked up with a tilt of her head. "Pearce used to be with the RAF Police, I think. One of those unassuming types that quietly knows where all the bodies are buried."

Hayley accepted a paper cup of tea from Sarah and sat on the edge of the low windowsill, staring out over the academy's narrow strip of lawn. A distant contrail sliced across the pale blue above, sharp and ghostly. For a moment, she imagined it was a Cessna again, or something larger—something she might one day fly. That thought never truly left her. It was an ember, burning steadily, impervious to the makeup and mimicry PanEuro imposed.

"So," Tannie said, nudging her gently, "when do you think you'll snap and leg it to easyJet? Or are you going to do a dramatic walkout at graduation, throw your gloves in Havers' face and declare, 'I am not a bloody mannequin!'?"

Hayley smiled despite herself. "I'll wait until I can do it with dramatic lighting. Maybe during the final practical, right as the evacuation slide deploys."

"You joke," Agatha said, "but I guarantee someone's tried to fake an ankle injury to escape this farce."

A movement at the doorway caught Hayley's eye. Mr Pearce re-entered, holding a battered file under one arm. He glanced around, not impatient, but waiting—watching.

"Ladies," he said, once most had resumed their seats. "We've had our laugh. Now for the serious part."

They returned to their places, laughter evaporating like mist. Hayley noticed the way Pearce seemed to carry a different kind of authority than Havers. Not loud. Not even intimidating in the usual sense. Just... resolute. Grounded. Like someone who'd seen things go wrong and refused to let them happen again.

"This," Pearce said, opening the file and pulling out a series of black-and-white photos, "is a timeline of one incident. You won't find it in your training handbooks. It's not glamorous. But it is instructional."

****

CHAPTER 12 – Graduation from Stewardess School
Friday 14th May 2021

The day had finally arrived, Hayley knew, the day where she was no longer beholden to the dragon that was Rosemary Havers, that she and her fellow trainees, minus Agatha, who had left and was now in Frankfurt, training to become a Lufthansa pilot, the 18 month training course the German operator had whisked her away in a blur of regulation, German efficiency, and a promise of proper flight deck time—were to don the full regalia of PanEuro Airways and graduate from Stewardess School. Graduation, of course, in the Haversian context, was not some light-hearted cap-and-gown affair. No, it was a performance, an ordeal, a pageant of vintage grooming and ceremonial compliance. And for Hayley Northcott, it marked the threshold between enduring a parody of 1960s air travel and entering the surreal, shimmering theatre of PanEuro's operations proper.

The morning began, like all mornings under Havers, with an inspection. Though Rosemary had promised to "soften her stance" for the sake of the graduation ceremony, no one believed her. She stood at the front of the Academy's main training room, which had been converted into a pseudo-departure lounge with faked Perspex boarding gates, marbled vinyl flooring, and a mannequin dressed in a 1970s PanEuro uniform propped near a lectern. Her heels clicked ominously across the linoleum as she surveyed her remaining cohort: Sarah Marsh, ever the former RAF pilot cloaked in impeccable poise; Emma

Lang, who had dialled down her once-raucous attitude to a tolerable sass; Poppy Knight, nervously adjusting her hat every ten seconds; Tannie Keyworth, who had somehow made it through the entire training with equal parts grace and gobsmackery.

"Northcott," Havers snapped, eyeing Hayley from behind her horn-rimmed glasses. "That hemline is precisely half a centimetre too long. The PanEuro silhouette demands precision."

Translation?

Havers either was on her time of the month, or had been left on read by an old flame from BOAC. Either way, Hayley had long ceased to take the constant barbs personally. It was all part of the ritualised psychodrama that had characterised every moment of the last six weeks. She gave a quiet nod, subtly adjusted the hem, and held her gaze on the faux flight information screen behind the lectern. 'PE001 – Departing to Manston – ON TIME' blinked in the corner, a bit of set dressing designed to evoke PanEuro's fictional golden age.

Next to her, Sarah Marsh stood rock still, shoulders squared, the faintest of smirks betraying her shared disdain. Emma Lang, ever the born performer, offered a silent theatrical shrug as Havers stalked down the line like an air marshal on inspection.

"Marsh, you're not in the RAF. You need to look like a hostess, not a heroine. Chin down, smile soft. This isn't a court-martial."

Sarah obeyed the instruction with a flicker of something almost like amusement. She inclined her head, just enough to satisfy the pantomime of submission, and offered a subdued smile — one that to anyone who'd known her longer would recognise as sardonic. She and Hayley had mastered the art of surviving Havers' barbed commentary with passive rebellion: internal mockery and impeccable outward obedience. It was the safest method of self-preservation in a school where eye-rolls could delay graduation and chipped nail polish could instigate a ten-minute monologue on "the standards that built an empire".

Havers finished her sweep of the line, circling back to the lectern like a lioness returning to her perch. Her voice rang out through the converted room, slicing the air like an announcement over a poorly tuned Tannoy.

"Today, ladies, you will graduate not simply from this training course, but from girlhood to the refined womanhood required of PanEuro Airways. You will step onto that stage as ambassadors of an era in which air travel was a luxury, not a bus journey. Remember that. Posture, precision, polish."

She glanced around, taking a moment to lock eyes with each of them. Tannie smiled too brightly. Poppy looked like she might combust under the pressure. Emma, behind a veil of forced serenity, was mouthing "help me" to Sarah when Havers turned her back.

"Now. To the dressing rooms. Uniforms, final touches, and do not—do not—emerge until you have been individually inspected by me. Mr Oslov will assist backstage. Dismissed."

Hayley could see the Ukrainian purser look like he wanted to slap Havers for being a condescending relic of imperial nostalgia, and as they walked out, he followed the group, muttering about 'old bags who failed at finishing school trying to recreate the 1950s with cheaper lipstick and a clipboard.' Tannie snorted. Sarah, ever the composed one, tilted her head slightly in his direction and muttered back, "Somewhere between Flight Attendant Barbie and Bridge on the River Kwai."

They reached the cramped dressing rooms, a space once intended for changing uniforms but which now functioned more as a ritual chamber for final transformation. The air inside smelled of hairspray, foundation powder, and a peculiar sort of nervous sweat. Rows of plastic garment bags lined the wall, each marked with their names and gowns, their uniforms already being on their persons and so all that was left was makeup, hair, and the final, farcical fittings that would determine whether they were "PanEuro ready".

"I'll be glad when we can get to the bases that we've been assigned to," Emma muttered, attacking her own reflection with a mascara wand like it owed her money. "Six weeks of mascara drills, lipstick inspections, and posture checks, all to be awarded a certificate printed on 200gsm stock and a lanyard. And possibly a lifetime of wedgies from regulation tights."

Hayley found her place in front of the mirror and unzipped her bag, revealing the regulation items issued on Day One of training: coral lipstick, PanEuro's exclusive shade of blush (somewhere between 'sunset optimism' and 'airport loo lighting'), a compact powder case stamped with the airline's golden wings, and the navy gloves she was meant to hold, not wear. The hat—oh, the hat—was perched upon its foam stand like a tiny fascist dictator, waiting to command obedience.

Hayley fitted the hat on her head with robotic precision, tilting it exactly 25 degrees as prescribed in the grooming manual. She caught sight of Sarah in the mirror, adjusting her own hat with a sigh that sounded more like the final exhalation of a prisoner being led to the gallows than a graduate about to celebrate. They exchanged a look— somewhere between solidarity and gallows humour. Tannie gave a dramatic groan as she tried to thread a hairpin into a painfully tight chignon, jabbing her scalp with the same vigour as Havers jabbing their souls.

"This bloody bun's pulling tighter than my last relationship," she hissed, and Emma barked out a sharp laugh before catching herself and glancing at the door. No sign of Havers. Yet.

Poppy, still fluttering about like a nervous debutante, held up her gloves like they were alien artefacts. "Do you think she'll actually check if we're holding them or wearing them?"

"She'll check," Hayley said, dabbing foundation under her eyes. "She's probably got a tick chart backstage. 'Knight: gloves held, not clenched. Minus five.'"

"She's got a ledger of grudges," Emma added. "Probably files us under 'most likely to wear non-regulation moisturiser'."

The mood was lighter than expected, a relief after six weeks of unrelenting performance. There was something about the finality of it all—knowing they were at the threshold—that loosened the tension. For Hayley, the last day wasn't an end; it was a reprieve. The real performance, she suspected, was yet to come once they were out in the skies, balancing champagne flutes and diplomacy with stag parties vomiting into sick bags and business class passengers demanding to speak to the captain because the Chardonnay was too warm.

She finished her makeup, affixed the tiny PanEuro wings to her lapel with the ceremonial reverence expected of her, and gave herself one last once-over. It was uncanny—how someone who had once flown left seat in a Cessna over the Channel could now resemble a bottle-blonde relic of 1971.

"Let's get it over with," Sarah said quietly, and led the way.

The backstage area of the 'departure lounge' was a surreal construction of muslin backdrops, fake airline banners, and a looping soundtrack of Frank Sinatra's Come Fly With Me, punctuated every few minutes by a pre-recorded boarding call in clipped RP English. Hayley caught sight of Dimitri Oslov, who was managing backstage like a disgruntled West End stage manager, clipboard in hand, his face obviously annoyed with the way he was being forced to act as a stagehand in a play he'd never auditioned for.

"Oh, darlings," he sighed, spying the group in their full uniformed regalia. "You look like the opening credits of a low-budget Channel 5 docudrama. All we need now is a voiceover: 'In the glamorous world of PanEuro Airlines, not everything is as retro-chic as it seems…'"

Hayley laughed at Dimitri's comment just as Rosemary Havers emerged from the wings, her face a mask of pride, condescension, and performative nostalgia. The laughter died down like a switch had been thrown. Dimitri took a theatrical step back, bowing with a flourish as if to introduce her.

"Ladies," Havers intoned, arms raised slightly as though conjuring an audience from thin air, "you may now proceed one by one for final inspection. Remember your deportment. This is not a race to the boarding gate. It is the stately procession of icons."

Sarah was the first to be summoned. She stepped forward, posture exact, her facial expression neutral save for the barest twitch at one corner of her mouth. Havers circled her like a museum curator admiring a particularly well-preserved artefact.

"Acceptable," she pronounced. "If only marginally lacking in charm. Next."

One by one, the others followed—Emma giving a hint of camp flair that stopped just shy of insubordination, Tannie attempting poise while muttering a silent prayer that her bun would hold, and Poppy trembling like she'd been called to a royal court. When Hayley stepped forward, she did so with calm certainty. Not confidence—she had long since had that whittled down by repeated critiques about her 'masculine energy' and 'unladylike gait'. But she held herself steady. She wasn't here for Havers anymore. She was here for herself.

Havers eyed her as though evaluating an off-brand gin in a First Class bar.

"You've at least learned how to stand still," she murmured. "Shame about the jawline—it makes you look defiant."

Hayley remained silent, lips closed in a perfect PanEuro smile. She knew that, by now, Havers' jibes were more habitual than personal. A form of theatre. The older woman gave a curt nod and waved her along. Behind her, Dimitri mouthed, *'Freedom awaits'* and made a chopping motion across his neck.

The ceremony commenced moments later. They were ushered out in single file onto the set that had once been the Academy's classroom. Now it resembled an airport lounge caught in amber—a tribute to an era that only truly existed in cigarette adverts and faded postcards. Faux-leather chairs, airline posters bearing long-defunct routes, a drinks trolley stacked with bottles of ginger ale and vintage tonic water. An audience composed of other PanEuro employees, executives, trainers, and even a smattering of "VIP passengers" who were clearly just HR reps with better tailoring and clipboard fetishes, lined the edge of the makeshift 'gate area'.

"Ladies and gentlemen," Rosemary's voice echoed through a fake intercom speaker mounted above the door, "welcome to Flight PE001, departing shortly to your dreams."

Hayley stifled a groan. Sarah didn't. The ceremony began in earnest: a theatrical parade of "duties demonstrations," from safety belt instruction to champagne pouring, all choreographed to the minute. Emma performed her safety card mime with dramatic flair, clearly enjoying herself now that the finish line was in sight. Poppy's hand trembled slightly as she demonstrated the use of the life vest, but she caught herself and corrected the motion with a practiced smile.

Hayley's role was the infamous "coat service" demonstration, a segment Rosemary had insisted symbolised "the personal touch PanEuro brought back to the skies." She stepped forward and mimed taking a guest's imaginary mink coat, folding it delicately, and placing it into a phantom wardrobe. All this while standing next to a dummy dressed as a 1975 PanEuro executive, complete with flared trousers and a moustache like a minor disco star.

As she stepped back, she caught sight of Sarah standing tall, waiting for her turn. The former pilot's eyes met hers, and for a moment they shared the same thought: *This is absurd—but we survived it.*

Eventually, all six remaining trainees stood in a line. The lights dimmed, and a trumpet flourish—pre-recorded and badly mixed—played from overhead speakers. Havers stepped forward with the ceremonial lanyards, each one attached to a faux-ivory badge embossed with the PanEuro crest. The effect was reminiscent of a Victorian Masonic ceremony dressed in airline drag.

She went down the line, pronouncing each name as though reading from a register of minor aristocracy.

"Marsh. Knight. Lang. Keyworth. Northcott."

Each woman stepped forward, accepted her badge with a bow of the head, and took her place back in line.

Afterwards, there was a staged "press moment," complete with a flashbulb camera effect and a man with a Polaroid pretending to be a reporter. They posed in front of a backdrop of a PanEuro A321LR with a laughably Photoshopped sunset and palm trees behind it.

When it was over, and the applause had died down, the graduates were finally allowed to step away from the stage and make their way to the adjacent reception lounge. A low-budget canapé selection waited—cheese straws, stuffed olives, and suspiciously glossy vol-au-vents, flanked by glasses of prosecco poured into vintage-style champagne saucers. There was music, too: a playlist of Sinatra, Ella Fitzgerald, and the occasional Andrews Sisters number piped through a tinny speaker system.

Hayley accepted a drink from Dimitri with a grateful nod. "Is this actually prosecco?"

"It's from a bottle," he replied. "It might even be Italian."

She laughed and took a sip, grateful for the chill. Nearby, Poppy was talking excitedly to one of the HR women, her nerves seemingly dissipated now that the ordeal was over. Tannie and Emma were at the snacks, arguing good-naturedly over which canapé would most likely give them food poisoning. Sarah, as ever, stood at the edge of the crowd, observing. Hayley joined her.

"Feels strange," she said.

"Which part?" Sarah asked. "The mock aircraft lounge? The fact that we just graduated from a vintage-themed hostage situation? Or the creeping sense that this is only the beginning of the madness?"

"All of the above."

They clinked glasses, and Hayley allowed herself the first real smile of the day.

"I've got my base assignment through," Sarah said after a moment.

Hayley raised an eyebrow. "Where to?"

"Manston, doing both short and long haul," Sarah said, sipping from her glass with the same casual neutrality she used when talking about engine failures or fuel misloads.

Hayley chuckled, as she had been assigned to Manston too, as it was her local PanEuro base.

The prosecco had warmed to a faint fizz in Hayley's glass, the effervescence fading with each passing minute. The surreal graduation ceremony was slowly giving way to quiet conversations and slightly less formal mingling. It was oddly calming to know the ordeal was behind them, even though, as Sarah had pointedly noted, the real madness likely lay ahead.

She looked around at the scene: Poppy was animatedly discussing uniform regulations with one of the HR representatives who appeared genuinely impressed by her grasp of the minute details of PanEuro's grooming standards. Tannie and Emma had moved from their canapé critique to covertly rating the looks of the pretend VIP passengers—clearly a coping mechanism after weeks of enforced decorum. Sarah still stood at Hayley's side, her posture finally easing into something resembling comfort.

Dimitri approached again, shaking his head theatrically, a mock tragic look on his face.

"Ladies, it has been an honour to shepherd you through this nostalgic nightmare," he said, handing them each a fresh glass. "I assume this calls for another round of suspiciously cheap fizz."

"You've read our minds," Sarah replied dryly, clinking glasses with Hayley.

"It's finally sinking in that it's over," Hayley said, sipping slowly. "No more inspections."

Dimitri chuckled softly. "Oh, my dears. Trust me, Rosemary's inspections are nothing compared to what you'll endure at 35,000 feet with a passenger who believes you're responsible for air traffic control delays, turbulence, and their existential dissatisfaction."

Hayley smirked, knowing Dimitri wasn't exaggerating by much.

Nearby, Rosemary Havers herself stood in the centre of the makeshift lounge, accepting effusive praise from one of PanEuro's more senior executives, a middle-aged man whose overly slicked-back hair seemed oddly matched to his dated tweed suit. Hayley watched Rosemary preen under the flattery, basking in the carefully cultivated illusion of timeless sophistication she had spent weeks trying to instil in her trainees.

"You think she'll miss torturing us?" Hayley asked quietly, nodding in Rosemary's direction.

"Miss it?" Sarah raised an eyebrow. "She's probably already plotting the next intake's psychological warfare."

Hayley smiled faintly, then glanced around the room again. She realised she felt strangely detached from the carefully choreographed reality PanEuro had constructed around them. After weeks of striving to become the perfect symbol of a bygone aviation era, it was hard to shake the sense of living inside someone else's nostalgic fantasy.

Her thoughts drifted to Agatha. Somewhere in Frankfurt, she was likely drilling checklists into her mind, immersed in aviation manuals, flight-planning software, and cockpit procedure. A pang of envy shot through Hayley, tempered immediately by a genuine sense of pride for her friend's achievement. Agatha had escaped this absurd pantomime for something truly real: a future in the flight deck.

Hayley's heart still longed fiercely for that herself, but she tried to hold it at bay—at least for tonight.

Emma suddenly approached, flinging an arm dramatically around Hayley's shoulders, the fizz evidently beginning to take effect.

"You know what this night needs?" Emma announced, slightly louder than necessary. "A proper bloody toast, ladies!"

Tannie, catching the vibe immediately, raised her glass with theatrical enthusiasm. "To Rosemary! For showing us precisely how not to inspire loyalty and affection!"

Giggles erupted, only slightly suppressed due to Rosemary's proximity. Poppy, still anxious about any transgression, widened her eyes comically and whispered, "Careful, she might hear!"

Dimitri, ever the mischief-maker, joined the huddle. "A toast, yes! To lipstick drills, mandatory smiles, and professional Stockholm syndrome!"

They clinked glasses, Hayley allowing herself to finally laugh freely. Sarah's normally composed demeanour cracked with amusement, and for a few glorious moments, the absurdity of it all bonded them in shared camaraderie.

As the group quietened again, Sarah leaned closer, voice low and serious.

"I don't know about you, but I'll be relieved to get out of this pantomime and onto an actual aircraft. Even if we're still serving drinks and demonstrating life jackets, at least it's real."

"I'm with you there," Hayley said firmly. "I'm not sure how many more pretend mink coats I can fold without snapping."

Sarah smirked, "Give it two weeks in economy class and you'll miss the mink coats."

Before Hayley could respond, Rosemary's voice cut through their quiet corner of relief, the piercing clarity of her elocution honed to a knife-edge.

"Ladies," she called, striding towards their group. "I believe congratulations are finally in order. Your performance today was...passable. And passable is, as you now know, the minimum PanEuro standard."

She stood rigidly in front of them, her scrutiny never entirely softened. Yet, in her own austere way, Rosemary seemed genuinely pleased.

"Tomorrow, you'll disperse to your respective bases. I trust you'll uphold the values I've endeavoured to instil. Remember, the vintage aesthetic is not mere nostalgia; it is our brand, our identity, and your new professional reality."

"Yes, Mrs Havers," they chorused obediently, more out of habit than genuine submission.

Rosemary gave a curt nod, adjusted her glasses slightly, and for one fleeting second, her gaze softened. "Good luck, ladies."

With that, she turned sharply and exited the makeshift lounge, heels clicking with precise finality. Once she had gone, Tannie exhaled dramatically, practically deflating into Emma.

"Well, that felt like being knighted by Margaret Thatcher," she groaned theatrically.

Emma grinned wickedly. "If Margaret Thatcher had a perm and an obsession with lipstick shades."

The group laughed again, louder this time, feeling finally free to indulge openly in their camaraderie.

Hayley's phone buzzed softly, and she glanced at the screen to see a message from Dani.

Dani Northcott: *Congrats, Hales! Now escape quickly before they start doing authenticity spot-checks!*

She smiled fondly. Her sister, flying transatlantic flights in her Virgin Atlantic uniform, was well-acquainted with corporate absurdity, albeit a more contemporary version.

Sarah nudged Hayley gently. "Your sister checking up on you?"

"Yeah," Hayley replied, pocketing her phone again. "She's reminding me not to let the PanEuro glamour go to my head."

"Oh, absolutely," Sarah deadpanned. "Wouldn't want you to develop Stockholm syndrome for vintage hats."

They lingered a little longer, slowly beginning to feel more like themselves again as the staged fantasy faded into the background. Eventually, Dimitri gently shepherded them towards the exit, visibly relieved himself that the charade was ending.

"Time to leave the stage, darlings," he announced with exaggerated gravitas. "The props are tired, the fizz is flat, and tomorrow you step into the slightly more tolerable madness of real airline life."

Outside, the evening air was cool and refreshingly ordinary. Hayley inhaled deeply, relieved by the absence of hairspray and faux nostalgia. Manston awaited her—a strange kind of homecoming, close enough to familiar comforts yet still entirely uncertain. She glanced at Sarah, knowing her friend felt something similar.

"Well," Sarah sighed, adjusting her hat one last time, "onto the next adventure."

"Yeah," Hayley echoed, eyes looking towards the horizon, "to the next adventure."

Together, they walked away from the academy, finally free from Rosemary's meticulous gaze, ready to embrace the unpredictable skies of their new PanEuro life.

****

CHAPTER 13 – Unexpected Guest
Wednesday 26th May 2021

It had been a week and half since Graduation from the PanEuro Stewardess Academy, and Hayley had to admit, the flights were getting busier by the day, each one becoming a little less surreal, and a little more routine. The initial flush of excitement at finally being airborne again was tempered now by aching feet, restless passengers, and the nagging feeling that she was somehow still adrift—so close to the cockpit yet stranded firmly in the galley.

This morning's early rotation to Prague had been uneventful, just another day spent pouring coffee and smiling politely at half-awake business travellers glued to their laptops.

Hayley had been assigned to the rear galley, to serve the 80 'classic class' customers that were on the Airbus A320neo that PanEuro operated on the Manston to Prague service, a predictable mixture of business passengers, a scattering of tourists eager to make the most of easing Covid restrictions, and a handful of aviation enthusiasts documenting their first flight in more than a year.

She leaned briefly against the galley wall, giving her tired feet a rest, and took a deep breath as she glanced down the cabin. Rows of weary travellers slumped into their seats, wrapped up in their own worlds. It wasn't exactly the glamorous life she'd envisioned, but at least it was flying. That thought alone kept her spirits buoyant—even during the most tedious of rotations.

Her quiet moment was abruptly shattered when the interphone chimed softly above her head. She picked it up immediately, assuming another routine request from the forward galley or perhaps a passenger issue.

"Rear galley, Hayley speaking," she answered professionally.

"It's Captain Kwiatkowski up on the flight deck," came the clipped, lightly accented voice through the interphone. "Hayley, any chance you could send the Purser up here please?"

Hayley's stomach gave a slight jolt of apprehension. It was unusual for the flight deck to request the Purser mid-flight, especially on such a routine rotation. But she quickly brushed aside her concern—aviation was filled with unexpected moments, and PanEuro's quirky internal procedures meant it could easily be something mundane. She smiled into the handset, forcing cheerfulness into her voice.

"Of course, Captain. I'll let Padraig know right away."

"Thanks, Hayley," Captain Kwiatkowski replied, his voice crisp but untroubled, reassuring her slightly. "Nothing urgent. Just a minor operational issue we'd like to discuss. No need to rush."

"Understood, Captain," Hayley replied professionally, returning the interphone to its cradle.

She peered forward through the narrow aisle towards the front galley, spotting Padraig Shaw, an Irishman who was formerly of Aer Arran and Stobart Air, the latter before the Connect Airways collapse the previous year.

Padraig, she noticed, was clearing trays with practiced ease, the Irishman in his three piece suit that male Stewards and Pursers at PanEuro were required to wear, managing somehow to look both dignified and approachable. She admired the deft manner in which he moved through the aisle, exchanging easy chatter with passengers as he balanced cups and trays without losing an ounce of his composure. Despite PanEuro's quirks, Padraig made it look effortless.

She quickly made her way down the narrow aisle towards the front of the cabin, offering polite smiles to passengers who barely registered her presence as they tapped away on their laptops or dozed, leaning awkwardly against window shades. When she finally reached Padraig, she placed a gentle hand on his shoulder, causing him to turn around with a questioning smile.

"Sorry, Padraig, Captain Kwiatkowski needs a word up front—said it's nothing urgent, just operational."

Padraig raised an eyebrow, curious but unperturbed. "Right you are, Hayley. Probably just a gate change at Prague. Can you hold the fort here?"

"No problem," Hayley replied, already mentally rearranging her duties. "I've got it covered."

Padraig handed her the half-filled tray, gave her a grateful nod, and moved swiftly towards the cockpit. Watching him go, Hayley felt a pang of envy. Any reason to visit the flight deck, even mundane operational discussions, felt like a tantalising glimpse of the world she was still fighting to rejoin.

She shook off the thought, refocused, and quickly continued clearing the remaining trays, making small talk where appropriate and projecting the careful, reassuring calm PanEuro demanded.

Ten minutes passed before Padraig returned, his face frowning. Hayley knew that look immediately—a blend of confusion and mild irritation that spoke louder than words ever could.

"What's up?" she asked quietly, moving aside to let him slip back into his workspace by the forward galley.

"Bit of an unusual request," Padraig said softly, his Irish accent lending even mundane statements a melodious charm. "We've got an extra passenger joining us in Prague for the return. A VIP."

Hayley's eyebrows shot up. "A VIP? Who? Since when do we pick up random VIPs out of Prague?"

Padraig smirked, glancing up and down the aisle to check they weren't overheard. "Some sort of last-minute arrangement. Apparently, he's being escorted to the aircraft straight from the ground, no need for security, but we've got to all be searched by the Bezpečnostní Informační Služba. All of the Executive class seats are to be blocked, and no Classic seats are to be filled by regular passengers"

Hayley blinked, processing the news. The Czech Security Information Service. She'd heard rumours, usually from

214

pilots over post-landing pints, of surprise VIPs whisked aboard last minute, but that was usually at Heathrow, Manston or Gatwick, not Prague—and never on a quiet Wednesday in May.

"All crew to be searched? In Prague?" she asked, her voice pitched low, more curious than anxious. "What, like a full security sweep?"

Padraig nodded, the lines at the corners of his eyes deepening. "Aye, so the Captain says. No details given, only that it's to be done on a remote stand."

Hayley exhaled, letting the implications settle in. A full sweep by Czech intelligence? For a single VIP? Her mind immediately conjured all sorts of scenarios—government minister, exiled oligarch, underworld figure being quietly moved under diplomatic cover. She almost laughed at herself for veering towards the melodramatic, but she knew enough about aviation to trust her instincts: if the security services were involved, it would not be for someone forgettable.

"Do we know who it is?" she asked, curious if it was a name anyone would recognise, or just another anonymous suit swept up in Eastern European politics.

"Something Babiš," Padraig said with a shrug. "Some political bigwig or businessman, is all they told the cockpit. And before you ask, no, I don't know why he can't just take a private jet. Must be something hush-hush." He smirked again, but the unease lingered in his eyes. "The manifest is just him, a dozen security agents and some staff, no other pax."

Hayley blinked, absorbing this. She tried to recall what she'd read about Czech politics—wasn't Babiš the controversial Prime Minister, always in and out of the headlines for some scandal or another? Or was it a relative, or a business partner? The Eastern European oligarch circuit was murky at the best of times, and the name alone conjured images of limousines, bodyguards with earpieces, and an air of constant tension.

"Guess it's our lucky day," she said lightly, tucking a stray wisp of hair behind her ear and scanning the forward rows of Classic Class, which were now, it seemed, about to become impromptu Executive. "Well, if he wants coffee, he'll have to make do with PanEuro's finest sachet, just like everyone else."

Padraig gave a tight smile, but his eyes were elsewhere, already running through the mental checklist of what this would mean for their duties. The galley, the passenger cabin, the service routine—they'd have to adjust on the fly. That was the thing about airline life: hours of tedium punctuated by sudden, inexplicable drama.

* - * - * - *

"...the temperature on the ground is expected to be a pleasant fourteen degrees, with scattered cloud and light winds out of the northwest," announced Captain Kwiatkowski as the A320 began its gentle descent towards Prague. The usual passenger rustle started—a slow, collective stirring as seatbacks clicked upright, laptops disappeared into bags, and overhead lockers snapped closed in anticipation of landing.

Hayley, who had spent the last half hour methodically preparing the galley and running her post-landing checks, found herself watching the other crew more closely than usual. There was a tangible tension to the atmosphere, a sense that this flight had just shifted from ordinary to the sort of situation that filled post-duty WhatsApp chats for weeks. Padraig had briefed the rest of the crew discreetly, outlining what little was known: a VIP boarding at Prague, Czech intelligence sweeping the plane, all standard procedures out the window for the return sector.

Looking on her phone, she noticed that there was a BBC headline about how Prime Minister Boris Johnson was, during the next few days, meeting with various EU leaders, as it was just under 5 months until COP26, the UN Climate Change Conference, and there were rumours that Czech Prime Minister Babiš himself would be flying to London for a behind-closed-doors summit. It was a strange, disorienting feeling to connect the dots: here she was, mere months out of a dead-end pandemic, poised to share a cabin with a figure who, for all intents and purposes, might be at the epicentre of half of Europe's backroom wheeling and dealing.

"You seen this?" Hayley asked Clara Osmond, a fellow Stewardess who she was working with, showing her the article on her phone. "Boris is meeting with several Euro politicians this weekend."

Clara glanced at the headline, then at Hayley, a flicker of incredulity in her eyes. "You think it's our Babiš? On this flight?" She lowered her voice, cautious even in the relative privacy of the galley.

Hayley shrugged, lowering the phone. "Stranger things have happened. And with all this extra security… it fits, doesn't it?"

Clara let out a low whistle, rolling her shoulders as she began folding away the last of the service items. "Suppose we'd best be on our best behaviour, then. Or as close as we can manage on two hours of sleep."

The rest of the descent passed in a kind of nervous silence, the normal routines now layered with a heightened sense of anticipation. Hayley found herself running through the sequence of post-landing checks twice, hands slightly trembling as she clipped the waste carts and locked the final cupboards. She caught Padraig's eye from the front galley, the Purser giving her a steady, reassuring nod.

She was grateful, in that moment, for his calm. If there was one lesson the skies had drilled into her, it was the value of a cool head in unexpected turbulence—on or off the flight deck.

The landing itself was uneventful; the A320 kissed the runway and slowed with that gentle deceleration that always seemed to signal a good day's work by the pilots. The engines whined down, and the familiar sequence began: seatbelt signs off, the thunk of doors arming, the symphony of passengers retrieving overhead bags.

But as the aircraft coasted towards its parking position, it was clear this was no ordinary arrival. They didn't taxi to the terminal, but instead swung onto a remote stand at the far edge of Václav Havel Airport, away from the usual bustle. Through the small window by the rear door,

Hayley could see a cluster of vehicles waiting—dark SUVs, a couple of white airport vans, and two police cars idling nearby. There were figures in suits, some with discreet earpieces, some with official-looking lanyards. One, with the unmistakable authority of a senior agent, paced beside the stairs, checking his watch.

Clara joined Hayley by the door, both watching as the jet bridge remained conspicuously absent. Instead, a set of steps was wheeled out, flanked by uniformed airport staff and what Hayley presumed were Czech intelligence officers.

"Well, that's our welcoming committee," Clara murmured, forcing a smile.

"Cheer up," Hayley replied quietly. "At least it breaks the monotony."

"Well, the last former Soviet state I was in where we had a VIP, the crew I was on got took into private rooms and got strip searched. So, let's just say I'm hoping for the less dramatic variety," Clara replied under her breath, though her nervous laugh didn't quite hide her unease.

It turned out, Hayley, realised as she walked out of a private room in Prague airport, that Clara's hope of a less dramatic search had not happened. Putting her bra back on, Hayley reflected wryly on the absurdity of it all. She'd just undergone the most thorough security check of her life, courtesy of the Czech Republic's BIS, and she hadn't even stepped off the aircraft in uniform before being escorted, individually, into a nondescript airport building for what the agents had termed a "routine VIP sweep."

Routine, her arse.

The windowless room had been sparse, clinical—just a coat hook, a folding chair, and two female agents who'd spoken little English but had gestured efficiently for her to remove her uniform in stages.

What was worse was that one of the agents even pressed their fingers in the most intimate areas of her body once Hayley had taken her underwear off, as if she was smuggling a microfilm or coded message taped somewhere obscene.

The fact she had unintentionally felt some pleasure while the intimate examination happened made her fume, and the urge to slap the BIS agent was one she had to resist.

"What the fuck are you doing," she growled as the Czech agent then gently adjusted her waistband again as if nothing had happened. But Hayley's glare could have cut glass.

"I'm a bloody stewardess," she hissed, more to herself than to the stony-faced woman opposite her. The agent merely nodded once, handed back her folded blouse with impassive precision, and stepped back towards the door.

It was over in less than ten minutes, though it felt far longer. As Hayley redressed, her face burned not just with indignation, but with an unfamiliar flicker of guilt. Why had that moment—the pressure, the clinical touch—provoked something that didn't feel entirely...

unwelcome? She slammed the thought back down where it came from and fastened her blouse with clipped, angry fingers.

"You know, I'm going to report this to the British Ambassador," Hayley snarled, her voice echoing slightly in the sterile, low-ceilinged, room. "He'll tell your President and Prime Minister-"

"We work for the BIS, and what the President or Prime Minister doesn't know cannot harm them," the Czech agent interrupted flatly, her accent cutting through the tension with dispassionate finality. "The Bezpečnostní Informační Služba does not care for your protests. And we would advise you not to tell the Prime Minister when he boards your plane, or there will be... consequences."

Hayley stared at the agent, her jaw tight, pulse hammering behind her temples. The sheer brazenness of it—the violation, the threat, the patronising way the woman spoke English like it was beneath her—left her momentarily frozen in place.

"What... what do you mean by consequences?" Hayley said, her voice firm but shaking ever so slightly, betraying the blend of fury and unease she was desperately trying to suppress.

The Czech agent didn't blink. "When your nations Prime Minister and Energy Minister both travel by commercial airliner, it becomes our job to ensure the plane is safe. If you create diplomatic complications, we will ensure you never enter the Czech Republic again, and that you will face you will face further consequences," the BIS agent concluded, her voice calm but edged with the kind of authority that didn't need to shout.

Hayley stared at her, breathing through her nose, knuckles white as she clutched her PanEuro blazer. She was no stranger to being talked down to—PanEuro's Stewardess Academy had trained her for that, if nothing else—but this felt different. Colder. More violating. More dangerous.

She bit her tongue and turned away to finish dressing, the air suddenly heavier than it had been a minute before.

She emerged into the corridor and was met by Clara, who looked just as rattled, though she gave a tight smile.

"Well, that was fun," Clara murmured, brushing a hand through her hair. "Feel like I've been through the bloody bootcamp at Sandhurst."

"Did they—?" Hayley began, but trailed off. She didn't need to finish. Clara's glance said enough.

"Bloody perverts made me take off everything, even my tights," Clara said under her breath, voice cracking ever so slightly with disbelief. "Then one of them... well, let's just say that my hus... boyfriend I mean... is the only one allowed to do what they did to me."

Hayley noticed the slip of the word husband, as, at PanEuro, being a cosplay of BOAC and Pan Am, banned its female Stewardesses from being married or even visibly partnered in public-facing roles, a draconian throwback that would have been laughable if it hadn't been enforced with actual penalties. Clara's correction said enough. It meant pretending, suppressing, conforming—for the sake of an aesthetic that suited an upper-management nostalgia trip. Now, layered on top of that, they'd been poked, prodded, and all but assaulted in the name of security.

"And then the bitch said that if I reported it to anyone, even the Ambassador or our own Captain, they'd blacklist me from Czech airspace," Clara finished, her voice a low tremble of fury. "What are we even doing here, Hayley? This isn't flying. It's theatre. It's a bloody costume drama with a side order of state intimidation."

Hayley could only nod. Her mind was still reeling from the encounter. Not just the violation, but the underlying current of control. As if their uniforms made them less human, more disposable. She knew, from stewardess school, from whispered stories over cheap bar wines in crew hotels, that flight attendants had long been seen as ornamental. But this was different. This was political. Weaponised femininity wrapped in a turquoise blazer.

A security agent down the corridor jerked his chin towards the exit. "Back to aircraft, please. Boarding soon."

The women shared a look—one that said more than words ever could—before falling in line with the other crew who were emerging from their respective rooms with similar dazed expressions. Padraig caught up with them near the hangar doors, and even he looked unusually rattled.

"They did the same to you?" Clara asked him quietly.

Padraig hesitated, then nodded, eyes dark. "And worse. One of their guys kept asking about my passport stamps.

Like being Irish and flying for a British airline somehow makes me suspicious. Tossers."

They crossed the tarmac under escort, the afternoon sun glinting coldly off the metal fuselage of their waiting A320neo. It looked surreal, bathed in light yet feeling like the stage for something clandestine. Hayley stared at it, unsure if she was walking back to work or into another layer of a story that had nothing to do with her.

"You know, I'm taking this up with the union," Kwiatkowski said with a frown. "Having some bloke go as far as they did, well, let's just say it crossed a line." His jaw was tight as he spoke to the crew just outside the aircraft door, arms crossed, still in his captain's epaulettes and hat. "The union will have everyone from BA to Wizz refusing to fly here if they get wind of this. You know Powers is a former shop steward at BA, right?"

Hayley knew that, as her dad, being a BA captain, knew Powers as the two were based at Heathrow on the senior captain roster, and that Powers was a tough man to intimidate. A former union firebrand in his time, Adrian Powers had been the bane of both Willie Walsh and Sean Doyle when he was still flying long-haul before being 'retired' sideways into PanEuro's bizarre retro-vanity project. If the Czech intelligence service thought they could intimidate British flight crews and get away with it, they clearly didn't know the names on the other end of the email chains that were about to erupt across Europe.

"BA would go on strike for any reason, to be fair," Hayley muttered, and she noticed that Kwiatkowski looked at her as if she had leaked something that only pilots knew.

"What? I spent some time in the flight deck at easyJet starting line training before the pandemic."

"Wait, you're A320 rated?" Kwiatkowski asked, his voice lowering with a trace of disbelief.

Hayley froze, just briefly, then gave a small, slightly embarrassed nod. "I was in the cadet programme with easyJet. Passed the sims, got the minimum hours to tick off the type rating but still needed the line training when the pandemic hit. Grounded. Then furloughed. Then made redundant. PanEuro was... something to do. A way to stay airborne." She paused. "Sort of."

Captain Kwiatkowski tilted his head slightly, regarding her with a more measured expression now. "Interesting," he said after a beat. "Padraig... Miss Northcott isn't staying in the galley for the flight. She's going to be in my flight deck in the jump seat. Simon?"

Hayley looked towards the First Officer, Simon Hobbs, who she knew was a former Air France A318 pilot and distinctly less chatty than most of the flight crew she'd worked with. Hobbs gave a noncommittal shrug, not quite a protest but not a warm endorsement either.

"It's your cockpit, Captain," he said simply.

"Good," Kwiatkowski replied, then looked back at Hayley. "We're not wheels-up for another half hour while they finish their dog-and-pony show. Get a bottle of water and meet me at the door. You'll ride jump seat. I want a third set of eyes, and as you've got rating... I presume you've got your meds and licence with you, right?"

Hayley nodded, as in her suitcase, which was on board the A320neo, was her flight bag. She always carried them, even though PanEuro's stewardess contract officially forbade any mention of her flight credentials. It was another relic of the airline's commitment to "heritage aesthetic": women in lipstick and heels were to be seen, not heard—not rated. Not capable. Not pilots. At least not while working the cabin.

"Yes, Captain," she said clearly, the words tasting more like affirmation than reply.

"Then let's go," he said, already turning back toward the airstairs. The Czech agents were still loitering on the tarmac, their dark suits and cold stares lingering like a bruise. Hayley followed Kwiatkowski without hesitation, each step feeling heavier and more deliberate, as though this short walk might finally drag her back towards the flight deck for good.

*_*_*_*

The cockpit door clicked shut behind her, that heavy, sealed sound she had missed more than anything in the past year. That little noise meant safety, solitude, purpose. Hayley stood just inside the threshold for a moment, letting the scent and hum of the flight deck settle over her like a balm. A subtle aroma of worn leather, avionics heat, and the faint tang of jet fuel clung to everything. She barely realised she was holding her breath.

Captain Kwiatkowski slid into the left-hand seat and began adjusting his headset, motioning towards the jump seat behind him with a nod. Hayley folded it down and took her place, strapping herself in quickly, hands steady despite her racing pulse. This was it. Not a simulator, not a dream, not some hollow pep talk in a crew room.

"You remember the basics?" Kwiatkowski asked, his eyes scanning the centre console.

"Yes, Captain," Hayley replied, her voice even, her RAF-style diction slipping into place almost unconsciously. "Checklists, flows, comms—I've kept current."

Simon Hobbs raised an eyebrow slightly but said nothing, his fingers dancing silently over the FMS as he cross-checked the new flight plan. The VIP's boarding was still underway below, their identities cloaked in layers of acronymed authority. Hayley glanced out of the windscreen to see several figures ascending the airstairs, surrounded by men in ill-fitting suits and mirrored sunglasses.

"Bloody circus," Hobbs muttered. "You'd think he was royalty."

"In this part of the world, he may as well be," Kwiatkowski replied drily. "ATC's been told to treat us as military-grade priority."

Hayley kept her reactions neutral, but her mind was racing. She knew what that meant—dedicated air corridors, no slot delays, even potential fighter escort if something went wrong. It wasn't common for European leaders to travel on commercial aircraft, and it was even less common for them to do so while pretending it wasn't a security issue.

She looked over the overhead panel, comforted by the rows of familiar switches and guarded buttons. The Airbus was like an old friend in a new suit. Her fingers twitched instinctively, mentally running through flows and scanning patterns.

"You're clear to monitor radio," Kwiatkowski said, flipping a switch to give her headset audio feed. "Don't touch anything, obviously. But if I ask you to confirm something, I want a straight answer. That clear?"

"Crystal, sir."

The boarding was completed in eerie silence. There were no announcements, no clatter of bags into overhead lockers, no chorus of rolling cases down the aisle. The security detail seated themselves in the forward cabin, flanking a man with silver hair and a stiff posture who Hayley recognised instantly from the news—Andrej Babiš himself.

He didn't look her way as he passed. His eyes were fixed on something distant, and his face wore the smooth non-expression of someone who had long since mastered the art of neutral politics. Still, seeing him there, breathing the same stale recirc air, drove home just how far this flight had diverged from routine.

"Cabin secure," Padraig's voice announced from the interphone. "All agents seated. Doors armed."

"Very well," Kwiatkowski responded. "Northcott, check our flight deck door is sealed and locked."

Hayley rose, checked the mechanism, and nodded. "Locked and sealed."

The captain adjusted his thrust levers gently and signalled for pushback. The aircraft shuddered as the tug latched on.

"Here we go then," Hobbs murmured. "Let's try not to start a war."

****

CHAPTER 14 – The Day After the Day Before
Thursday 27th May 2021

It had been 24 hours since the Prague incident and Hayley knew two things were wrong. One was that it was the start of her usual time of the period—her body reminding her with a dull ache and a heavier-than-usual exhaustion that seemed to pool behind her eyes, her skin prickling with irritability and fatigue she could not quite shake. The other was less physical but more insistent: the sensation of something wrong and unresolved, a residue of anger and humiliation that stuck to her like stale cabin air. Sleep had been little more than a sequence of fretful dozes, each one dissolving into dreams where BIS agents in ill-fitting suits asked her for her passport and a smile. She'd woken at half three, sweat-soaked and clammy in Theo's arms, the two in his Birmingham home, having caught a Manston to Birmingham shuttle that was in the late evening when she had finished, as he had been on a Doha return that day.

It was ironic, Hayley knew, that despite the coronavirus restrictions being in the final stages of ending, that the Prime Minister, Boris Johnson, had just been on the news the night before, smiling in a mask, shaking hands with the German Chancellor and making breezy promises about travel corridors and "Global Britain." Yet here she was, one day out from having her own corridor—a narrow, sterile hallway in the depths of Václav Havel Airport, complete with a state-sponsored strip search and the kind of cold, administrative violence that never made it onto the Six O'clock News.

She hadn't told Theo the details. Not the intimate ones, anyway. She'd simply muttered, "Security in Prague was out of order. I'll be writing it up," and left it at that, her voice brittle enough that even Theo—usually quick to tease her about bringing work drama home—had just squeezed her shoulder and let her be. He'd run her a bath, poured her a glass of cheap red wine, and then retreated to his own side of the bed, scrolling quietly through flight deck memes until she'd slipped, finally, into some kind of uneasy half-sleep.

Now it was morning, and she was awake before him, lying on her side and watching the watery grey light creep across the ceiling, the dull ache in her lower back reminding her of everything: of the cabin, the corridor, the chill of clinical hands on her skin. She resisted the urge to check her phone—there would be emails from the union, she was certain, and probably something vague and threatening from PanEuro's HR. Instead, she closed her eyes and counted backwards from fifty, letting the numbers anchor her to the present.

And then the cramps decided that they were going to start.

Yes, she knew the irony, that she had even been fingered by the BIS agent and sexually stimulated, the day before her cycle started, and that she had, even though it was, in her mind, was disgusting, and that, yes, she knew that she hadn't asked for any of it, nor had she been able to stop it, nor did she owe herself shame. And yet, shame had crept in anyway, crawling under her skin in the small hours, refusing to be shrugged off. Hayley curled in on herself, one hand pressed against her stomach, feeling both the unremarkable, biological pain of her period and the more complicated, inarticulate burn of violation.

She stared up at the ceiling of Theo's flat when her WhatsApp decided to ping, the screen lighting up in a quiet corner of the room. She rolled onto her back and glanced over at the phone on the nightstand. Even before she checked, she could guess: crew chat, maybe the union, maybe her mum—though, God forbid, she'd confide in Karen about this. The last thing she needed was her mother's acid commentary on the indignities of modern flying, delivered at full volume from a kitchen strewn with unwashed coffee mugs and old Flight International magazines.

Hayley thumbed the phone open, careful not to disturb Theo, who was still sleeping deeply, face half-buried in the pillow, his hair sticking up at odd angles like a cartoon boy. He looked almost peaceful in sleep, which only sharpened the ache she felt inside—wishing, for a moment, that she could step out of her own mind and join him there, just for a bit.

Dave Parsons (Unite the Union): *Morning, all. Those on the PRG rotation yesterday, we've had some updates. Seems that BIS were acting alone, not with the President's knowledge—though of course management are claiming 'full compliance' with local regulations. If anyone needs to make a statement, please contact me directly. We're pushing for a formal apology and a full review, however, we're going to be honest, there is political pressure, and we don't expect much more than the usual vague 'lessons will be learned' line. Your safety and dignity are our priority—please look after yourselves and each other. If*

Hayley read Dave's message three times over, letting the union man's blunt, northern courtesy wash over her like a blanket. She could hear his voice in her head—the low, well-meaning rumble she'd learned to trust after years in and out of crew rooms, a comforting fixture even in chaos. Dave always ended his bulletins with look after yourselves and each other, as if solidarity could be conjured by repetition alone. Sometimes, she almost believed it.

She knew that her dad, Alan, as a BA Captain who was one of their workplace BALPA reps, would be itching to get his hands on the details. She could almost picture the conversation already—Alan standing in the cramped galley of some long-haul 777 to Miami, squinting at his phone and muttering, "Absolute bloody disgrace, that. You write it up, Hales. Don't let the bastards off the hook." He would, she knew, want her to be angry, not ashamed. That didn't make it easier.

She put the phone down, and turned over, the cramps still gnawing at her from the inside, radiating outwards in heavy, sullen waves, only to tall onto Theo's morning wood. That was, Hayley had to chuckle, ironic, as she was a 'no go' zone while she was on her period, and Theo— bless him—was horny.

Not just horny, but persistent, Hayley thought with a faint, private smile. That, at least, was a comfort: the sheer normality of it, the awkward, adolescent hilarity of two pilots trying to sync their bodily clocks, libido, and moods to a 24-hour cycle ruled by airport curfews, minimum rest, and now, evidently, the whims of foreign security services. It felt almost retro in its own way—a reminder that underneath the uniform, the airline, the news cycle, she was still allowed to be a living, breathing, desiring human.

"Cabin crew, prepare for landing," he muttered, and then Hayley felt him reach out as if he were going for an Airbus side stick, instead grasping her breast, and start caressing it. However, as she knew that they would be sore over the next few days, she gently guided his hands onto his erection, a grin on her face as she knew he'd find it funny.

She swung her legs out of bed, careful not to disturb Theo, and padded to the bathroom. The light was harsh, too white, but she avoided looking at herself in the mirror. Instead, she rummaged through the toiletries, found some paracetamol, and swallowed two with a quick gulp of water. She sat for a moment on the closed lid of the loo, breathing through the pain, reminding herself that she was safe, now, at least. Just a flat in Birmingham, in a quiet cul-de-sac, a world away from airport corridors and stern-faced agents.

Hayley lingered in the bathroom longer than necessary, the chemical taste of paracetamol still on her tongue. She listened to the muffled drone of the city waking outside—the distant clatter of a bin lorry, the whine of a bus changing gear somewhere along the Stratford Road, and the thin, metallic squawk of a wood pigeon on the windowsill. It was the kind of ordinary morning noise that, after a spell of airport hotels and endless rotation, still felt faintly miraculous. No 4am wake-up call, no industrial-strength air conditioning, no distant jet roar thrumming through the walls. For a moment, she let herself just listen, eyes closed, hands pressed flat against the cool, chipped surface of the sink.

After a few moments of stillness, Hayley ran the tap and let the water run cold before splashing her face, the shock a welcome jolt to her foggy senses. Her phone vibrated again on the edge of the sink—once, then again, the distinctive double-buzz that signalled a new message from the PanEuro crew app. She ignored it, at least for the moment, determined not to let the day be hijacked by corporate platitudes or the perfumed poison of HR's "checking in" emails. Today, she decided, could wait.

She lingered in the bathroom until the edges of the mirror had begun to mist, then finally forced herself to look up. Her face was pale, puffy at the cheeks, the greyish cast that came with a run of poor sleep and stress. She bared her teeth experimentally, then rolled her eyes at her own reflection. Get a grip, Northcott, she thought, channelling the inner voice that sounded suspiciously like Sarah Marsh back in training: "It's not the end of the bloody world. You're just tired and pissed off."

She ran her hands through her tangled hair, gathered it up into a messy ponytail, and padded back into the bedroom. Theo had rolled onto his back and was snoring lightly, mouth open, one hand flung across his bare chest. For a moment, Hayley was struck by the sheer normality—the morning laziness, the mild embarrassment of having a partner who snored, the sunlight puddling on the rumpled duvet. She pulled the duvet up around his shoulders, a fond smile curling her lips, then headed for the kitchen.

There was precious little in the fridge—an unopened bottle of orange juice, a block of cheddar, and the remains of a supermarket lasagne. She made a mental note to grab groceries later, then settled for a mug of instant coffee and two slices of toast, which she ate standing by the sink, gazing out over the backs of terraced houses and the shimmering roofs of parked cars. The city was still coming alive, a few early dog-walkers trundling past, a cyclist weaving through puddles left by last night's drizzle.

Walking back in, she noticed that Theo was masturbating, and that he was randomly calling out calls, as if he was the pilot flying and not the pilot monitoring. Hayley had to suppress a laugh—there was something surreal, almost comforting, about the way aviation bled into every aspect of their lives, even the intimate and absurd. Theo's eyes were still closed, but his hand was moving with distracted enthusiasm, and the words that tumbled from his lips were a dreamy mixture of cockpit callouts and half-formed nonsense.

"V1... rotate... positive rate... gear up..." he muttered, and Hayley had to chuckle, as, today, they would both be on a series of Belfast to Birmingham and Belfast to Manston shuttles, as, in the past week, PanEuro had decided to revise its interworking of flights, so instead of planes doing Manston to Berlin to Birmingham, then a ferry flight to Manston all in a day, now they'd split the rotations in strange, circuitous loops that seemed designed purely to keep crew rostering software from ever learning a routine. It meant that tonight, both she and Theo would end up together in Hayley's family home at Broadstairs, where Dani, who was on a JFK overnight, would be absent.

Hayley let him get on with his sleep-wank. She wasn't about to risk blood on the sheets and besides, her libido was somewhere between "go away" and "if you so much as look at me wrong, I'll ground you for a week." She padded back to the living room, phone in one hand, toast in the other, and sat cross-legged on the carpet by the window where a little square of sun had crept in and was slowly warming the threadbare rug. This, she thought, was as close to mindfulness as she was likely to get this week.

Her phone buzzed again—this time the group chat: 'PanEuro Gals 🍷 ✈'. She braced herself for the day's onslaught.

Poppy Knight: *Please tell me someone else has seen the email from Havers about skirt length and 'galley posture'? Is it 1963 again or did I time travel?*

Emma Lang: *Skirt length? As long as I get Charlie on my JFK from Doncaster tonight, I'll be happy. Y'know he's got a big cock?*

Hayley groaned at the message from the former Bee Manic presenter, who was known to, during her time at the Manchester radio station, have slept with anything with a pulse, male or female, and at least three that could only be described as "uncertain." Emma's running tally of conquests had been the unofficial background noise of

PanEuro training, a mix of horror, awe, and morbid fascination for the rest of the cohort. It was, Hayley reflected, a distinctly modern way of coping with the antique nonsense that was PanEuro's aesthetic.

She started to type a reply, then thought better of it, knowing that sarcasm could easily spiral out of control before she'd finished her coffee.

Tannie Keyworth: *Can someone please explain how I'm supposed to "stand poised" in the rear galley when the only thing to lean on is a boiling water urn and half a trolley of shortbread biscuits? Havers would have us all balancing books on our heads like debutantes.*

Tannie's message had barely landed when Sarah Marsh finally chimed in.

Sarah Marsh: *Pretty sure Havers wants us all to morph into Stepford Stewardesses. Next week it'll be eyelash inspections and mandatory girdles.*

That got a few laughing emojis, and Hayley cracked a faint grin. She could see it vividly—Sarah standing stock still at the front of a mock 737, arms crossed and glowering while Havers paced the aisle with a clipboard, inspecting people's calves.

Hayley Northcott: *Still waiting for her to enforce "lipstick at 36,000ft" as a safety requirement.*

Emma Lang: 😊 *Hayley don't give her ideas.*

Hayley let her thumb hover over the keyboard, feeling the odd comfort of the chat bubbling in her palm. There was something about the collective gallows humour that made the worst parts of the job—strip searches, endless galley drills, the chronic ache in her knees—just about bearable. She glanced at the clock. Still an hour before she and Theo needed to leave for the first hop up to Belfast.

A message popped up from Agatha Dean, who'd recently started her Lufthansa conversion course in Frankfurt, via a DM, and Hayley sighed as she read it.

Agatha Dean: Hey, Hales, how's things at PE?

Hayley paused, thumb resting on the screen, thinking how to answer Agatha honestly without descending into a torrent of bitterness or, worse, melodrama. The urge to type out a graphic, line-by-line account of the Prague indignity was strong. But something held her back—a sense that putting it in writing, even in a supposedly private DM, would only make it feel more real, more permanent. Besides, Agatha was out of the PanEuro madness now, living in the reassuringly ordered world of Lufthansa, with its tectonic efficiency, clear manuals, and HR departments that, at the very least, paid lip service to crew welfare.

Hayley Northcott: *Honestly, mate? It's… eventful. PE keeps finding new ways to remind me this isn't flying, it's survival with lipstick. The crew are still keeping me sane. (Just about.) How's life with the Germans? Are their security searches less… intimate?* 😂

Agatha replied almost instantly, the typing dots bouncing.

Agatha Dean: *Honestly, you'd love it. Even the worst day here is like a spa compared to PE. We get actual food,* *you can wear trousers if you want (!!!), and nobody cares if your hair is in a bun or a ponytail. No one's tried to grope me at security, unless you count a very enthusiastic Golden Retriever. Heard a PanEuro flight had the Czech PM on yesterday. You on that rotation? The gossip here is that you guys got 'special' treatment. Hope you're ok. Let me know if you want to talk—don't bottle it up. x*

Hayley's chest tightened as she read Agatha's message, the flood of half-suppressed memory mingling with the dull ache in her abdomen. She stared at her phone, thumb hovering, and for a moment, she wondered whether to say it—really say it. That yes, she'd been there, that yes, she'd been strip-searched by the Czech intelligence services, that yes, it had left her feeling both violated and furious, that the anger seemed to come in sudden, unpredictable squalls. But the moment passed. She'd talk, she decided, but not now. Not through a phone screen. Maybe in person, over a pint, on a day when her period and the world weren't quite so heavy.

She typed instead.

Hayley Northcott: *Thanks, Aggs. Yeah, that was our rotation. Long day, bit intense, but survived it. Will take you up on that beer—could use one! Glad Lufthansa is treating you well. x*

She pressed send, took a steadying breath, and forced herself to focus on the day ahead. She was due on a Belfast to Birmingham, then a quick hop to Manston. Theo would take a later Birmingham–Belfast leg and join her on the Manston rotation home, assuming the ever-fickle PanEuro rostering gods didn't throw another last-minute swap her way. The thought of seeing her parents' house—Broadstairs, Kent, always smelling faintly of sea salt and roast coffee—was a small comfort. Home, she thought, wasn't always peaceful, but at least it was known.

She put her phone away, finished her lukewarm coffee, and padded back to the bedroom. Theo was awake now, his boxer shorts, or lack thereof, as he had discarded them mid-wank, lying halfway down the bed. He gave her a sheepish, lopsided grin, blinking blearily at the daylight leaking through the blinds. For a moment, Hayley simply stood in the doorway, arms folded, and gave him the sort of look that said: don't even start.

He held up a hand in mock-surrender. "Sorry, Captain Northcott. Uncommanded thrust event." His voice was thick with sleep, but his eyes were bright, mischievous. She snorted—she couldn't help herself.

"Be careful, or I'll report you to Engineering," she said, dropping her phone on the bed and sitting beside him, the mattress dipping beneath her weight.

Theo stretched, grimacing as he did, and shifted up onto his elbows. "You alright, Hales?" There was something serious in his tone now—a softness that cut through the early morning banter.

She didn't answer straight away. Instead, she stared at her bare knees, pale in the soft light. Finally, she shrugged. "Yeah. Just tired. Period's started, which is why, for the next few days, my body is no entry, flyboy."

Theo offered her a commiserating little grimace, the sort that only people who live with pilots—or are pilots themselves—seem to perfect. He rubbed her knee gently, his hand warm, a grounding weight.

"Want a cup of tea?" he asked, voice low. "I'll do the tea. You did the night-waking and the tossing and turning."

Hayley shook her head but smiled anyway. "You're a good man, Theo Sullivan. Go on, then. Strong. Builder's. Two sugars. I'm not above bribery today."

He saluted, a clumsy, theatrical gesture, and rolled off the bed, padding—naked, careless, the way only a man at home and loved can be—into the kitchen. Hayley watched the play of muscle across his back, the tattoo of a tiny Airbus on his hip, and allowed herself, just for a moment, the small comfort of familiarity.

Her own body felt like alien territory today—cramping, heavy, her skin too tight, everything faintly raw. She pulled her knees up to her chest and hugged them, staring at the swirl of duvet and the tangle of their discarded uniforms—her scarf askew, Theo's white pilot shirt half-off a hanger, black shoes abandoned at the door. The detritus of two lives lived in endless rotation. There was a poetry in it, she thought. Or maybe just a mess.

The kettle clicked on in the kitchen; Theo hummed tunelessly, a half-remembered melody, probably something from the radio the day before. Hayley closed her eyes and let the ordinary noises settle around her, the domestic soundtrack of a life lived around the margins of flight. Bin lorry. Kettle. The gentle burble of Theo's voice as he muttered something about the tea bags. The squeak of the cutlery drawer.

It struck her, not for the first time, that aviation had become less a job than a lens through which she saw the world: every small act a checklist, every emotion a CRM scenario, every minor inconvenience a line item on some invisible safety card. There were worse ways to survive, she thought. At least it gave you something to hold onto, when the world tilted.

Theo returned with a steaming mug, set it down on the bedside table, and perched beside her. He looked her over, gentle, assessing. "You don't have to talk about it, you know," he said softly. "Whatever it was in Prague."

Hayley's lips twitched in something like gratitude. She met his eyes—blue, earnest, forever two parts boy to one part grown man. She let out a breath. "Yeah. I know. Not yet."

He nodded, not pressing, just being present. "Alright. We'll get through the day. Then you can go full Northcott on them if you want."

She smiled properly this time, feeling something unfurl in her chest. "Full Northcott is reserved for the truly deserving."

He reached out and tucked a stray strand of hair behind her ear, a feather-light touch. "Save it for Havers, then. Or whoever wrote that crew bulletin about 'galley posture.'"

They both laughed—a low, exhausted, conspiratorial sound.

Hayley sipped her tea, wincing at the first, too-hot mouthful, but grateful for its grounding heat. The world felt just a little less hostile, the day a little less long.

* _ * _ * _ *

Their morning together was spent in the usual haze of pre-roster logistics: uniforms checked for errant lipstick stains, shoes buffed in the hallway, lanyards untangled, flight bags zipped and re-zipped as they hunted for missing epaulettes or a spare packet of paracetamol. It was a rhythm, if not a ritual—punctuated by the occasional snarky aside or the resigned mutter of "bloody PanEuro."

In the cab to the airport, Hayley stared out at Birmingham's streets as they woke: corner shops opening up, delivery vans nosing through puddles, an old man in a flat cap shuffling his dog across a zebra crossing. She found her gaze caught on the passing glimpses of ordinary life—families loading school bags, workmen in hi-vis huddled by a steaming tea urn. It always surprised her, the strange dislocation of crew life: how you could spend so much time away from home that even a suburban morning felt exotic.

Theo squeezed her hand in the backseat, his thumb tracing the back of her knuckles. "You want me to handle check-in with the dispatcher?" he offered. "You look knackered, Hales. You could do with five minutes and a doughnut before you go through security."

Hayley shook her head, managing a smile. "No, I'll do it. Although, to be fair, I'd call fatigue, but the morons in charge don't recognise female issues as being a protected characteristic, so I'd just end up on the "fit to fly" list anyway."

Theo gave her a knowing grin—half empathy, half that uniquely aviation breed of gallows humour. He squeezed her hand one more time before letting go, both of them slipping back into their public selves as the cab rolled under the airport canopy.

Inside Birmingham Airport, the air was thick with the mingled scents of industrial-strength disinfectant and burnt filter coffee. Social distancing stickers were beginning to peel at the edges, and the plexiglass screens at check-in were smeared with fingerprints. The terminal was busier than Hayley had expected for a Thursday; half-term was looming, and families in matching tracksuits were already squabbling in line for the Jet2 check-in.

She kept her head down, mindful of the PanEuro insignia glinting on her scarf—a lightning rod for every passenger who wanted to moan about mask mandates, cancelled flights, or the price of a meal deal. She joined the crew queue, nodded to the bored-looking woman behind the desk, and tapped her ID on the counter with the air of someone who'd done this a thousand times before.

The dispatcher, a new lad with a nervous stammer, barely glanced at her before printing the flight plan. "You're off to Belfast first, right?"

"That's right," Hayley replied, mustering as much warmth as she could. "Then Manston."

He fumbled with her paperwork. "Watch out for the crosswinds. They've been a bit lively on approach this morning."

She thanked him and moved on, resisting the urge to correct his pronunciation of "Manston." She was already feeling the slow, coiling fatigue that marked the first day of her period, the ache in her back pulsing in time with her footsteps.

At security, she hesitated, stomach tightening as she remembered the Prague corridor, the click of latex gloves, the deliberate, humiliating pause before the search began. She shook her head, forced herself to keep breathing, and stepped through the archway, arms raised. The Birmingham staff were, as always, cheerfully indifferent, more interested in scanning for stray bottles of water than the psychic detritus of international indignities.

Theo caught up with her in the airside Costa, balancing two coffees and a pair of paninis. "Pre-flight briefing, First Officer?" he teased, sliding into the seat beside her.

Hayley took the coffee, grateful for the distraction, and glanced over the flight plan. The Manston run was simple enough—an hour in the air, thirty minutes on the ground, back again. Cabin full of business types and a handful of families. The Belfast sector would be the same—a carousel of faces, all of them wanting something, all of them believing that their journey mattered most.

Theo tapped the paper. "We'll have a strong tailwind on the return. Could shave ten minutes off, if ATC don't hold us over the Wash."

She nodded, letting the details wash over her, finding comfort in the routine. In aviation, it was always the small things that anchored you: a good briefing, a joke in the galley, the way a familiar aircraft felt beneath your hands.

****

CHAPTER 15 – A Near Miss
Sunday 6th June 2021

PanEuro Flight 154 Manston to Moscow was going well, so far, Hayley knew, as, although she was technically the stewardess for the flight in the Executive Cabin of the Airbus A321LR that was operating this service, it was Captain Adrian Powers who was on the flight deck, the Chief Captain for PanEuro presiding over the flight, with First Officer Oliver O'Day as the co-pilot. Unofficially, that meant that Hayley was sitting in the right hand seat, and Oliver was spending the flight relaxing in the Executive cabin, as it was empty due to last-minute cancellations from a Russian diplomatic delegation.

As soon as she had boarded the flight following the pre-flight briefing, Powers had told her that she was to report to the flight deck, and that if the purser, Lauren Andrews, gave her grief, she was to redirect the grief back to him.

"Tell her to fetch me a coffee if she has a problem," he'd muttered with a grin, half-shielded by the brim of his cap.

So, Hayley had done as she was told. She'd tucked her crisp hat into the overhead locker at the front of the aircraft, rolled her sleeves once just to give herself some breathing room, and stepped through the reinforced door onto the flight deck, greeted by the scent of strong coffee, cockpit heat, and that odd, electric thrum that always emanated from a live aircraft.

Adrian Powers was already in the left-hand seat, running through a set of checklists for cruise while speaking in clipped, precise phrases. The man, although technically a desk jockey as he was the Chief Pilot and Head of Flying, meaning that when Operations needed crews for a flight, the would fear speaking to him as he was a pilots pilot, a former British Airline Pilots' Association shop steward, and would make sure that if a pilot needed their legal rest, needed to self-report any medical issue, or simply refused to operate outside legal hours, that they would be protected. He was known throughout PanEuro as someone who brooked no nonsense, especially from management, even if, ironically, he now was management.

Even if it was mainly doing a desk job for all but a few selected flights. And today, this Manston–Moscow sector was one of them.

Hayley slid into the right-hand seat, familiar now with the layout of the Airbus, but still buzzed with a flicker of nerves every time she stepped into the cockpit proper. Powers gave her a quick glance and a wry smile.

"Right," he said, stabbing a thumb towards the pedestal. "You're on radios. ATC's Russian today, so that should be fun. Let's see if you can decode vodka-speak."

She smirked. "Iain had me do this sector last week, so I'm familiar with the Moscow Centre dialect," Hayley replied, sliding the headset on. "Mind if I depart on 10, or shall I do runway 28?"

Hayley knew that, even though departing on Runway 10 had become her favourite out of Manston, as it was the runway which was eastbound departure, westbound arrival, over the village of Manston and the town of

Ramsgate, flying an Airbus A321LR, the longer range variant with wing mods and extra fuel tanks, would require the full runway, and a tighter gain of height compared to the departure of runway 28, which was westbound departure, eastbound arrival, over the Birchington, Herne Bay and Whitstable coasts.

Hayley's remark had been part-joke, part-test, and Captain Adrian Powers knew it. He glanced over with a smirk tugging at the corner of his mouth.

"Nice try," he replied. "Runway 28 it is. Full length, flex take-off. Nice right hander as we climb to FL340. We'll be up before we cross the Estuary. Keep the power smooth—those tanks make her a bit tail heavy on rotation."

Hayley nodded, reaching for the Flight Management Guidance System interface and double-checking the flight plan as it scrolled across the primary display. "Copy that. Wind was five knots cross from the north-northeast earlier. Still holding?"

Powers gave her a nod, tapping the METAR printout wedged into his knee board. "Marginal drift, nothing to correct for too heavily. You'll feel it as a tickle in the sidestick. She's loaded light for once—only seventy-two pax down back, nothing in Executive. Fuelled for contingency plus alternate into Helsinki, St Petersburg or Khrabrovo Kaliningrad, the latter if the worst comes to the worst."

Hayley knew that Khrabrovo Airport, in the Kaliningrad Oblast of the Russian Federation, was not one of the more frequented alternatives for diversions, but it was a backup. It sat perched on the edge of the country, flanked by Poland to the west and Lithuania to the north, offering little in the way of luxuries but a reliable stop if the need ever arose. She had flown over the region before, and despite its strategic importance, it always felt slightly eerie—an isolated point on a map, far from any major urban centre.

As Powers continued running through his checks, Hayley reviewed the fuel and weight calculations again. Everything was in order—nothing out of the ordinary. This should be a routine flight, but something about it still felt oddly charged. There was a distinct, electric hum in the air, something Hayley could never quite shake when operating with minimal passenger loads. With so few people on board, the aircraft felt more like a machine than a carrier of people, and the absence of noise—the hum of passengers, their voices, their movements—seemed to accentuate the machine's presence. It always felt like a blank canvas for the potential of something going wrong. A phantom fear, really, but one Hayley couldn't help acknowledging.

"Ready to roll when you are, Captain," she said, tapping the comms button as she keyed in the departure codes.

"Manston Control, this is PanEuro Flight one-five-four, requesting taxi to runway 28 for departure," Hayley heard Powers say over the radio, his voice calm and authoritative, a stark contrast to the anticipatory energy building in Hayley's chest. The monotony of the radio check, the usual shuffle of sounds from ATC, soothed her nerves. Powers' steady professionalism had always been a grounding influence, and she admired his no-nonsense approach to flying.

"PanEuro Flight 154, Manston Control, taxi to runway 28, cleared for take-off," came the response. A pause, then, "Good luck."

The aircraft, a sleek and slightly intimidating Airbus A321LR, began its slow crawl towards the runway. Hayley adjusted the thrust levers, making small but deliberate adjustments as they moved down the taxiway. It was moments like these, the quiet hum of the engines, the steadying roll of the aircraft beneath her feet, which made her feel most alive—completely in control yet at the mercy of physics and metal. It was a delicate balance that made the job so thrilling.

"You seem quiet, Northcott," Powers observed, breaking the silence that had settled over them. His voice was casual but laced with the keen observation of someone who had spent decades in the cockpit. "Something on your mind?"

Hayley shrugged, though she wasn't sure why she felt a sudden bout of uncertainty. "Nothing, just… I've been thinking a lot about the flight ahead. It's odd flying with such a light load, no VIPs or diplomats this time. Makes it feel different somehow."

Powers chuckled softly, a sound that was both reassuring and infectious. "Ah, I know what you mean. Too quiet, huh? Don't worry, you'll get used to it. More time for us to chat, eh?"

The banter was easy, and soon enough, they reached the runway threshold. Powers adjusted the seatbelts, ensuring everything was in place for their departure. With a final check of the instruments, he pushed the throttles forward, and the powerful engines of the A321 roared to life. The aircraft surged forward with the familiar pull of acceleration, the ground beneath them a blur as they moved down the runway.

"Power's yours, Northcott," Powers instructed, and Hayley's fingers danced over the controls, her eyes flicking between the instruments and the runway ahead.

The aircraft lifted off smoothly, the nose rising sharply into the air as the wings sliced through the cool morning sky. Hayley's heartbeat matched the rhythm of the aircraft's climb, the sheer force of it exhilarating. The whine of the engines seemed to fade as they reached altitude, the cockpit suddenly quieter than it had been on the ground.

"Positive climb, 300 feet," Powers called, making sure the climb rate was holding steady.

"Altitude set to FL340," Hayley responded, adjusting the autopilot as the aircraft began its steady ascent0

For the next few hours, the flight proceeded as planned. The rhythmic hum of the engines was a familiar companion, a gentle reminder of the power beneath them. The clear skies and smooth air gave Hayley time to reflect on her career, the long months of waiting and the frustrations of lockdown. She thought about her training, about the setbacks she had faced, and how, despite everything, this was where she was meant to be. In the air, in control, alongside pilots like Powers, who had seen it all and still found joy in every take-off, every landing.

The silence between her and Powers was comfortable, the kind of silence that only comes when two people are perfectly in tune with each other. She glanced at him occasionally, noting the ease with which he manipulated the controls, his focus entirely on the instruments in front of him.

* _ * _ * _ *

It was over Kaliningrad when Powers unbuckled his seatbelt, climbed out of his seat, and stretched his legs. His shift was almost over, and the planned handover to Oliver O'Day was coming up soon. Hayley, still monitoring the controls, glanced over at him, knowing he was about to step away for a break.

"Taking five?" she asked, her voice light but professional.

Powers nodded, smiling slightly. "Yep, but don't go getting too comfortable. O'Day's up next, and you'll need to brief him when he takes the seat."

"Ask him if he can grab an extra cuppa when he comes back," Hayley replied with a playful smirk, recalling how Powers had teased her earlier about the coffee. She couldn't help but feel a sense of ease in the cockpit, despite the lack of passengers and the looming stillness. Everything felt almost too calm, but she was grateful for the break from the usual buzz of passengers and their demands.

Suddenly the intercom for the secure door to the flight deck came to life, and Hayley knew that it was O'Day starting his part of the shift.

"Ollie, you coming in?" Powers asked, and as soon as O'Day appeared at the cockpit door, the familiar face of the First Officer greeting them with a relaxed grin. He was a few years older than Hayley, 25 to her 22, meaning that he had already clocked up more flight hours and had a far more seasoned approach to cockpit protocol. Despite his experience, though, his youthful energy and laid-back manner were always a welcome contrast to Powers' more intense presence.

"Ready to take over?" Powers asked, giving O'Day a playful nod as the younger officer replaced him in the left hand side. "Hayley'll brief you with what you need to know, and I'll get Lang to bring a pot of coffee before I head back," he added, standing and stretching as he prepared to vacate the seat.

"Cheers, Captain," O'Day responded, flashing a grin at Hayley before sliding into the captain's chair. His manner was easy-going, almost careless at times, but there was no mistaking the professional focus that slid into place the moment his hands touched the controls.

Hayley passed over the briefing notes she'd been keeping track of, her eyes briefly scanning the instruments to ensure that all the parameters were still within normal operating ranges. "Right, Oliver. We've got a smooth ride ahead," she began, her tone professional as she briefed him on the current status. "We're on course for Moscow, FL340, with about two hours to go. Crosswind's minimal, so there shouldn't be any surprises. Fuel's good, and the alternate fields are ready if anything changes."

O'Day nodded, absorbing the information with the usual precision of a pilot. "All sounds straightforward. Let's keep it that way." He adjusted his headset as Powers gave him a final nod and left the flight deck.

With Powers gone, the cockpit fell into a more relaxed rhythm, though it wasn't long before Hayley's keen instinct for slight anomalies began to prickle at her attention. As O'Day settled into the flight, his casual chatter about his recent break, plans for a weekend in Brighton, and off-duty banter started to fill the space. She could hear the easy, comfortable hum of the air conditioning and the occasional call from Moscow Centre, when suddenly a MiG-31 suddenly appeared, making an aggressive manoeuvre in the airspace to their left, just as they passed into Lithuanian airspace, along with Turkish F-16 fighter jets on their tail, both planes gliding into position with a menacing precision. It was the kind of near miss Hayley had heard about in training, but never expected to encounter herself.

"What the fuck!" Oliver exclaimed, before pressing a button which would get the Purser on the intercom. Hayley's heart skipped a beat as she stared at the radar screen. The two military jets — a MiG-31 and a pair of Turkish F-16s — were now dangerously close to their flight path. The planes were clearly on an intercept course, moving with precision that suggested they had been directed to position themselves in close proximity.

Although she hadn't been ordered to, she had a feeling that transmissions through VHF on the emergency channel would order her to deploy her landing gear shortly, to prove that it was a civilian airliner and not a military aircraft. Hayley felt a surge of adrenaline as she snapped her attention to the radio frequencies, her fingers already adjusting the controls. The cockpit, which had felt calm just moments before, now buzzed with tension.

The next thing she knew, Arrows was at the door on the other side, buzzing to access the flight deck. Hayley quickly glanced at O'Day, who buzzed the Captain into the cockpit, his face a mix of concern and urgency. The situation was escalating faster than any of them had anticipated, and Hayley could feel the tension in the air as the two fighter jets closed in.

"I don't like this," Arrows muttered, and Hayley knew that if the most senior pilot in the PanEuro fleet was feeling concerned, things were serious. He had seen enough in his years of flying to know when something was wrong. "We're going to divert to Helsinki as a precaution. Hayley, get Moscow Centre on the comms."

Hayley's hands were already moving, reaching instinctively for the comms panel. Her voice was calm, clipped, professional—far more so than she felt inside— as she keyed in the correct frequency.

"Moscow Centre, this is PanEuro Flight one-five-four, squawking seven-seven-zero-zero, we are being intercepted by unidentified aircraft—MiG and Turkish F-16s—in Lithuanian airspace. Request immediate confirmation of airspace integrity and clearance to divert. Repeat, requesting clearance to divert. Over."

There was a long pause on the frequency. Too long.

The cockpit was now a pressure cooker of rising tension. Oliver O'Day was gripping the sidestick a little too tightly, his eyes fixed on the heads-up display as the MiG-31 eased closer, less than a hundred metres off their wingtip. A ridiculous, impossible distance at 36,000 feet and over 450 knots.

Powers, back in the jump seat now, had one leg crossed over the other with forced calm. "Gear down, Hayley. Let's not wait for the request. Show them who we are."

She nodded, her thumb flicking the gear lever downwards. There was a subtle thud and drag as the landing gear extended into the thin upper atmosphere, useless at this altitude but unmistakable to a trained military radar operator. The message was clear: we are not combatant.

Hayley caught the ghost of a smirk on Powers' face. "Always best to overcommunicate in a language they understand."

Then, finally, the F-16 called out on radio, in English, with a Turkish accent.

"PanEuro one-five-four, be advised, you are entering contested airspace. We are Baltic Air Policing, and you are being escorted due to Russian military activity ahead. Recommend you divert to Helsinki or Tallin."

Hayley knew that Powers had already made that decision — Helsinki was close, the airspace was clear, and PanEuro procedures were very clear about one thing: don't argue with supersonic military hardware, even if you're in the right.

She immediately keyed back into ATC.

"Moscow Centre, PanEuro one-five-four, acknowledging vector instruction from Baltic Air Policing. Request clearance to deviate northbound for Helsinki Vantaa. Re-routing now. Squawk remains seven-seven-zero-zero, for identification. Please confirm radar contact and notify Finnish ATC."

O'Day was already punching new coordinates into the FMS, eyes flicking with laser focus across the multiple screens, while Powers was now standing behind them both, one hand resting on the back of O'Day's seat, the other holding a paper cup of coffee he'd picked up en route from the galley.

"Good choice," he muttered approvingly. "You alright, Northcott?"

"I'm fine," Hayley replied, her voice taut but steady. "Just… alert."

He grinned wryly. "That's the correct mode. Alert, not panicked. Let's keep it that way."

The aircraft banked slightly, altering course towards the Gulf of Finland. The MiG-31 peeled away as quickly as it had arrived, vanishing into a bank of high-altitude cirrus like some dark omen, while the Turkish jets held station a little longer, one moving ahead of the Airbus while the other slid slightly behind and below, a silent chaperone through uneasy skies.

There was no mistaking it now — this wasn't a training sortie or some miscommunication on an international level. There was something going on in the air over Russia's western edge, and PanEuro 154 had come dangerously close to being in the wrong place at the wrong time.

*_*_*_*

"You was almost going to be another MH17," Max Livingstone, who had been on a Manston - Helsinki flight that had departed after the Moscow flight said as the Flight 154 crew walked into the staff lounge that various airline used for their short layovers at Helsinki-Vantaa. "One of the Finns who speak Russian told me that Kaliningrad was lining up SAMs at your flight. Funny how there was no NOTAMs and that the flights were being authorised to run and yet nobody thought to put a broadcast out until after you were already in the air."

Hayley sat down heavily on the worn-out sofa, the plasticky cushions hissing slightly beneath her. She looked across at Max, blinking in stunned silence for a moment before removing her cap and laying it on the armrest beside her.

"Cheers, Max," she said dryly. "That's exactly what I needed to hear."

Captain Adrian Powers, now with his jacket off and collar open, was on the phone to PanEuro HQ, while also writing on his tablet a report which was 99% the truth, but with Hayley's name not mentioned due to the archaic policy of only men being permitted by PanEuro's backers to fly the aircraft—at least officially. She knew it, and he knew it, and between the two of them it was a silent agreement: she'd done the job, and done it well, but nobody at the boardroom level would ever hear of it. At least, not in a way that reflected reality.

Hayley looked around the crew lounge. A couple of Finnair pilots were asleep under a fleece blanket, a KLM stewardess was FaceTiming someone in what sounded like Indonesian, and someone had left a vending machine coffee steaming atop a discarded tabloid. The mundanity of it all felt at odds with the chaos that had just unfolded in the skies. The world, she thought, really didn't care about your close calls—unless, of course, you didn't survive them.

Powers ended the call and walked over, his expression unreadable as he flicked through a few final lines on his tablet and tapped 'Send'. He handed it to O'Day to co-sign.

"Filed," he said. "Command knows what happened. We'll be in the papers by morning, but with a controlled statement. I made sure of that."

O'Day rubbed a hand through his hair, still pale under his tan. "I'll be honest, that was the closest I've ever felt to a mid-air incident. Never seen a MiG in the flesh before. Never want to again."

Hayley finally allowed herself to slump into the sofa, pulling a crew blanket over her lap. "I think I've sweated out most of my insides."

"You handled yourself well," Powers said, turning to face her. "Cool under pressure. Right decisions at the right time. You've got instincts."

"Instincts don't show up on paper," she replied, tired and more bitter than she intended. "And you made sure not to put me on any."

Powers didn't blink. "I protected your licence. The board would have roasted you for touching a control. You want a career here? You play the long game."

As Powers said that, Hayley's phone sounded, a WhatsApp notification from her sister, Dani. Opening her phone, she read the message.

Dani Northcott: *Did you hear about the PanEuro flight that almost got downed by a SAM over Kaliningrad? People at Virgin are talking about it already. Rumour is they were two seconds from scrambling Typhoons to intercept if the MiG didn't back off.*

Hayley stared at the screen, jaw slightly slack.

Hayley Northcott: *That was me.*

There was no reply from Dani for nearly a minute. Then a response came through.

Dani Northcott: *What the ACTUAL fuck.*

Hayley gave a dry chuckle that turned into a quiet sigh as she held the phone loosely in both hands. That summed it up perfectly. Somewhere between her panic and precision, reality had finally caught up with her. It was real now—not just adrenaline in the moment or autopilot reflexes. She had almost been a footnote in an international incident.

Her thumbs hovered over the keys.

Hayley Northcott: *All good now. Diverted to Helsinki. MiG gone. Turkish jets escorted. Bit shaken but fine.*

She hesitated before adding:

Hayley Northcott: *Don't tell Mum and Dad yet.*

The reply was near instant.

Dani Northcott: *Too late. Dad already heard about it through the ATC grapevine. He's calling you in 10.*

Hayley winced. Of course he had. Her father, Alan Northcott, was one of British Airways' senior long-haul captains, and his network of friends included ATCOs, ex-military, and more than a few who moonlit on airspace advisory boards. If a jetliner diverted due to intercept near Kaliningrad, he'd know before the ink dried on the NOTAMs.

And sure enough, her mobile rang seconds later.

"Hi, Dad," she answered before the phone had even reached her ear.

Alan's voice was immediately stern, clipped, and no-nonsense—the tone he reserved for debriefings and disciplinary briefings.

"Are you alright?"

"Yeah. Bit rattled but we're down safe."

"What happened?"

Hayley quickly summarised: the calm sector over Denmark, the handover to Baltic Control, then that moment—an eerie silence on the airwaves before the flash of the MiG and its silent dance beside their aircraft. She tried to keep it factual, procedural, as if that would make it less terrifying.

Alan was quiet for a moment.

"They shouldn't have been there. That corridor was declared green last week. Somebody's playing politics again."

"It wasn't a mistake," Hayley said quietly. "They were too coordinated. It felt… planned."

Her father sighed heavily on the line. "You did the right thing. Gear down was textbook. That's the signal that says, 'I'm civilian. I'm not a threat.' Whoever's in that MiG will have recognised it. Proud of you."

Hayley blinked fast, suddenly fighting tears she hadn't realised were there.

"Thanks," she whispered.

"Get some rest. I've got a sector to JFK tomorrow. We'll talk more when I get back."

"Love you."

"Love you too. Stay sharp, Hales."

She hung up and stared at the muted television across the room. News tickers were already starting to scroll: *PANEURO FLIGHT DIVERTED AMID MILITARY INTERCEPTION OVER BALTICS*. Beneath the headline, stock footage of an Airbus—wrong model, she noticed— was paired with a file image of a MiG. Even the news was being clumsy.

Across the lounge, Powers was now scrolling through Reuters on his own phone.

"They've already sanitised the narrative," he muttered. "Calling it an 'airspace confusion'. Says Baltic Control were warned of 'military exercises' but failed to relay it to commercial carriers."

Hayley snorted. "So, they're blaming Lithuania?"

Powers didn't answer. He just handed her the phone.

"In response to increased military exercises along NATO's eastern flank, Russian Federation defence sources confirmed that interceptors were scrambled as 'a precautionary measure' against unidentified air traffic near Kaliningrad's ADIZ. No hostile intent was declared."

Hayley read it, lips tightening. "I suppose they're not wrong. We were near Kaliningrad. And we were 'unidentified' if no one told them we were cleared."

"That's the trick," Powers replied. "They want plausible deniability. MiG shows up, rattles a few windows, then disappears. No missiles fired, no borders crossed. Everyone goes home and says it was a misunderstanding."

"But it wasn't."

"No," Powers agreed. "It wasn't."

****

CHAPTER 16 – The Strike Choice
Tuesday 8th June 2021

It had been two days since the incident with the MiG, and Hayley was at her family home in Broadstairs when her dad, Alan Northcott, suddenly got up from off the sofa, as it was his day off from British Airways, and Hayley's rostered day off from PanEuro. The lounge was filled with that particular hush that only a household of aviators could muster—news muted on the telly, mugs half-full of Yorkshire Tea abandoned on coasters, and the family Labrador stretched across the rug, oblivious to the low thrum of tension in the air. It was a pale, briny Monday, the June sun making a brief, uncertain appearance between the scudding clouds that rolled in off the sea.

"Karen," Alan said as Hayley watched the elder Northcott walk into the kitchen, phone in hand. "I've got to nip down to Heathrow. The shop stewards have called a BALAP union meeting for 3. We're balloting over refusing to work Moscow's, Prague's and any Baltic rotations. Not just us either. Iberia and Aer Lingus crews are going out as well. As one of the reps, I need to be there for the meeting. Looks like your story's made the rounds faster than a Ryanair turnaround, Hales."

Hayley looked at her dad, who was now grabbing his BA Captain's blazer, and she knew that, when he wore that, he was not just dressing for Heathrow, but putting on the uniform of the whole profession—especially when a union meeting was brewing. She watched him slip into the dark jacket with a deft movement that still carried the formality of years, even in the easy chaos of their seaside home. Her mum, Karen, was standing by the hob, stirring a pot of soup and eyeing the proceedings with a blend of worry and seasoned resignation.

Alan paused at the kitchen door, phone pressed to his ear. "I'll be back by seven if all goes to plan. But you know what these things are like—could be all night."

He then gave Hayley a look, half-proud, half-worried. "You did right by yourself up there. Just be ready if things get noisy. Press are still sniffing, and I've heard a few too many questions from the Daily Mail's 'aviation editor' for my liking."

Karen caught Hayley's eye over the rim of her glasses. "If they call here again, I'll tell them you're on a run to Vladivostok. Or the Falklands," she said, with the kind of dry humour Hayley had grown up around, and which always made her feel safe, no matter what was swirling outside.

Hayley smiled weakly, but there was an ache at the back of her chest—a deep tiredness that even home couldn't quite reach. The events over Kaliningrad still replayed in her mind in little flashes: the cockpit's dim blue glow, the staccato Russian on the radio, the thrum of adrenaline in her hands. She'd slept badly since, waking at odd hours and reaching, by reflex, for the missing headset or checklist.

"Any chance of a lift, Dad?" Dani then asked, coming down the stairs. "I've got a Shanghai in 6 hours, and the Union has called, wanting all FOs on a Zoom in half hour, so I can't exactly drive and take part in that at the same time." Dani, Hayley's older sister, was already half-in, half-out of her navy Virgin Atlantic uniform, red scarf draped around her neck with the artful carelessness of someone who had long since made a performance of being crew. Her suitcase trundled along the hallway behind her like a well-trained dog. "Anyway, Air France have done another walk out."

Hayley heard the laughter of her father, as it was well known that Air France, as well as the French Air Traffic Control, would strike at the drop of a hat. It was, everyone in the aviation world knew, an almost stereotypical reaction from the SkyTeam member to, if the wind blew even one mile per hour in the wrong direction, threaten a walkout, just like when British Airways, if BALPA, the pilots union, wanted to cause a bit of grief to management, could bring the system to a halt with a single ballot. It was a family joke that the French called strikes like the English called for tea—often, with ritual, and mostly to remind the world of their relevance.

Alan's laughter was brief, already half-absorbed into pilot mode, his mind on the coming union business and Dani's logistical needs.

"You know, Alan, love, you could just hire a Cessna from the new flying school at Manston and land at Denham, get an Uber to Waterside," Karen called after him, arching an eyebrow with a hint of a smile. "Might be faster than the M25."

Hayley couldn't help but snort. There was something absurdly comforting in her mum's suggestion—the idea that a mid-ranking BA captain might just jump in a light aircraft and skip London's endless ring of misery. But then, in their world, it didn't sound wholly unthinkable. Hayley watched her dad button the last of his blazer and grab his battered black holdall, the one with frayed piping and a faded Speedbird badge stitched by some long-forgotten BA stewardess on a cold layover night.

Alan glanced once more at the family before ducking out. "If you see the news getting out of hand, text me. And don't answer the landline unless it's one of us."

"Don't worry, we'll run radio silence," Dani said with a theatrical salute. She turned her eyes to Hayley. "You okay, Hales? Not too rattled still?"

Hayley shrugged. "Not sure. My brain feels like a VOR in a thunderstorm—never quite centres, just keeps spinning."

"Give it time." Dani's look was softer, stripped of the usual banter. "I'll WhatsApp when I'm at LHR. Don't watch Sky News, it'll just wind you up."

They stood in silence, listening as Alan's car rumbled away down the quiet crescent, the sound momentarily displacing the hush that had settled over the house. It was a silence Hayley had come to know intimately—what her father called "the holding pattern". Life after an incident in aviation was rarely a straight descent. There was always the wait: for reports, for decisions, for the all-clear or the next storm to break.

She wandered into the kitchen, mug in hand, and hovered by her mother, who was now spooning soup into bowls with the measured grace of someone for whom routine was a bulwark against the chaos of airline life.

"Will you go if PanEuro ballots?" Karen asked, quietly. "If they call a strike?"

Hayley looked at her mum, then at the calendar on the wall—already blotched with rosters and layover scribbles, their colour-coding bleeding into each other like a tube map run in the rain.

"I don't know," she admitted. "It's different, isn't it? Dad's lot, they've got clout. BA can't move a plane without the pilots. I mean, I'm Unite because of being a bloody Stewardess, even though if I was at easyJet, I'd be on the flight deck, I'd be in BALPA, and I'd probably vote yes in a heartbeat. But PanEuro...? I don't know if striking would change anything. Feels like we'd just get replaced by temps flown in from Romania or Latvia, or they'd sack us. I mean, they think that BOAC and TWA were the best thing since sliced bread, but they treat us like we're on zero-hours at Poundland. Even when we're flying over the bloody Baltic being chased by MiGs."

Karen gave her daughter a look that was both knowing and sad, her eyes creasing in sympathy as she set a bowl in front of her. "You know what your gran used to say? 'A strike's only as strong as the story behind it.' If it's just for pay, people get bored. If it's about dignity, or not getting shot down in airspace that's one wrong squawk away from a BBC Breaking News banner, that's different. And besides, love, even PanEuro can't staff a summer with nothing but temp Romanians and giddy nostalgia."

Hayley spooned her soup, the steam catching on her fringe. "I know. I keep thinking about two things, that incident in Prague when the BIS agents strip searched me, and even… y'know, erm… stimulated me while doing it, and then the MiG incident, and it just feels like this whole job—this whole life—is running on borrowed time. But then, what do you do? I can't not fly. Even now, after everything, the idea of just… walking away feels more frightening than a pair of afterburners on the TCAS."

Karen set herself down opposite, a gentle thud of mug on table. Her face softened. "You're like your dad and sister, you love the air, love the job. But you're not wrong to wonder. Look, Hales, you know your rights. The union won't leave you high and dry. Not this time, not after what you went through. If it comes to it, you'll have to do what feels right for you—whatever side of the picket line you end up on. And anyway, I don't see you walking away from the cockpit for good. You're too much like your dad. Stubborn as sin. It's the Northcott way."

Hayley couldn't help but smile at that. There was a strange comfort in the ordinary rhythm of the kitchen— her mother's voice, the clink of spoons, the far-off rumble of an airliner on approach to Manston, ghosting through the open window with the tang of salt and jet fuel. Outside, the wind had picked up, and the clouds had gathered into a bruised mass over the Channel.

She sipped her soup and stared down into the swirl of carrots and potato, letting herself drift for a moment, imagining herself somewhere at FL350, looking out over a sun-struck sea of clouds, the noise of the galley and the drone of the engines her only company.

The phone buzzed on the countertop, snapping her out of her reverie. Karen picked it up and glanced at the screen.

"It's Theo," she said, sliding it across the table.

Hayley blinked and accepted the call, forcing herself to sound a little brighter than she felt.

"Hey," she said, tucking a strand of hair behind her ear.

Theo's voice came down the line, his accent softened by fatigue. "Hales. You at home? How's your dad?"

"Off to Heathrow. Union business. How's Brum?"

There was a pause, the faint sound of an intercom in the background.

"Edgy," Theo said, finally. "Ops are tense. Everyone's watching what BA does. Word's gone around about your flight, the MiG, the ATC chaos. People are rattled. We're briefing extra security on all Eastern flights. You'd think we were back in the Cold War."

Hayley let out a low sigh. "Feels like it sometimes."

"Look," Theo went on, his tone dropping to something more intimate, "don't let them get to you. You did everything right. We're all behind you. Even the grumpy ones. If it comes to a ballot, we'll walk together."

There was a long, quiet moment, the sort that hung between people who'd weathered storms together.

"I'll let you know what PanEuro are saying if anything drops," Hayley said. "For now, just—stay safe, alright?"

"You too, Hales. Text me if you want to talk later. Or if you want a distraction. I can read you the world's most boring MEL if you like. Got one about a broken coffee machine that'll make you question humanity."

She smiled despite herself. "Maybe later. I'll hold you to it."

They hung up, and Hayley found herself gazing out of the kitchen window, the fields beyond the garden merging with the grey of the sky, her mind flickering with the competing currents of dread and loyalty that defined her life since she'd first put on a uniform.

* _ * _ * _ *

"Lydd Tower, this is Golf Romeo Delta Echo Romeo, inbound for a full stop, request join instructions."

Hayley flicked the push-to-talk with a thumb that was steadier than she felt. The Robin DR400/180 Regent that she had hired from the newly formed Manston Aero Club, a tiny, battered little French workhorse, burbled its way eastwards over the Weald of Kent, the world outside a patchwork of fields and hedges sliding beneath her wings. She'd needed to get up. She'd needed to fly. When the ground felt unsteady—when life below was chaos and rumour—airborne was the only place that still made sense.

She listened as the radio crackled in her headset, the local controller replying with calm, measured clarity.

"Golf Echo Romeo, join right base for Runway 21, report two miles."

"Will join right base for Two-One, Golf Echo Romeo," Hayley responded, her voice steadying further, gaining that professional cadence that had been drilled into her by a dozen instructors and twice as many check rides.

She scanned the sky, dropping her left wing just enough to catch the glint of the English Channel on the horizon. Below, Romney Marsh was a green-brown blur. She could see, off to the west, the angular shapes of the Dungeness nuclear power station, a reminder that—despite all the romance people attributed to flying—aviation lived cheek-by-jowl with the business of the modern world.

She throttled back, set carb heat, trimmed out. Her hands moved with economy and purpose, the product of years. In the cockpit, Hayley could almost forget the storm that swirled below—unions, ballots, headlines, the ache of old humiliations. In the air, she was just a pilot again. Not a pawn, not a headline, not a symbol for a cause she hadn't chosen.

She rolled out on the base leg, calling: "Golf Echo Romeo, right base, Two-One."

The Tower came back: "Golf Echo Romeo, surface wind 210 at 7 knots, clear to land."

"Clear to land, Golf Echo Romeo."

The rest was simple muscle memory: undercarriage fixed, mixture rich, flaps down, a last glance at the ASI—seventy knots. Then that moment of hush, the transition from flying to floating, the world pausing before the main wheels kissed the tarmac. A chirp, a gentle squawk from the tyres, and she was down, rolling out gently, the Robin's nosewheel bumping over the cracks in the little airstrip.

She taxied in with the window open, letting the sea air whip away the last vestiges of nerves. Lydd was nearly deserted, save for the odd flying club Cherokee and a single parked Islander that looked as if it had flown direct from 1978 and never left.

Once parked, Hayley sat in the cockpit a long moment, letting the ticking of the cooling engine fill her ears. Out here, nobody knew her. No press, no union reps, no cabin crew managers with their thinly veiled warnings and pastel PowerPoints. Just the slow exhale of a propeller unwinding and the faint, sweet stink of Avgas.

She eventually climbed out, taking her logbook and a battered satchel, and walked to the little clubhouse, where a pair of instructors were arguing quietly over a Met report. They barely glanced up as she passed. The young man at the desk gave her a nod and a smile—nothing more. For a few moments, she was anonymous, just another pilot out for a day's solo, seeking the sky not as a cause but as a home.

She signed the movements book, paid her landing fee, and—on a whim—ordered a mug of builder's tea at the club counter, drinking it on the wooden veranda. Across the grass, a Cessna was turning onto final, the sun glinting off its wings. Hayley sat back, her legs dangling, and let the wind—salty, rough, persistent—strip away some of the exhaustion. Above her, gulls wheeled and cried.

Her phone buzzed again. This time it was a message from Theo.

Theo Sullivan: *Hey, you fancy meeting me for a date? I'm due back in Brum in an hour off my CDG.*

She almost laughed at the message—part disbelief, part gratitude. The world could be falling in around them, and still, Theo could find a moment for something as simple, as sweet, as a date. The fact that she had hired the Regent for a whole 24 hour period, as she had decided an hour after her dad had gone for his union meeting, having seen the roster and noticing that tomorrow, she was on a St Petersburg, that she was going to call in using fatigue as a reason. The irony that she was using a legitimate fatigue report to buy herself breathing space wasn't lost on her. The industry had drilled into her the importance of duty, the fiction of resilience, but never the legitimacy of vulnerability. Today, she was taking a little back for herself.

Hayley Northcott: *Unless you fancy some VFR flying, flyboy. I've got a Regent for the next 23 hours and plenty of fuel in the tanks. I'm at Lydd, but if you want to meet me at Coventry, we can go for a flight somewhere while there's light.*

Theo Sullivan: *Ha! You know I can't say no to some stick time. Coventry it is. Can you be there for half four? I'll try to beat the French out of CDG and I'll get an Uber from BHX to Coventry airport. Make sure you file your PPR.*

PPR, or Prior Permission Required, was a running joke in GA circles—some airports enforced it like a point of honour, others used it as a not-so-subtle deterrent to keep out students and spotters. Hayley grinned, thumbed out a quick response.

Hayley Northcott: *Roger that—see you at Coventry. Don't let the cheese-mongers delay you.*

Finishing her tea, she looked up the phone number for Coventry airport, dialled in, and after the briefest of exchanges with a cheerful old-school ops controller— who seemed more excited by the prospect of "a bit of interesting traffic" than any formalities—she had her PPR sorted. It felt gloriously normal: the tangle of clearances, squawk codes, and airspace chatter, the low-stakes ritual of light aviation. Here, nobody cared about the latest union ballot or her name in a press headline. She was just Golf Echo Romeo, routing north, a line on a chart, a voice on the radio.

She ambled back across the apron, logbook in hand, the Robin's wings gleaming under the uncertain June sun. For a moment, she paused, gazing out at the sweep of sky above Dungeness, and wondered, not for the first time, how everything could feel so terribly complicated on the ground and so beautifully simple aloft.

* _ * _ * _ *

Climbing back into the cockpit, she went through the ritual of preflight checks with careful deliberation. Controls free, fuel checked, mixture rich, mags both, trims set, hatches secure. Even the familiar whiff of burnt avgas and upholstery was a comfort. Engine started on the second try, she taxied out, radioed for departure, and with a last, longing glance at the Channel, lined up for take-off.

Full throttle. The little Robin surged forward, lifting from the short strip and into the forgiving blue-grey sky. Once airborne, the world contracted to dials and horizon, a thin thread of cloud and the occasional drone of traffic. For the first time in days, Hayley felt almost herself.

The flight north to Coventry was peaceful, the radio busy but not frantic—an undercurrent of professional chattiness that was balm to her nerves. As she skirted the South Downs, the Kent fields gave way to the urban sprawl, then the languid, rolling Midlands, Coventry's spires rising like old bones from the new-build estates and ring roads.

She joined right base for runway 23, careful to follow the circuit with all the propriety of someone who had been drilled in the etiquette of busier skies. The touchdown was light, barely a chirp, and she taxied in, radioing her stand as if she were lining up for a BA long-haul, not some windswept slab of Coventry tarmac.

Theo was waiting near the flying club, phone in hand, the standard-issue crew bag at his feet, his hair mussed by the wind, uniform jacket slung over one shoulder. He looked tired, but when he spotted her, his face lit up with something almost like boyish glee. "You actually brought the Robin. Bloody hell, Northcott, you're a woman of your word."

Hayley, suddenly aware of how dishevelled she must look—hair tousled by the slipstream, cheeks windburnt—managed a smile. "Couldn't pass up the chance. Besides, I needed to remember I'm more than just a headline."

Theo's reply was gentle, but had an undercurrent of steel: "You're not a headline. You're the one who kept it together when it mattered." Then, with a sideways grin: "Now, where are you taking me?"

"Manston, do a few circuits round Thanet, and maybe head to my folks for a shag?" she said, kissing her boyfriend.

Theo's laugh echoed off the Robin's wing, not in the laddish, mocking way of bored flight crew on a delayed rotation, but in that sudden, unselfconscious relief you feel when the world tips back onto its axis, however briefly. "Northcott, you're incorrigible. Not sure your parents will approve of me pitching up in uniform for that sort of layover."

"Please. My mum will throw you a towel and tell you to wash your hands before dinner. You're already in the good books for putting up with me." Hayley winked, then glanced away, not quite able to sustain the bravado as a gust buffeted the light plane. "But seriously, let's just fly a bit, yeah? I want a sky with nobody else in it."

"Your wish is my checklist." Theo dropped his crew bag in the back, glancing at the fuel gauges with the quick, precise scan of a man who knew the value of double-checking everything—especially when it belonged to someone else. He slipped into the right seat, rolling his shoulders and settling in with a sigh. "Been a while since I did anything that wasn't Airbus-shaped. This thing even have an autopilot?"

"You're looking at her," Hayley quipped, flicking the master on and running through the after-start checks. The ritual, between them, was oddly comforting: transponder set, flaps tested, carb heat checked, the symphony of little switches and dials grounding them in a world where things made sense and every action had a reason.

They taxied to the holding point. The air was alive with birds and the distant rumble of jet traffic, but here, behind the glass, they were in a bubble: pilots first, partners second, and everything else—unions, news, the weight of events—somewhere on the far side of the perimeter fence.

The take-off was smooth, a quick climb-out into the late-afternoon light. Hayley glanced over, caught Theo grinning as he watched the patchwork below, the fields and housing estates giving way to the gentle smudge of distant hills. "Forgot how loud these things are," he said, yelling to be heard over the Lycoming's cheerful racket.

"Not everything comes with noise-cancelling headsets and decent catering!" Hayley shot back, but her heart wasn't in the banter. She felt herself relax as the altimeter wound upward, as the Midlands unspooled beneath them and the air smoothed out to something close to peace.

They flew in companionable silence for a while, tracing lazy turns over the countryside, Theo handling the radio with the casual fluency of someone who'd once flown Cessnas before Airbus took over his logbook. The Robin was slower, more honest than the jets they both worked: every movement meant something, every bump and whistle of wind a reminder that this was flying as their grandparents would have known it.

After a while, Theo broke the quiet. "Do you want to talk about it?"

She hesitated, hand resting lightly on the yoke. "Not really. But I can't think of a better place to try."

So she did, in fits and starts. The MiG, the radios, the cold sweat as they squawked and descended, her hands locked on the controls and Adrian Powers's voice snapping commands she'd followed on instinct. The strip-search in Prague, the way fear never quite left you afterwards—how, even now, she checked and double-checked everything, as if the next disaster might hide in the gap between muscle memory and panic.

Theo listened, only asking the odd question when she faltered. When she finished, she let out a shaky breath, surprised by the sudden surge of relief. "I keep waiting for someone to tell me I'm making a fuss. Or that I should just get over it."

He was quiet a moment, then shook his head. "You're allowed to feel what you feel, Hales. You kept your crew and passengers safe. That's all that matters. If anyone tries to tell you otherwise, send them my way. I'll give them the world's longest lecture about CRM and dignity and what it means to be a proper aircrew."

****

CHAPTER 17 – Fatigue City
Monday 21st June 2021

It was now three weeks since the MiG incident, and Hayley Northcott's life had returned to something resembling normal—or at least, the kind of normal that passes for it in the airline world.

Especially as BALPA, the pilots union, and Unite, the cabin crew, maintenance and ground staff union, had told all their members to take action short of a strike when it came to flights to Russia. That, of course, was code for working to rule, calling out for fatigue when a Russia bound flight was rostered, and even quietly turning the screw on management by sticking religiously to every last procedural nuance, from crew rest regulations to the most arcane detail in the OM-A.

And it wasn't just PanEuro whose crews were taking the same action. British Airways, Virgin, easyJet, Jet2, Iberia, Air France, KLM, Lufthansa, Aer Lingus, and, surprisingly, ITA, all were following suit, albeit in their own national styles. BA pilots cited the letter of every CAA and EASA regulation, clogging up ops with paperwork and making a minor art form out of the Fatigue Risk Management System. The Spanish, after a brief spell of chest-puffing, quickly adopted a kind of Mediterranean work-to-rule: mysterious "unwellness" on any sector east of Warsaw, a rash of non-specific gastroenteritis sweeping through the crew rooms of Madrid and Barcelona. The French simply called a meeting, blocked the doors with a pile of baguettes, and declared themselves en grève—regardless of whether anyone had actually scheduled a strike.

Of course, for the public, the official reason from BAPLA and Unite was pay, pensions and the usual gripes about working conditions, but everyone in the airline world knew the true source of tension. The escalation of hostilities, and the increasingly precarious geopolitical situation, had left crews caught between the absurdity of the airlines' operations and the ever-present possibility of something far worse than a crew rest violation.

"Scabs," Hayley heard a BA pilot mutter, sitting in the multi airline crew canteen at Madrid–Barajas Airport, and she knew why.

An Iberia crew were sat in the corner, a crew who she had heard were non-unionised, were planning an Iberia flight to Moscow, one of the few ones where non-union crews were still being scheduled, though word was it was only because management had offered triple pay.

The BA captain's voice was low, thick with disdain, but even so it carried through the hum of the crew canteen— a familiar sort of drama in the air. Someone from KLM, long-legged and weary, raised an eyebrow and muttered something in Dutch about "another week in Fatigue City". Nobody laughed, but several exchanged glances. Everyone knew that every airline, no matter the livery or national myth, ran on the invisible union of human frailty and institutional stubbornness.

"You know no one from Finnair or Brussels Airlines are running any Russia flights at all, even though both the

Finn and Belgian national teams are playing their Group B games in St Petersburg," another BA Captain said to his Irish counterpart, an Aer Lingus Captain. "And the Danish ATC have told Aeroflot their planes aren't welcome today, even though Denmark and Russia are in Copenhagen."

"At least our game tomorrow is at Wembley against the Czechs," Hayley muttered, as she knew that the Euro 2020 schedule was, unlike normal years where the tournament was held in one nation, was instead being spread out across the continent in a feat of logistics only UEFA could think "practical". The effect in the crew canteen was a low, rolling grumble: pilots and cabin crew from every flag carrier and budget airline clustered in little national knots, each group fiercely invested in its own cocktail of fatigue, football, and frustration.

Hayley stirred her tea, half-listening to the chatter as she kept an eye on the departures screen, which was an unending dance of delays and substitutions. Moscow—DELAYED. St Petersburg—CANCELLED. Prague—PENDING. Overhead, the Tannoy called yet another crew to the ops desk, while an exasperated Jet2 supervisor muttered, "Fatigue City" as though it were both a destination and a diagnosis.

A group of Vueling cabin crew sat nearby, bright yellow scarves askew, looking as knackered as Hayley felt. Their laughter—shrill, tired—was a desperate kind of cheerfulness. One of them was clearly explaining to a new joiner how to report unfit for duty in just enough English, Spanish, and mime to get the point across. Hayley caught "cansancio extremo" and "no Moscow" before the group broke up, heading for the vending machines in a tired, slightly limping parade.

Looking at her roster on her phone, she knew that she had another hour before the return flight, a Madrid to Doncaster, and then a Doncaster to Copenhagen flight which was an overnighter, she knew that, as a Stewardess, not flight attendant as per other airlines, she had to drag herself back into the retro-liveried hell that was PanEuro's themed Airbus cabin and pretend, again, that she was part of the "golden age" of flying. But right now, she felt more like a half-melted tray of 1960s prawn cocktails in 37C tarmac heat.

She leaned back in the cracked plastic chair, her cabin bag wedged under the table, and tapped out a WhatsApp message to Theo.

Hayley Northcott: *Madrid is 33°C and the coffee's weak. Can I swap this uniform for an ice bath and your hands.*

She knew that he was on a Birmingham to John F Kennedy run, the young First Officer being assigned to work with Hiram Lethenshaw, a former BA Captain who had been part of the EuroFlyer setup before the pandemic started, was flying for PanEuro with the kind of weary gallows humour only Gatwick veterans possessed. Theo wouldn't see her message until cruise, but it made her feel better just to send it—to reach across the sky to someone who understood that their job, for all its high-altitude glamour, had more in common with trench warfare than Champagne and silk scarves.

The crew canteen aircon sputtered overhead like a dying APU, never quite cutting through the simmering heat and underlying exhaustion. Somewhere near the vending machines, a Lufthansa senior purser let out a sound between a sigh and a laugh—"Der müde Streik," Hayley thought she heard—The Tired Strike. That about summed it up.

Her PanEuro Captain for the return to Doncaster was a new name on her list—Captain Jeremiah Jones, ex Virgin Atlantic, a training captain who she knew that Dani, her sister, had been mentored by when she was starting out at the airline. Jeremiah was known in crew circles as "JJ"—a towering, Welsh-born, fiercely proud product of the long-haul glamour days, now awkwardly shoehorned into PanEuro's performative nostalgia project. Word from her sister was that he took everything in his stride: turbulence, terrible catering, and corporate idiocy alike, with the same blend of dry wit and resigned dignity.

He was also the BALPA representative at Manston, meaning that he walked a constant tightrope between duty and dissent. The irony that he, along with Powers, who was the Chief Pilot, and several other senior Captains at the airline were BALPA reps in their past lives at BA, Iberia, Aer Lingus and Virgin, meant that management was effectively he walked a constant tightrope between duty and dissent.

Hayley sighed and took another sip of her lukewarm tea. Across from her, a Norwegian Air Shuttle crew were trading gossip about the latest budget carrier collapse—rumours swirling that FlyBosnia had finally thrown in the towel, and that there were rumours one of the Romanian

ACMIs, an aircraft, crew, maintenance and insurance firm, were getting a new client, an ultra-low cost start-up that wanted to do intra-European and UK to EU flights from the late summer season.

"The new ULCC is apparently ran by people from Wizz, Easy and Ryanair," one of the Norwegian cabin crew was saying, her English inflected with the clean Nordic cadence of someone who had learned it young but precisely.

"The Unholy Trinity," a Jet2 pilot muttered from a nearby table, barely looking up from his tuna sandwich. "You just know they'll call it something tragic like ZipGo or Jettix. And God help us when they start undercutting us on Gatwick slots."

Hayley listened with half an ear, her mind flickering from the absurdity of the airline naming conventions to her own aching feet. She had worn through her third pair of regulation heels this month—cheap leather dyed to match the company's arbitrary retro shade of "PanEuro Coral", a colour that had no business existing in daylight, let alone in uniform policy. She'd taken to stuffing plasters into the lining of her shoes like a soldier preparing for the trenches.

Her phone buzzed.

Theo Sullivan: *Just passed FL310 over Shannon. Lethenshaw's doing his monologue about how the management are dinosaurs who should respect the fact that women are just as good as men at the controls and if he had his way, he'd be installing women pilots* *throughout the flightdeck. Told him you'd appreciate the sentiment.*

Hayley snorted, earning a look from a serious-faced Air France steward—who clearly disapproved of anyone showing visible amusement before 14:00.

That or he had been sentenced to a Moscow with a full aircraft and no hotel layover—a fate Hayley wouldn't wish on her worst enemy.

She thumbed a reply.

Hayley Northcott: *Tell him he's my new favourite dinosaur. Can we clone him and replace half the clowns at PanEuro HQ?*

She could imagine Theo grinning. FL310, cruising just north of the North Atlantic Tracks, probably watching some patchy cloud over Ireland dissolve into early evening sun. The difference between her day and his was stark.

While Theo was flying a real transatlantic run for PanEuro, working with seasoned captains, she was about to do another themed trolley dash down the aisles of a half-empty aircraft, pretending that she was a Pan Am stewardess for the same airline.

Hayley dropped her phone back on the table and let her head fall back, staring at the tiled ceiling above like it might yield a portal out of this heat-soaked purgatory. Theo's text had made her smile, but even that warmth couldn't offset the creeping fog of weariness settling over her limbs like a damp blanket. It had been creeping up for weeks, this fatigue, like a low cloud descending after sunset—subtle, persistent, eventually all-consuming.

"Fatigue City," she muttered aloud, echoing the Jet2 pilot's earlier phrase. She didn't even try to hide the bitterness in her voice.

"You and the rest of us," came a voice from behind her.

She looked round to see a tall figure in a PanEuro captain's cap with silver braid. JJ. Jeremiah Jones. She stood reflexively, out of habit more than protocol, but he waved her down with a brief flick of the hand.

"Sit, sit. Not expecting deference unless you're planning to bow and curtsey as well. And I've had enough of that from this airline's design committee," he said, his voice dry as a California vineyard. "Is this seat free?"

She nodded, shifting her bag beneath the table with a heel. "Captain Jones."

"JJ, if you please. Titles are for the ops briefings and media disasters." He took the seat across from her with a groan that betrayed years of long-haul landings. "Anyway, are you in the union?"

Hayley blinked, caught off guard by the bluntness of the question. She wasn't used to captains opening conversations with union affiliations.

"I'm… technically Unite, but I was BALPA when I was... well, training with easyJet. Line training that is, A320 family," she admitted, stirring the last remnants of her tea.

"Good," JJ said, with the air of a man ticking boxes in his head. "And I'm not just being nosy. We've got a lot of people sitting on the fence right now, not knowing whether to back management or keep their heads down and hope this all blows over. But it won't. Not this time."

Hayley frowned. "You really think it'll come to a proper strike?"

JJ gave a noncommittal shrug, the kind that experienced captains had perfected for flight delays and political discussions. "It already has, in all but name. This 'action short of strike' lark? It's just a polite way of saying no one wants to fly to Moscow unless someone explains how we're not going to get shot down, sanctioned, or stranded in airspace owned by people who think transponders are optional."

He paused to glance at the departures board, then back to her. "You were on that Kaliningrad flight, weren't you? With Adrian Powers?"

Hayley nodded, slowly. "Yeah. I was… unofficially in the right-hand seat. Oliver O'Day was off-duty in the back."

JJ's eyebrows lifted. "Unofficially," he repeated, with the carefully neutral tone of someone who understood exactly what that meant. "I've seen the internal reports. Well, the bits they haven't redacted into oblivion. Word is Powers was impressed. That you kept your head."

"I just did what I was trained to do," Hayley replied quietly.

JJ gave her a long, appraising look, then nodded. "Good answer. But that doesn't make what happened any less serious. Or any less of a ticking bomb under this whole Russia scheduling mess."

He sat back and rubbed a hand through his greying hair. "Listen, Hayley… you know what I think the real problem is? It's not just the routes or the geopolitics. It's that this airline wants to pretend it's 1965 when the rest of the world's on the edge of Cold War II. You can't wear white gloves and push chicken or beef when the country you're flying into has missile batteries pointed at your nosewheel."

Hayley managed a small laugh, bitter but appreciative. "Tell that to Havers. She would blow a head gasket when one of us at Stewardess School forgot something as minor as our girdles or even a hair out of place under the pillbox hat. Bombs and border tensions weren't on the curriculum. But they definitely insisted on lipstick matching the cabin trim."

JJ smiled faintly. "Ah yes. The Iron Lipstick. She used to run a finishing school, the kind where the tray placement mattered more than thermal runaway. I heard she was rejected from British Caledonian for being 'too draconian'—and that's saying something. Still, it's the PanEuro way, isn't it? Style over substance, as long as the Instagram feed looks good."

Hayley rolled her eyes. "Don't forget the checklist on how to angle your ankles during turbulence so the heels stay photo-ready."

JJ laughed, the sound warm and tired. "We're flying aircraft into contested airspace in vintage get-up, asking the cabin crew to serve chicken supreme with a smile while missiles play tag overhead. You couldn't make it up."

"Nope," Hayley agreed. "If you did, they'd call it satire."

They sat in silence for a beat, the hum of the canteen and the clink of plastic cutlery filling the space between them. Then JJ leaned forward, elbows on the table.

"Off the record," he said, "BALPA's preparing for a coordinated strike vote. Not just us. BA, Virgin, Lufthansa, the lot. The day before the Euro final."

Hayley's eyes widened slightly. "The day before the final? Won't that cripple everything? That's going to hit everything—airports, hotels, transfers, the works."

"That's the point," JJ said, his voice low, calm, but edged with the steely conviction of someone long past caring about the fallout. "It's not about wrecking the game. It's about reminding the government—and the airlines—that without us, there is no game. No tourists. No travel bubble. No million-pound sponsorship deals being ferried on the backs of sweat-drenched crews pretending that missile evasion is part of the inflight service routine."

Hayley nodded slowly. "You're not wrong. But half the crew room won't back it. Not with everyone hanging onto jobs by their fingernails."

"True," JJ acknowledged, "but the other half have had enough. Look, I was in BA when they grounded the fleet during the pensions standoff in 2003. I remember the looks we got. Some of the newer FOs were terrified. But the sky didn't fall in. It never does. Airlines survive. Crews get tired of being threatened into silence. Eventually, someone stands up."

He checked his watch and stood. "We're on gate 17. Push in thirty-five minutes. You okay for preflight?"

Hayley stood, brushing crumbs off her skirt, and felt the heaviness of fatigue set back into her legs like lead shot in her shoes. "Yeah, I'm good. Just… don't expect me to pour tea with a smile."

"Wouldn't dream of it," JJ said with a wink. "If anyone asks, tell them I authorised a temporary suspension of Stepford Stewardess Mode."

Together, they made their way through the terminal, slipping between families heading back to Manchester and students carting overstuffed backpacks, their tan lines already fading under the harsh strip lighting of the departures lounge. As they boarded the A320 at the stand, Hayley did the usual scan of the cabin—mint-condition faux-wood panels, adverts masquerading as heritage posters, coral curtains so synthetic they probably violated three environmental treaties—and shook her head.

"Every time I walk into one of these," she muttered to herself, "I feel like I'm about to be filmed in black and white."

JJ heard her and chuckled. "We're all extras in someone's nostalgia fetish, Hayley. Anyway, briefing in five, so don't be late or they'll start knitting your replacement from polyester and passive aggression."

"Would you like beef, chicken or the vegan stroganoff substitute?" Hayley asked, smiling tightly as she leaned across the narrow aisle, one hand gripping the trolley, the other offering a tray.

The man in 4D, one of the Executive Class rows on the Airbus A320neo, looked up from his newspaper—an actual paper newspaper, Hayley noted with a flicker of incredulity—and frowned as if he'd just been asked to choose between types of dental surgery.

"Which one is least likely to give me food poisoning?"

Hayley resisted the urge to sigh. "They're all fine, sir. Our catering was loaded fresh in Madrid. The beef is in a mushroom sauce, the chicken is in a cream-based reduction, and the vegan option is lentil stroganoff."

He looked at her name badge. "Hayley. Which one would you pick?"

Hayley gave the rehearsed smile she reserved for such moments. "I usually go with the chicken, sir. It's light and reheats well."

"Fine," he said, as though making a painful concession. "Chicken, then. And can I get a G&T?"

"Certainly, sir," she said, handing him the tray. "I'll ask the Purser to bring it along shortly." She smiled again—refined, mechanical, practised—and moved down the aisle before he could offer further commentary on the airline's retro dining selections.

Behind her, the trolley squeaked slightly with each jolt of the aircraft's light turbulence. The cabin was dimly lit in the PanEuro sepia tone that tried desperately to recreate a 1960s aesthetic, all gold-edged seat numbers and pastel lighting that was meant to be warm but only served to deepen the sense of weariness clinging to every surface. The scent of reheated food mingled with the synthetic tang of the aircraft air, and Hayley could feel her blouse starting to cling unpleasantly beneath her arms. Fatigue City.

Back in the galley, she found Dimitri Oslov, the flamboyant purser with an uncanny knack for theatrical timing and vintage sarcasm, lining up miniatures on a tray like a bartender preparing for a themed wedding.

"Ah, Hayley, my radiant assistant from the land of culinary diplomacy," he said, selecting a bottle of Tanqueray with a flourish. "Who requires embalming with juniper?"

"4D," she replied. "One of those who thinks sarcasm is a substitute for personality."

Dimitri nodded sagely. "Ah yes. The Boarding Gate Philosopher. I shall deliver his G&T with all the grandeur of a Versailles footman."

She gave him a tired smile, then leaned against the sidewall for a second, eyes closed. "How are we doing on timings?"

He glanced at the FAP screen. "We're twenty-six minutes to Doncaster, barring any ATC japes. Captain Jones said we may be held a little—some congestion due to a Ryanair inbound from Gdańsk and a Jet2 returning from Alicante."

Hayley groaned softly. "Classic. Shall we do another round of teas and coffees, or declare hot drinks emotionally unavailable for the rest of the flight?"

Dimitri smiled. "I'd vote for the latter, but alas, the PanEuro Charter of Quaint Delusions insists we must offer everyone 'a taste of mid-century hospitality'. Which means, dear one, we brew and smile."

Back down the aisle, the lights flickered gently as the aircraft dipped into a soft descent curve. Overhead, the PA clicked to life.

"Ladies and gentlemen, this is your captain speaking—Jeremiah Jones here. We're just starting our descent into Doncaster Sheffield Airport, currently expecting to be on stand in approximately thirty-five minutes. Slight delay due to traffic ahead of us, but we'll do our best to minimise it. Temperature on arrival is a not-so-balmy twelve degrees, so we do recommend jackets if you've become accustomed to Madrid's summer. We'd like to thank you for flying with PanEuro today—where nostalgia meets necessity."

A chuckle broke out in the galley.

"Did he just *roast the company* over the PA?" Dimitri whispered gleefully.

"Yep," Hayley said. "Subtle. Polished. Lethal. JJ's a master."

Dimitri winked. "He can ride shotgun with me anytime."

Hayley knew that Dimitri was gay, and that being openly supportive and flamboyant was Dimitri's subtle rebellion against the dour expectations of PanEuro's retro-cosplay command structure. But she also knew he meant it as the highest compliment. Captain JJ had managed to walk the tightrope—professional but wry, respectful but unsparing. It was a hard line to tread in an airline that wanted its captains to sound like they were reading Shakespeare while marching into a Cold War.

The cabin lights flicked to a soft orange hue as descent continued, that synthetic twilight shade the company believed evoked "first-class elegance", though in Hayley's opinion it made everyone look faintly jaundiced.

By the time they were wheels down in Doncaster, the passengers had mostly sunk into that pre-arrival stupor familiar to every short-haul flyer: bags clutched in laps, seat belts clicked, eyes glazed over as though waiting for a school bell. The soft bump of the gear touching tarmac was met with the usual round of polite British applause from row 8 back—though whether it was for the smooth landing or sheer relief to be off the plane, no one could quite say.

Hayley did her final walkthrough with that practiced panache of someone who knew every inch of the cabin and could execute the required inspections while balancing a tray, dodging elbows, and subtly checking for left-behind passports.

The moment the aircraft doors opened, and the jet bridge clicked into place, she was hit with that signature UK terminal draught—the one that smelled faintly of bacon rolls and a misplaced sense of optimism.

Dimitri passed her a disarmingly hot paper cup of tea as she disembarked behind the last of the passengers.

"You look like you're about to throttle the next person who says 'vintage charm,'" he said.

She sipped the tea and hissed. "Not if I throttle myself first."

As they passed through the crew channel and emerged into the back corridor behind Doncaster arrivals, JJ was already waiting, a leather flight bag over one shoulder, peering at his phone with the resigned posture of someone trying to make sense of crew scheduling chaos.

"Well done, all," he said without looking up. "I'm told we've got 1 hour 40 minutes before wheels-up for Copenhagen. Ops says it'll be a quick turnaround. I suspect they mean we're doing the turnaround ourselves."

Hayley groaned. "Of course."

Dimitri, cheery as ever, gave her a conspiratorial look. "Darling, I hope you didn't get too attached to sitting down. Then again, this is the golden age of aviation. Nothing says glamour like lugging waste carts and empty

Prosecco bottles through security because catering forgot to reload the bins."

Hayley snorted, managing a weak smile as they trudged along the corridor. The linoleum floor had that faint stickiness unique to regional airports, and the fluorescent lights overhead buzzed like mosquitoes. The fatigue in her bones had shifted from dull ache to something sharper, like her muscles were starting to protest in earnest.

They passed a side corridor marked "Crew Operations" where a whiteboard was still scrawled with notes from a previous shift: "Ryanair turnarounds → bay 4 ONLY," and beneath it, a crude sketch of a stick figure crying beneath the word "Madrid".

JJ held open the door into the ops lounge for them, nodding to a ground handler hunched over a clipboard. "Looks like we're parked remote. Bay 8. Bus in twenty."

Hayley dropped her cabin bag next to a couch upholstered in a fabric so garish it could have doubled as camouflage in a 1970s disco. She collapsed beside it and unzipped the top flap, pulling out a protein bar that had probably passed its best-before during the Obama administration.

"Does it count as self-care," she said, "if I eat this and cry at the same time?"

JJ chuckled from across the room as he poured himself a Styrofoam cup of coffee. "Only if you hydrate between sobs."

"Too late," Dimitri said, lowering himself into a sagging armchair. "My tear ducts are on strike."

"Don't blame them. BALPA would walk out over that," Sarah muttered. "That and Unite."

"Don't give Unite any ideas," JJ replied. "They'll start issuing tissues with slogans. 'Wipe away your fatigue— Vote Strike.'"

The room was quiet for a moment, save for the soft crinkle of Hayley's protein bar wrapper and the distant rumble of another aircraft spooling up on the apron. Somewhere down the corridor, the low chime of a Tannoy announcement called for a crew to report to gate two. Probably Jet2. They were always moving.

Hayley leaned back, resting her head against the wall. "So, night stop in Copenhagen. Nice. Where are we booked.

JJ nodded. "Layover at the Clarion near the station. Not bad. Bit of a hike from the airport but clean beds, good breakfast."

Hayley didn't respond. Her brain had started to dull again, folding in on itself like crumpled paper. Even with the promise of a hotel bed in Copenhagen, the layers of exhaustion didn't feel like something sleep alone could fix. They were cumulative. Woven into the rhythm of an airline trying to do too much, with too few people, under the pretence of glamour.

JJ seemed to read her silence for what it was. He watched her for a beat, then spoke without his usual humour.

"This job takes everything from you if you let it. Don't let it."

Hayley blinked. That wasn't a line from a safety briefing. That was the voice of someone who'd watched bright-eyed cadets become weary long-haulers, who'd seen careers and marriages buckle under the weight of fuel plans, missed Christmases, and the thousand indignities of an industry that sold dreams and delivered delays.

She nodded slowly, words failing her. Dimitri, for once, said nothing.

****

CHAPTER 18 – The Slap Heard Around the World
Friday 25th June 2021

The flight on the Airbus A321LR between Manston and John F Kennedy was meant to have been a normal one, Hayley knew. She had done this three times now as a stewardess, a trip over the Atlantic, a 24-hour drop back, and then the next day return to Manston and then a pair of short-haul flights to maximise the legal duty hours. It was a schedule that PanEuro had become notorious for—relentless, tight, and occasionally soul-crushing. But Hayley, grateful for the hours and still doggedly pursuing a way back into the flight deck, bore it all with the resilience of someone who had once been closer to her dreams.

Today had started much like the others. She had arrived at Manston in the thin silver light of an early Kent morning, the salt of the sea in the air as she parked in the designated crew area beside a battered Fiat 500. Inside the terminal's staff entrance, Toby was stood there, a frown on his face.

"We've got Roger Hargreaves as Captain today," he said, and Hayley could see the dread on his face as he said that.

Unlike most pilots based at Manston, Hargreaves was known to be a traditional pilot, who, when he joined PanEuro, instantly agreed with the airline's ethos of men on the flight deck, women in the cabin, and not much else. He was a throwback, a fossil from the days when pilots still smoked in cockpits and called flight attendants "girls." Worse still, he was homophobic and also had wandering hands and was not averse to groping stewardesses when they entered the flight deck to serve refreshments to the flight crew.

"He's currently shagging a non-union flight attendant off the Moscow rotation, something about how a 'young, willing, and pliable bird does wonders for a pressurised man.'" Toby had spat the words with barely concealed disgust, his jaw clenched so tight that Hayley feared he might crack a molar.

She knew that the Moscow rotation, officially a Manston flight deck and a Doncaster cabin crew, done because the plane would do Doncaster to Moscow in the morning, and then Moscow to London Manston in the evening, with a different aircraft doing the opposite loop, something to do with Manston having an Airbus technical team, whereas Doncaster was light maintenance, as there were rumours the airport was closing and things would be moving to Leeds-Bradford or Newcastle, was an awkward one, as officially, pilots were one pool where they could be assigned to any route at their base, whereas the cabin crew were fixed on a 3 day on, 3 day off rotation.

This, Hayley knew, meant that she would not be getting any time at the controls, as she had sometimes done, even though, unofficially, and in her personal logbook, she had done 50 hours under "unofficial line training", even though the flight deck was, from the brass who owned the airline, male only and Hargreaves enforced it meticulously.

"Pity Iain, Max, John or one of the others isn't on our flight as Captain today," she muttered, looking at her best friend with a sigh. "I only need another unofficial 150 hours to shed the line check requirements, and then someone like Livingstone, Powers, Jones, Harvester or Lethenshaw could sign me off for completion of line training, so I can get a FO post at Wizz or Easyjet and finally be back where I belong."

Toby looked at her, sympathy tugging at his features as they queued up at the crew checkpoint. "If it makes you feel better," he said in a low murmur, "I had a word with Powers, and he's going to get you, Sarah and a few of the others placements at Easyjet Gatwick. They're hiring now, so he's going to write you all internal references. Said it's time we stop wasting hours with Captain Dinosaur and his airline of Stepford hostesses."

Hayley glanced over, eyes narrowing with a mixture of surprise and cautious hope. "Powers said that?"

Toby nodded, ushering her past the scanner with a practiced flick of his ID badge. "He said he'd seen enough of you flying unofficially to know you've got the chops. You just need to get out before this place sucks out the last bit of joy you've got left."

Hayley didn't reply immediately. It was hard to hope too hard in a place like PanEuro, where the shine of retro glamour was little more than a smokescreen for rot underneath. Instead, she offered a small smile and turned her focus to the flight ahead.

Walking through the crew corridor, Hayley passed under the velvet-framed PanEuro propaganda posters: images of peroxide-blonde stewardesses from the sixties smiling vacantly with martinis, next to slogans like "Style in the Skies" and "Serving Elegance Daily.

Their aircraft that morning, Princess Anne, named after the daughter of HRH Queen Elizabeth II, was parked on stand, nose gleaming under the sunrise, but of course, first up, Hayley knew it was the crew briefing that she needed to sit through—a ritual part pre-flight procedure, part psychological endurance test. Especially when Roger Hargreaves was leading it.

The atmosphere shifted palpably the moment Hargreaves strode in. He was wearing his aviator sunglasses indoors, which he only removed after making an exaggerated show of scrutinising the female cabin crew with a smirk that should have been illegal. A few of the younger stewardesses squirmed slightly. Hayley, sat beside a stone-faced Sarah Marsh—ex-RAF and the only person on the crew list who might survive hand-to-hand combat with the man—made eye contact with Toby, who was deliberately looking down at his tablet, jaw tight.

"Right," Hargreaves began, clapping his hands together like a games master at a girls' boarding school. "Manston to JFK. Eight hours thirty outbound, nine hours forty-five return. Weather's fine over the Atlantic, one jet stream crosswind at FL370, shouldn't be too sporty. We've got ten in Executive, one hundred in Classic, a full hold of cargo, and apparently a baby giraffe in the rear cargo— don't ask, I didn't."

Hayley knew that the A321LR, like the A320, was 7 rows of 2+1 seating in Executive Class and the remainder being 2+2 but she wasn't really listening to the seating arrangement. Not when Hargreaves was prowling the perimeter of the table like a hawk sizing up prey. His voice continued, smooth as melted plastic.

"Now ladies... and queers..." he said, looking at Toby for the latter, "this is a PanEuro flight. Not bloody Ryanair, not a Pride march, and not a goddamn hen do out of Liverpool. So, I expect full poise, full service, and none of the politics, yah? I want heels polished, lipstick matte, smiles on and knees together. We are not here to serve personality; we are here to serve prestige."

There was a beat of silence, the kind that seemed to choke the air from the briefing room. Haylcy's hands curled tightly around the edge of her laminated briefing sheet. Across from her, Sarah Marsh's eyes narrowed a fraction, but the ex-RAF officer didn't speak—yet. She shifted in her seat, subtly straightening her back.

Hargreaves continued, either oblivious or indifferent to the discomfort around him. "Right then. Hayley, you've got front galley, so don't screw up the welcome tray again. Emma, aisles one to ten. Tannie, eleven to twenty. Sarah, rear galley and emergency duties. And remember—any issues with the customers, you nod, you smile, and you report it to me or First Officer Shirtlifter and then go back to your seat. We are not in the business of opinions, objections, or confrontations. That sort of nonsense stays with the Guardian readers on the ground."

Hayley felt the bile rise in her throat, but she kept her expression neutral. Years of training—both in aviation and in surviving male-dominated spaces—had taught her how to weather such moments. Still, there was a pressure building behind her eyes, a flicker of something volcanic. She glanced at Sarah, whose jaw had tightened ever so slightly, her eyes cool and calculating like a fighter pilot waiting to be cleared for take-off. If Hargreaves pushed just a little further, Hayley suspected the RAF might invade.

With the formalities of the briefing done, they moved as a unit out to the tarmac, the team of PanEuro glamour-bound souls in sky-blue coats and retro-heel shoes walking in step towards the Princess Anne, her livery gleaming white and gold with that faintly ridiculous crest emblazoned by the nose. Hayley had always loved this part—the moments before boarding, with the quiet hum of ground crew, the soft hiss of the wind over the apron, the smell of jet fuel catching in her throat.

This, she thought, sighing, *is going to be a long flight.*

* - *- * - *

It was an hour into the flight when it happened, when Hargreaves pushed his luck once too many times.

Hayley had just finished serving the final tray of canapés in Executive and was preparing the soup course—an overly ambitious chilled gazpacho served in glass ramekins too shallow for turbulence and too stylish to be practical. She worked briskly, aware of every passing minute and the subtle way the nose of the aircraft edged further over the vast Atlantic. The lighting in the galley was soft and blue, diffused through the curved plastic that framed the overhead lockers, while the gentle hum of engines offered a strange calm.

She'd just balanced the ramekins on the polished steel service cart when the curtain at the front of the galley was swept aside with the dramatic flourish of a man who thought himself the star of every room he entered.

Roger Hargreaves.

He leaned in the doorway, arms folded, a smug grin on his lips.

"Ah, Northcott. Very attentive today," he said, glancing at her with that leery tone he reserved for stewardesses he thought had 'potential'—a term that, in his world, had nothing to do with aviation skill.

Hayley turned, managing a tight, professional smile. "Service is proceeding on schedule, Captain."

"Good girl," he said. Then, stepping in without invitation, he touched her breast.

And she instantly kneed him, slapped him, and then reached for the duct tape that was in a hidden compartment on the galley's inner wall—the same compartment where cabin crew were trained to keep first-aid kits and security equipment.

The slap was sharp. Not the playful sting of a flirtation rebuffed, not a theatrical stage act, but a full, open-palm, flush-to-the-cheek *crack* that rang out like a gunshot through the front of the cabin. It echoed down the aisle. It silenced the nearest passengers, drew heads from behind first-class partitions and even made the baby in 2A stop crying for a heartbeat.

Hargreaves reeled slightly, clutching the side of his face where five perfect crimson stripes had bloomed. He looked stunned, not because of the pain—though there was likely plenty—but because someone had dared. Someone had, in front of crew and passengers, struck *him*.

"Are you mad, you stupid girl?!" he bellowed, his voice pitched high with disbelief. "You'll never fly again!"

"Good," Hayley replied coldly, her voice steel. "Because if flying means being felt up by a dirty old pervert in uniform, then it's not worth the wings."

Undoing the tape, she knew instantly what she was going to do, she was going to tape his hands and mouth if he tried anything else.

She knew that, as she was restraining the Captain of the flight, Toby would have to know, so he could arrange a divert to Belfast, Shannon or Dublin, as they had barely entered the Atlantic, and so they needed to get onto the ground quickly, as the flight was by a British airline, and so the CAA would investigate immediately. But right now, she didn't care. There was a raw, electric clarity surging through her limbs—adrenaline, justice, and the long-stifled scream of too many silenced women.

She stood firm, shoulders squared, as Hargreaves staggered back against the galley bulkhead. The passengers in Executive were watching now. A businessman in 1A had pulled off his headphones. A woman in 2C clutched her flute of sparkling wine in wide-eyed horror. The cabin was no longer a stage for glossy service and polite smiles—it had become a theatre of confrontation.

And Hayley, burning with years of indignation, had just thrown open the curtain.

Sarah Marsh was there within seconds, her long strides cutting across the carpeted aisle as if she'd been waiting for this very moment. Her jaw was tight, fists clenched, but her voice, when she spoke, was a low, commanding growl.

"What the hell just happened?"

"He assaulted me," Hayley replied, still holding the duct tape. "Touched me. Without consent."

Sarah's eyes flicked to the Captain, who had straightened now and was adjusting his tie like a cartoon villain trying to reassert control.

"She hit me!" he barked. "Assaulting the Captain is mutiny—it's a criminal offence. You're done, Northcott. You're out of aviation. I'll make sure of it!"

Hayley knew that there was a CCTV camera that was in the galley area, as it was right by the cockpit door, and used both as a security and safety measure. It recorded all activity within view of the cockpit, particularly during inflight service when the reinforced cockpit door had to be opened for meal delivery or cabin crew communication. Hayley stepped slightly aside, letting her hand fall to her side as she gestured calmly at the lens overhead.

"Then let the footage speak for itself," she said. "Security feed's running. You want to press charges? Let's do it. Let the CAA, the CAAIB, and the press see exactly what happened. I'll be the face of every training module on boundary violations for the next twenty years. You're finished."

For a long, trembling moment, silence ruled. Hargreaves' nostrils flared. Behind him, one of the curtain flaps fluttered slightly with the movement of the aircraft through a patch of mild chop, but it may as well have been thunder. The moment swelled with something elemental—history grinding slowly into gear, ready to flatten or free.

Then Sarah stepped closer. "We're diverting," she said. "I'll tell Toby. Shannon's the nearest. I've flew a Typhoon there, I know the approach vectors, so if Toby needs a co-pilot, I'll take the right-hand seat and help bring her down."

Hargreaves' eyes widened, mouth gaping. "You can't be serious—you're cabin crew!"

"I was Flight Lieutenant Marsh," Sarah snapped. "RAF No. 6 Squadron, Lossiemouth, so if you ever pull that line again, I'll make sure you're the one grounded. Permanently." Her voice was quiet, steady, and more terrifying than any raised shout. "Am I clear?"

Hargreaves looked at Sarah, and Hayley knew that the feeling of his hand touching her blouse would be the last vestige of power he would ever try to wield in uniform.

His hand dropped. His shoulders sagged. For the first time in his blustering, grotesque career, Roger Hargreaves looked… small.

"Fine," he said, almost spitting the word, though it carried no weight. "Divert. Get your show trial over with."

He turned as if to stride back to the cockpit, but Sarah was already ahead of him, arms folded in front of the flight deck door.

"No. You're not getting near the controls again. You're done."

"Who the hell do you think you are, girl?" Hargreaves snapped.

Hayley saw it then—that twitch in Sarah's jaw, the little crack of restraint that hinted at a woman whose restraint was no longer being rationed for diplomacy's sake. Sarah didn't flinch, didn't move.

"You're relieved of duty, Captain. You're a risk to safety and crew welfare. Toby has command now."

It was as though something ancient broke in the air—like the walls of a stone castle that had withstood generations of abuse had finally given way to floodwater. Hayley didn't realise she was trembling until Sarah touched her gently on the arm and whispered, "Go sit. I've got this."

Hayley nodded, too stunned to speak. The sound of the engines, the ambient cabin announcements, the rustle of seatbelts—it all seemed so far away now. She slipped past the drawn curtain and took a seat in the jump seat by the forward door, the galley still behind her. Her hands were shaking, her mind racing.

But she'd done it.

She'd finally done it.

*_*_*_*

Touching down at Shannon, Hayley turned her phone on and sent a text message to Dani, telling her what had happened. No filters. No euphemism. Just the cold, hard fact.

Hayley Northcott: *Captain groped me inflight. I kneed him in the bollocks and then slapped the wanker. We've diverted to Shannon.*

Hayley knew that her sister would have just finished her pre-flight debriefing from her Virgin Atlantic flight from Heathrow to JFK, and so the reply pinged in barely a minute later.

Dani Northcott: *Jesus Christ. Are you okay? That's bloody disgraceful. Have you informed Dad yet?*

Hayley stared at her screen, fingers trembling, emotions oscillating between fury and a strange sort of catharsis. The events aboard the flight had shaken her more deeply than she initially realised.

Hayley Northcott: *Not yet. Don't know how he'll react.*

Dani's reply was immediate.

Dani Northcott: *He'll back you. Dad might be old-school, but he's never tolerated bullies or bastards. Call me as soon as you can. And stay strong, sis—you've done the right thing. You're a bloody hero.*

Hayley exhaled slowly, letting her sister's words settle over her like a balm. Hero? She certainly didn't feel heroic.

Hayley Northcott: *Thanks. Love you.*

Then she locked the phone again, pocketing it with a sigh as she glanced out the small oval window. Shannon Airport stretched wide and green beneath grey Irish skies, clouds gathered dark and brooding, as if summoned to witness the end of something monumental. In the distance, a solitary Gardaí patrol car had already arrived, blue lights pulsing gently beside the PanEuro Airbus now parked on stand. Ground crew hurried to affix wheel chocks, moving briskly beneath the wings as if the urgency of the moment was contagious.

Hayley looked back down the aisle, now eerily quiet as passengers sat in silent bewilderment. Some murmured softly amongst themselves, heads bent conspiratorially towards neighbours. She wondered how much they'd seen or heard, and how much had rippled through social media already. Soon, the whole world would probably know.

Toby stepped out of the cockpit, his face set in a determined expression. He made eye contact with Hayley, nodded gently, then raised the PA handset. His voice was calm but resolute as it echoed softly through the cabin.

"Ladies and gentlemen, this is your First Officer speaking. Due to an incident involving crew safety, we have diverted to Shannon, Ireland. There's no threat to passenger safety, and we apologise for this unexpected stop. Irish authorities will assist us, and our ground team is already arranging alternative onward travel. We thank you for your understanding and cooperation."

Hayley watched him replace the handset, realising the weight that now rested on his shoulders. A First Officer commandeering a transatlantic flight, removing his Captain mid-route—that was career-defining. Yet Toby had done it without hesitation, drawing a line clearly and decisively.

"You alright?" Sarah approached, her tone softer now, sympathetic eyes reading Hayley carefully.

"Not really," Hayley admitted quietly, her throat tight. "But better now it's done."

****

CHAPTER 19 – Questioning
Friday 25th June 2021

Hayley knew that the Gardaí would come for her first.

Not because she had done anything wrong. She was clear on that. But because that was how it worked. The woman who made the accusation. The woman who struck out. The woman whose slap had rung through the pressurised silence of an Airbus Cabin like a fire alarm. She was the anomaly, and anomalies were always interrogated first.

She stayed in uniform. That was something she clung to. The smart PanEuro skirt, the heels she had sworn at while striding up and down the aisles, the little pillbox hat that had stayed jammed in her crew bag for most of the flight. She brushed down her lapels, fastened her jacket again, and pulled her badge lanyard from where it had been tucked away during service. If she was going to be questioned like a criminal, she would go in looking like a professional.

A pair of officers approached the aircraft stairs with crisp strides and expressions neutral enough to belong in a training manual. They were both young, perhaps mid-thirties, in dark uniforms with high-vis jackets zipped down just far enough to expose their insignia. One of them had a clipboard, the other a voice recorder already primed. Hayley stood by the door, flanked quietly by Sarah, who didn't say a word but made it abundantly clear she wasn't going anywhere unless she was physically moved.

The wind on the steps was cold for June, sharper than it had any right to be at Shannon, where the cloud always seemed to hang low, stubbornly clinging to the runway and soaking everything in a thin, salty mist. As Hayley waited, she watched the Gardaí exchange a word with the ramp agent, who glanced at her, then away again, as if anxious to be uninvolved. She straightened her spine a fraction more, head high. Sarah gave her a subtle nod, the kind of silent encouragement that says: I've got your back.

"Miss Northcott?"

The officer with the voice recorder offered a half-smile, all careful professionalism. His colleague stood just behind, the clipboard tucked in the crook of her elbow. "I'm Detective Sergeant Foley, and this is Garda Dunne. Could we have a word with you, please?"

"Of course." Hayley's voice did not tremble. She stepped forward, letting the wind snatch a stray wisp of hair as she moved. Sarah made as if to follow, but the officers paused her with a gentle shake of the head.

"It'll just be a few minutes, Miss Marsh. You're next, but we'd like to speak to Miss Northcott alone first."

Sarah didn't push. She simply nodded, eyes unwavering, the quiet force of her RAF heritage showing in the set of her jaw. "I'll be here, Hayley."

Walking through the airport, Hayley felt as if she were being treated like a perpetrator and not a victim, even though Foley had told her that she wasn't.

Eventually they arrived at their destination, an interview room within the Gardaí section of Shannon Airport.

Inside the small, draughty interview room set aside for crew debriefs and the occasional drunk footballer, the lights were too bright, bouncing harshly off whitewashed walls and cheap laminate furniture. Hayley was offered a bottle of water, which she accepted but did not open.

Detective Foley set the voice recorder on the table between them. "This is just a statement at this stage," he said quietly. "It isn't a formal interview under caution. We're here to understand what happened onboard. Can you walk us through it?"

Hayley took a steady breath, then another. She began with the boarding at Manston, the crew briefing, the dread that had coiled in her gut the moment Hargreaves had entered the room and started on with his usual jokes and directives. She described the feeling, the sickening certainty of what might happen. She gave them the facts, clinical and clear: Hargreaves had touched her. She had defended herself. She had slapped him. The rest was a blur of shock and adrenaline.

She didn't sugar-coat it, nor did she editorialise. "He put his hand on my breast, Sergeant. Without consent. I reacted. I'm not proud of how, but I'd do it again. I don't want to pretend it didn't happen. And there's CCTV, if you need it."

Foley nodded, making a note. "Were there any prior incidents with Captain Hargreaves?"

Suddenly the door opened, and a man Hayley recognised as PanEuro's Head of Legal, Adam Carter, a slight, grey-templed man in a suit that looked as if it had survived the

Eighties and everything since, stepped in without a care in the world. He carried a battered leather folder, the sort that seemed purpose-built for bad news. He didn't try to sit; he hovered just behind Hayley's left shoulder, deliberately close enough for her to feel his presence, but far enough away that it couldn't be construed as intimidation. Hayley didn't know whether to be relieved or appalled.

"Gentlemen, this interview stops immediately," he said, without any preamble. "Miss Northcott is under a NDA which means that she cannot, without the permission of PanEuro Airlines Limited, comment on any alleged incidents relating to the conduct of flight crew, ongoing HR matters, or reputationally sensitive events, including but not limited to those which might lead to disciplinary action or criminal proceedings, without representation or prior approval from the company. I'm sure you understand."

Detective Sergeant Foley did not move the recorder. He didn't even blink, but his tone took on the crisp, iron calm of someone well used to being stonewalled by men in suits. "We are currently investigating an incident which occurred within Irish jurisdiction, Mr Carter. Miss Northcott is not under arrest, and she has not been cautioned. This is a preliminary statement. Her rights to legal counsel are not in dispute. But PanEuro's internal policies are subordinate to Irish law."

Carter gave a tight, corporate smile. "Then I will be filing an injunction with the Irish courts by the end of business today, should this interview proceed without a company representative present."

Carter then fixed Hayley with a look that was supposed to be reassuring, but was too carefully neutral to be of any comfort. "For your own sake, Miss Northcott, I should not answer any questions, should you wish to avoid being subject to a lawsuit for breach of confidentiality. I'm sure the Gardaí understand we all want the best for our crew."

Hayley fought the urge to roll her eyes, biting down the childish retort that trembled on her tongue. The man's loyalty was not to her, not even to the facts. It was to PanEuro's bottom line, to the reputation that might yet weather one more storm, provided it could keep the truth at bay. She had seen enough company briefings, enough risk management memos, to know exactly how this would play out: delay, deny, defend. Always in that order.

Detective Foley kept his gaze steady on her. "Miss Northcott, you're entitled to legal advice. You're not obliged to say anything without it, but equally, you're not obliged to comply with a company NDA that prevents you from reporting a crime. If you wish, we can pause the statement while you speak to your representative, or you can continue. It's entirely up to you."

The battle lines were suddenly, chillingly clear.

Hayley knew that she didn't want Carter anywhere near her, that the non-disclosure agreement that she had signed was just another line in a handbook meant to protect the company, not her. She also knew that the Gardaí, here in neutral Ireland, weren't interested in playing corporate games or company politics. In this room, with the harsh light and the cheap water and the dull thud of her heart in her chest, she realised that this was the line in the sand. If she backed down now, if she allowed herself to be silenced by a legal document drawn up in a London office, the story would be told without her, and it would not be one she recognised.

She took a careful breath, then looked directly at Detective Foley. "I would like to finish my statement. I am reporting a crime, and I will deal with PanEuro's lawyers later."

Carter's mouth opened as if to protest, but something in Foley's gaze—a silent, iron patience—warned him off. The Head of Legal gave a small, infuriated sigh, flicked his folder closed, and retreated to the corner. He stayed, watching, making notes with a pen that never seemed to move quickly enough to keep up with his agitation.

Hayley resumed her statement. She explained, as simply as she could, the pattern: how Hargreaves had a reputation among the crew, how she and others had learned to avoid him, to whisper warnings about which flights he was rostered for, how the culture of PanEuro enabled him. She described how, in the moment, she had not felt like she had a choice. "If you don't stand up," she said, her voice taut with the effort not to cry, "it just happens again. Maybe to someone younger. Maybe to someone who can't say no."

Foley listened with the sort of focus that suggested he had heard this before, too many times. "Thank you, Miss Northcott. You say there is CCTV. Is that something your airline has custody of?"

Hayley nodded. "The galley cameras. By the cockpit door. I know for a fact they run all the time the cockpit is locked or being serviced. It'll be on there."

Foley made a note, and Dunne, the younger officer with the clipboard, added, "We'll request the footage through the proper channels."

Carter, from his perch in the corner, interjected at last. "That footage is the property of PanEuro Airlines and subject to data protection laws."

Foley didn't even look at him. "And subject to a criminal investigation in the Republic of Ireland. If you do not comply with our request, we will seize the recording. I'm sure you understand, Mr Carter."

There was a taut silence in the room. Hayley realised, almost with relief, that she was not the only one tired of being managed by men like Carter.

The questions continued. "Did you feel threatened before today?" "Had Captain Hargreaves ever touched you before?" "Did you see anyone else witness the incident?" Hayley answered each, calm, factual, never straying into drama. When she finished, Foley thanked her quietly and said, "You may have to stay local tonight. If you need a safe hotel, we can arrange it. There's an official from the British consulate coming to assist with your rights and any support you need."

Hayley nodded, the adrenaline ebbing now, leaving her hollow. She was led from the room, back out into the echoing linoleum corridor, where Sarah waited, arms folded, like a sentinel. "You alright?" Sarah murmured.

"Getting there," Hayley managed. She blinked hard, willing herself not to collapse now, not in front of anyone. "Just need to have a few days to relax and hopefully get my head in the game."

* - * - * - *

Hayley and Sarah sat side by side in a small, sterile waiting area near the Gardaí offices in Shannon Airport. The room felt like every other airport backroom Hayley had seen: overly bright lights, plastic chairs bolted to the floor, and the stale air of institutional coffee and bleach. Outside, through a narrow strip of reinforced glass, Shannon's apron bustled with routine aviation movements—a stark contrast to the chaos unfolding inside Hayley's life.

"I didn't realise how tired I was," Hayley murmured, rubbing her temples.

Sarah offered a sympathetic glance. "Adrenaline crash. Happens after combat flights too. One minute you're flying high on clarity, next minute it's like hitting turbulence at Mach one."

Hayley allowed herself a faint smile. "I never imagined I'd end up in a Gardaí interrogation room. I mean, I knew PanEuro was retro, but this feels medieval."

Sarah shifted, stretching her legs out in front of her, heels squeaking against the polished floor. "At least it's real police asking the questions—not some PanEuro kangaroo court."

Hayley grimaced. "I think I'd prefer the kangaroo at this point. That lawyer was worse than useless."

A door opened sharply, cutting off their conversation. Adam Carter emerged, his demeanour icy as he approached them. "Miss Marsh, you're next."

Sarah stood smoothly, her posture impeccable, eyes unwavering. Carter's eyes flickered over her briefly, clearly evaluating how much trouble she might cause. "Please remember—"

Sarah interrupted calmly, her voice cool. "With respect, Mr Carter, I'm well aware of my obligations. I don't require guidance on how to report truthfully."

Carter's face darkened slightly, but he stepped aside, lips thinning into a tight line as Sarah moved past him, shooting Hayley a quick reassuring glance. "Be right back."

Hayley watched the door close, feeling strangely vulnerable without Sarah's reassuring presence. Alone now, her thoughts spiralled into uncomfortable territory. Had she really just destroyed her own career? Would PanEuro truly dare to sue her, to bury the incident beneath layers of litigation? She knew what had happened, knew she'd acted rightly, but rightness rarely mattered in aviation politics. Especially at PanEuro.

The silence stretched on. Hayley fumbled in her crew bag, pulling out her phone. The notifications had exploded— text messages, missed calls, and WhatsApp alerts from crew members who'd clearly heard rumours already spreading through Manston and Doncaster. She ignored them all, instead opening Dani's message again.

Dani had always been the more decisive sister, and in moments like this, Hayley envied that. Her sister's certainty that their father, Alan Northcott—ex-BA Captain, and rigorously old-school—would back her felt oddly comforting. But the thought of confronting her father with this mess brought another wave of nausea.

Finally, she tapped her father's number. The phone rang once, twice, three times.

"Hayley?" Alan's voice was calm, familiar, instantly grounding. "I saw your sister's message. Are you alright?"

"No," she admitted, her voice faltering for the first time. "Not really. I've caused a diversion, Dad. Slapped a Captain who assaulted me."

There was a pause—brief, but weighty. "Are you safe now?" Alan's voice was softer, fatherly, devoid of judgment.

"Yes," she said quietly. "I'm with the Gardaí at Shannon."

Alan exhaled slowly, carefully. "Hayley, listen closely. You did the right thing. Full stop. No matter what PanEuro's HR drones tell you. Anyone who lays hands on crew forfeits his stripes. You're a Northcott. We don't apologise for standing up."

Relief rushed through her chest like oxygen after a depressurisation. "Thank you, Dad."

"I'm on my way. Stay put, Hayley. We'll face this together."

Hayley blinked tears away, grateful for her father's swift decisiveness. "See you soon."

She ended the call, staring numbly at the floor. Alan's words resonated like a gentle echo, reinforcing her shaky resolve. It was the first real glimmer of hope in a day rapidly descending into chaos.

* _ * _ * _ *

The hours blurred into monotony. Sarah returned from her questioning, coolly composed, giving Hayley a thumbs-up. Other crew members filtered in and out, their interviews shorter, less fraught. Finally, a Garda came over, offering to escort them to the hotel arranged by PanEuro.

Stepping outside, the Shannon sky had darkened to slate grey, the wind cooler now, cutting through Hayley's thin uniform jacket. The hotel shuttle waited, its driver looking bored, oblivious to the turmoil unfolding among his passengers.

Arriving at the hotel felt surreal. Hayley's mind was foggy from exhaustion. Her room was blandly corporate, with crisp sheets and anonymous décor. She sat numbly on the edge of the bed, realising she was still clutching her lanyard, the PanEuro logo mocking her silently.

Opening her laptop that was in her suitcase, she logged onto the easyJet website, where, a few days earlier, she had filed an application to re-join their training program, s she had only needed the line training element of it to be complete, and she was then a fully signed off First Officer. After all, she had done the Ground School, the A320 type rating and the majority of things, it was just the final elements of line training before she could be free to fly.

The easyJet application screen stared back at Hayley, impersonal yet oddly comforting, its bright orange banner almost aggressive in its optimism. It felt surreal to return here after everything that had unfolded. A week ago, applying for a cockpit role had seemed like an act of quiet rebellion—a way to reclaim control over her aviation destiny. Now, after today, it felt like her only escape route from the stifling confines of PanEuro's backward-looking culture.

She scrolled slowly through her application details, scanning the neatly organised sections of flight experience, qualifications, and references. Toby had promised that Captain Adrian Powers had already vouched for her and Sarah. He'd said it with such conviction earlier that day, and yet now, with the adrenaline ebbing and fatigue setting in, doubt whispered cruelly in her mind.

Would easyJet even want her now? Would anyone want a pilot candidate who'd slapped a captain mid-flight? Aviation was a small, tightly knit world, and news travelled faster than a Concorde. Even if she'd acted rightly—heroically, according to Dani—reputations were fragile things. She was branded now, whether she liked it or not, as trouble.

She logged out, snapping the laptop closed with a frustrated sigh. She knew there was nothing more she could do tonight. The fatigue that clawed at her bones felt heavier now, amplified by the sterile anonymity of the hotel room. But her mind wouldn't stop spinning, replaying every moment of the incident in excruciating clarity.

A sharp knock at the door pulled her back into the present. Heart thudding, she opened it cautiously. Toby stood there, holding a 16 inch pizza, a wry smile on his face.

"Room service for the world's bravest stewardess-slash-pilot-in-waiting," he said, voice low but coloured with a kind warmth that threatened to unravel Hayley entirely. "I thought you might be running on fumes."

Hayley stepped aside to let him in, her gratitude wordless. Toby moved with the tired fluidity of a man who'd done three sectors in a day, but even he looked hollowed out by the gravity of what had happened. He set the pizza on the small table beside the window, glancing out at the brooding Irish dusk.

Neither of them reached for the food right away. Hayley perched on the edge of the bed, hands clasped tightly, and Toby sat down across from her, elbows on his knees.

"Well," he said after a moment, "that was a day for the logbook, eh?"

Hayley snorted, a brittle sound that still managed to be more laughter than sob. "I don't think they have a section in the logbook for 'diverted due to sexual assault, mutiny, and world-class slapping'."

Toby managed a smile. "Maybe they should. Christ, Hayley, I've seen some messes, but… he deserved it. You know that, right? Don't let anyone, not Carter, not some stuffed shirt in Manston, tell you otherwise."

She nodded, biting her lip. "I just—" The dam threatened to burst, so she steeled herself, forcing the words to be careful, measured. "I keep thinking about what's next. Not just for me. For everyone. For you, for Sarah, the rest of the crew. What if—what if PanEuro comes after us all? What if this is the end?"

Toby's eyes softened. "PanEuro can try all they like, but we've got the truth on our side. The CCTV. Witnesses. Even the bloody passengers, half of whom probably already posted about it before we landed. And anyway," he shrugged, "do you really want to keep flying for a place where this is even a worry?"

The silence between them hummed with mutual understanding. It was Sarah who had said it best earlier, as they'd sat in the waiting area: sometimes you have to lose everything before you can start to rebuild. Hayley found herself wondering if this was what rebuilding looked like—pale hotel lights, cardboard-tasting pizza, and exhaustion that scraped right down to the bone.

They ate in companionable silence, each lost in their own thoughts, chewing methodically, as if simply processing calories could somehow replenish the soul as well as the body. When the pizza was gone, Toby wiped his hands on a napkin and turned to her.

"There's a rumour," he said, voice suddenly lighter, conspiratorial, "that Captain Hargreaves has already called every union rep in the book. Trying to claim he was the one attacked, that you assaulted him unprovoked. But—" He lifted a hand, forestalling her protest, "—the Gardaí aren't idiots. And neither are we."

Hayley's anger spiked, then fizzled into resignation. "It's what I expected. He'll spin it, say I'm unstable, emotional. That I brought shame to the uniform." She looked down at her own lapels, at the neat rows of wings and the faux-gold buttons. "But this—this isn't the uniform I want to wear anymore. Not if it means swallowing it all down just to stay in the air."

Toby gave a small, sad smile. "No one joins for the uniforms, Hayley. We join because flying's in the blood. Whatever logo's on your chest, it's you who's got the right stuff. PanEuro can't take that away."

"I know Toby, but I'm just worried about how my application to easyJet would look now, after all this."

She trailed off, staring at the remnants of the pizza, the greasy box and the slightly burnt crusts a stark reminder of reality's messiness. She felt the sting of injustice—the sense that even when you did everything right, the world had a way of punishing you for standing your ground.

Toby leaned forward, his elbows on his knees, voice soft but steady. "Look, if easyJet has any sense at all, they'll see exactly what happened. And if they don't—well, then sod them. Someone else will. There's not a pilot or cabin crew in Europe who wouldn't back you up after today, Hayley. You know that, don't you?"

She wanted to believe him. She really did. But faith came hard, in the sterile quiet of a chain hotel room, far from home, with her career on a knife-edge and the sharp tang of betrayal still burning in her mouth. She thought of the way Hargreaves had looked at her—like something disposable, like a thing he could use and discard. Then she thought of Sarah, of Toby, and her father's words, resolute and fierce and loving, cutting through the gloom like a searchlight.

"I hope you're right," she whispered.

Toby squeezed her shoulder. "I am. And if not, we'll just set up our own bloody airline. Call it Northcott Airways. Motto: 'Touch the crew, get the shoe.'"

She managed a weak smile at that. "You can be CEO. I'll just sit in the left-hand seat and never, ever, let a Captain like Hargreaves on board."

"Deal," Toby grinned, eyes bright. "I'll make a flight safety video starring Sarah. She'd terrify the CAA."

A wave of fatigue washed over her—real, bone-deep, the kind that comes not from hours on duty but from the sudden, shattering collapse of everything familiar. She ran a hand through her hair, feeling the tangles, the sweat and tiredness and ache of a day that seemed it would never end.

"I need to shower," she said softly. "And sleep, if I can."

Toby nodded, rising with the easy grace of a man used to making exits. "I'll leave you to it, then. Ring me if you need anything. Seriously. Even if it's just to tell me to bugger off."

"Thank you, Toby," she said, meaning it more than she could ever express. He smiled, lingering in the doorway a moment, then let himself out, leaving her alone once more.

Hayley moved through the motions—unpacking the smallest things, a toothbrush, her toiletries, laying out tomorrow's clothes with the mechanical precision that had kept her sane through countless time zones and crew hotels. The shower was scorching hot, the pressure just enough to pummel her skin clean of the day. She stood beneath it, eyes closed, letting the water wash away the tears she refused to shed in front of anyone else.

Afterwards, she curled up on the bed, still in her PanEuro pyjamas—navy blue, with a tiny embroidered logo that felt more like a scar than a brand. She tried to sleep, but her mind replayed the day in staccato bursts—boarding, briefing, Hargreaves' sneer, the shock of his touch, the slap, the aftermath. She heard her own voice, trembling and strong, telling the truth in the Gardaí interview room. She saw Sarah's steady presence, Toby's concern, the endless, unspooling anxiety about what would come next.

When sleep finally claimed her, it was fitful and brief, haunted by dreams of flying—a cockpit empty but for herself, the sky outside black as pitch, a warning light blinking red in the corner of her vision.

One that would not go away.

****

CHAPTER 20 – Suspension
Saturday 22nd June 2021

The email that Hayley had received was not what she had expected at all. After all, when, the day before, you slap a Captain, ignore the orders of the Head of Legal and a NDA that you never properly read, and find yourself sitting in a cheap Irish airport hotel, you tend to expect an email filled with HR-speak, bullet points, and "regrettable but necessary" wording. What you do not expect is an email that determines the next two weeks of your employment

From: *acarter@paneuro.aero*

To: *hales34314bleak@hotmail.com*

Subject: *Suspension of Employment and Suspension of Employment and Notice of Investigation*

Hayley read the subject line again, as if, by re-reading, she might find some subtlety she'd missed—a softened edge, a get-out clause, a hint of solidarity. But Adam Carter, Head of Legal at PanEuro, was nothing if not precise. She could imagine him, at his desk in the glass-walled office at Manston, tie tight, eyes fixed on a regulation font. She pictured his fingers on the keyboard, not quite touching as he dictated to a junior, his sentences cold and efficient.

"Dear Miss Northcott,

Following the incident that occurred on PE001 Manston–JFK, you are hereby suspended from all duties with immediate effect, pending the outcome of a full internal investigation.

Please do not attend PanEuro premises or contact other employees during this period.

You will be contacted in due course with further details of the investigation.

Regards,

Adam Carter

Head of Legal, PanEuro"

The words seemed to blur as she read them again, her heart pounding, knuckles white where she clutched her phone. She lay back on the pillow in the hotel room—a room with sickly yellow light, walls too thin, and a single window that looked out onto a car park still slick with Irish rain. She could hear the distant thunk of trolleys and the flat laughter of a stag party downstairs.

Suspended. Not sacked. Not yet.

Hayley tried to parse the relief from the humiliation, and found only exhaustion. Every muscle ached from the adrenalin of the day before: the slap, the interrogation, the hour in the windowless room at Shannon Airport with the Gardaí and Adam Carter, the knowledge that her future in aviation now hung by a thread. She forced herself up, knees creaking, feeling every bit the displaced pilot, the stewardess in exile.

She checked the time. 05:34. Barely four hours' sleep since she'd fallen into the bed, uniform skirt abandoned on the chair, jacket hung askew. The little travel kettle gurgled as she made a tea, hands trembling slightly as she poured. The room was silent except for the distant hum of a motorway and the occasional gust of wind rattling the window. Her mind, still racing through possibilities and regrets, seemed louder than all of it—a kind of tinnitus of what-ifs and half-remembered radio calls. Hayley Northcott, suspended. She let the words settle as the steam curled around her face.

For a moment, she considered phoning her father, or Dani, or even Theo, but the urge passed. What could she say that would make any of this easier? That she'd finally stood up for herself—and been sent packing for her trouble? That a man who'd groped her mid-flight was likely still on PanEuro's books, while she was not? The thought stung, a blend of anger and shame that threatened to spill over if she lingered too long.

The tea was strong and bitter, but she forced herself to drink it, savouring the heat. It was something to do. In the silent, airless cocoon of her hotel room, Hayley willed herself to move—first to shower, then to dress in yesterday's jeans and a borrowed Ryanair T-shirt (a joke from Dani, never worn until now). She glanced at her PanEuro blazer, slumped forlornly across the back of a chair, and turned away.

The morning stretched ahead, featureless and undefined. She had no return ticket, no plan, no reason to linger in the terminal beyond the uneasy knowledge that she was persona non grata.

Checking SkyScanner for flights, she decided that, if she was being suspended, then she might as well fly on some random flight to somewhere, hoping that the ID90 that

PanEuro had given her, as she was still technically an employee, would still work. The idea of sitting idle in Shannon, stewing in her own frustration, was intolerable. Anywhere was better than here—anywhere, she thought, where she might feel less like a criminal and more like herself.

Noticing an Aer Lingus flight back to Heathrow, Hayley knew that as her dad was a BA Captain, and BA and Aer Lingus were part of the same labyrinthine alliance, she might just be able to charm her way onto a standby seat.

Hayley Northcott: *Dad, do you know what's on the EI SNN-LHR later?*

Alan Northcott: *Should be an A320, departs 09:25. Why?*

Hayley Northcott: *Been suspended by PanEuro. Don't suppose you heard from Dani what's happened?*

Alan Northcott: *No, I've just come off a long-haul and haven't spoken to her yet. Suspended? Are you alright?*

Hayley Northcott: *Yeah, apparently slapping a captain who decided my breasts were an in-flight navigational aid isn't quite the career move the manuals recommend.*

Alan Northcott: *Christ, Hayley. Want me to fly out?*

Hayley Northcott: *No, Dad. Not unless you fancy a full Irish at Shannon departures and a coffee that tastes of jet fuel. I'll get myself back. Can you ping crew travel for a standby on EI384?*

Alan Northcott: *Give me ten minutes.*

Hayley placed her phone face down on the thin duvet and exhaled, the adrenaline finally draining away and leaving only the prickling aftertaste of shame and indignation. She closed her eyes, tried to slow her breathing. She pictured the cockpit, the gentle green glow of the panels, the comforting certainty of levers and dials, the world ordered and comprehensible, unlike the Kafkaesque disaster her career had become. She missed it so much it hurt.

She was showered, dressed, and drinking a second cup of aggressively black tea when her phone pinged again.

Alan Northcott: *You're on the list. They're tight today—looks like a decent load, but there's always the odd no-show. You'll need to be at the gate by 08:50 latest. Want me to ring Dani?*

Hayley hesitated, thumb hovering over the reply icon. She wanted Dani's comfort, but she also wanted to keep this mess contained—at least until she knew what happened next.

Hayley Northcott: *Not yet. I'll let you know when I'm home. Any chance of a lift from LHR, or are you back home yet? Otherwise its hire a car, or get a NX into Victoria and one to Canterbury.*

Alan Northcott: *I'll be around Waterside until 12, as I've got BALPA rep work to do, so I'll pick you up if you text me when you land.*

Hayley set her mug down, savouring the comfort that came with knowing someone, at least, was in her corner. The thought of her father at Waterside, BA lanyard around his neck, making phone calls on her behalf—it was at once reassuring and oddly infantilising. But today, she'd take any kindness she could get, even if it was just a text promising a ride home.

Packing her few belongings was a matter of shoving things into her bag with little care for neatness. The PanEuro blazer she folded carefully, almost ritualistically, and buried beneath her jeans and a leftover crew jumper. There was a strange finality in the gesture: as though she were not just leaving Ireland, but putting her entire career as a stewardess on ice, along with everything else the last months had contained.

Heading to the shower, she took a moment to study herself in the mirror, steam fogging the glass, her reflection ghostlike in the early morning light. The face that stared back at her was drawn, the under-eye circles showing the tiredness that she was suffering, the irony that, had she been flying, she would have called fatigue due to minimum rest. She gave a thin, humourless smile, thinking how even her own personal standards for fitness to fly had been eroded by the past 24 hours, from boarding the flight at Manston to the moment her palm met Hargreaves' jowl, that shocking flash of contact echoing over and over in her mind. Her hair, once perfect per PanEuro's draconian grooming manual, was in wild curls; her eyes, green and flecked with amber, looked both older and sharper than she remembered. The marks of one long, unsparing day in aviation.

* _ * _ * _ *

Walking up to the ticket desk, Hayley held the details that her dad had sent her of the flight, along with her passport and her PanEuro crew ID—tucking the latter deep into her bag, not keen to advertise the name of an airline now suspended her in disgrace. She could feel a prickle of nerves beneath her skin as she approached the Aer Lingus desk, the functional, quietly harried young man behind the plexiglass barely glancing up from his terminal.

"Morning," she said, mustering the clipped cheerfulness of a seasoned non-rev, "I've been advised there's a standby reservation for EI384, name on the list under Northcott, H.," she continued smoothly, smiling the bland, practiced smile of crew everywhere trying not to look like trouble.

The man flicked his eyes up, registered the name, then down again to the keyboard with the apathy of someone who'd already dealt with five people late for their Ryanair flights, one irate pensioner demanding a refund for a cancelled jet, and at least one sozzled hen party confusing Shannon with Stansted.

"Yeah. You're there. Space might open up. Go to Gate 7A around boarding. That's about half eight. Flight's showing on time."

"Thanks," Hayley said, and moved off before he could change his mind or ask questions. Gate 7A. She checked the airport screens. Still listed. No gate change. Boarding 08:50. So far, so survivable.

She made her way to security, keeping her head down, the weight of her crew ID like a guilty badge in her pocket. She could hear the tinny clang of the trays, the occasional barked instruction from security staff, and the sound of wheels dragging across linoleum. Everything felt oddly heightened, as if her senses had become too sharp, too attuned to any hint of danger or exposure.

She passed through with the ease of someone who'd done this hundreds of times—shoes off, liquids out, laptop separate. She didn't even flinch when the metal detector buzzed; just spread her arms and let the bored security woman wave her down with the wand.

Inside airside, she bought herself a croissant that looked better than it tasted and a bottle of overpriced water, then found a seat near the windows where she could watch the ground crews move about beneath the leaden grey Irish sky. There was something comforting about the choreography—fuel trucks and baggage carts, orange-vested men waving their marshalling wands like symphony conductors. Here, at least, was something that made sense. Movement, routine, purpose.

By the time the gate opened, she was one of a knot of maybe fifteen non-revs and standbys lingering near the front, clutching coffee cups and phones like talismans. The gate agent began calling names, ticking them off, and Hayley felt her pulse pick up with every syllable.

Finally—finally—"Northcott? Miss Hayley Northcott?"

She stepped forward.

"You're in luck. 1 Alpha alright for you?" the gate agent asked and Hayley knew that 1A meant business class—Aer Lingus's version, which, on the A320, was little more than a normal seat with a spare place beside you and a few inches more legroom, but to Hayley, after the last twenty-four hours, it felt like the height of luxury. She tried not to look too relieved, offering a thank you with just enough warmth to pass as polite, and headed down the jet bridge. The familiarity of the aircraft, the scent of jet fuel and the distant whine of APU bleed air, brought her a peculiar, aching comfort.

She tucked herself into 1A, stowed her bag, and buckled in, letting her head rest back as the world outside the window bustled and moved, perfectly indifferent to the dramas of one weary, out-of-uniform stewardess. The cabin filled with the usual murmur of boarding— businessmen, a retired couple, a harried woman with a toddler who glared at Hayley as if pre-emptively apologising for any tantrums. Hayley offered a tired smile, her mind drifting between the present and the sting of yesterday's events.

A male cabin crew member came down the aisle, smiling with the particular bland cheeriness of a professional well into his shift. "Welcome aboard. Tea or coffee before take-off?"

"Tea, please," Hayley replied automatically, the ritual comfortingly familiar. She tucked her feet under her, closed her eyes for a moment, and allowed herself—just for a heartbeat—to imagine that she was a passenger on holiday, not a suspended employee adrift between disasters.

The safety demonstration was a background hum; she could have recited it backwards in her sleep. The engines spooled up, the aircraft nudged away from the gate, and Hayley felt the gentle thrum of power running through the airframe as the plane taxied out towards the runway. For a moment, as the aircraft turned at the threshold, she pressed her palm flat against the armrest, feeling the old, bright surge of anticipation: the promise of escape, of movement, of a new horizon, even if only for an hour.

As the Airbus rotated, Hayley felt a strange sense of weightlessness, more emotional than physical, as though the suspension from PanEuro had left her untethered, floating above her own life. She gazed down as the fields of the west coast slipped by beneath the wing, waterlogged and green, and wondered where she would land next, in every sense.

The in-flight service was perfunctory—no silver trays or linen, just a croissant, a hot drink, and a courteous word. Hayley ate and drank, her mind half-blank with fatigue, half-racing with plans and contingencies. What did you do when the airline you'd broken yourself for suddenly broke you back? Where did you go when home wasn't the sky, or Manston, or even your family home in Broadstairs, right near Bleak House of all places? She pressed her face to the window, breathing shallowly, feeling more like a stowaway than a passenger. Every bump in the sky was a nudge: What now? What next?

* _ * _ * _ *

Hayley knew that, due to the terminal closures at Heathrow due to the pandemic, Aer Lingus, was joining its stablemates within IAG, Iberia and BA, in the "fortress" terminal of Terminal 5—a quiet irony that had not escaped her, considering its long history of BA dominance and the bitter jokes among crews that you could get lost inside and never be seen again. She gathered her things quickly, keeping her head down as she passed through the cabin, giving a nod of thanks to the Aer Lingus crew, who barely registered her as anything but another harried, slightly rumpled non-rev. Disembarking into the glass-walled pier, she was hit by the sour tang of disinfectant and the hollow acoustics of a terminal half-empty, the pandemic's echo everywhere: shuttered Pret a Mangers, vinyl arrows on the floor, Perspex screens and the Tannoy's hollow bark of "Face coverings must be worn at all times."

Border control was efficient, her British passport waved through the e-gates. She was in that strange post-flight limbo: at home, but not home, her fate still undecided. She kept her phone close, checking for a message from her father. As she walked the long, echoing corridors of Terminal 5—glass and steel, too much light, the silent shuffle of passengers with nowhere in particular to hurry—she couldn't help but feel like a ghost haunting her own life.

Her phone buzzed.

Alan Northcott: *Should be finished in an hour. I've got a meeting with the big bosses over the usual pay and conditions drama.*

Hayley chuckled, as she knew that when it came to British Airways, and pay and conditions, there was no such thing as "finished in an hour"—the entire history of modern aviation seemed to be written in the time BA and its unions had spent squabbling in the walls of Waterside. Still, it meant she had some time to kill.

She found a seat near one of the big windows overlooking the apron, where a parade of A320s and the odd 787 shimmered under the low, pewter-coloured clouds of a London morning. Hayley sat with her knees tucked up, clutching her bag like a talisman, letting her mind drift in and out of the moment. Around her, Terminal 5 was both eerily quiet and, in pockets, suddenly loud—an American family wrangling children, the hiss and clatter of a distant cleaning crew, the crackle of a Tannoy announcing a flight to nowhere she wanted to be.

Her phone sat on the armrest, silent. She toyed with the idea of checking the aviation news, but couldn't face it: too many headlines about strikes, COVID, the odd union mutiny or summer meltdown. She closed her eyes and tried to listen to the quiet instead.

Of course, she had only been sat five minutes when a Metropolitan Police officer, in the distinctive blue vest and slightly scuffed shoes that bespoke far too many hours patrolling the airport, wandered up the concourse and paused in her eyeline. Hayley tensed instinctively, fighting the urge to shrink back or look guilty—never mind that she hadn't done anything wrong, not here. The sense of being on the wrong side of authority lingered from yesterday, like the bruise on her palm from Hargreaves' stubbled jaw.

The officer, a woman perhaps in her late thirties, made eye contact, nodded, then walked on. Hayley let out a breath she hadn't realised she was holding. In her exhausted state, every encounter felt like a threat. She caught herself in the reflection of the window: hair still wild, skin sallow, eyes ringed and wary. She looked like any other lost young woman in transit—a survivor of some unspoken disaster, but no longer the centre of attention.

For a few long minutes, she watched the ground crews ballet-dance their way around a newly-arrived Dreamliner. The ritual was soothing: Hi-Viz jackets moving in unison, fuel trucks weaving amongst catering vans, baggage hatches yawning open and shut. There was something about it that steadied her, even if she could not be a part of it for now.

Her phone vibrated with a new message.

Dani Northcott: *Heard from Dad you're at T5. I'm doing a VS out of JFK in a bit, and its lightly loaded still, so want anything from Upper Class, as it'd otherwise be wasted. I've also got some Delta goodies if you want some.*

Hayley grinned at her sister's message, heart squeezing with a cocktail of affection and envy. Dani, always on the move, thriving in her own way—Upper Class banquets and Delta's American quirks, a world away from yellow-lit Irish hotel rooms and punitive HR emails. For a second, Hayley could taste the freedom, the heady mix of exhaustion and exhilaration that came with long-haul: a world she'd once been certain she'd inhabit, before COVID, before PanEuro, before everything had gone so utterly sideways.

She replied, trying to sound casual:

Hayley Northcott: *If you can pilfer any of those mini salt-and-pepper shakers, I'm starting a collection. And a* *proper teabag, not whatever Aer Lingus calls "breakfast blend." See you soon, jetsetter. x*

She hit send, then tucked her phone away, curling deeper into her seat. There was a time when this—waiting in an airport, watching planes from behind glass—had filled her with longing, the ache of anticipation for what was next. Now, suspended in every sense of the word, she felt only the weary patience of someone who knows the world won't move for her, not this time.

Hayley drifted in and out of reverie, the sterile comfort of Terminal 5 serving as both sanctuary and prison. For years, airports had been portals—promises of elsewhere, of upward movement, of another city or continent awaiting just past the clouds. Today, the liminality of the place pressed in on her: she was neither crew nor passenger, neither sacked nor secure, not even sure whether she belonged on the landside or airside of her own life. The seat, narrow and hard under her, might have been a pew in some secular church devoted to delay and lost time.

She checked the clock on her phone—just after ten. Another hour to kill. In a fit of something close to restlessness, she stood and wandered the length of the pier, rolling her neck and stretching out stiff legs. She passed closed shops—Mulberry, Tiffany, shut up tight like dreams she couldn't afford. Even Boots had the atmosphere of a place waiting for a new shift, shelves pillaged by anxious travellers for last-minute masks and paracetamol. She drifted into WHSmiths, scanned the headlines (COVID. Delays. Football. More COVID), and bought a bottle of water with the change in her pocket. It tasted faintly of plastic.

The departures board scrolled through the day's exodus. Malaga. Nice. Berlin. Helsinki. Lisbon. Even now, at the ragged end of June 2021, the illusion of normality lingered: families in shorts, a scattering of businessmen, the odd couple in matching luggage. But to Hayley, every announcement, every flicker of a gate change, felt like another reminder of her exile. She was an aviator grounded—not by the weather, but by the fallout of doing what was right.

She found herself back by the window, knees up on the vinyl, watching a 777 push back in the rain. She tracked the subtle ballet of the tow truck, the perfect choreography of the headset guy, the slow, cautious nod of the captain's salute through the windscreen. That language, silent but exact, was hers—except it wasn't, not today, not for as long as PanEuro wanted her silenced, invisible, out of mind.

She took a long, deliberate breath, reaching into her bag for her battered notebook—the one she'd started in her earliest days as an easyJet cadet. It was creased, stuffed with boarding passes, dog-eared, the spine cracked and half the pages a palimpsest of SOPs, weather codes, and crude caricatures of airline managers. She let the pen hover, then wrote:

22/6/21

Terminal 5, in exile.

First time suspended, first time for violence. Am I proud?

Not sure. Angry, yes. Tired, always. Would do it again?

Probably. Hargreaves deserved worse.

Dad says I did the right thing. I know I did. But what if "the right thing" costs you your wings?

Dani's in New York again. I'm jealous, but glad she's out there—someone's got to be.

What's left if they sack me and easyJet say no because of it? Freelance flying? Teaching? Bloody aviation journalism?

Would rather flip burgers than pour another PanEuro gin & tonic for a creep in 3A.

I miss the sky.

Her handwriting was spidery, the ink smudged by the heel of her hand as she wrote, but the act steadied her. She closed the book and slipped it away, allowing herself to drift for a while—lost in the simple comfort of watching jets rise and bank into the grey.

A movement in her peripheral vision brought her back— her father, Alan Northcott, weaving through the seating, recognisable instantly by his BA-issued pilot's roller bag and that indefinable air of contained fatigue. He looked, she thought, older than he had last week, the lines at the corners of his eyes deeper, his uniform crisp but worn-in, a man who lived in and out of hotel rooms and briefing suites.

He caught her eye and gave a little half-salute, a gesture both teasing and affectionate.

"All present and correct, Captain Northcott?" he said, voice pitched low, a smile flickering.

She got up, letting herself be enveloped in a quick, fierce hug.

"I see you survived Irish exile," he murmured.

"Only just," she replied, forcing a smile. "Thank you for sorting crew travel. The Aer Lingus tea nearly killed me, though."

He huffed a laugh, slinging an arm around her shoulders as they made their way towards the car park.

They made their way in companionable silence, the routine of travel—lifts, escalators, the dull trudge towards the outside world—so ingrained it barely needed words. When they were finally in the car, Alan fiddled with the air con, his gaze flicking across to his daughter as if weighing how much to ask.

"So—do you want to talk about it?" he said at last, as they pulled out onto the ring road.

Hayley stared out at the rain-streaked glass, then shrugged. "What's to say? Hargreaves was—Hargreaves. He groped me. In the galley. In front of passengers. I slapped him. He threatened me. I stood my ground. Head of Legal tried to shut me up. The Garda were surprisingly decent, actually. But now I'm suspended. And—" She trailed off, words running out, anger and shame twining together like barbed wire.

Alan was silent for a moment, hands steady on the wheel. "You did the right thing. Doesn't matter what the company says, not really. I'll have a word with BALPA— see if they can get you some advice. And—" he hesitated "—if you want, I'll ring Dani, get her home for a few days."

Hayley shook her head. "Let her fly. She'll just worry, and you know what she's like—she'll storm the offices at Manston with a sword if you let her."

He smiled faintly. "Maybe that's what PanEuro needs. A good, old-fashioned mutiny."

They drove on, the city giving way to the rolling, damp landscape of Kent, the fields washed pale and green in the June sunlight.

Hayley let the familiar landmarks roll by—the M25 flyover, the sign for Canterbury, the first glimpse of the sea—her heart heavy and restless.

She let the silence hang for a while, before breaking it. "Dad—if I lose my job, what do I do? I can't go back to being cabin crew for another airline. Not after this."

He glanced at her, concern shadowing his features. "You won't. If they sack you, it'll look bad—for them, not you. I've seen it before. We'll get you something—maybe a ferry pilot gig, or something in operations until this blows over. You're a Northcott. We always come back."

The words were meant as comfort, but Hayley felt only the ache of uncertainty.

She was tired of "blowing over"—of waiting for men in glass offices to decide whether she got to fly or not.

****

CHAPTER 21 – A Surprise Interview
Friday 18th June 2021

The irony that, being dressed in her PanEuro blouse and blazer, while being at London Luton Airport, a destination that PanEuro certainly would avoid with extreme pleasure, was not lost on Hayley.

Instead, she was, where 14 months earlier, had been told that her line training, which she was doing at the time, was being terminated due to the "ongoing uncertainties" around the COVID-19 situation and easyJet's resulting need to "adjust its operational footprint".

It was, Hayley remembered, the worst day of her life, that she was being "furloughed", initially, and then a month later being told that she was no longer part of the airline's future plans. Not even a redundancy package. Just a curt email from a faceless HR officer, followed by radio silence. She'd cried in the car park, a grief so profound it had startled her—because for people like her, flying wasn't just a job, it was everything. That orange tailfin had once been the pinnacle of her ambition, the thing she'd trained and fought for through cadetship and sim checks, through grotty flat shares and seven-day blocks of back-to-back standbys. And here she was again. Full circle. Dressed in someone else's polyester blazer, feeling like an imposter on borrowed time.

Today was different, though. At least she hoped so.

She had, the previous afternoon, received two phone calls. Three, if she counted the one where she was told by Adam Carter that she was being reinstated effective 21st June on probation. The first one had been from Wizz Air's recruitment team, a chirpy Hungarian-accented woman named Petra who called her "Miss Hay-lee" and invited her to a walk-in assessment day "just for a chat" at their Luton base. The second call, rather more unexpectedly, was from the recruitment office at easyJet.

"Hi, is that Hayley Northcott? You came through our Generation easyJet cadet programme, and were furloughed last year?"

She'd recognised the accent immediately—Luton, Home Counties, overworked and unbothered.

"I—yes. I was. Until… the, er, Covid situation."

"Well, we've got some simulator time booked next week, and we're re-reviewing some of the former cadets who didn't get to complete line training. Would you be interested in coming in for a catch-up assessment and an informal interview? Tomorrow?"

Hayley had managed not to cry until she hung up. After that, the dam burst.

Now, with Luton Airport's low ceiling humming with budget holiday energy, toddlers wailing and hen parties beginning their decibel ascent before boarding had even been called, she stood in the Arrivals meet-and-greet zone, clutching a print-out of her email confirmation, the cheap PanEuro blazer itching at her neck.

The polyester was scratchy and ill-fitting, having been designed for someone who'd never needed to reach an overhead locker or sprint for a gate change. Hayley shifted awkwardly, aware of how she looked—PanEuro-styled but out of place, a Frankenstein of airline cultures. Her makeup was minimal but tidy, her hair pinned up in the precise style the grooming manual demanded. But it wasn't PanEuro she was trying to impress today.

It was them.

The orange.

easyJet.

She remembered the way the corridors had smelled—coffee and aircraft-cleaning fluid, the plasticky tang of hi-vis vests and the dry scent of recycled air in the crew room. She'd loved it all once. And she had never expected to be back.

A woman with a tablet approached, glancing down at Hayley's badge before addressing her with a perky half-smile. She wore a charcoal easyJet fleece over her smart trousers, the unmistakable lanyard swinging from her neck.

"Miss Northcott? Hi! You're here for the re-entry interview?"

"Yes," Hayley said, voice hoarse from the nerves she hadn't admitted until just now. "That's me."

"Great. If you want to follow me through, we'll take you up to the old training wing. It's still all a bit make-do—the main recruitment team's still part-remote, so today's fairly low-key. Nothing to worry about."

Nothing to worry about. As if.

They passed through the staff security gate—Hayley's PanEuro ID got her a look, but the easyJet escort waved her through easily enough. It was strange how her body remembered the rhythm of airside movement, even as her brain buzzed. Every beep of a staff door, every coded push-button sequence, it all came back in sequence, like she'd never left.

The corridors upstairs were oddly quiet. Not like the old days, where crew would be clustered in break rooms, joking over stroopwafels brought back from AMS or griping about the latest round of crewing emails. There were fewer people now, and the silence carried a ghost of 2020's stillness.

"You're with Captain Orla McBride and Chris Wharton," the escort said, pausing by a glass-walled office with a whiteboard proclaiming Cadet Re-acclimatisation Assessments – Week 25. "They'll do a short chat, and if that goes okay, you might get some sim time early next week."

Hayley nodded, not trusting herself to speak. Her stomach felt like it had been hollowed out and lined with vibration. She stood in front of the door for a second longer, straightened her blazer out of reflex, and knocked.

"Come in!"

The voice was female, strong, Irish.

HayIey stepped in.

The woman behind the desk rose and extended her hand. She was in full uniform, four stripes, hair in a neat bun.

Her handshake was firm. "Orla McBride, Fleet Standards Captain. This is Chris, he's our recruitment lead."

Chris was younger than she expected, maybe thirty-five, in a crew polo with an easyJet lanyard cluttered with badges. He gave her a quick smile. "Nice to meet you, Hayley. Thanks for coming in."

She perched on the edge of the chair they offered, hands clasped loosely in her lap. She tried not to wrinkle the PanEuro blazer too much. That felt important for some reason.

"Before we start," Orla said, flipping through a thin sheaf of papers, "I just want to say—this isn't a formal assessment. We're not marking you, you're not under exam conditions. It's more of a chat. We want to understand where you're at and what you've been doing since furlough. You were Generation easyJet, yes?"

"Yes, Ma'am," Hayley said, her voice clear but quieter than she'd hoped. "I started in 2019, graduated early 2020. I'd just begun line training when COVID hit. My last sim was February. I'd done… about seven sectors before we were grounded."

"And you haven't flown since?"

Hayley hesitated.

"I haven't flown from the flight deck. I—well, I took a position with PanEuro. Cabin crew."

Chris blinked. Orla didn't.

"We've seen that," Chris said lightly, gesturing to the CV in front of him. "Interesting operation."

"Mm." Orla's tone was more non-committal. "It must have been… a contrast."

Hayley allowed herself a smile, albeit a brief one. "Let's just say the CRM was more… theatrical than procedural. I must warn you that officially, I was… well, suspended from PanEuro"

That earned a huff of amusement from Orla. Chris, too, looked up with a grin.

"I had to do something to stay in the industry," Hayley continued, more seriously. "It wasn't ideal. But I kept up with my CBTs, my licenses. My Class 1's still current. I flew right-seater on a few ferry and passenger flights. Unofficially, I mean—I was in the jump seat, but I monitored radios, helped with checklists. Just to stay sharp."

"You say you were suspended from PanEuro," Orla prompted, leaning forward slightly. "May we ask why?"

Hayley didn't flinch, though her stomach rolled.

"There was an incident," she said, choosing her words carefully. "On a transatlantic sector to JFK. The Captain I was flying with—Roger Hargreaves—made an unwanted physical advance during the service. In the galley. In front of passengers."

Chris's eyebrows rose. Orla's expression remained impassive.

"I reacted. Instinctively. I slapped him. Immediately afterwards, I reported it to the First Officer and the senior cabin crew. The flight was diverted to Shannon. The Gardaí got involved. I was questioned, gave a statement, and then—well, I was suspended. Pending internal investigation. That's where it stands."

A pause stretched. For a moment, Hayley regretted her honesty. She could have softened it—called it a 'disagreement' or an 'HR matter.' But some deeper instinct refused. This was who she was now.

Orla gave a single nod, slow and deliberate.

"Well," she said at last, "that's the most honest answer we've had in a while. Thank you."

Chris scribbled a note, but his face remained neutral. "And how are you feeling about potentially returning to the flight deck?"

Hayley took a breath. "It's all I've wanted, since I was a teenager. Since before I could legally drive, let alone fly. And the last year and a bit… I mean, I've done things I never thought I'd do, just to keep close to aviation. I've learned a lot. About the industry, yes. About how it treats women, definitely. But also about myself. I want to come back to the flight deck more than ever. And I think I'd be a better pilot for everything I've had to go through."

Orla nodded again, more slowly. "I've seen pilots get derailed by furlough and never recover. I've also seen ones come back stronger. The fact you were willing to do cabin crew just to stay connected says a lot. Not all Captains would see that as a plus, but I do."

"Likewise," Chris added. "We're in a rebuilding phase. And we're not just looking for stick-and-rudder types— we want people who bring resilience, who understand the bigger picture."

Hayley offered a tentative smile. "Well, I've served gin and tonic to Russian oligarchs, told stag parties to sit down during turbulence, been groped by BIS in Prague and even been nearly intercepted by Russian MiGs over Lithuania. If that doesn't count as 'understanding the bigger picture,' I'm not sure what does."

There was a beat. Then Orla let out a breath—a short, sharp exhale that turned into a laugh. It wasn't mocking. It was the kind of laugh women in aviation sometimes shared when words failed and absurdity took over.

"Well," she said, glancing to Chris, "she's not dull."

Chris looked down at her file again, flipping through it more slowly this time. "The way we're handling these assessments, Hayley, is that we'll do a short sim profile with a TRI or a TRE present—nothing formal, just a chance to see where you're at. Muscle memory. Scan rate. CRM. No tricks. We've got a slot in an hour if you're interested, or we can bring you back in early next week. Up to you."

Hayley felt her throat tighten. She'd come expecting a conversation, maybe a pencilled-in date, perhaps a follow-up email in three working days. Not this.

"In an hour?" she repeated, her voice carefully neutral.

Chris nodded. "It's a 320 sim, fixed-base but with full visuals. Orla's already briefed the TRI. You won't be flying anything wild. Just a few circuits out of Bristol, maybe a raw data ILS, a little engine out on the climb. We just want to see your handling. Doesn't need to be polished—just give us a sense of your fundamentals."

Hayley's mouth was dry. The tea she'd nursed on the train up that morning felt a century ago. She'd worn her PanEuro blazer as a disguise, a kind of protective mimicry. But if she said yes now, it would be stripped away. They'd see what she really was—or wasn't.

"I'd like that," she said. "Let me just... freshen up?"

Orla gave a nod. "Use the flight crew washroom down the corridor—code's 2511. When you're ready, we'll take you through. Just one question, do you have to give a notice period or are you already free to join if this goes well?"

Hayley managed not to snort. "I've been reinstated at PanEuro, technically. But I think the writing's on the cabin wall. They've slapped me with probation and told me not to talk about the incident—although I have to give a month notice. I'd rather resign with dignity than wait for another HR ping disguised as a wellness check."

Orla gave her a long look—assessing, sympathetic, professional. "Fair enough. Let's see what today brings, shall we?"

Hayley stood, her legs stiff from tension and too much stillness. She gave a polite nod and slipped out of the office, her PanEuro blazer brushing the frame as she went.

The corridor was quiet, lined with motivational posters left over from a time when optimism was printed in Helvetica and laminated. One read "It's not just a job—it's a journey," with a sunset and a stylised orange tailfin. She gave it a dry look as she passed.

The crew washroom was where she remembered it—compact, bright-lit, with the faint scent of antiseptic soap and the soft drone of an extractor fan. The mirror above the basin was unforgiving. Hayley braced both hands on the sink and studied her reflection.

This was it. No more nostalgia. No more clinging to the flight deck by proximity or pretending that handing out meal trays in heels and lipstick was "staying current." This was now or never.

She removed the PanEuro blazer and carefully folded it, stuffing it into her tote bag. Beneath, she wore a plain white shirt—not regulation but sharp enough—and the skirt, the PanEuro skirt, that she hated with a passion. She re-tightened her bun and splashed her face with cold water. The airline-grade concealer beneath her eyes had held up, but she dabbed at the corners with a tissue and reapplied a hint of mascara. If she was going into the sim, she was doing it as herself—not as some cartoon stewardess in retro drag.

When she stepped out, Orla was already waiting.

"Feel alright?" the Captain asked as they walked down the corridor towards the training suite.

"As ready as I'll ever be," Hayley replied, hoping it sounded less brittle than it felt.

Orla led her into a side room where a uniformed man in his mid-fifties, silver at the temples and with the neat, square build of a military-trained pilot, stood reviewing a laminated profile sheet. He looked up as they entered.

"Hayley, this is Captain Colin Marten. He's one of our longest-serving TRIs and does all our cadet re-acclimations."

Colin extended his hand. "Welcome. No pressure—just a short sim, more to see where you are than to test you. Treat it like a line check minus the clipboard."

Hayley smiled tightly. "Understood, Captain."

"Excellent," Colin said, returning the smile. "We'll do Bristol to Exeter. Take-off, vectors, engine failure after V1, then some general handling and raw data ILS. Nothing fancy. You're left seat. I'll role-play FO duties for simplicity's sake."

Hayley's brain kicked into gear. Left seat. Manual handling. Raw data. She knew the drills, but it had been over a year. Her last proper sim had been 2020, just before everything unravelled. But she nodded. "I'm good with that."

They stepped into the fixed-base simulator, a familiar shell that managed to conjure real muscle memory even without the motion platform. The scent of rubber matting, the subtle ozone tinge from the electronics—it was enough to stir old instincts. Hayley reached out and ran a hand along the sidestick before settling into the seat.

Colin settled in beside her, flipping switches with casual confidence. "I'll be here the whole way, doing callouts. Don't overthink it. Ready when you are."

Hayley took a breath. Battery on. ADIRS aligning. She moved with mechanical precision, not out of panic but ritual—setting up the MCDU, scanning the ECAM, flexing her memory muscle like she had in the sims all through cadet school. Within minutes, they were configured for departure.

"Bristol, runway 09. Wind 080 at 6. Cleared for take-off."

Her voice didn't waver. "Cleared for take-off, 09. Hayley Northcott."

She advanced the thrust levers, feeling the simulated whine build, the vibration humming through the rudder pedals. "Man flex. SRS. Runway."

"Checked," Colin replied calmly.

The aircraft accelerated. "100 knots."

"Checked."

"V1."

"Rotate."

She pulled back gently, watching the nose rise on the display, the attitude just shy of 15 degrees. "Positive climb."

"Gear up."

Then came the jolt—engine 2 failure. No warning beforehand. Just the judder, the shift in thrust, the instinctive grip on the stick.

"Engine failure," Colin confirmed. "You have control."

"I have control," Hayley responded, heart thudding, but hands steady.

She did everything by the book—rudder, pitch, climb out. The memory came back like a tide—initial climb, acceleration altitude, ECAM actions. She kept breathing, stayed ahead of the aircraft, and when Colin passed her the failure checklist, she was halfway through the items already.

"Nice work," he said quietly.

Once levelled off, he gave her vectors for Exeter, then vectored her back in for a raw data ILS.

"Just hand-fly this one," he said. "No flight directors. Just scan, trim, feel."

Hayley grinned. For the first time in a year, she felt something ignite—a flare of joy, of clarity, of belonging.

The ILS wasn't textbook-perfect—she dipped a touch low before correcting—but the approach was stable, speed nailed, and the flare surprisingly smooth.

"Not bad at all," Colin said as she ran through the shutdown sequence. "How'd that feel?"

"Better than expected," Hayley admitted. Her forehead was damp. Her left leg was trembling under her trousers, but it didn't show. "I mean… a few rough patches."

"Nothing worrying," he said. "Scan rate's good. Stick and rudder skills are still there. Your CRM's sharp—you worked the problem instinctively."

He stood and offered his hand. "We'll write up the feedback and pass it on to recruitment. But between you and me, if this were a line sim, you'd have passed. With margin."

Hayley shook his hand, her smile real now. "Thank you, Captain."

Orla met her outside the sim bay, arms folded, weight resting on one leg. "Well?"

Hayley exhaled. "It's still in there. I can feel it. Like waking up from a long sleep."

Orla tilted her head. "And do you still want this?"

"I want it more than ever."

"Good. Because the industry needs more pilots who know what it's like to be thrown out of the flight deck and still claw their way back."

She handed Hayley a printed sheet—a feedback summary and a handwritten note from Colin scrawled in pen: "Would recommend for line requalification assessment. Excellent CRM. Handled engine failure with precision."

Hayley's eyes stung, but she kept her composure.

"We'll be in touch early next week," Orla said. "HR will need to do the usual checks. Assuming no surprises, you'll likely be rostered to start line training again within the month. And Hayley…"

"Yes?"

"Leave PanEuro. It doesn't deserve you."

* _ * _ * _ *

Back outside, the noise of the terminal hit her like a wave. She walked to the station, phone clutched in her hand, staring at the feedback form. It wasn't a job offer. Not yet. But it was the closest she'd been in eighteen months to having wings again.

The moment she boarded the Thameslink back to St Pancras, she slumped into a window seat, pulled her bag tight to her chest, and finally let the emotion hit.

It wasn't sobbing. Not really. Just a slow, steady stream of tears she couldn't quite stop, mingled with a grin she couldn't quite suppress.

As the train pulled away from Luton Parkway, she opened her phone and typed a message.

Hayley Northcott: Guess what, Theo?

She hovered over the send button, her thumb trembling with something that was half adrenaline, half disbelief. Even now, hours after the sim, she wasn't sure whether she was floating or falling. The bright streak of hope that had blazed through her during the sim session was already fraying at the edges, replaced by the usual doubts that clung to her like a worn-out hi-vis vest: Was I good enough? Did I look desperate? Did they see through me?

The Thameslink juddered south, the landscape rolling past in a blur of warehouses, car parks, and the suburban hinterland of Bedfordshire. She tucked her knees up on the seat, resting her head on the glass. Around her, the carriage hummed with the everyday theatre of English rail travel: students in oversized headphones, families with too many bags, a woman quietly weeping into her phone. No one paid Hayley any attention, not even when she let out a low, shuddering breath. In a world where nobody knew or cared what a requal sim meant, her own drama felt both enormous and invisible.

The phone vibrated. Theo, of course, replied immediately.

Theo Sullivan: Let me guess—you found a new way to get yourself sacked from an airline? Or are you about to tell me you finally got those PanEuro pyjamas dry cleaned? x

She laughed, really laughed, for the first time in days.

Hayley Northcott: Neither! Did the easyJet sim. It went… well. Better than well. They want me back for line training. Not official yet, but I think it's happening. Feels like I might be a pilot again.

She stared at the words for a moment, as if trying to anchor them in reality, then hit send before she could talk herself out of it.

Theo Sullivan: Bloody hell, Hales, that's brilliant! You smashed it, didn't you? Proud of you. Want to celebrate?

My shift ends at Manston tonight, so… if you're not too busy being a legend…

The wink emoji at the end of his message made her smile wider, despite herself. For a moment she let herself imagine it—Manston, a battered Fiat in the car park, the salty tang of the Kent coast. Theo, arms open, teasing her about her blazer, his hair still ruffled from a headset, his own troubles shelved for an evening.

The fact that it meant that she would be bringing him home, while Dani was also bringing her partner, an Alitalia First Officer, back home, meaning that the Northcott house would be having two couples, three Hayley had to admit if she counted her parents, meaning it would be an aviation house-share the likes of which only the summer of 2021 could provide. She allowed herself a small, daft grin at the thought: the house in Broadstairs, groaning under the weight of flight bags, hi-vis jackets, and airline uniform hangers on every available hook, tea always brewing, the dishwasher full of airline coffee mugs and mismatched catering cutlery.

She wiped her eyes with the sleeve of her PanEuro blazer, catching a whiff of the hotel room air freshener that had clung to it since Shannon. She thought about all the places this jacket had been: Berlin, Moscow, Prague, Rome, back and forth to JFK and Madrid and Copenhagen, more layovers than any cabin crew should see in a year and a half. Each city haunted by the memory of a crew bus, a hotel room, a duty-free aisle, the soft "ding" of a PA, the dull ache of her feet at the end of another day.

She felt, not for the first time, as if she existed in the liminal spaces of aviation—neither fully pilot nor wholly cabin crew, a ghost on the edge of someone else's story. For months she'd lived in fear that she would never get back to the flight deck, that she'd always be a stand-in, an imposter whose only claim to aviation was knowing the words to "Doors to manual and cross-check" in three different languages.

Now, for the first time since February 2020, she let herself believe that maybe she belonged again. Maybe the sky hadn't finished with her after all.

****

CHAPTER 22 – Serving Notice
Monday 22nd June 2021

The email came as quick as Hayley thought, but the way it had, if she was honest, was inconvenient.

Not because she didn't want the job at easyJet, because she did, but because she and Theo were laying in bed, her bed, in the Northcott family home, and she could feel his erection poking her, his snoring loud, while his arm was blocking her ability to actually reach her phone. Sunlight was already peeking through the half-drawn curtains, casting a rectangular glow across the duvet and illuminating the ever-growing mound of aviation detritus that had colonised her childhood bedroom. She could just about see the tips of her easyJet confirmation email on the lock screen—a faint orange glimmer between Theo's knuckles and her old Beanie Babies.

She wriggled sideways, not quite enough to wake him but sufficient to dislodge the pressure on her ribs, and managed, after a few contortions, to free her hand. The phone buzzed again; another notification from easyJet Recruitment. It felt unreal. For months, she had become a connoisseur of corporate silence: the kind where HR promised to "be in touch" and then vanished into an admin abyss, and the kinder, more honest kind, where no one pretended to care. This—this was action. Certainty.

Her heart beat a little faster. She swiped up, careful not to drop the phone or elbow Theo in the face, though she doubted he'd wake up if she did. Overnight roster duty had left him dead to the world, dribbling faintly onto the pillow. She loved him for it, especially as it was his weekend off, and he, and her, were both on the Manston to Berlin rotation with Captain Lucius Herringbow, a Canadian captain who had, prior to the pandemic, been a American Airlines Airbus A321 captain and, more usefully, had taken a great liking to British humour, Kentish real ale, and the phrase "Alright, sunshine?" delivered in a dubious Toronto lilt.

She felt Theo's other arm, the one that was under her, cup her breast, the unintended action being due to the half-conscious fidgeting of a man who'd learned the art of sleeping through every noise known to the Stansted crew hotel, but not the presence of a new job confirmation three inches from his hand. Hayley eased herself away, disentangling from his reach, careful to avoid the zone of maximum snore volume. She glanced at the clock: 06:21. Outside, she could hear gulls shrieking, a dustcart rumbling along the high street, and, faintly, the sea—her childhood soundtrack, and now the white noise of her anxious transition.

The phone screen glowed.

From: *easyJet Recruitment*

To: *hales34314bleak@hotmail.com*

Subject: *Your Re-Entry – Offer and Next Steps*

Dear Miss Northcott,

We are pleased to confirm your successful completion of the Generation easyJet Cadet acclimatisation assessment. Following your recent simulator session and interview, we would like to offer you a place in our next line training cohort, commencing Monday 26th July 2021 at London Gatwick.

Further details are attached, including your training schedule, pre-course reading, and a digital contract for signature.

Please confirm your acceptance by replying to this email and returning the signed contract by Friday 25th June. Should you require additional time, contact Recruitment as soon as possible. If you have any queries regarding your roster, uniform, or training requirements, do not hesitate to reach out.

Welcome back, Hayley. We look forward to seeing you return to the flight deck.

Kind regards,

Chris Wharton

easyJet Recruitment

Hayley felt Theo's fingers twisting her nipples as she was trying to concentrate on reading the email, trying to take in the news, trying to take in the fact that in just over 1 month, she would be back, officially, in the simulators, back in the cockpit, not as a hopeful, not as a redundancy statistic, but as a pilot once more. The word itself—pilot—felt almost foreign now, like a term she'd overheard in a terminal rather than one that truly belonged to her. She let herself savour the moment: the orange glow of the easyJet logo on her screen, the memory of the sidestick beneath her hand in the sim, the hush of anticipation that even now fluttered in her chest.

And then Theo's arm that was resting on the free side moved. Not up, but lower, towards her panties. She paused for a moment as Theo's fingers crept downward— still unconscious, still accidental, still very much in the way of her attempt to process life-changing news.

She let herself close her eyes, just for a moment, letting the truth settle. It was done. The humiliation, the months of feeling like an imposter, the last year and a half of navigating other people's aisles, the endless deflections— *I'm just keeping my hours in, just staying current, just paying the bills*—all of that could, perhaps, start to lift. She had a place on the flight deck again. Her place.

And then she opened her eyes, just as Theo's involuntary movement went into her panties, the feeling of his fingers on her hips, his erection behind her, the-

"No, Hales," she muttered to herself, half-amused, half-exasperated, "not the time, darling." She considered the merits of gently elbowing Theo awake, but decided she needed a moment longer in her own head before dealing with his inevitable blend of morning wood and teasing affection.

But before she could do anything, the sound from the bedroom next to hers, the one Dani slept in, started a symphony of groaning, sexual energy, as Dani's Alitalia partner was again in residence, as he had been on another, over the weekend, set of Rome to Heathrow runs, while Dani had been doing A330 runs between Brussels and Heathrow for Virgin Atlantic, the cargo only service that the transatlantic Virgin contract had rendered both tedious and, in Dani's words, "good for the thighs, bad for the brain.".

"Fuck, Lorenzo, harder!" Dani's voice rang out through the thin wall, accompanied by a cacophony of bed springs and a distinctly Italian expletive that required no translation. Hayley let out a stifled laugh, half mortified, half resigned. Of course, in the Northcott house, privacy was a theoretical concept—more observed in the breach than the practice. It was a running joke among their friends: you could always tell which Northcott sister was home by the soundscape. If it wasn't the heavy-footed shuffle of her father Alan trundling down the corridor to put the kettle on at 6 a.m., it was Dani's soundtrack of transnational romance, delivered in surround sound through the paper-thin plasterboard. "No, I don't want a condom this time!"

Hayley groaned at her elder sister's blithe disregard for subtlety, burying her head under the pillow with a soft groan that managed to be both laughter and despair. Theo, still deeply unconscious, chose that exact moment to insert three fingers in her, and the feeling of them going in, wholly uninvited and yet with a bizarre accuracy that suggested a pilot's instinct for controls even while asleep, snapped Hayley's fragile concentration like a snapped speed brake.

And as he had got her button, the immediate place where she knew that the climax would come whether she wanted it or not, Hayley gasped and reached down to gently prise his hand away.

"V1," he muttered, and Hayley chuckled, as she knew that sometimes he would call out, in his sleep, the take-off procedure or the flap setting or some bit of Airbus trivia that would have made any non-pilot run for the hills. Only in this house, she thought, could sex and Standard Operating Procedures overlap with such chaos and comfort. "Rotate," he then said, and Hayley could feel his breath against her neck, the sleep-heavy rasp and the vague but unmistakable thrust of his hips, as though his unconscious mind was half-flying a jet and half-making love to her.

"Fuck, Harder," Dani's voice through the wall shouted out again. "Knock me up, you Italian stud!"

Hayley gasped at that, as she knew that getting pregnant while being a First Officer, especially Dani who had 3 years under her belt but a contract that made maternity leave about as generous as Ryanair's crew hotel policy, was an act of either true romantic abandon or terminal short-term thinking. She grinned, shaking her head, and tried—without much success—to ignore the growing chaos both inside and outside her bedroom.

"Setting AP2," Theo then said as his fingers inside her started to move rhythmically, his sleep-buried mind blending cockpit automation with the most intimate automation of all. Hayley stifled a laugh, squirming half in pleasure and half in sheer disbelief at the surreal aviation sitcom that her life had become. This, she thought, was not how most people found out they'd reclaimed their dream job—sandwiched between a boyfriend's somnolent Airbus checklist and her sister's latest bid for the Italian citizenship test through highly practical means.

"Shit, number 2 engine just dropped off," Theo murmured into her hair, his fingers increasing their speed, and Hayley could feel the pleasure withering through her, sharp and spiralling.

"Breed me you Italian bastard," Dani's voice from the next room crescendoed with a vigour that made Hayley question whether the walls were actually structural or merely symbolic. It was like living in a house built out of cardboard, with every sound conducted directly into her skull, every intimate moment a shared family affair whether anyone wanted it or not.

Theo's fingers were still working her, the rhythm now oddly in sync with the creaking headboard from Dani's room, as though the Northcott house had been converted into some kind of percussive, pan-European love machine. Hayley, caught between laughter, mortification, and the involuntary roll of pleasure, tried to extricate herself once more, but Theo's arm was heavy, his body warm.

And then it happened, the pleasure causing her to wither, the apex of her body's response surging up with such inevitability that Hayley half-choked on her own suppressed moan. She buried her face in the pillow, clutching at the duvet as Theo's sleepy, uncoordinated but undeniably effective fingers pushed her over the edge. Her climax was a tremor she tried—utterly in vain—to keep silent, a low whimper lost amid the thunder of Dani's performance and the distant call of the morning gulls. Her toes curled, her legs tensed, and she bit down on the pillow, desperate not to join the Northcott family chorus with an aria of her own.

Theo, still half-asleep, withdrew his hand and shifted with a groan, turning onto his back and flinging an arm over his eyes. "Checklist complete," he muttered in his sleep, and began to snore again. Hayley stared at the ceiling, breathless, a hand pressed to her racing heart. She tried to will her body back to calm, to gather herself for the day ahead.

She lay there, a ridiculous smile on her face, staring at the whorls in the paint above her bed, and realised she would always associate the moment she truly returned to the flight deck with the scent of Theo, the chorus of her sister's love life, and the sting of cheap polyester on her skin. It was, she reflected, utterly on brand.

*_*_*_*

Getting out of bed was a tactical exercise in its own right. Hayley manoeuvred out from under Theo's sprawling limbs, her body still tingling with aftershocks and amusement. She retrieved her phone and—after a final glance at the easyJet email—tiptoed past the explosion of shoes, uniforms, and battered flight bags that marked her and Dani's return home. She paused at the door to Dani's room, and saw that she was now being squashed against the wall, and that she was being entered from the rear.

"Fuck, pound me into next week!" Dani shrieked, her voice rising in a way that surely must have carried out through the sash windows and down into the garden, where, on previous mornings, their mother had been known to do her stretches. "Stretch my fucking arse."

Hayley groaned as she walked into the bathroom, as she knew that she would, inevitably, have to face her parents at breakfast with whatever residual flush lingered on her cheeks. She shut the bathroom door behind her, locking it with the gentle precision of someone who grew up in a house with no true boundaries. Her reflection in the mirror showed tousled hair, smudged mascara, and an expression halfway between exhaustion and euphoria. She ran the tap, splashed cold water on her face, and exhaled—long and slow.

Today, she thought, everything changes. For real, this time.

She took a few moments to herself, breathing in the familiar scents of the Northcott family bathroom: the vaguely medicinal aroma of her mother's rosewater face spray, the ever-present trace of her father's shaving foam, and the faint, briny hint of sea air that seemed to permeate every corner of the house. It grounded her, as did the scratchy towel she used to dry her face and the pale sunlight that filtered through the frosted window.

She checked her phone again, scrolling through the attached documents from easyJet: the contract, the pre-course reading pack, a list of uniform suppliers ("for your reference"), and a PDF with the roster for her cohort. The sight of her name, Northcott H, on an official easyJet document, made her heart stutter. All at once, she wanted to cry, to shout, to tell the whole house—perhaps the whole street. But dignity prevailed.

There would be time for celebration later. First, she had business to attend to. Grim, overdue business: serving her notice to PanEuro.

Hayley went back to her room, only to see Theo sleep masturbating, his hand acting as if he was gripping a A320 sidestick, the jerking motion oddly reminiscent of a touch-and-go at Rotterdam. She didn't even try to stifle her laugh this time. It was just another data point in a life where Airbus ergonomics seemed to bleed seamlessly into the most private moments.

"Control, this PanEuro 531, we're coming up against a severe wind shear, 20 miles north of Charles de Gaulle," Theo murmured, lost to the world, his erect member showing pre cum, and Hayley decided to head to the bed, to get down on her knees, as she sometime occasionally enjoyed the spirts of-

"No, Hales, you've got to get downstairs, you've got to email HR at PanEuro to give your notice, you've got to email easyJet, and you've got to stop letting everyone else in this house shag their way into your concentration," she muttered, pushing her fringe back with both hands.

She scooped up her laptop from the floor and, laying it on the bed while she grabbed a Virgin Atlantic pyjama top that Dani had liberated from the 'to be wasted due to COVID' pile at Heathrow, Hayley wrapped herself in it for comfort. The soft, slightly over-washed cotton, striped in understated red and grey, felt oddly like a suit of armour—a reminder of family, of Dani's successes, of all the hours spent in cockpits and crew rooms, of the strange, shifting hierarchy of airlines in which, finally, she might be back on top, at least for a while.

She padded quietly out of the room, tiptoeing past Theo's recumbent form—one arm flung wide, the other clutching at a phantom sidestick—and into the hallway. Downstairs, the kitchen was a scene of aviation chaos and domestic normality, the two blending as naturally as they always had in the Northcott household.

Her father, Alan, was already up, his laptop out, watching Mick Lynch on the television talking about the latest planned rail strike while simultaneously checking the BALPA electronic notice board for the latest union guidance on pay negotiations and the never-ending saga of post-pandemic rostering. A mug of tea steamed beside him, the handle turned precisely toward the edge of the table in the way only a pilot's sense of order could demand. Karen, her mother, was at the counter making toast, one eye on her husband and one on her phone, replying to a WhatsApp group that seemed to be solely for the purpose of coordinating family arrivals and departures at various UK airports.

Alan looked up as Hayley entered, squinting slightly over the top of his glasses. His hair, greyer than ever, stuck out at odd angles, and he wore his battered BA fleece, the one he always swore he'd replace but never did.

"You're up early, love," he said, the tone gentle. "Y'know, Hales, why I've got the telly up loud?"

Hayley grinned, rolling her eyes. "Because you can't stand the sound of Dani's sex life any more than the rest of us?"

Karen chuckled. "Yes. You know she was telling me that thank goodness it isn't hers and your time of the month, as you're both on the same cycles, as she's... well, let's just say there's always been a reason your dad prefers Sydney runs once a month."

Hayley snorted, feeling that bubble of laughter, that warmth, which was somehow always present in the Northcott household even when the world outside seemed intent on turning to ash. "She'll be lucky if she's not on a different sort of cycle in nine months at this rate," Hayley said, and her mother shot her a warning look over the top of the toast.

Alan took a sip of tea, set it down, and fixed Hayley with that particular paternal gaze—half mock-stern, half concerned. "So, what's got you up at this ungodly hour then? More interview prep? Or are you running from the crosswind upstairs?"

Hayley slid into the seat opposite him, careful not to dislodge the pile of flight planning printouts and union bulletins that had colonised the end of the table. "Neither. Well, not really. I, uh…" She glanced at her phone again, as if needing to see the orange logo one more time to believe it was real. "I got the offer. From easyJet. Proper offer—contract attached, start date, the lot."

Karen paused, half a slice of toast in mid-air, and Alan's face cracked into a rare, genuine smile—one that seemed to erase a few years from the lines around his eyes. "Oh, Hales," Karen breathed, setting the toast down and coming around the table to wrap her in a hug. Alan stood too, awkward in his affection but pulling her close. For a moment, Hayley let herself be folded into their arms, three Northcotts pressed together in the familiar kitchen with the low hum of BBC Breakfast on in the background and the smell of burnt crumbs and fresh tea filling the air.

"Well done, kiddo," Alan said quietly, his voice thick. "I told you, didn't I? You'd be back. You're too bloody stubborn not to be."

Karen squeezed her one last time before releasing her. "When do you start?"

Hayley grinned, suddenly shy, like she was sixteen again and about to admit to skipping school. "End of July. Line training at Gatwick."

Karen's face lit up. "We'll have to celebrate. Properly. None of this tepid Prosecco nonsense. Dani will want to know the minute she surfaces. Though I suspect Lorenzo will be somewhat... distracted."

At the mention of Dani, a fresh chorus of squeals and Italian exclamations echoed down the stairs. Alan winced, turning the television up another notch.

Hayley took a breath, steeling herself. "First, though, I need to email PanEuro. Give notice. I can't quite believe it's happening." She shook her head, feeling the disbelief flutter through her again. "After everything. I'm finally... free."

It was then Hayley realised that she had left her laptop in her bedroom half-naked, sprawled on top of her duvet, no doubt drooling on the pillow she liked best. She could picture the way he'd look if she walked in now—mouth open, hair a ruffled tangle, probably still talking to imaginary ATC in his sleep. Her family, mercifully, didn't bat an eyelid at the occasional boyfriend emerging in only boxer shorts or a rogue PanEuro T-shirt. Still, Hayley hesitated. For a second, she was just a woman in her childhood kitchen, needing her laptop, with the weight of a career decision clutched quietly in her chest.

Alan, catching her pause, arched an eyebrow. "You alright? You look like you're about to steal something valuable."

"Just realising I left my laptop up there," she said, grabbing a crust of toast. "And I'm pretty sure Theo's turned the bed into an Airbus training device."

Karen snorted, pouring more tea. "You better hurry. If Dani and Lorenzo surface first, you'll have to mount a rescue mission. Remember last time? The walk of shame with your laptop and his pants in the hallway."

Hayley grinned. "Fine, but if I run into naked Italians, I'm blaming you both."

She hurried upstairs, and, as Dani's room was at the top of the stairs, she saw Dani still being anally penetrated by Lorenzo, who was now calling her his "Bellissimo angelo volante" while he thrusted into her like an Airbus A330. Shaking her head, she walked past, into her own bedroom, where Theo was now laying on his chest, his body half covering her laptop with it resting on the edge of the bed.

The fact that Theo was now snoring heavily, meaning that he was in the final phase of his deep post-roster sleep, was oddly reassuring. Hayley crept towards the bed, gingerly sliding her laptop out from beneath his forearm, careful not to jostle him or the heap of crumpled bedsheets any more than absolutely necessary. He didn't stir, only let out a low, satisfied grunt and burrowed further into the pillow. With laptop in hand, she retreated, closing the door behind her with a soft click and leaning against it for a moment— just to breathe.

She padded back downstairs, Virgin Atlantic pyjama top still draped about her shoulders, feeling the early-morning cool of the hallway beneath her feet and the strange lightness that comes with big, irreversible change. In the kitchen, her father had migrated to his emails, the family dog, now having been in the garden, laying in the corner of the room, her mother now stirring porridge and listening with half an ear to the hum of family and domestic routine. Hayley settled at the end of the table, opened her laptop, and—after a brief check of WhatsApp, just in case the world had fallen apart overnight—opened a new email draft.

From: *hales34314bleak@hotmail.com*

To: *hradminsystems@paneuro.aero*

Subject: *Notice of Resignation – Hayley Northcott*

Dear HR Team,

I am writing to formally give notice of my resignation from my position as Stewardess with PanEuro, effective in accordance with the notice period stipulated in my contract. My last working day will be Sunday 25th July 2021.

I want to thank you for the opportunities given to me during my employment, and for your understanding.

Please confirm receipt of this email.

Kind regards,

Hayley Northcott

She knew that it was short, simple and to the point—no histrionics, no burning bridges, just what was needed. It was perhaps a little colder than she'd have liked, but after everything, Hayley wasn't sure she owed the airline any more than that. She'd played her part in their mid-pandemic pantomime, smiled and sashayed through the aisles, endured the retro uniforms and the even more retro management style, and now she was finally taking off—not as a passenger, not as a fallback, but on her own terms. It was all she'd ever wanted.

Hayley sat back, the email cursor blinking at her. She read it over once, then again. For a fleeting moment, she considered adding a line about "valuing her colleagues" or "cherishing the opportunity to serve," but she stopped herself. It would be a lie, or at least an exaggeration, and she'd promised herself long ago—long before PanEuro, long before easyJet, long before COVID and redundancy and all the chaos in between—that she wouldn't build her career on half-truths. She'd always wanted to fly, not flatter.

She attached her signature, hit "send," and watched as the message whisked itself away into the digital ether. There was no immediate rush of euphoria, no triumphant soundtrack swelling in her mind. Instead, a curious sense of calm settled over her, like the moment a plane crests through turbulence and finds smooth air on the other side. She took a long, slow breath, letting her fingers drum lightly on the edge of the keyboard. Done. Really done.

Across the table, Alan's phone buzzed. He glanced at it, then at Hayley, his face registering a kind of paternal pride that he'd always struggled to express in words. "Good for you, Hales," he said quietly. "No point hanging around somewhere you're not valued."

Karen, too, nodded her approval, though her eyes glistened with the tears she always seemed to keep ready for family milestones—no matter how big or small. "I'll make something special for dinner tonight," she announced, her voice resolute. "Something orange, perhaps." She winked.

Hayley laughed, the sound bright and a little wild in the morning hush. "As long as it's not airline chicken supreme, I'll eat anything."

There was a knock at the back door, and a second later, Dani swept into the kitchen, hair wild, face flushed, wearing nothing but a Virgin Atlantic pyjama set. She was followed, sheepishly, by Lorenzo, who at least had the decency to pull on some pyjama bottoms and a T-shirt that read "I ♥ Roma."

"Buongiorno, famiglia!" Lorenzo said, with the kind of ebullience that only an Italian can muster before 7 a.m., especially after such athletic exertions.

Dani, undeterred by her own state of undress, beamed at Hayley. "You look like you've just won the lottery."

Hayley grinned, catching Dani's eye, and held up her phone. "I did. Sort of. easyJet offered me the job. I start line training next month."

For a heartbeat, Dani's smile faltered, just a crack, before she launched herself across the kitchen to hug Hayley hard. "You bloody legend. You absolute orange legend!" She squeezed her sister tight, then stepped back, eyes shining with the sort of pride that only a sibling can truly muster. "About time they saw sense. I hope you made them sweat for it."

Lorenzo, a man who understood both sisters' need for banter, patted Hayley on the back with all the solemnity of a Vatican priest. "Brava! You see, in Italia, we say—if you want to fly, you need wings. And you have many wings."

Hayley laughed, feeling something light and fizzy bubbling up in her chest. "I have wings, Dani has—well, let's just say she's flying this morning."

"Shut up," Dani hissed, but she was grinning, and Hayley knew she'd just given her sister fresh ammunition for at least a week's worth of teasing.

Alan, ever the captain, tapped his mug thoughtfully. "Well, that's two Northcott girls flying the flag for British aviation. Now all we need is your mother to get her dispatcher's ticket reinstated and we'll have the full set."

Karen snorted. "Not likely. I've served my time. Anyway, someone has to keep the home fires burning." She gestured at the bubbling porridge and the cluttered table, the tokens of domestic life that grounded them all.

Hayley felt herself flush with happiness, the worries and doubts of the past months melting away in the warmth of her family's kitchen. For a brief moment, she allowed herself to imagine the future—not just the immediate chaos of notice periods and uniform fittings and acclimatisation packs, but the longer view. Flying again, properly. The feeling of the yoke in her hands, the world dropping away beneath her, the hum of the engines and the rhythm of checklists and radio calls. It all seemed close now, tantalisingly within reach.

And then, inevitably, her phone vibrated again.

A new email, this time from PanEuro HR. She tapped it open, curiosity mingling with a strange, bittersweet nostalgia.

From: hradminsystems@paneuro.aero

To: hales34314bleak@hotmail.com

Subject: Re: Notice of Resignation – Hayley Northcott

Dear Hayley,

Thank you for your email. We acknowledge receipt of your notice of resignation, effective Sunday 25th July 2021, as per your contract.

We are sorry to lose you as a member of our team. Please advise of any outstanding annual leave so that this can be factored into your remaining rostered duties. You will receive details of your final pay and any outstanding benefits in due course.

We wish you all the best in your future endeavours and thank you for your contribution to PanEuro during these challenging times.

Best regards,

The HR Team

PanEuro

It was, she supposed, about as warm as any HR department ever got. She forwarded the message to her private email, for her own records, and then set the phone aside. That was it. She was out.

****

CHAPTER 23 – Three Lions on the Plane
Sunday 11th July 2021

Of all the inane things PanEuro could do, Hayley Northcott mentally swore, as she boarded the Airbus A321neo G-PANT, the unfortunate registration that everyone sniggered at, putting on special runs between Rome and Heathrow, where several coaches were waiting at a specially reopened Terminal 3 for passengers from Italy to get to Wembley in time for the Euro 2020 final, this surely topped the lot.

Of course, there were some England supporters mixed in with the Italian fans, though not as many as she might have expected. Most of the flights that morning had carried Italian nationals—flushed with hope and nerves, arms brimming with banners, flags and daft hats, their animated voices bouncing around the airbridge like the racket of a piazza. Today, Hayley wasn't a pilot, nor an FA in any recognisable sense; she was a prop in what the media officer had dubbed "the glory shuttle"—a phrase delivered with the kind of forced bonhomie that made her toes curl.

The footballers themselves weren't on board, of course, but a fair number of WAGs were, along with sponsors, UEFA delegates, and assorted media people. The England contingent, squeezed in alongside the Italians, looked vaguely apologetic, as though sheepish about their luck in getting seats at the last minute. A few quietly hummed 'Three Lions', eyes wide as they drank in the sense of occasion, but it was the Italians who dominated. Hayley could hear the words 'Forza Azzurri!' shouted at random intervals from the back of the plane as she slipped on her gloves, adjusted her hat—never had she felt less like herself—and went to join the rest of the cabin crew at the forward galley.

Up front, she knew, was Theo and Captain Hiram H Lethenshaw, a career pilot who had been at, previously, British Airways and Aer Lingus, and knew every corner of Heathrow like the back of his hand, but still referred to Rome's Fiumicino as "Leonardo" with the proprietary pride of someone who'd spent half his working life drinking espresso in Terminal 1. Lethenshaw had greeted the morning with the air of a man dispatched from another era—his moustache as neat as his cap, posture as upright as the Queen's Guard, blue eyes twinkling with amusement at the spectacle before him.

Hayley, for her part, could only marvel at the carnival taking over the jet bridge. Each step she took towards the forward galley was greeted by some new surge of noise: a snatch of Fratelli d'Italia, the crash of a suitcase up against the bin, an enthusiastic "Viva l'Inghilterra!" from one cheeky Brit in the midfield. Everywhere, colours: azure, white, the occasional red-and-white cross of St George looking rather lonely amid the ocean of tricolores.

She exchanged a look with Emma Lang, who rolled her eyes beneath the strict sweep of her PanEuro bob, lipstick flawless, composure only just holding. "Glory shuttle," Emma whispered, her voice low, sardonic. "I'd rather shuttle Boris Johnson's dog through rabies quarantine than do another one of these."

Hayley suppressed a laugh. The shift had been thrown together at the last minute, as PanEuro had decided, just this once, to "let the plebs on", as Emma had summed up, in the company WhatsApp group, to mild outrage from HR and universal agreement from everyone else on the roster. Today, "the plebs" were an odd, churning mix—well-heeled enough to have scored a ticket, yet boisterous as any Ryanair stag do, united in obsession and anticipation. It was the sort of crowd that blurred the lines between VIP and economy, between post-pandemic caution and a longing for old communal rituals. Pandemic or not, football and flying brought out something primal in people.

"Chicken, beef or vegetarian," she said to a passenger in Executive, who was dressed in an Italy shirt and had paint all over his face, his smile enormous and expectant.

"Pollo, per favore!" he beamed, and Hayley handed over the tray, relieved to find her muscle memory carrying her through the ritual. The galley was chaos—tin trays clattering, voices ricocheting in half a dozen languages, colleagues weaving around each other, Carter Pembleton, the Purser, talking on the interphone to the flight deck about the latest disruptive passengers, a quartet of England fans who were chanting "Is this a library?" at the top of their lungs while waving inflatable lions.

"I swear to God, Captain, if we don't land soon, then I'll have to get the speed tape and restrain four grown men with three catering carts and a packet of Hobnobs," Carter's voice barked down the line, his usual clipped confidence taking on a slightly frazzled edge. Hayley smothered a grin and continued sliding trays into their slots, nodding at Emma who, without looking, passed her a fresh stack of napkins.

"I'll go check on them," Hayley said. She tugged at her jacket hem and eased herself down the aisle, dodging arms, flags, and feet stretched out like tripwires. The chant of "Southgate you're the one" drifted from a group of English lads halfway down the aircraft.

And then the person behind her, an Italy fan, decided now was the right time to grope her.

Turning round, Hayley resisted the urge this time to slap him full in the face—she'd learnt, after her last altercation and subsequent union meeting, that violence was for the truly dire moments, and PanEuro was, if nothing else, currently running out of tolerance for PR disasters.

Instead, she marched up to the front, where Carter was still on the interphone with the flight deck, and intercepted him with a look that required no translation.

"Seat 14D," she murmured tightly, "wandering hands. Needs a word, not a spectacle. He's the row in front of the England fans singing Southgate's praises."

Carter's mouth hardened, the set of a man who'd seen every variety of mid-air buffoonery. "On it." He smoothed his uniform, squared his shoulders, and, with the sort of unhurried grace usually reserved for swans, began his march down the aisle, projecting an aura of calm authority that stilled the giggling around him.

Sarah noticed that, as he moved down the aisle, Carter did have the speed tape, and the hush that followed him as tangible as the fragrance of airline coffee and aftershave. He didn't break stride for the flailing arms of an overexcited passenger or the hesitant tug of a woman wanting her wine refilled. His presence—his height, his solidness, the unspoken aura of someone who'd done this job across decades and continents—was usually enough to settle most incidents before they began. As he approached row 14, Hayley paused, half-turning, careful not to stare, and watched him crouch beside the offender, his voice measured, his hand resting not on the seat, but on the edge of authority.

She caught just enough. "We're here to get everyone to Wembley, not to the tabloids. Hands to yourself, mate, or you're spending the final with the met police instead of your friends. Now, if you do it again, I'm going to tape your hands, arms and gob up so much, that you'll need an Amazon Prime parcel station to get out. Understood?" The threat, delivered with dry wit and absolute seriousness, had its intended effect. A few nervous titters drifted down the aisle from the England fans. The offender, cheeks flushed redder than his Italian scarf, managed a mumbled apology and kept his hands conspicuously in his lap for the remainder of the flight.

Hayley gave Carter a nod of gratitude as he returned, now with a wry smile creasing the lines at his eyes. "You know," he murmured as he passed, "one day they'll invent a cabin class for people who need a time-out." Hayley nearly laughed, but the sound was lost amid another round of boisterous singing, this time a mashup of "Sweet Caroline" and "Volare" that only football could make seem natural.

She pressed forward, collecting stray rubbish, topping up drinks, and issuing the thousand small reassurances that kept an aircraft full of sports fans from tipping over into full-scale anarchy. Emma, who had a natural gift for tactical retreat, stationed herself near the mid-cabin exit and distributed bottles of water with the clinical precision of a medic in a field hospital. Occasionally, she exchanged glances with Hayley—glances that communicated a whole silent conversation about the madness of the day.

Unfortunately, Hayley knew, this was flight 2 of 8 for the day, however they were 20 minutes away from Heathrow, and so she let herself breathe—just a little. The ritual of descent was always a comfort, a return to the old certainties of flying, whatever uniform she wore. Theo's voice crackled through the PA: "Cabin crew, twenty minutes to landing. Let's get everything stowed and locked. And—" There was a pause, the barest hint of amusement in his tone. "—could someone please collect the remainder of the inflatable lions? Apparently there's a betting pool on whether we can get them through customs."

A ripple of laughter ran through the front galley, but it was more relief than anything. The end was in sight; soon, this impossible, feverish mixture of hope and rivalry, of longing and homesickness and sport, would tip out of the jet and into the roiling chaos of Wembley.

As the cabin prepared for descent, Hayley and Emma worked in practiced silence, eyes flicking from doors to latches, from stray plastic cups to rogue banners. The choreography of landing was drilled deep into their bones—no matter the pandemonium, the routine held.

"Last round," Emma said, her voice steady. "You take starboard, I'll do port?"

Hayley nodded, squeezing past Carter as he checked the lav. "Any more trouble?"

He shook his head. "Our Italian friend is chastened. And the England fans are too busy singing about Baddiel and Skinner. The power of sport, or something like it."

Hayley allowed herself a small smile as she walked the aisle one last time, gathering the detritus of the journey. She found herself stopping beside a boy, maybe twelve, face painted half in the English cross, half in Italian tricolore, who was kissing a girl the same age, and she had to chuckle at how the pre-teens were somehow more restrained, more gracious, than the grown men who'd tried to turn the cabin into a lager-fuelled battleground. She slipped them each a PanEuro-branded chocolate with a conspiratorial wink, watching their shy grins widen before moving on. The whole aircraft now throbbed with a nervous, celebratory energy—an uncertain blend of hope, rivalry, and jet-lagged surrealism.

Hayley moved with a sense of duty, her movements brisk but gentle as she checked overhead bins, straightened seatbelts, and exchanged smiles with passengers. Many were glued to their phones, following every rumour, every lineup leak, and every viral video. She noticed how, even now, the English and Italian fans leaned together, sharing streaming links and tips about the quickest way to

Wembley, the friction between them more fraternal than hostile.

She paused briefly at row 17, where an older couple sat side by side, their hands entwined on the armrest. The woman, Italian, wore a faded Azzurri scarf. The man, his St George's tie slightly askew, gave Hayley a wry grin. "We've survived 42 years of marriage and four World Cups," he said. "I think we'll make it through this flight—though she may leave me if it goes to penalties."

The woman gave Hayley an arch look. "He snores through all the matches anyway. This time I made sure he was awake for every minute."

Hayley grinned, squeezing her way towards the galley, the easy humour of the couple softening the edges of her exhaustion. She felt, for the first time that day, something like optimism. The job might grind her down, the uniform might feel like a costume, but this—this mingling of lives, dreams, and old rivalries—was why she loved flying, however thankless it sometimes seemed.

The interphone buzzed, and Hayley knew that it was either Lethenshaw, who was one of the captains who were so liberal when it came to ladies in the cockpit, he was likely to offer a spare seat for landing.

Then there was Theo, her boyfriend, who was the First Officer, and also a liberal with regards to female visitors in the flight deck—provided you were type rated on the A320 family.

She pressed the button for the cockpit, catching Emma's knowing look as she did so. "Hayley Northcott for the front office," she announced softly, the code-phrase that, between her and Theo, meant a spare seat was going for landing and not to bother with the usual permissions.

Hayley ducked her head as she slipped through the forward galley, deftly sidestepping the stack of empty meal trays and the faintest scent of over brewed coffee clinging to the air. For a fleeting second, she almost felt like herself again—a pilot, not just another moving part in PanEuro's high-gloss machine. At the door, Emma shot her a last, sideways smirk.

"Don't let them start singing 'It's Coming Home' in the flight deck," Emma muttered, sotto voce, "or I'll come in there and unplug the radios myself."

"Promise," Hayley whispered back, and then, without pausing to gather her dignity, she rapped the door and heard the lock whir open with a sound she would never tire of.

Inside, the calm of the flight deck was a world away from the roiling carnival outside. Lethenshaw sat in the left seat, hands resting on his knees, posture perfect even in turbulence, a faint smile carving creases into his weathered cheeks. Theo, however, was strapping himself into the jump seat, and she knew what this meant.

She was going to be Pilot Monitoring for the inbound leg into Heathrow, a role she relished even if unofficial, and Lethenshaw—who, as the senior man aboard, had final say—had decided to give her the front-row seat for the show. Hayley knew that several of the PanEuro Captains were keen on letting the female cabin crew who had

APTL, either in frozen or full licence form, up front for landing, a minor act of resistance against the pantomime of retro sexism that still clung to the PanEuro operation like the last sticky dregs of boiled sweets. Lethenshaw was one of them, old enough to remember when women in the cockpit were novelty, and progressive enough to have decided that novelty was vastly preferable to the alternatives.

"Miss Northcott, you're with us for arrival," Lethenshaw announced with the faintly theatrical tone of a man used to getting his own way. "Right hand, doing the radios and checklists, Hayley?"

"Certainly, Captain," Hayley replied, slipping into the right-hand jump seat and adjusting her headset. She felt the familiar, electric thrill as the cockpit door slid shut behind her—closing out the chaos, the chanting, the fumes of lager and perfume, and dropping her into the cool hum of aviation professionalism.

Lethenshaw's blue eyes twinkled as he ran a practised scan across the instruments. "Theo, let's do the approach brief," he said, voice clipped but warm. The man's presence was somehow both calming and energising, his command of the flight deck absolute, but never oppressive.

Theo flicked her a grin. "Welcome to the pointy end, Hales. Let's hope there's no airspace stack—London Control are holding everyone today, and the Italians in the back might storm the flight deck if we're late for kick-off."

Hayley matched his grin with one of her own. "That's what the inflatable lions are for. Crowd control."

A chuckle rumbled from Lethenshaw. "I'll have you know, Miss Northcott, the last time I flew an England final, we were still on TriStars. If we could land those at the old Northolt, we can do Heathrow in a stiff breeze with a cabin full of singing Italians."

The next few minutes were brisk, businesslike. Hayley worked through the checklists with Theo, running through altitudes, runway assignments, expected weather. Lethenshaw dictated vectors, predicted a ten-mile final, and shrugged off any nerves about the wind—"just a stiff crosswind from the west, nothing we can't handle." ATIS was checked, fuel balances reviewed, and the holding patterns over Lambourne and Ockham discussed, just in case.

"PanEuro 9438, this is London Control, please be advised that you are number five for the approach to 27 Left. Expect holding over Ockham, standard pattern, estimated delay ten to fifteen minutes. Winds at Heathrow currently 260 at 18 knots, gusting 25. Report established."

"London Control, understood number 5 for approach, 27 Left, holding over Ockham, standard patter, wind 260 at 18, gusting, delay 5 to 10 mins, 9438, over," Lethenshaw repeated over the radio, making notes on both a written notepad that Hayley knew he kept with him for his records and the electronic flight log, his handwriting a neat, looping script reminiscent of a different era. Hayley watched, quietly impressed by the ease with which the old captain married the digital with the analogue. Even the most seasoned Airbus pilots rarely bothered with ink and paper now, but Lethenshaw insisted on tradition—"It keeps me honest," he'd once told her. She rather liked it. It was the sort of thing her father would do.

Theo handled the MCP, punching in the new hold at OCK, and Hayley updated the FMS. Outside, clouds stacked themselves in great bruised tiers over southern England, their undersides tinged pink by the late afternoon sun. Hayley glanced at the clock—nearly 18:30 local, two hours before kick-off, though the airwaves had already begun to buzz with Wembley's looming presence.

A chime from the cabin. Carter on the interphone: "Flight deck, just a heads up—we've got an England supporter attempting to negotiate a truce with half the Italian cabin, using duty-free limoncello as leverage. So far, peace talks are progressing, but I'll let you know if we need to declare a UN intervention."

Lethenshaw grinned, pressing the transmit button. "Thank you, Carter. Do let me know if the Treaty of Ockham is ratified before touchdown." He replaced the handset, rolling his shoulders. "Right, time to brief the approach one more time. Miss Northcott?"

Hayley leaned forward, voice professional, slipping effortlessly into the rhythms of a job she still craved. "ILS approach 27 Left. Initial altitude at 6,000, OCK hold as per chart. We'll plan for the full procedure, no shortcuts, given the traffic load. Go-around is published to Lambourne, left turn, maintain 3,000. Weather's crosswind but VMC, should be a straightforward landing, but we'll keep an eye for windshear on short final. Minimums set, runway clear."

"Good, good. Hopefully easyJet, Wizz or Iberia open training for UK based cadets before the next World Cup, as you should be up here full time, not stuck asking if chicken, beef or vegetarian is a sufficient life choice," Lethenshaw said, glancing over at her with that peculiar mix of irony and quiet encouragement that only the best captains managed. "I suspect you'll be logging more stick time before the year's out, Hayley. You have the temperament for it. Never forget it."

She let the words settle. Sometimes, a small act of faith meant more than a dozen LinkedIn endorsements or the passive-aggressive silence from HR after yet another rejected application. "Thank you, Captain," she murmured, matching his formality.

Theo leaned in, his tone conspiratorial but gentle. "And if they don't, I'm defecting to Ryanair and taking you with me. God knows, they'd probably give us a base at Southend and a brand-new Max." His smile was just visible beneath the headset.

"Nah, I don't like the Max, especially after the MCAS thing." Hayley shot him a wry look, but her hands moved deftly over the panels, checking each instrument in turn. "The A320 is far safer in my opinion, and to be fair, having the side stick means that sometimes flying manually, it is an interesting way to remind yourself you're still a pilot, not just a human autopilot babysitter." She let her hands rest on her knees, feeling the subtle vibration of the aircraft—a living, breathing thing, even now, even in a sky stacked with metal and noise and anticipation.

Below, the patchwork fields and winding rivers of Surrey looked as eternal and detached as ever, serenely ignorant of the thousands of football-mad souls crammed into aircraft above them. Hayley felt, just for a moment, entirely apart from the madness—alone with her longing, her love of flight, the secret she nursed in her chest that all she wanted, in the end, was this: the quiet before landing, the certainty of approach, the cockpit chatter, the sense of possibility.

"Cabin crew, prepare for landing, thirty minutes to touchdown." Lethenshaw's voice carried into the intercom, measured and warm, barely a tremor of the carnival behind the flight deck door.

Hayley's headset crackled. Emma's voice, half-joking, half-wearied, drifted through. "Starboard secure. All lions caged. If anyone asks, I'm defecting to Alitalia."

"Copy that, Emma," Hayley replied, and then glanced at Theo. He grinned, the two of them perfectly in sync.

* _ * _ * _ *

The hold at Ockham was mercifully brief—just two lazy, sweeping turns over the woods and motorways, a gentle reminder that even the busiest airspace sometimes worked in your favour. On the radio, London Control was all professional calm, slotting them in between a BA 777 inbound from Milan and a Virgin A350 from Delhi. Hayley's hands fluttered over the radios, catching snatches of ATC chatter, her heart thumping with the old familiar adrenaline that came with every approach.

"PanEuro 9438, this is London Control, please be advised that your sequence is now established, descend 4,000 feet on the Ockham Three Alpha arrival, maintain speed 210 knots. Contact Heathrow Director 120 decimal 4. And folks, it's coming home."

Theo shot Hayley a sly grin, twisting in his seat so his lips wouldn't catch the microphone. "Even ATC is in on the football fever," he murmured.

Lethenshaw, ever the professional, keyed the mic: "Descending 4,000 on the OCK3A, 210 knots, over to Director, PanEuro 9438. Thank you, London, and we'll pass on the message."

The ritual of descent now entered its purest form. The engine note shifted, the nose dipped, and the aircraft began its gentle, unhurried drop towards the metropolis sprawled beyond the haze. Hayley adjusted her seat, cross-checking the ILS frequency against the plate, confirming the localiser was alive and well. On the right, Theo took care of the ECAM, his fingers flying over the switches with a dexterity born of habit and confidence.

"Checklist to landing," Hayley intoned, and together they worked down the list: seat belts, signs, altimeters, cabin call, approach briefing, everything by the book, everything precise and calm.

A shudder ran through the fuselage as the first hints of turbulence bit into the descent, but Lethenshaw's hands on the stick never wavered. "Nothing more than a few leftovers from yesterday's convection," he remarked, as though discussing the remnants of a dinner party, and Hayley felt a wave of calm soak through her bones.

In the cabin, a final round of singing broke out—this time "It's Coming Home" and "Notti Magiche" in a kind of musical truce. Even the boisterous Italians, who had spent most of the flight ribbing their English seatmates, were now offering each other swigs of limoncello and high-fives over the headrests.

The approach cleared, gear down, flaps set, Hayley managed the radio: "Heathrow Director, PanEuro 9438, descending four thousand, with you."

"9438, roger, continue descent 2,500 feet, reduce speed 180 knots to 8 DME, cleared ILS 27 Left. Traffic ahead is a British Airways 777, wake turbulence caution. Expect a short taxi—Terminal 3 is reopening for this flight."

Theo raised an eyebrow. "All for the football," he muttered.

"All for the football," Hayley echoed, as she began her scan: airspeed, descent rate, check and recheck, the numbers flowing through her hands and mind. She could feel the press of the city below, the importance of the day—not just for those on board, but for everyone about to pour out into London's streets.

The approach was textbook, the kind that made you believe flying could still be effortless. The city slid into view as they broke through the lowest deck of cloud: London shining, glass and brick, Wembley's arch ghostly on the horizon, an omen and a promise.

"Contact Tower, PanEuro 9438, good luck again," Heathrow Director intoned, with a note of warmth rare for an ATC handoff.

"Switching, 9438," Hayley replied, and flicked the selector. "Heathrow Tower, PanEuro 9438, ILS established, 27 Left."

"9438, wind two-six-zero at two-zero, runway 27 Left, cleared to land. Welcome home—bring it back for the lads."

"Cleared to land, 27 Left, 9438," Lethenshaw confirmed, his voice lighter now, a subtle pride threading through every syllable.

Theo dialled the final approach speed, eyes flicking across the PFD, and Hayley found herself watching, just for a heartbeat, the way his hand steadied on the throttle. It was the look of someone who'd done this a thousand times and yet never took it for granted.

Below, the city unrolled like a painted canvas—Kew Gardens, the Thames' slow meander, rows of rooftops and matchbox gardens. For a moment, Hayley's heart squeezed tight: she'd landed here as a cadet, as a passenger, as a displaced aviator in the middle of a pandemic. Now, she was returning as almost-but-not-quite the real thing—a pilot, not in name, but in deed.

The wheels thumped down, the spoilers leapt from the wing, and the roar of reverse thrust echoed forward. In the cabin, the singing peaked—then, as the aircraft slowed, fell away into spontaneous applause, the kind that felt entirely unscripted. Hayley barely heard it. She was scanning the instruments, running the after-landing checks, already shifting gears to the next ritual.

"Beautiful work," Lethenshaw murmured, and for the briefest second, Hayley felt like she'd come home.

****

CHAPTER 24 – Going Orange, Going Easy

Wednesday 21st July 2021

"I can't believe we're both going today," Hayley heard as she filled in the sheet which had what food and drink was being offloaded her flight, PE341 from Madrid to Manston.

Turning around, she saw Sarah, sitting down, taking her heels off. The Airbus A320neo they had been on, G-PANE, had just pulled into stand 4 at Manston after the late evening arrival from Barajas. The crew were working through their final checks, stripping galley carts and filling in the usual piles of paperwork. The cabin had long since emptied of passengers, and the once-buzzing aircraft was quiet now, lit only by the overheads and the faint flicker of lights on the apron outside.

Hayley offered a tired smile. "Barely feels real, doesn't it?"

Sarah let out a dry chuckle. "More than real. My feet are reminding me every minute."

"Only one more rotation, this time to Charles de Gaulle and back as stewardesses for this bloody heritage scheme airline," Hayley replied, her voice equally wry. "Then that's it. Me off to do the last bit of line training and you to start your shortened course to become a First Officer. Which base you applied to do your training at?"

"Gatwick," Sarah said after a pause, stretching her legs under the jump seat and sighing as if trying to drain away the weight of the day through her limbs. "I can't believe easyJet gave me the nod to do a shortened pilot, type rating and FO course which would see me fully qualified by next February."

Hayley leaned back against the galley wall, her clipboard held loosely in one hand, the other tugging at the top button of her blouse. "Well," she said, voice low and fond, "you've earned it. Every second. Anyway, I hardly think you need Ground School, having done QRA for years, and then this stint playing make-believe at this bloody airline. You heard about the court case that's coming up for PanEuro and RiverOak?"

Sarah looked up, eyes darkened by exhaustion but glinting with curiosity. "The one about staff contracts and working conditions? Or the CAA audit complaints?"

Hayley nodded, brushing a loose strand of hair from her temple. "Slots. Seems that a new ULCC wants slots here, and RiverOak's been a bit too generous handing out access to PanEuro without proper transparency. The new entrant—Sprint Air, I think—has formally complained. They say they're being blocked from a fair go."

Sarah raised her eyebrows. "Sprint Air? Never heard of them."

"Nor had I until this morning. Some ex-easyJet, Ryanair and Wizz people behind it, supposedly."

Hayley shifted her weight from one foot to the other, feeling the ache spread through her calves. The long day was catching up with her, but the conversation sparked enough interest to keep her going.

"They've apparently got a Romanian ACMI running some flights from Lithuania while they apply for their Air Operators certification," Hayley continued, lowering her voice as she checked over a galley inventory sheet with a biro that barely worked. "I overheard Linda talking to Ops about them. Sprint wants a foothold here at Manston, but PanEuro doesn't want a 'bloody low cost shithouse with peasants', their words, not mine, clogging up the apron with half-painted 737s and gaudy A320s," Hayley said, rolling her eyes. "Yet PanEuro uses A320s and A321s, so they can hardly claim superiority just because they slap on some retro livery and force us to wear lipstick while slinging roast chicken at row 18B."

Sarah snorted, rubbing her eyes. "God, don't remind me of that chicken. I'm convinced it's just rebranded leftovers from some motorway service station."

"I'm not denying it." Hayley snapped her clipboard shut, glancing towards the open L1 door where a cleaning crew hovered, waiting to begin their turnaround. "Still, this is it. One last trip pretending we're flying in 1973 before we get to be real aviators again. I thought I'd be more nostalgic, but... I'm just glad to get out with my sanity intact."

"Ladies," Dimitri Oslov's unmistakably camp drawl cut through the murmur of the galley. The purser stood at the foot of the forward aisle, his camp, flamboyant style, completely on show. "We've got 2 hours until our Parisian pantomime. Best find some sparkle before the next act. I'm going to miss you pair, you know."

Hayley smiled, a flash of warmth cutting through her fatigue. Dimitri, for all his melodrama, had been a kind of guardian angel through the absurdities of PanEuro. He knew how to make the impossible palatable—with one-liners, runway-ready flair, and a shade of lipstick always too perfect to be accidental.

"We'll miss you too, Dimitri," she said genuinely. "Well… mostly. What are you planning on doing?"

Hayley knew that the flamboyant purser was moving internally within PanEuro, and that this was his last flight from Manston.

Dimitri tossed his scarf with theatrical elegance over one shoulder, winking at them both. "Darling, please. You know me. I'll either be running a drag brunch in Barcelona or forming a union by Christmas. Possibly both." He sashayed into the galley, his clipboard appearing from nowhere like a conjuring trick. "Anyway, I'm moving to the Doncaster airport base next month, so there's no escaping me. I'll be pestering you lot for a decade at least."

Sarah laughed softly, shaking her head as Dimitri disappeared into the back galley. "Doncaster, really? Not far from Coningsby."

Hayley knew that Sarah was referencing the RAF station in Lincolnshire where she'd once scrambled Tornadoes for intercepts. The contrast couldn't be more surreal. Back then, Sarah had been in a pressure suit, strapped into a jet streaking toward threats over the North Sea. Now, she was reapplying lipstick in a 1970s-styled galley, discussing chicken trays and corporate theatre.

"World's gone mad," Hayley muttered, tossing a sealed catering log into the grey bag at her feet. "Anyway, at least you'll be getting back into something that goes faster than a milk float."

Sarah cracked her neck. "Honestly, I'm not sure what's more exhausting—G-forces or galley gossip. At least when I was RAF, if someone tried to stab you in the back, they had the decency to do it in a debriefing room."

Hayley smiled tightly. She knew the feeling too well. Their time at PanEuro had been like treading a tightrope of forced nostalgia and real-world fatigue. The uniforms were polyester, the culture was Mad Men meets mini-break, and the ethos seemed to think dignity could be sewn back into aviation with pillbox hats and beef consommé. But the magic of flight—the real stuff—still clung around the edges like vapour trails on a winter morning. That, and the people. Dimitri, Theo, and even a few of the crustier captains who'd served on real Tridents back in the day, had kept it all just barely human.

*_*_*_*

"You alright Hales?" Theo Sullivan, the First Officer and her boyfriend, asked. It was 20 minutes until block time on PE342, their final Paris rotation. Hayley was sat at the front of the aircraft in seat 1C, legs crossed, head resting against the bulkhead partition. Her eyes were open but unfocused, gazing at nothing in particular. The hum of ground power beneath the fuselage was rhythmic, calming almost, but it didn't mask the hollow twist in her stomach.

"Yeah," she said without looking at him. "Just… thinking."

Theo slid into 1B, as the 'Executive' cabin was a 1-2 configuration, meaning that he could sit beside her without intruding on anyone's space. He rested his forearms on his knees and tilted his head slightly, watching her. "Nerves?"

Hayley gave a slow nod. "Not the flying. Just… this. All of this ending."

Theo didn't reply at once. The quiet weight of the moment hung between them, buffered by the subtle hiss of conditioned air and the occasional beep from the avionics testing. Outside, the sky was soft with twilight, the last of the golden light catching on the wingtips of other aircraft dotted around Manston's freshly resurfaced apron. The airport was trying its best to look like a real hub again.

"You'll be in a flight deck again soon," Theo offered gently, brushing his knuckles against hers. "This gig was just a detour."

"A bloody long detour." Hayley's voice cracked, not from emotion but fatigue. "And surreal, too. All that effort just to be back where I was meant to be in the first place."

"You've come out of it sharper, stronger," he said. "And more stylish. Anyway, you do remember that I'm stopping here at PanEuro, right?"

Hayley gave a little snort, her lips curling with affectionate exasperation. "Oh, don't remind me. You and your shiny epaulettes, lording it over everyone with your eighties hair and your beloved Airbus checklists. You'll be the last one left turning the lights off when they finally work out that nostalgia can't pay for Jet A-1."

Theo's lips twitched. "We'll see. I don't fancy joining the orange army just yet."

She eyed him, more warmth in her gaze now. "You'd miss the food. Or the uniform. Or Dimitri's lipstick, maybe."

"I'd definitely miss Dimitri's lipstick," he agreed, smiling. "Besides, where else do you get to work with a bunch of ex-RAF pilots, failed radio DJs, and women who could break your neck with a safety demonstration?"

He let the words hang for a moment, his eyes searching hers for any sign of laughter. When she didn't respond, he shifted closer, lowering his voice. "You alright, really?"

She looked away, watching a baggage tug trundle past the window, its little flashing beacon the only real sign of urgency in the creeping dusk. The emptiness of the airport struck her — this was Manston, supposedly the reborn gateway to Britain's past and future, and yet most of the stands sat empty, the lights burning pointlessly above puddles of tarmac. Somewhere across the airfield, a lonely bird chirped, as if protesting the sudden quiet after the day's endless traffic.

"I just... thought I'd feel different," she said at last. "I thought I'd feel relief. Or pride. Or something. But all I feel is tired, and a bit... well, flat."

Theo put an arm around her shoulders, gently. "It's normal. Everyone gets it. You give your best years to a place and when it ends, it never feels like the films, does it?"

She let her head rest against his shoulder for a moment, the familiar feel of his uniform shirt soft against her cheek. "No. Never does. Maybe tomorrow, when I'm packing for Luton and a million miles from the galley carts and the endless announcements, maybe then it'll hit me. That I'm free. That it's over."

He kissed her temple, soft and lingering. "And then you'll be a pilot again. Not a stewardess in heels. You'll be back up front. Where you belong."

She squeezed his hand, wordlessly grateful.

Behind them, the rest of the crew were gathering at the forward door, ready for the Paris rotation. Sarah appeared, hair already pinned up, heels swapped for flats in preparation for another long sector. Dimitri breezed past, offering a glimmer of his usual camp flourish, but even he looked a little less luminous than usual, the weight of a last flight at Manston dulling his sparkle.

"Boarding in five, girls," he trilled, clipboard at the ready. "Let's give them a show, one last time."

Hayley straightened, rolling her shoulders and smoothing the front of her uniform with the practised efficiency of habit. Theo squeezed her hand once more before standing, the moment slipping away as quickly as it had arrived.

The theatre of flight, the choreography of duty, was ready to begin again.

* _ * _ * _ *

The taxi out was as uneventful as every other Manston departure, but Hayley felt a prickling sense of nostalgia as the little airport slipped behind them. She watched the hangars, the floodlit stands, the single empty row of parked cars — and then, with a lurch and a whine, the A320neo spun up and lifted away from Kent's flat expanse, climbing into the purple velvet of a July night.

Service to Paris was brisk and mostly uneventful, the load light — just fifty-eight passengers, a mix of French tourists, businessmen, and a handful of "heritage" aviation geeks snapping photos of the cabin. Hayley made her way down the aisle with the trolley, her routine automatic, body remembering each gesture before her mind caught up.

"Bonsoir, monsieur," she smiled, offering a miniature bottle of Merlot to an elderly Frenchman in a flat cap, who responded with the kind of courtesy that made her wish all passengers could be so polite.

As she moved past row 15, she caught sight of Sarah, expertly juggling coffee orders and dispensing smiles with a deftness honed by years of dealing with fighter pilots and low-cost airline stag parties. Their eyes met for a second, and Sarah's quick wink was enough to remind Hayley of how much she'd miss this — the camaraderie, the gallows humour, the quiet understanding that only comes from surviving madness together.

Galley banter drifted down the aisle in snatches. Dimitri held court as always, his stories even more outrageous now that the end was nigh. He described his plans for Doncaster, the perils of northern weather, and his theory that PanEuro was secretly run by a cabal of failed 1970s TV presenters.

Hayley stifled a laugh, handing out plastic glasses of still water and watching the rows go by. Each face was a blur; she felt herself drifting, just slightly out of step with the world. The clock was ticking down now — not just on this sector, but on a chapter of her life.

At the forward galley, Theo appeared, the First Officer with a grin on his face. "You know we've got 7 minutes until we're due to start our descent, right?"

Hayley grinned, as she knew what her boyfriend was thinking, the fact that they had been more sexually active over the past month and half being a key source of their happiness, but also a private little joke between them, a running tally of illicit kisses stolen behind bulkheads and late-night flights spent swapping whispered fantasies in crew hotels from Nice to Newcastle. It was the sort of thing that would have horrified the PanEuro management if they'd known, and perhaps that made it sweeter still.

She nudged him with her hip as she passed, eyes glinting. "Don't start what you can't finish, Sullivan. Or I'll have you filing passenger complaint forms for the rest of the month."

"Sarah's in the cockpit with Powers, so if you fancy a snog in the lavs... or more?" he whispered in her ear, nibbling the top of her ear with a cheeky grin. Hayley could feel his erection as he got closer to her, the privacy and adrenaline of these last flights making everything more vivid and reckless. She knew that this and the return trip the duo would be able to let loose a bit, away from the prying eyes of officious supervisors and the exhausting charade of the retro airline image. For all the discipline and performance demanded of them, these stolen moments with Theo felt like a liberation. Hayley found herself grinning despite the tiredness, her body relaxing as she leaned back against the galley partition.

"Steady, tiger," she murmured, shooting him a sidelong look that was equal parts warning and invitation. "Remember, Paris is supposed to be the city of romance, not the site of a CAA disciplinary hearing."

Theo laughed, eyes crinkling at the corners. "All the more reason to make the most of it. Who knows how much longer we'll be able to get away with it once you go orange. Especially with Stelios lurking somewhere in the Geneva shadows, ready to spring an NDA on any ex-PanEuro crew caught fooling around in the EasyJet break room," he quipped, lowering his voice but unable to hide the laughter. He ran a hand through his hair, a lock falling artfully over his brow, the very picture of boyish mischief in his starched PanEuro uniform. "Come on, you know you'll miss the drama."

Hayley rolled her eyes, but her smile was real. "I'll miss bits of it. Not the miniskirt. Not the shoes. Maybe the— no, definitely the people. And maybe the absurdity. When else do you get to be a time traveller and an airline skivvy in the same twelve-hour shift?"

Theo's hand brushed her hip for the briefest, secretive second. "Next time I see you in orange, I expect the same attitude. Just better catering."

She snorted, glancing down at the galley counter scattered with untouched cheese triangles and those odd little biscuits PanEuro insisted on offering, a relic from some 1970s boardroom decree. "You're an optimist, Sullivan."

"Better than that pervert Hargreaves. There's only one person who can touch your arse, gorgeous, and that's your hot, flyboy, boyfriend."

Hayley chuckled, as she knew it was rare for Theo to be self-conscious and flirty, as often he was more serious, more careful about boundaries. "You know we've only got the flight back to Manston and then I'm officially done as a trolley dolly, right?" she said, flicking a glance at him, trying not to let the bittersweet weight of the moment overwhelm her. "This bloody girdle is killing my tits."

"Don't worry, I'll still fancy you in orange, even when you're up front where you belong," Theo murmured, voice softer now, carrying beneath the low hum of the galley chillers. He tucked a loose strand of her hair behind her ear, lingering there a second too long, before the spell was broken by the familiar sound of the internal phones, where the flight deck could communicate with the galley without passengers knowing that there was ever a crisis, a delay, or just a mundane check-in. Hayley reached to answer, brushing her uniform straight, composure settling over her like a familiar mask.

"Forward galley," she said crisply.

Powers's voice, crackling and accented by the faint hum of background avionics, sounded almost jovial for once. "We're five from the top of descent. Expect a little chop, but nothing your side can't handle. Weather's clear, Paris looks golden. Could you do us a favour and send your boyfriend back here, as he's the FO and so we're rather hoping he fancies landing the aircraft?"

Hayley smirked, covering the mouthpiece. "Your chariot awaits, Sullivan. The captain wants his favourite right-seater at the helm for our grand Parisian arrival."

Theo gave her a mock salute and a surreptitious squeeze of the hand. "See you on the ground, trouble." He slid past her, shoes soundless on the galley vinyl, and disappeared behind the flight deck door. The hiss and click of the locking mechanism was oddly final.

Hayley stood for a moment, bracing herself against the galley's cold stainless steel, feeling the judder and subtle dip of the airframe as the pilots eased back the thrust levers. She had performed this dance so many times, and yet tonight each step felt weighted with memory: last looks, last rituals, last times.

She moved methodically, ensuring everything was stowed and locked, the curtains snapped back, the cabin ready for landing. She glanced towards row 1, where Sarah had returned from the flight deck behind her, already securing the forward lockers, her RAF precision apparent even in the way she tied off the blue curtain and checked the jump seats with military efficiency.

"Ready?" Hayley asked, her voice low and calm.

"Ready as I'll ever be," Sarah replied, a touch of mischief flickering in her eyes. "Let's land this relic and get ready for one last turnaround."

The descent into Paris was gentle, the Airbus carving slow, wide turns above the Île-de-France as dusk fell, the city's lights emerging like gold veins in the encroaching blue. Hayley found herself craning for a glimpse of the Eiffel Tower, though she knew it would be barely visible from the approach path. There was something both grounding and bittersweet about it—this city where she'd first learned, as a trainee years before, how little romance there really was in commercial aviation, and yet how much you still clung to, in spite of it.

Cabin secure, galley latched, she took her seat on the forward jump seat beside Sarah for landing. As the aircraft began its final approach, Sarah offered her a sideways glance and a smirk. "Feel like making an announcement, for old time's sake?"

Hayley raised an eyebrow. "You want the nostalgic version, or the honest one?"

Sarah grinned. "Dealer's choice."

Hayley pressed the PA handset, dropping her voice into the clipped, honeyed tones of the PanEuro script: "Ladies and gentlemen, as we make our final descent into Paris Charles de Gaulle, please ensure your seatbelts are fastened, your tray tables stowed, and your seatbacks upright. On behalf of Captain Powers, First Officer Sullivan, and all the crew, we'd like to thank you for flying PanEuro Airways, where every journey is a step back in time."

She clicked off, and without missing a beat, leaned closer to Sarah and added, sotto voce, "And if you're lucky, you'll forget the past forty minutes of cabin service ever happened."

Sarah snorted so hard she had to muffle it in the crook of her elbow, drawing a startled look from a passenger in the front row. Hayley caught the glance and flashed a professional smile. The mask was still in place—just barely.

The landing was smooth, a real greaser, and Hayley felt a swell of pride. She could picture Theo's hands steady on the sidestick, his concentration written in the tautness of his jaw, the familiar little ritual he had before every touchdown—right hand tapping twice on the thrust levers, like a pianist counting himself in. She'd watched him do it a thousand times now, both in the jump seat and on grainy hotel Facetimes from airports all over Europe.

As the aircraft taxied in, she caught his eye through the open flight deck door. He gave her a tiny, tired thumbs-up. She replied with a conspiratorial wink, all the words they couldn't say written in that shared moment.

On stand, the routine resumed with clockwork inevitability: doors disarmed, L1 opened to the glassy jet bridge, the slow exodus of passengers with their bags and their stories and their grumbles about the price of coffee. In the galley, Hayley busied herself with the paperwork, ticking boxes and counting catering trays, while Sarah handled the final farewells with the brisk efficiency of a woman already halfway out the door in her head.

Dimitri arrived, a tornado of scarves and sarcasm. "Well, darlings, that's Paris. No riots, no bomb scares, not even a single passenger who tried to light up in the loo. Frankly, I'm insulted."

Hayley smiled. "Don't jinx the return sector."

He pouted. "Too late. This airline's been jinxed since the day it opened. But at least we go out with some class." He paused, then added with genuine warmth, "You're both wasted on orange."

Hayley felt a lump form in her throat. "We'll come back and visit when you're running Doncaster."

"Assuming Doncaster's still standing after another winter," Sarah deadpanned, rolling her shoulders and pulling her blazer straight. Her gaze flickered around the emptying cabin, as if she were mapping it for the last time.

Dimitri winked. "There's always room for more rebels up north. If you ever tire of Stelios's orange shackles, you know where to find me."

Their layover at Charles de Gaulle was predictably joyless—a dark, echoing corridor of a terminal, all brushed steel and bad lighting, the kind of place that seemed designed to sap glamour out of even the most devoted trolley dolly. The crew room PanEuro used was a windowless bunker beneath the arrivals hall, lined with battered sofas and a coffee machine that coughed up grey, unspeakable sludge.

Hayley flopped onto a seat, unpinning her hair and letting it fall loose around her shoulders. "If you ever want to cure someone of their aviation fantasies, lock them in this room for half an hour."

Sarah grimaced as she massaged her ankles. "If this is what the future holds, maybe I should have reapplied for the RAF."

Theo, standing by the vending machine, cracked a can of Fanta and offered it to her. "Don't let them break you. You're both too stubborn for that."

Dimitri, perched on a battered armchair, surveyed them with mock solemnity. "Darlings, you need a little perspective. When I started out, you were lucky if the staff room had a functioning bog, let alone Wi-Fi. These are the good times. Relatively speaking."

Hayley snorted. "Maybe for you, Dimitri. Some of us still have to survive the easyJet induction."

He grinned, wide and wicked. "Just remember, orange is the colour of revolution. And questionable design choices."

****

Books by Thomas Brant

Broadcasting Boundaries
BROADCASTING BOUNDARIES
BROADCASTING CHAOS
BROADCASTING DISRUPTION

The Wirral Gal
IN SPEKE
NOW A MAM

Fallen
IRELAND IS DOWN

PanEuro
STICK AND LIPSTICK

Standalone Manic Novels
THE BROOKES BABES
THE DAY THE QUEEN DIED
VIXEN
THE MANIC COLLECTIVE CANDIDATE